C

Regency

BALLROOM

Deb Marlowe

MILLS
BOON
&

Mills & Boon, an imprint of Harlequin (UK) Limited,
Eton House, 18-24 Paradise Road, Richmond, Surrey TW9 1SR

CINDERELLA IN THE REGENCY BALLROOM
© Harlequin Enterprises II B.V./S.à.r.l 2013

Her Cinderella Season © Deb Marlowe 2008
Tall, Dark and Disreputable © Deb Marlowe 2009

ISBN: 978 0 263 90618 9

052-0713

Harlequin (UK) policy is to use papers that are natural, renewable and recyclable products and made from wood grown in sustainable forests. The logging and manufacturing processes conform to the legal environmental regulations of the country of origin.

Printed and bound
by CPI Group (UK) Ltd, Croydon, CR0 4YY

Deb Marlowe grew up in Pennsylvania with her nose in a book. Luckily, she'd read enough romances to recognise the true modern hero she met at a college Halloween party—even though he wore a tuxedo T-shirt instead of breeches and tall boots. They married, settled in North Carolina and produced two handsome, intelligent and genuinely amusing boys. Though she now spends much of her time with her nose in her laptop, for the sake of her family she does occasionally abandon her inner world for the domestic adventure of laundry, dinner and car pool. Despite her sacrifice, not one of the men in her family is yet willing to don breeches or tall boots. She's working on it. Deb would love to hear from readers! You can contact her at debmarlowe@debmarlowe.com.

In The Regency Ballroom Collection

Her Cinderella Season

Author Note:

For many years the Dreadnought Seamen's Hospital provided health and welfare services to 'all distressed seamen' and the people who lived and worked in port communities. The hospital's very first home was on board *HMS Grampus*, afloat on the River Thames. Here a small staff dedicated themselves to those who made their lives on the sea. They took in their first patients in 1821.

By 1830 the hospital had outgrown the *Grampus*. The Royal Navy generously donated the ex-warship *HMS Dreadnought*, from which the hospital thereafter took its name. In 1870 the Dreadnought moved ashore in Greenwich. It became an important part of the local community, and treated sailors from all nations and locals alike until it closed its doors in 1986.

I admit to fudging the dates a bit in *Her Cinderella Season*, when I had the staff of *HMS Grampus* taking J. Crump in several months earlier than the hospital officially opened its doors. Once I knew Crump and realised he was dying, I longed for him to end his days in a place of caring and dignity. I hope you'll forgive the poetic licence.

For my Grandpap—
a real-life hero for the ages

Chapter One

Jack's hand held steady, his aim unwavering. His pistol was pointed straight at Hassan's evil heart. This time he would kill the bastard. This time he would.

But something moved in the shadowy dreamscape. A soft rustle sounded, impossibly close—just as his sleeping mind had known it would. Not Aswan. Smaller. Jack caught the faint scent of gardenias just a moment before he felt the press of cold steel at his temple.

A flood of fury and frustration swamped him. God damn it, now the innocent girl below him would die. *He* would die all alone up here in the pitch blackness of the Egyptian Hall gallery and an ancient treasure would fall into the worst of hands.

As it always did, night after night, an indescribable flurry of movement erupted as Aswan intervened. A woman's cry. A bright flash of light in the near darkness. And a searing pain that exploded in his arm and knocked him backwards.

Someone loomed over him. The sinister face swam in the darkness, but somehow he knew it was not the woman who'd shot him, nor was it the villain Hassan—it must be Batiste. Captain Batiste, the silent, invisible mastermind behind much of the plot to hurt his friends. The shadow began to laugh, and an old, cold rage burned deep in Jack's gut.

'So disappointing, Jack,' the figure whispered. 'I expected more of you.'

He scrambled backwards. It was not a stranger's voice reaching for him out of the darkness, but his father's.

Gasping, Jack jerked awake.

That damned dream again. He shook off the remnants of the nightmare and glanced at the clock on the wall—early afternoon. Had he fallen asleep in his chair? A heavy tome rested painfully against his injured arm. He tossed it on to the floor and scrubbed his free hand against his scalp, trying to chase away the fuzziness in his head.

That night at the Egyptian Hall had not been his finest moment. Perhaps that was the reason he relived it repeatedly in his dreams. He heaved a massive sigh. He didn't regret mixing himself up in Lord Treyford's misadventures, and yet…

Trey and Chione had taken their family back to Devonshire. Soon they would be leaving for Egypt, embarking on an adventure that Jack couldn't help but envy. He'd held his breath, hoping to be asked along, but Trey and Chione were occupied with each other, and caught up in the wonder of what awaited them.

Jack had been left behind and he'd found himself strangely unsettled. He pressed his good hand hard against his brow. His preoccupation with Batiste had grown, becoming something closer to obsession. The villain had slipped away on the tide, leaving Hassan and his other confederates to be caught up in Treyford's net. The man's escape nagged at Jack incessantly.

He stood. He was due to meet Pettigrew, to test those devilishly bad-mannered bays the baron was trying to sell. Jack cast a rueful glance down at his arm. This was not the most reasonable course of action, but, damn it, the man had baited him. At any other point in his life, Jack would have ignored the baron's desperate manoeuvre. Not this time. Instead he had risen like a trout to a well-crafted lure. A stupid response. Immature. And yet another maddening symptom of his recent erratic temperament.

Jack struggled into his greatcoat and decided to stop by White's and pick up his brother along the way. Charles was in town to further his reform causes before the Parliamentary session closed, and to conveniently avoid the domestic chaos brought on by a colicky baby. And since he had been the one to introduce him to Pettigrew, then riding along with a crippled driver and an unruly team was the least he could do.

As he set out, a chill wind began to gust. The cold blast of air made his arm throb like an aching tooth. Jack huddled a little deeper into his coat and rifled in his pocket for Pettigrew's hastily scribbled address. He stopped short. The baron's dire financial straits had led him to take rooms in Goodman's Fields. An unsavoury neighbourhood it might be, but it was conveniently located near enough to the London docks—where the offices of Batiste's defunct shipping company were located.

Jack quickened his step. This might not be a wasted day after all.

Lily Beecham glanced at her mother from the corner of her eye. Mrs Margaret Beecham had turned slightly away from her daughter, avoiding the brightest light as she concentrated on her needlework. Slowly, surreptitiously, Lily tilted her head back and directly into the path of the afternoon sunshine.

Though it wasn't the least bit ladylike, Lily loved the warmth of the sun on her face. The burst of patterned radiance behind her closed eyelids, the brush of the breeze on her heated cheeks; it took her back, every single time. For a few seconds she was a girl again, in her father's arms, giggling like mad while he spun her round and his rich, booming laugh washed over her. Sometimes she could hear its echo still, the liquid sound of pure love.

Not now, though. Now she heard only the unnecessarily loud clearing of her mother's throat. 'Lilith, this is a public thoroughfare, not the back pasture at home.'

'Yes, of course, Mother.' Lily straightened in her seat. She glanced down at her copy of *Practical Piety*, but she'd read Hannah More's work many times over already and now was not the time to risk her mother discovering the thin volume she'd tucked inside. She got to her feet and began to pace behind the table they'd been asked to tend for Lady Ashford's Fancy Fair and Charity Bazaar.

The majority of the booths and tables in the countess's event had been strung along Rotten Row in Hyde Park, where they were sure to catch the attention of those with both the in-clination and the wherewithal to purchase ribbons, bonnets and embroidered penwipes in the name of charity. The Book Table, however, along with the Second-Hand Clothing and the Basketry tables, had been pronounced more likely to appeal to the masses, and had thus been placed outside the Grosvenor Gate, right alongside Park Lane.

'It is somewhat frustrating, isn't it, Mother—that we've sat here all day, just outside the most famous park in London, and we've yet to set foot inside?'

'Not in the least. Why should such a thing vex you? This park is full of grass and trees just like any other.' Mrs Beecham's needle did not pause as she glanced up at her daughter. 'We should count ourselves fortunate to have been asked to help today. It is an honour to be of service to such a noble cause.'

'Yes, of course you are right.' Lily suppressed a sigh. She

didn't know why she should be surprised at the disappointments of the day. The entire trip to town had been an exercise in frustration.

Long ago her father had talked to her of London. He had perched her on his knee, run his fingers through the tangle of her hair and spoken of great museums, elaborate theatrical productions and the noisy, chaotic workings of Parliament, where the fates of men and nations were decided. He had spun fanciful stories of her own future visits to the greatest city in the world, and she had eagerly absorbed every tale.

But her father had died before his stories could come true and Lily's busy, happy life had been abandoned for sober duty and sombre good works. And so, it seemed, had her dream of London.

Her hopes had been so high when her mother had announced that they were to travel to town and spend the month of May. But over the last weeks, joy and anticipation had dwindled. She had trailed her mother from one Reformist committee to another Evangelical meeting and on to an Abolitionist group, and the dreadful truth had dawned on her. Her surroundings had changed, but her situation had not.

'Mr Cooperage will make a fine missionary, don't you agree?' her mother asked, this time without looking away from her work. Lily wondered if it was giving her trouble, so intent did she appear.

'He will if the fancy work inside the park proves more profitable than the Book Table. Even with the Cheap Repository Tracts to sell, we haven't raised enough to get him a hackney across town, let alone passage to India.'

Her mother frowned.

Lily sighed. 'I don't mean to be flippant.' She stood on her toes to peer past the gate and into the park. 'There does seem to be a bigger crowd gathered inside.'

Her mother's scowl faded as a young woman strolling past on a gentleman's arm broke away to approach their table. Lily returned her friendly smile and admired the white lute-string trim on her violet walking dress.

'Good afternoon,' the young woman said brightly. 'But it seems as if you are out of A. Vaganti?' She nodded towards Lily's chair and the volume now peeking from the staid pages of Mrs More's work. 'I've already read *The Emerald Temple*. I was wondering if you might have the newest Nicolas adventure, *The Pharaoh's Forbidden City*?'

Mrs Beecham darted a sharp glance in Lily's direction. 'No, but we have several more improving works. Bowdler's Shakespeare, for instance, if fiction is what interests you.'

The young lady gave a soft, tinkling laugh. 'Oh my, no! Surely it is a shame to allow that man to chop apart the works of our great bard? What harm is there in Shakespeare? It seems I've read or seen his works from the cradle!'

She tilted her head engagingly. 'Forgive me for being bold, ma'am,' she said with a smile. 'How wonderful you are to give your day to helping Lady Ashford's good cause.' She dropped a curtsy. 'I am Miss Dawson.' She cast an encouraging glance at Lily.

Hurriedly, Lily returned the curtsy. 'My mother, Mrs Margaret Beecham.' She gestured and smiled back. 'I am Miss Beecham.' Something about the girl's friendly countenance had her blurting out, 'But please, you must call me Lily.'

'Beecham?' the girl asked with a frown of concentration. She eyed Lily curiously. 'You test my recollection of our ponderous family tree, but I believe we have relatives of that name. Might you come from Dorset?'

'Indeed, yes,' Lily replied. 'We are in town for a few weeks only.'

'It's a pleasure, Lily.' She looked over her shoulder as her

companion called her name. 'Oh dear, I must run.' She leaned
in close. 'That is my betrothed, Lord Lindley. We both adore
A. Vaganti, but he would never admit to it in public.' She
grinned and, reaching across the table, pressed Lily's hand. 'I
feel sure we shall meet again.'

Lily watched the young lady take her gentleman's arm and
head into the park. A little sigh escaped her. She might have
been friends with a girl like that, had her father not died. She
let herself imagine what might have been, for just a moment:
friends, novels, walks in the park. Perhaps even she might
have had a beau? She flushed and glanced at her mother, who
regarded her with a frown.

'I hope you are not still mooning about participating in the
social whirl?'

Lily took notice of the sharp note in her mother's voice and
then she took her seat. She picked up her book, and gazed down
at it for several long seconds. 'No, of course not,' she answered.
A soft breeze, warm and laden with the green scent of the
park, brushed her cheek. With sudden resolution, Lily pulled
the adventure novel from its hiding place and opened it.

The heavy weight of her mother's gaze rested on her for
several long seconds. Suddenly her mother let out a sigh that
echoed her own. 'I do hope that young lady will buy something
inside. Mr Cooperage's work is so important. Think of all
those lost souls just waiting for him!' She resumed her needlework, then paused to knot her thread. 'We've had so little
interest out here, I had begun to wonder if Lady Ashford might
better have chosen the Hanover Square Rooms for her fair.'

'I'm sure it will all turn out well,' Lily soothed. 'You know
the countess—she will have it no other way.' She smiled.
'And the crickets were singing away when we arrived, Mother.
That's a definite sign of good fortune.'

Her mother's needlework went down, but her brow lowered

even further. 'Lilith Beecham—you know how it upsets me to hear you spouting such nonsense!' She took a fortifying breath, but Lily was saved from further harangue by a shrill cry.

'Mrs Beecham!'

They turned to look.

'Mrs Beecham—you must come!'

'It's Lady Ashford,' Lily said in surprise. And indeed it was the countess, although clad as she was in various shades of blue and flapping a large white handkerchief as she sailed towards the gate, she resembled nothing so much as a heavily laden frigate storming a blockade.

'My dear Mrs Beecham…' the countess braced her hand on the table for support while she caught her breath '…it is Mr Wilberforce himself!' she panted. 'He has come to thank us and has brought Mr Cooperage along with him.' She picked up one of the Repository Tracts and began to fan herself with it.

Lily looked askance at her mother's stunned expression. William Wilberforce, the famous abolitionist and one of the leading members of the Evangelical movement, was Margaret Beecham's particular idol.

Mrs Beecham found her tongue. 'Oh, but, Lady Ashford—Wilberforce himself! What a coup!' She stood and pressed the countess's hand. 'How wonderful for you, to be sure.'

'And for you, too, Mrs Beecham,' Lady Ashford said warmly, recovering her breath. 'For I have told Mr Wilberforce how easily the charity school in Weymouth went up, and how thoroughly the community has embraced it. It was largely your doing, and so I told him. I informed him also of your tremendous success in recruiting volunteers. He wishes to meet you and thank you in person! His carriage is swamped right now with well wishers and so I have come to fetch you. He means to take us both up for a drive and he'll drop you right here when we've been round the park.'

'A drive?' Lily saw all the colour drain from her mother's face. 'With Mr Wilberforce?'

'Come now!' Lady Ashford said in imperious tones. 'We must not keep him waiting!'

'Oh, but I—' Mrs Beecham sat abruptly down again.

'Come, Mother,' Lily urged, pulling her back to her feet. 'You've worked long and hard. You deserve a bit of accolade.' She smiled at the odd mix of fear and longing on her mother's face. 'It is fine,' she soothed. 'He only wishes to acknowledge your efforts.'

'We must go now, Mrs Beecham!' Lady Ashford had done with the delay. She reached out and began to drag Lily's mother along with her.

'Oh, but Lilith—' came the last weak protest from Mrs Beecham.

'The girl will be fine. The ladies from the other tables are here and she's not some chit barely out of the schoolroom. She'll know how to handle herself.'

'Goodbye, Mother!' Lily called. 'Do try to enjoy yourself!' She watched until the ladies disappeared into the crowd, and then took her seat, knowing the futility of that last admonition.

Traffic in the street ahead of her began to pick up. Shining high-perch phaetons wheeled through the Grosvenor Gate into the park. Gorgeously groomed thoroughbreds and their equally handsome riders followed. Ladies dressed in rich, fluttering fabrics paused at the tables, or giggled as they passed them by. Lily watched them all a bit wistfully. Surely they were not all so empty-headed and frivolous as her mother believed? Lady Ashford certainly thrived with one foot firmly in the thick of the *ton* and the other in the Evangelical camp.

She fought back a shudder as she glanced down at her plain, brown, serviceable gown. What did those men and women of society think when they looked at her? They could not see inside, where her true self lay. Did they see the girl who loved a bruising ride, and a thrilling novel? Could they conceive of her secret dreams, the longings that she'd buried so deep, she'd forgotten them herself? No. They could not. Why would they?

Lily straightened, shocked by a sudden idea. She'd been so excited to come to town, sure this was the chance she'd awaited: the long-anticipated sign of change and good fortune. But what if the sign had been meant for her mother instead? This disturbing thought kept her occupied for several agonisingly conflicted minutes. Of course she wished her mother happy. Hadn't she thrown herself into an attempt to please her for the last seven years? She'd done all she could to ease the blow of her father's loss. She'd settled down, acted the lady, given up all the rough-and-ready activities of her youth, all because she was eager to please a mother who had always seemed uncomfortable with and somewhat perplexed by her spirited daughter.

Only now did Lily realise how significant the prospect of change had become in her mind—now when the possibility appeared to be fading fast away.

'My dear Miss Beecham, here you are at last!'

'Mr Cooperage.' Lily shook off her disturbing train of thought and tried to rally a smile for the missionary approaching from the park. 'How nice to see you. I'm sure your presence is a boost to all of our volunteers.'

'Naturally,' he agreed. Lily tried not to wince. Everything about the missionary, from dress to manner, spoke of neatness and correctness. Yet Lily did not find him a comfortable man. His tendency to speak in pronouncements unnerved her.

'Will you step away a little with me?' he asked in his forceful tone. 'I gave up my seat in my friend Wilberforce's barouche for your mother. What better recompense, I asked myself, than to seek out her lovely daughter?'

'I should not leave my table,' she hedged. 'I should not wish to miss a sale.'

He glanced significantly about. Not a soul appeared to rescue her.

'We shall not stray far,' he insisted. 'We shall stay right here near the gates.'

Lily sighed, laid a hand on the gentleman's arm and allowed him to lead her a few steps down the street.

'You, my dear Miss Beecham, are a fortunate young lady,' Mr Cooperage told her in the same tones he might use from the pulpit. 'I confess myself to be a great admirer of your mother's.' He took care to steer her away from the busy traffic in the street. 'Your mother, much like Wilberforce himself, has lived in the world. They each knew years full of frivolities and trivial pursuits. How much more we must honour them for having turned from superficiality to a life of worthiness.'

Lily stared. 'I must thank you for the compliment to my mother, Mr Cooperage, but surely you state your case in terms too strong?'

'Impossible!' he scoffed. His voice rang so loud that several passers-by turned to look. 'I could not rate my respect for the woman your mother is now any higher, nor my contempt for those who cling to a life of vanity and mindless amusement—' he flicked a condemnatory wave towards the park and the stream of people now entering '—any lower.'

Had Lily been having this conversation yesterday, or last week, or at any given time in the last seven years, she would have swallowed her irritation and tactfully steered the missionary to a less volatile topic. But today—there was something different about today. Perhaps she'd had too much time to think, or perhaps she had for some time been moving towards an elemental shift, but today the rebel in her—the one with the taste for adventure novels—had got the bit in her teeth.

She sucked in a fortifying breath and straightened her spine. 'Firstly, Mr Cooperage, I feel compelled to tell you that my mother has been worthy of your admiration, and anyone else's, for her *entire* life. Secondly, I would ask that you not be so quick to disparage the pleasure seekers about us.' She cocked her head at him. 'For is that not what today is all about—the happy mix of amusement and altruism?'

Displeasure marred his pleasing features, but only for a moment. He chuckled and assumed an air of condescension. 'Your innocence is refreshing, Miss Beecham.' He sighed. 'The sad truth is that if it would give them a moment's pleasure, most of these people would as soon toss their coin in the gutter as donate it to our cause.'

'But surely you don't believe that merriment and worthiness are mutually exclusive?' Her father's image immediately rose up in her mind. His quick smile and ready laugh were two of her most cherished memories. 'I'm certain you will agree that it is possible to work hard, to become a useful and praiseworthy soul and still partake of the joy in life?'

'The joy in life?' Mr Cooperage appeared startled by the concept. 'My dear, we were not put on this earth to enjoy life—' He cut himself abruptly off. Lily could see that it pained him greatly. She suspected he wanted badly to inform her exactly what he thought her purpose on this earth to be.

Instead, he forced a smile. 'I will not waste our few moments of conversation.' He paused and began again in a lower, almost normal conversational tone. 'I do thank you for your efforts today. However they are gained, I mean to put today's profits to good use. I hope to accomplish much of God's work in my time abroad.'

'How impatient you must be to begin,' she said, grateful for a topic on which they could agree. 'I can only imagine your excitement at the prospect of helping so many people, learning their customs and culture, seeing strange lands and exotic sights.' She sighed. 'I do envy you the experience!'

'You should not,' he objected. 'I do not complain. I will endure the strange lodgings, heathen food and poor company because I have a duty, but I would not subject a woman to the hardships of travel.'

She should not have been surprised. 'But what if a woman has a calling such as yours, sir? What then? Or do you not believe such a thing to be possible?'

He returned her serious expression. 'I believe it to be rare, but possible.' He glanced back towards the park gate. 'Your mother, I believe, has been called. I do think she will answer.'

Her mother had been called? To do what?

'My mission will keep me from the shores of England for a little more than a year, Miss Beecham, but your good mother assures me that there are no other suitors in the wings and that a year is not too long a wait.' He roamed an earnest gaze over her face. 'Was she wrong?'

Lily took a step back. Surprise? He had succeeded in shocking her. 'You wish my mother to wait for you, sir? Do you mean to court her?'

He chuckled. 'Your modesty reflects well on you, my dear. No—it is you who I wish to wait for me. You who I mean to court most assiduously when I return.' His eyes left her face, and darted over the rest of her. 'Your mother was agreeable to the notion. I hope you feel the same?'

Lily stood frozen—not shocked, but numb. Completely taken aback. Mr Cooperage wished to marry her? And her mother had consented? It must be a mistake. At first she could not even wrap her mind about such an idea, but then she had to struggle to breathe as the bleak image of such a life swept over her.

'Miss Beecham?' Mr Cooperage sounded anxious, and mildly annoyed. 'A year is too long?' he asked.

She couldn't breathe. She willed her chest to expand, tried to gasp for the air that she desperately needed. She was going to die. She would collapse to the ground right here, buried and suffocated under the weight of a future she did not want.

Her life was never going to change. The truth hit her hard, at last knocking the breath back into her starving lungs. She gasped out loud and Mr Cooperage began to look truly alarmed. Seven years. So long she had laboured; she had tried her best and squashed the truest part of her nature, all in the attempt to get her mother to look at her with pride. Was this, then, what it would take? The sacrifice of her future?

Lily took a step back, and then another. Only vaguely did she realise how close she had come to the busy street behind her. She only thought to distance herself from the grim reality of the life unfolding in front of her.

'Miss Beecham!' called Mr Cooperage. 'Watch your step. Watch behind you!' he thundered. 'Miss Beecham!'

A short, heavy snort sounded near her. Lily turned. A team of horses, heads tossing wildly, surged towards her. Her gaze met one wild, rolling eye. A call of fright rang out. Had she made the sound, or had the horse?

'Miss Beecham!'

Chapter Two

~~~~~~~~~~~~~~~~~~~~~~~~~

Jack Alden pulled as hard as he dared on the ribbons. Pain seared its way up his injured arm. Pettigrew's ill-tempered bays responded at last, subsiding to a sweating, quivering stop.

'I warned you that these nags were too much for that arm,' his brother Charles said. His hand gripped the side of the borrowed crane-neck phaeton.

'Stow it, Charles,' Jack growled. He stared ahead. 'Hell and damnation, it's a woman in the street!'

'Well, no wonder that park drag ground to a halt. I told you when it started into the other lane that this damned flighty team would bolt.'

'She's not moving,' Jack complained. Was the woman mad? Oblivious to the fact that she'd nearly been trampled like a turnip off a farm cart, she stood stock still. She wasn't even looking their way now; her attention appeared focused on something on the pavement. Jack could not see just what held her interest with near deadly result. Nor could he see her face, covered as it was by a singularly ugly brown bonnet.

'You nearly ran her down. She's likely frozen in fear,' Charles suggested.

'For God's sake!' Jack thrust the reins into his brother's hands and swung down. Another jolt of pain ripped through his arm. 'Hold them fast!' he growled in exasperation.

'Do you know, Jack, people have begun to comment on the loss of your legendary detachment,' Charles said as he held the bays in tight.

'I am *not* detached!' Jack said, walking away. 'You make me sound like a freehold listing in *The Times*.'

'Auction on London Gentleman, Manner Detached,' his brother yelled after him.

Jack ignored him. Legendary detachment be damned. He was anchored fully in this moment and surging forwards on a wave of anger. The fool woman had nearly been killed, and by his hand! Well, that might be an exaggeration, but without doubt the responsibility would have been his. He'd caught sight of her over the thrashing heads of the horses—standing where she clearly did not belong—and fear and anger and guilt had blasted him like lightning out of the sky. The realisation that his concern was more for himself than for her only fuelled his fury.

'Madam!' he called as he strode towards her. The entire incident had happened so fast that the park drag had still not manoeuvred completely past. People milled about on the pavement, and one florid gentleman glared at the woman, but made no move to approach her.

'Madam!' No response. 'If you are bent on suicide, might I suggest another man's phaeton? This one is borrowed and I am bound to deliver it in one piece.'

She did not answer or even look at him. 'Ma'am, do you not realise that you were nearly killed?' He took her arm. 'Come now, you cannot stand in the street!'

At last, ever so slowly, the bonnet began to turn. The infuriating creature looked him full in the face.

Jack immediately wished she hadn't. He had grown up surrounded by beauty. He'd lived in an elegant house and received an excellent education. From ancient statuary to modern landscapes, between the sweep of grand architecture and the graceful curve of the smallest Sèvres bowl, he'd been taught to recognise and appreciate the value of loveliness.

This girl—she was the image of classic English beauty come to life. Gorgeous slate-blue eyes stared at him, but Jack had the eerie certainty that she did not see him at all. Instead she was focused on something far away, or perhaps deep inside. Red-gold curls framed high curving cheeks, smooth, ivory skin gone pale with fright and a slender little nose covered with the faintest smattering of freckles.

And her mouth. His own went dry—because all the fluids in his body were rushing south. A siren's mouth: wide and dusky pink and irresistible. He stared, saw the sudden trembling of that incredibly plump lower lip—and he realised just what it was he was looking at.

Immense sorrow. A portrait of profound loss. The sight of it set off an alarm inside of Jack and awoke a heretofore unsuspected part of his character. He'd never been the heroic, knight-in-shining-armour sort—but that quivering lower lip made him want to jump into the fray. He could not quell the sudden urge to fight this unknown girl's battles, soothe her hurts, or, better yet, kiss her senseless until she forgot what upset her and realised that there were a thousand better uses for that voluptuous mouth.

He swallowed convulsively, tightened his grip on her arm…and thankfully, came back to his senses. They stood in the middle of a busy London street. Catcalls and shouts and several anatomically impossible suggestions echoed from the surrounding bustle of stopped traffic. A begrimed coal carter had stepped forwards to help his brother calm the bays.

Several of society's finest, dressed for the daily strut and starved for distraction, gawked from the pavement.

'Come,' Jack said gently. Her steps wooden, the girl followed. He led her out of the street, past the sputtering red-faced gentleman, towards the Grosvenor Gate. Surely someone would claim her. He darted a glance back at the man who had fallen into step behind them. Someone other than this man—who had apparently left her to be run down like a dog in the street.

Lily was lost in a swirling fog. It had roiled up and out of her in the moment when she had fully understood her predicament. *Her life was never going to change.* Just the echo of that thought brought the mist suffocatingly close. She abandoned herself to it. She'd rather suffocate than contemplate the stifling mess her life had become.

Only vaguely was she aware that the stampeding horses had stopped. Dimly she realised that a stranger led her out of the street. The prickle of her skin told her that people were staring. She couldn't bring herself to care.

'Lilith!' Her mother's strident voice pierced the fog. 'Lilith! Are you unharmed? What were you thinking?'

Anger and resentment surged inside of her, exploded out of her and blew a hole in the circling fog. It was big enough for her to catch a glimpse of her mother's worried scowl as she hurried down from Mr Wilberforce's barouche, and to take in the crowd forming around them.

Her gaze fell on the man who had saved her from herself and she forgot to speak. She stilled. Just at that moment a bright ray of sunlight broke free from the clouds. It shone down directly on to the gentleman, chasing streaks through his hair and outlining the masculine lines of his face. With a whoosh the fog surrounding her disappeared, swept away by the brilliant light and the intensity of the stranger's stare.

Lily swallowed. The superstitious corner of her soul sprang to attention. Her heart began to pound loudly in her ears.

The clouds shifted overhead and the sunbeam disappeared. Now Lily could see the man clearly. Still her pulse beat out a rapid tune. Tall and slender, he was handsome in a rumpled, poetic sort of way. A loose black sling cradled one arm and, though it was tucked inside the dark brown superfine of his coat, she noticed that he held it close as if it ached.

His expression held her in thrall. He'd spoken harshly to her just a moment ago, hadn't he? Now, though his colour was high, his anger seemed to have disappeared as quickly as her hazy confusion. He stared at her with an odd sort of bated hunger. A smile lurked at the edge of his mouth, small and secretive, as if it were meant just for her. The eyes watching her so closely were hazel, a sorry term for such a fascinating mix of green and gold and brown. Curved at their corners were the faintest laugh lines.

So many details, captured in an instant. Together they spoke to her, sending the message that here was a man with experience. Someone who knew passion, and laughter and pain. Here was a man, they whispered, who knew that life was meant to be enjoyed.

'Lilith—' her mother's voice sounded irritated '—have you been hurt?'

Lily forced herself to look away from the stranger. 'No, Mother, I am fine.'

Her mother continued to stare expectantly, but Lily kept quiet. For once, it was not she who was going to explain herself.

Thwarted, Mrs Beecham turned to Mr Cooperage, who lurked behind the strange gentleman. 'Mr Cooperage?' was all that she asked.

The missionary flushed. 'Your daughter does not favour…' he paused and glanced at the stranger '…the matter we discussed last week.'

'Does not favour—?' Lilith's mother's lips compressed to a foreboding thin line.

Mr Cooperage glanced uneasily at the man again and then at the crowd still gathered loosely around them. 'Perhaps you might step aside to have a quiet word with me?' His next words looked particularly hard for him to get out. 'I'm sure your daughter would like the chance to…thank…this gentleman?'

'Mr…?' Her mother raked the stranger with a glare, then waited with a raised brow.

The stranger bowed. Lily thought she caught a faint grimace of pain in his eyes. 'Mr Alden, ma'am.'

'Mr Alden.' Her mother's gaze narrowed. 'I trust my daughter will be safe with you for a moment?'

'Of course.'

The crowd, deprived of further drama, began to disperse. Lily's mother stepped aside and bent to listen to an urgently whispering Mr Cooperage. Lily did not waste a moment considering them. She knew what they discussed. She remembered the haze that had almost engulfed her. It had swept away and left her with a blinding sense of clarity.

'I admit to a ravening curiosity.' Mr Alden spoke low and his voice sounded slightly hoarse. It sent a shiver down Lily's spine. 'Do you wish to?' He raised a questioning brow at her.

'I'm sorry, sir. Do I wish to what?'

'Wish to thank me for nearly running you down in the street while driving a team I clearly should not have been?' He gestured to the sling. 'I assure you, I had planned to most humbly beg your pardon, but if you'd rather thank me instead…'

Lily laughed. She did not have to consider the question. The answer, along with much else, was clear at last. 'Yes,' she said, 'even when you phrase it in such a way. I do wish to thank you.'

He looked a little taken aback, and more than a little interested. 'Then you must be a very odd sort of female,' he said. She felt the heat of the glance that roamed over her, even though he had assumed a clinical expression. 'Don't be afraid to admit it,' he said. He leaned in close, as if confiding a secret. 'Truly, the odd sorts of females are the only ones I can abide.' He smiled at her.

She stared. His words were light and amusing, but that smile? It was wicked. 'Ah, but can they abide you, sir?'

The smile vanished. 'Perhaps the odd ones can,' he said.

The words might have been cynical, or they might have been a joke. Lily watched his face closely, looking for a clue, but she could not decipher his expression. His eyes shone, intense as he spoke again.

'So, tell me…' He lowered his voice a bit. 'What sort of female are you, then?'

No one had ever asked her such a thing. She did not know how to answer. The question stumped her—and made her unbearably sad. That clarity only extended so far, it would seem.

'Miss?' he prompted.

'I don't know,' she said grimly. 'But I think it is time I found out.'

The shadow had moved back in, Jack could see it lurking behind her eyes. And after he'd worked so hard to dispel it, too.

Work was an apt description. He was not naturally glib like his brother. He had no patience with meaningless societal rituals. A little disturbing, then, that it was no chore to speak with this woman.

She stirred his interest—an unusual occurrence with a lady of breeding. In Jack's experience women came in two varieties: those who simulated emotion for the price of a night, and those who manufactured emotion for a tumultuous lifetime sentence.

Jack did not like emotion. It was the reason he despised the tense and edgy stranger he had lately become. He understood that emotion was an integral part of human life and relationships. He experienced it frequently himself. He held his family in affection. He respected his mentors and colleagues. Attraction, even lust, was a natural phenomenon he allowed himself to explore to the fullest. He just refused to be controlled by such sentiments.

Emotional excess invariably became complicated and messy and as far as he'd been able to determine, the benefits rarely outweighed the consequences. Scholarship, he'd discovered, was safe. Reason and logic were his allies, his companions, his shields. If one must deal with excessive emotions at all, it was best to view them through the lens of learning. It was far more comfortable, after all, to make a study of rage or longing than to experience it oneself. Such things were of interest in Greek tragedy, but dashed inconvenient in real life.

Logic dictated, therefore, that he should have been repelled by this young beauty. She reeked of emotion. She had appeared to be at the mercy of several very strong sensations in succession. Jack should have felt eager to escape her company.

But as had happened all too frequently in the last weeks, his reason deserted him. He was not wild to make his apologies and move on. He wanted to discover how she would look under the onslaught of the next feeling. Would those warm blue eyes ice over in anger? Could he make that gorgeous wide mouth quiver in desire?

'*Mister* Alden.'

His musings died a quick death. That ringing voice was familiar.

'Lady Ashford.' He knew before he even turned around.

'I am unsurprised to find you in the midst of this ruckus, Mr Alden.' The countess skimmed over to them and pinned an eagle eye on the girl. 'But you disappoint me, Miss Beecham.'

The name reverberated inside Jack's head, sending a jolt down his spine. *Beecham*? The girl's name was Beecham? It was a name that had weighed heavily on his mind of late.

They were joined again by the girl's mother and the red-faced Mr Cooperage, but Lady Ashford had not finished with the young lady.

'There are two, perhaps three, men in London who are worth throwing yourself under the wheels of a carriage, Miss Beecham. I regret to inform you that Mr Alden is not one of them.'

No one laughed. Jack was relieved, because he rather thought that the countess meant what she said.

Clearly distressed, the girl had no answer. Jack was certainly not fool enough to respond. Fortunately for them both, someone new pushed her way through the crowd. It was his mother, coming to the rescue.

Lady Dayle burst into their little group like a siege mortar hitting a French garrison. Passing Jack by, she scattered the others as she rushed to embrace the girl like a long-lost daughter. She clucked, she crooned, she examined her at arm's length and then held her fast to her bosom.

'Jack Alden,' she scolded, 'I could scarcely believe it when I heard that you were the one disrupting the fair and causing such a frenzy of gossip! People are saying you nearly ran this poor girl down in the street!' Her gaze wandered over to the phaeton and fell on Charles. He gave a little wave of his hand, but did not leave the horses.

'Charles! I should have known you would be mixed up in this. Shame on the pair of you!' She stroked the girl's arm. 'Poor lamb! Are you sure you are unhurt?'

Had Jack been a boy, he might have been resentful that his mother's attention was focused elsewhere. He was not. He was a man grown, and therefore only slightly put out that he could not show the girl the same sort of consideration.

Mrs Beecham looked outraged. Miss Beecham merely looked confused. Lady Ashford looked as if she'd had enough.

'Elenor,' the countess said, 'you are causing another scene. I do not want these people to stand and watch you cluck like a hen with one chick. I want them to go inside and spend their money at my fair. Do take your son and have his arm seen to.'

'Oh, Jack,' his mother reproved, her arm still wrapped comfortingly about the girl. 'Have you re-injured your arm?'

Lady Ashford let her gaze slide over the rest of the group. 'Elenor dear, do let go of the girl and take him to find out. Mr Cooperage, you will come with me and greet the women who labour in your interest today. The rest of you may return to what you were doing.'

'Lilith has had a fright, Lady Ashford,' Mrs Beecham said firmly. 'I'll just take her back to our rooms.'

'Nonsense, that will leave the Book Table unattended,' the countess objected.

'Nevertheless…' Mrs Beecham's lips were folded extremely thin.

'I shall see to her,' Lady Dayle declared. 'Jack, can you take us in your… Oh, I see. Whose vehicle are you driving, dear? Never mind, I shall just get a hackney to take us home.'

Mrs Beecham started to protest, and a general babble of conversation broke out. It was put to rout by Lady Ashford. 'Very well,' she declared loudly and everyone else fell silent. 'You can trust Lady Dayle to see to your daughter, Mrs Beecham. I will take you to fetch the girl myself once the day is done.'

She paused to point a finger. 'Mr Wilberforce's barouche is still here. I'm certain he will not mind dropping the pair of them off,' she said, 'especially since he has only just made you a much larger request. I shall arrange it.' She beckoned to the missionary. 'Mr Cooperage, if you would come with me?'

Everyone moved to follow the countess's orders. Not for

the first time, Jack thought that had Lady Ashford been a man, the Peninsular War might have been but a minor skirmish.

With a last, quick glance at the girl on his mother's arm, he turned back to his brother and the cursed team of horses.

But Lady Ashford had not done with him. 'Are those Pettigrew's animals, Mr Alden?' she called. She did not wait for an answer. 'Take yourself on home and see to your arm—and do not let Pettigrew lure you into buying those bays. I hear they are vicious.'

'Thank you for the advice, Lady Ashford,' he said, and, oddly, he meant it. Charles stood, a knowing grin spreading rapidly across his face.

'Not a word, Charles,' Jack threatened.

'I wasn't going to say a thing.'

Wincing, Jack climbed up into the rig and took up the ribbons. Charles took his seat beside him and leaned back, silent, but with a smile playing about the corners of his mouth.

'The girl's surname is Beecham.'

Charles sat a little straighter. 'Beecham?' he repeated with studied nonchalance. 'It's a common enough name.'

'It's that shipbuilder's name and you know it, Charles. The man who is supposedly mixed up with Batiste.'

His brother sighed. 'It's not your responsibility to bring that scoundrel of a sea captain to justice, Jack.'

Jack stilled. A wave of frustration and anger swept over him at his brother's words. He fought to recover his equilibrium. This volatility was unacceptable. He must regain control.

'I know that,' he said tightly. 'But I can't focus on anything else. I keep thinking of Batiste skipping away without so much as a slap on the hand.' Charles was the only person to whom Jack had confided the truth about his wound and the misadventures that had led to it. Even then, there were details he'd been honour-bound to hold back. 'It's bad enough that the man is a thief and a slaver as well. But by all accounts the man is mad—I worry that he might come after old Mervyn Latimer again, or even try to avenge himself on Trey and Chione.'

It wasn't Charles's fault that he couldn't understand. Though he knew most of the story, he didn't know about the aftermath. Jack didn't want him—or anyone else—to know how intensely he'd been affected. Charles must never know about his nightmares. He didn't understand himself how or why all this should have roused his latent resentment towards their cold and distant father, but one thing he did know—he would never burden Charles with the knowledge. His older brother had his own weighty issues to contend with in that direction.

'Would you like me to make some inquiries?' Charles asked.

'Both Treyford and I already have. Batiste has disappeared. He could be anywhere. All the Foreign Office could give me was that name—Matthew Beecham. A young shipbuilder—an Englishman from Dorset who moved to America to pursue his craft. Somehow he became mixed up with Batiste, and found himself in trouble with the American government. He's disappeared as well. The Americans have made a formal complaint against him. They want to question him and have asked that he be detained, should he show up back at home.'

'So? Does the girl hail from Dorset? Did you ask her if she has a relative named Matthew?'

'Not yet.' Jack watched Charles from the corner of his eye. 'I would dearly like to talk to the man. He's the only link I've been able to find. I'm not going to be able to rest until Batiste is caught and made to pay for his crimes.'

Perched ramrod straight now, Charles looked earnest as he spoke. 'You know, Jack, I've never known you to fall so quickly into something so…dangerous, as you did with Treyford.'

Jack bristled slightly.

'Now, forget that it is your older brother speaking and

calm yourself,' Charles admonished. 'There must have been a reason for it, something that drew you into the fray.'

There had been, of course, but he was not going to share it with his brother. Once Jack had heard Treyford's story of a band of antiquity thieves menacing Chione Latimer and her family, he'd known he had to help. He and Charles were both all too aware of the difficulties of living with an unsettled sense of menace.

'Whatever the reason, I, for one, am happy to see you out from behind your wall of books.' Charles's gaze slid over Jack's sling. 'I'm sorry that all you appeared to get from your adventure was a bullet hole, but I would neither see you slide back into your old hibernating ways nor allow yourself to become embroiled in something even more complicated and hazardous.'

'What would you have me do, then?' Jack asked with just a touch of sarcasm. 'Embroidery? Tatting?' He raked his brother with an exasperated glance. 'I've already told you, I have neither the inclination nor the patience for politics.'

Charles rolled his eyes. 'Why don't you just relax, Jack? It's been an age since either Mother or I have been able to drag you out of your rooms. Have a break from your work. Not everyone is fascinated with your mouldy classics.'

'They should be,' Jack said, just to tweak his brother.

Charles ignored him. 'Look about you for once,' he continued. 'Enjoy the Season, squire Mother to a society event or two.' He grimaced. 'Or if the thought of society is too distasteful, you can help Mother and Sophie with their charitable efforts. If you had paid attention, you would see that Mother is slowly becoming more and more involved with the work that the Evangelical branch of the Church is doing. This charity bazaar she is helping with is just a small example of their work. Their presence is only growing stronger as the years pass. Who knows? They might actually succeed in changing the face of society. And you might even find whatever it is you were looking for.'

'The only thing I'm looking for is Batiste.'

Charles sighed. 'Well, look again, little brother.' He leaned back again, his grip on the side tightening as the bay on the left shied from a calling-card vendor.

Jack was forced to watch the pair closely once more. His mind was awhirl. Perhaps he should consider something different from his usual classical studies—and if his new path also brought him closer to finding information on Batiste, then so much the better. If this Beecham girl and his mother were both involved with the Evangelicals, then perhaps he could look into them as well. Charles could believe what he liked about Jack's need to find something he was missing. He knew the truth of the matter and it involved nothing so mawkish or sentimental.

And neither, he told himself firmly, did it have anything to do with the shine of red-gold hair or the taste of soft, plump lips.

Chapter Three

A stranger inhabited Lily's skin. Or perhaps it had only been so long since determination had pumped so fiercely through her veins, it felt as if it were so. But this was the old Lily—her father's daughter, sure and strong, confident that whatever she wished for lay within her reach. Almost as if it were happening to someone else, she watched herself talk, smile and climb into Mr Wilberforce's barouche. He and Lady Dayle were soon engaged in a spirited debate over reform. Fortunate, since this left Lily free to turn her rediscovered resolve to answering Mr Alden's troubling question: *What sort of female are you?*

She barely knew where to start, but she did discover that some aspects of the new Lily—her mother's daughter—were not so easily discarded. And all of them were firmly fixated on the sudden burst of light that had shone down on Mr Alden for one dazzling moment. Surely it had been nothing more than a stray sunbeam?

Perhaps not. Her nurse's superstitious Cornish wisdom had been a constant in her life and it had taken firm root in Lily's mind while she was still young. In recent years it had flourished into a guilt-ridden tangle.

So often she'd worried that she'd missed some forewarning of her father's tragic death. The storm that ultimately killed him had been immense. Nurse had moaned that his loss had been punishment for their failure to heed several unmistakable portents of doom.

Lily had vowed never to make another such mistake. But surely a bright beam of light was no portent of doom. Then what could it possibly mean?

With every fibre of her being, Lily wanted it to mean the change she longed for. It had touched on Mr Alden. Could it be that he would be an instrument of change? She flushed. Or was it possible that he might be something more?

'Lady Dayle,' she spoke up into a pause in the conversation, 'I fear that your son has re-injured his arm because of my inattention. I wish you would convey my apologies.'

The viscountess patted her arm. 'Do not fret yourself, my dear. Jack should not have been driving those cantankerous animals in the first place. I dare say his brother told him so. But Charles should have remembered that the instant he counselled against it, it would become the single thing in the world that must be done.'

Lily smiled. She'd grown up with her cousin Matthew and he had acted in just the same way. 'How did Mr Alden first injure his arm?'

Lady Dayle frowned. 'Oh, he got caught up in that trouble at the Egyptian Hall, at Mr Belzoni's exhibition. I haven't the faintest idea how or why—I had no inkling that Jack even knew Belzoni or Lord Treyford. It was just a few weeks ago perhaps you heard of it?'

Lily shook her head.

'Yes, I heard of it,' Mr Wilberforce intervened. 'A ring of international art thieves, or something similar, was it not?'

'Something like,' Lady Dayle agreed. 'Jack will barely

speak of it—even to me. And believe me, when her son is shot, a mother wants to know why.'

'Good heavens,' Lily said. She stirred in her seat. 'Shot? Mr Alden must lead quite an exciting life.'

'But that is just it! The entire thing was so patently unlike him. Jack is a scholar, Miss Beecham, and a brilliant one at that. At times he is all but a recluse. He spends more time closeted with his ancient civilisations than with anyone flesh and blood.' She shot Mr Wilberforce a significant look. 'He is my inscrutable son, sir, and too reserved and detached from society to cause me much concern—especially compared to the rigmarole his brothers subjected me to.'

Mr Wilberforce laughed, but Lily fought back an undeniable surge of disappointment. A scholar? Inscrutable and reserved? It didn't fit the image she'd already built around that wicked smile.

But what did she know of men? An image of her father flashed in her mind. He dwelled heavily in her mind today— a natural reaction on a day when her past and her future appeared destined to collide. On the rare occasion she allowed herself to dream, the portrait she drew of a husband always shared important traits with George Beecham: twinkling eyes, a ready smile and a never-ending thirst for the next new experience. Never would she have conjured up a dry, dusty scholar who hid from life behind his books.

Lily had been hiding for seven long years. She'd done with it. She wasn't her father's little girl any more, but neither would she continue as her mother's quiet handmaiden. She fought back a surge of guilt. She didn't mean to abandon her mother, nor did she wish to give up the good works she had done along with her. She only wanted the chance to live her own life, while she worked to help others better theirs. Superstition would not make that chance happen. Neither, it seemed, would Mr Alden. She clenched her fists. She would find a way, and do it herself.

It was time she melded the two halves of her soul and finally answered that pesky question. It was time she discovered who Lily Beecham was.

Jack kept his senses alert, his eye sharp for movement in the roadway ahead. This was likely not the best time to be skulking about the East End, especially not on his own. But his eagerness for his brother's company had waned after listening to his admonitions and advice this afternoon. Charles would only have tried to talk him out of coming down here at all.

So Jack had dropped off his brother and then returned Pettigrew's nasty bays, and now he found his feet taking him towards the river, towards the reputedly abandoned shipping offices of Gustavo Batiste.

Little Bure Street was not exactly a hotbed of activity in the late evening. A pair of prostitutes propositioned him from a doorway, but he shook his head and continued on. No doubt anyone with legitimate business in these dockside buildings had long since gone home, but the full swing of the illicit enterprises of the night had not yet begun. It didn't matter; the alleyway he sought lay just ahead. Jack slipped in and stood a moment, allowing his eyes to adjust to the deeper blackness before he moved forwards cautiously. He flexed his sore arm as he went. The narrow space was more a passage than a street, but it opened on to a small walled courtyard at the end. Opposite him a rickety set of wooden stairs led to an office. Across the doorway sagged a crooked sign: *G. Batiste & Co.*

Mervyn Latimer and Treyford had both warned him this would be a waste of time. The offices had been deserted for months. But Jack had a need to see for himself. He eased up the stairs, careful to keep his footsteps quiet.

The door was not locked. Jack pushed it open with his free hand and was forced to stop again and adjust his eyesight. It was pitch black in the small anteroom. It took several long moments for his eyes to adapt, but there was nothing to see once they had. A listing table, a couple of small chairs and dust lying thick on every surface. He shook his head. What had he expected? He was grasping at straws. His obsession with Batiste was not logical, his involuntary association of the villain with his dead father utterly without a rational basis.

From the back of the building came a thump and a muffled curse. Jack froze. His pulse began to race. Slowly he reached down and pulled a knife from his boot. He'd taken to keeping it there, since his misadventures with Treyford. It felt awkward and unbalanced in his left hand, but it was better than nothing.

A closed door lay to the right of the broken table. He eased it open and found another narrow hallway. Several more doors were closed on either side, but the last one on the right stood cracked open, a faint light shining from within.

Who could it be? Silently he made his way there. He flattened himself against the wall and eased his arm from the sling. From inside the room came the sound of rustling papers and opening drawers. Grimacing at the strain, he placed his right hand on the doorway and gripped his knife tight with the other.

Thwang. Jack stared in shock and fascination as a wickedly vibrating blade abruptly sprouted from the opposite doorframe.

'I got another o' those,' a voice rasped from within. 'But this building's cheap and that wall is paper thin. I'm thinkin' it might just be easier to shoot you through it.'

The tension unexpectedly drained out of Jack, replaced by a rising flood of relief. He knew that voice.

'Eli!' he exclaimed. 'It's me, Jack Alden.'

The door flew open. The erstwhile sea captain turned

groom stared at him in surprise. 'Jack Alden! What in blazes are ye doing here?'

'I might ask the same of you, old man!' Jack pocketed his own blade and thumped the grizzled old sailor on the shoulder. Eli grunted and crossed back to the desk he'd been rifling through. The rap of his peg-leg on the wooden floor sounded loud in the small office. Jack pulled the blade from the doorframe.

'How's the arm?' Eli asked. 'Ye look a sight better'n the last time I saw ye.'

'It's healing. But why aren't you in Devonshire with Mervyn and Trey and Chione and all the rest of them? They've all got to be busy, what with a wedding to plan and one hell of trip coming up.'

'Aye, 'tis a madhouse at times.' He held out a hand and Jack gave back his knife. With a sigh he slammed a drawer shut and sat in the seat behind the desk. 'Mervyn and Trey sent me up. Something's astir.'

'Batiste?' Jack asked, with a sweep of his hand.

'You know Mervyn's ways. He's got ears everywhere and hears every bird fart and every whisper o' trouble. He's got word that some of Batiste's men are on the move. Here. In England.'

Anger surged in Jack's gut. 'God, it eats at me, knowing he got away,' he said. The low and harsh tone of his voice surprised even him. He struggled again to rein in his emotion. 'I hate the thought of it—him sitting back, silent and scornful, manipulating us like so many puppets.' His eyes narrowed. 'After all he's done to Mervyn, he needs to be brought to justice.'

'What he's done to Mervyn's bad enough. But he's done others far worse. What worrit's me is the idea of him having time to stew. Revenge is his favourite dish and he'll be spittin' mad at how we foiled him.'

'So what do you hope to find here?'

Eli glanced at him. 'The same thing you were, I s'pose.

Some hint o' where he might be hiding out. With the Americans after him as well as the Royal Navy, he's got to lie low for a while.'

'The bastard's got a ship and the whole world to hide in.' Jack sighed.

'Trey thinks he won't go too far. He didn't get what he wanted, and he thinks he'll try again. Like any man, he'll have a spot or two he goes to when his back is against the wall. Trouble is findin' it.'

Jack stood a little straighter. 'I might have a lead on that shipbuilder, Beecham. Perhaps he knows where Batiste would go to hide his head.'

'Do what ye can, man.' Eli sighed. 'I know Trey hates to ask ye—especially after ye got hurt the first time. But won't none of us be truly safe until that man is caught and hung.'

'I will. Tell Trey I will handle it.' He stared at the old man with resolution. 'In fact, I think it should be possible for me to begin right now.'

'Mr Wilberforce asked you to do what?' Lily's dish of tea hovered, halfway up. The evening had grown late. Lady Ashford and her mother had arrived to fetch her, and Lady Dayle had pressed them to stay for a cold supper.

'To make a tour through Surrey and Kent, speaking with local groups of Evangelicals along the way,' her mother repeated.

'Your mother has accomplished wonders in Weymouth, Miss Beecham.' Lady Ashworth accepted a slice of cheese from the platter Lady Dayle offered. 'She can share her methods and be an inspiration to many others.'

'Of course.' Lily's mind raced. This was just exactly what she'd wished for; a chance to travel, to see new places and meet new people. Her breathing quickened and her pulse began to beat a little faster. 'Mother, I'm so proud of you.'

'Congratulations, Mrs Beecham,' said Lady Dayle. 'You shall be one of the leading ladies of a very great movement. And to have the request come from Mr Wilberforce himself is quite an honour, is it not?'

'Thank you, it is indeed an honour.' Her mother looked exhausted. Lily felt a twinge of guilt. She'd spent a perfectly lovely afternoon with the viscountess and her mother had not even had a chance to celebrate her accomplishment.

'Will we be returning home first, Mother? Or shall we leave straight from town?' she asked. 'Either way, we must be sure that you rest beforehand. I can see you are quite worn out.'

An uncomfortable look passed across her mother's face. 'I'll be leaving from London in a few days, dear. Lady Ashford has graciously agreed to accompany me.' She met Lily's eye with resolve. 'You will be returning home.'

'What?' This time she was forced to set her cup down with shaking hands. 'You cannot mean that!'

'We've been away from home too long as it is. Someone needs to oversee the Parish Poor Relief Committee. The planning needs to begin now for the Michaelmas festival. We cannot abandon our duty to those less fortunate.'

'There are plenty of ladies at home willing and able to take care of those things,' Lily argued. 'Mother, please!' Resentment and disbelief churned in her belly. It was true that her mother had found less and less joy in life over the years. Her father's death had been a blow to them both. Grief and guilt were heavy burdens to bear, but Lily had been forced to cope alone. Sometimes she felt she had grieved twice over, for her quiet, reserved mother had sunk into a decline and a militant stranger had climbed out the other side.

Restrictive, distant, hard to please—yes. But Lily had never suspected her mother of deliberate cruelty before today. First Mr Cooperage and now—

She stopped, aghast. 'Does Mr Cooperage factor into this decision, Mother? Because I tell you now that I am not interested in his views on any subject!'

'Lilith!' her mother gasped. 'We will not discuss it further. This is entirely inappropriate!'

'Well then, it appears I have arrived at the perfect time,' an amused masculine voice interrupted.

Lily turned to find Mr Alden framed handsomely in the doorway. An instant flush began to spread up and over her. Was she doomed to always encounter this man at a serious disadvantage?

He advanced into the room and she tried to collect herself. Not an easy task. Poetic—that was the word that had sprung to mind earlier. Brooding was the one that popped up now. Darkly handsome and brooding. Though he had a sardonic smile hovering at the corner of his mouth, the effect was ruined by the rest of him. She just could not be entirely intimidated by anyone in that rumpled state. He looked as if his valet had dressed him in the height of fashion, in only the best silk and superfine, and then laid him down and rolled him repeatedly about on the bed. She tightened her mouth at the image evoked and her flush grew stronger yet. A great many women, she strongly suspected, would enjoy rolling Mr Alden about on the bed.

'Jack, darling.' Lady Dayle rose to welcome her son. 'Do come in and join us. The ladies have only just finished with the fair and we are taking a cold supper.'

He kissed his mother on the cheek and made an elegant bow to the rest of the ladies. Lily shifted slightly away as he took the chair directly next to hers.

'I should thank you right away, Miss Beecham,' he said with a quirk of a smile in her direction. 'Usually I am the one for ever introducing inappropriate topics to the conversation.

My brother informs me that virtually no one else cares for my mouldy ancients.' He leaned back. The seating was so close that Lily could feel the heat emanating from him. 'But you have saved me the trouble.' He raised a brow at her. 'Which distasteful subject have you brought to the table?'

'Never mind that, Jack,' scolded his mother. 'Mrs Beecham has been granted a singular honour. We are celebrating.'

Lady Ashford explained while Lily fumed.

'My heartfelt congratulations,' Mr Alden said to her mother when the countess had finished. He turned again to Lily. 'I'm sure you will enjoy the journey, Miss Beecham. There are some amazingly picturesque vistas in that part of the country.'

'I am not to go, Mr Alden.' Lily could not keep the anger completely from her tone. 'I am instead sent home like a wayward child.'

She noticed that he grew very still. 'Where is home, if I might ask?'

'In Dorset, near Weymouth,' she answered, though she did not see the relevance of the question.

'Ah.' He steepled his fingers and thought a moment. 'I suppose I can understand your mother's point of view.'

Irritation nearly choked Lily. She glared at him.

'You can?' asked her mother in surprise.

'Yes, well, it is only fair to consider both sides of the argument, and you must admit that travelling with an innocent young girl must always be complicated.'

'Innocent young girl?' Lily objected. 'I am nearly three and twenty and I have seen and done many things in the course of my volunteer work.'

'I do not doubt you, but the fact remains that you are a young, unmarried lady. As such you will most likely require frequent stops to rest, and special arrangements for private parlours to shield you from the coarser elements. If you stay at private homes, there will have to be thought given as to whether or not any single gentlemen are in residence. Not to mention that you will have to have a chaperon for every minute of every day. Without a doubt, two older, more mature ladies will travel easier alone.'

Lily gaped at him.

'You can see the logic of the situation.' He nodded towards her.

'There are so many things wrong with that litany of statements that I must give serious consideration on where to begin,' she responded.

'Do tell,' he invited. That lurking grin spread a little wider.

'I could refute your errors one by one, but instead I will merely ask you if you have any sisters, Mr Alden?'

'Nary a one.'

'Then I fail to see where you might have come by any experience travelling with *innocent* young ladies,' she said hotly. 'And if you are in the habit of consorting with other types, then I would only beg you not to equate me with them!'

'Lilith!' Her mother was clearly scandalised.

Lady Dayle, however, laughed. 'Bravo, Miss Beecham! You have routed him in one fell swoop. But now you are both guilty of introducing inappropriate topics to the conversation, so let us talk of something else.' She frowned at her son. 'Do not tease the dear girl, Jack. I believe it is a real disappointment for her.'

Mr Alden nodded at his mother, then spared a glance for Lily. Mortified, she avoided his eye.

Lady Ashford offered him the tray of biscuits. He took one and Lily saw him blink thoughtfully at the countess. '*Will* the two of you exceptional ladies be travelling alone?' he asked in an innocent tone.

'In fact, we will not,' the countess answered. 'Mr Cooperage will accompany us. We thought it possible to also raise money for his mission as we travel.'

'I knew it!' Lily exclaimed. 'Only today he informed me that he did not approve of ladies travelling from home.' She cast a disparaging glance at Mr Alden. 'I just did not expect to find other gentlemen in agreement with such an antiquated notion.'

'I said no such thing,' he protested. 'I said it was complicated, not that it should not be done. Is Mr Cooperage the gentleman from Park Lane, the one who was with you when you had your...near accident?'

'He is.'

'And he is an Evangelical, is he not?'

'He is. Why do you ask?'

Mr Alden drew a deep breath. He sat a little straighter. For the first time Lily noticed true animation in his face and a light begin to shine in his eye.

'I ask because I admit to some curiosity about the Evangelicals. For instance, I find their attitudes towards women to be conflicting and confusing.'

'How so, Mr Alden?' Lady Ashford bristled a little.

'Hannah More argues that women are cheated out of an education and are thus made unfit to be mothers and moral guides. She advocates educating women, but only to a degree. Evangelicals encourage women to confine themselves to domestic concerns, but when their important issues take the stage—abolition of the slave trade, or changing the East India Company's charter to allow missionaries into India—they urge them to boycott, to petition, to persuade.'

'Women are perfectly able to understand and embrace such issues, Mr Alden.' Now Lily bristled at the thought of this dangerously intelligent and handsome man negating the causes she had worked for.

'I agree, Miss Beecham. In fact, in encouraging such participation, I would say that the Evangelicals have opened the political process to a far wider public.'

Understanding dawned. She cast a bright smile on him. 'Yes, of course you are correct,' Lily said, turning to her mother. 'You see, Mother, I have petitioned for change, educated people about the work that needs done and laboured myself for the common good. What is a little trip through Kent when compared to all of that?'

'That was not my point,' Mr Alden interrupted. 'On the contrary, I counsel you ladies to proceed with caution. People are noticing the good that you have accomplished. But if they begin to suspect that Evangelicals encourage women to rise beyond their station—not my words, by the way—then you could have a public uprising on your hands.'

'Like the Blagdon Controversy,' breathed Mrs Beecham, referring to the extensive public outcry against Hannah More's Sunday Schools as dangerous and 'Methodist'.

'It could be far worse,' Mr Alden said. 'Women do not rate any higher on the Church of England's scale than Methodists.'

'Thank you, Mr Alden,' Lady Ashford intoned. 'You have given us a great deal to consider. We shall proceed with care.' She fixed a stern gaze on Lily. 'You can see that it would indeed be best for you to stay home, Miss Beecham. Old warhorses like your mother and I are one thing. We would not wish to be accused of corrupting young ladies.'

Lily lowered her gaze. Hurt and dismay congealed in her throat, choking off any protest. She barely knew Mr Alden; it was ridiculous to feel this bone-deep sense of betrayal. But she could not stem it, any more than she could hold back the rising tide of anger in her breast. She raised her head and met Mr Alden's gaze with a steely one of her own.

'I cannot see where sending Miss Beecham home on the mail coach is any kinder or gentler than carting her around

Surrey.' Mr Alden's eyes never left hers as he spoke. 'Clearly, the best thing for her to do is to remain here.'

Lily forgave the irritating man everything on the spot. 'Oh, yes! What a marvellous idea!'

Lily's mother sniffed. 'Well, I cannot see that a residence with a single gentleman in London is any less dangerous than one in Faversham.'

'But the Bartleighs, Mother!' Lily exclaimed.

Lady Ashford sent her an enquiring look and she hastened to explain. 'Very dear friends of ours, from home,' she said. 'They are due to arrive in London soon, for a short stay. Mother, you know they would not mind if I stayed with them.'

'Lilith Beecham,' her mother scolded, 'the Bartleighs are travelling to town to consult with the doctors here, not to chaperon you. I wouldn't ask it of them, even if they were due to arrive before we are gone, which they are not.'

But Lady Dayle was nearly jumping out of her seat. 'Oh, but Lily must stay with me! You need not worry, Mrs Beecham, for Jack has his own bachelor's rooms. I scarcely see him at the best of times, and now he talks of burying himself in his books for his next research project.'

Lily watched her mother and began to hope.

'It will be just Miss Beecham and I,' the viscountess continued. 'How perfect! She can help to introduce me to some of the worthy causes you ladies support, and I can introduce her a little to society.'

Lily's heart sank. That had been the absolute wrong thing to suggest.

'We are honoured by your invitation, my lady, but I do not wish for Lilith to go into society.' Her mother's mouth had pressed so tight that her lips had disappeared.

'Come now, dear Margaret.' The unexpected, coaxing tone

came from Lady Ashford. 'It will not do the girl any harm to gain a little polish. She'll likely need it in the future.'

Her mother hesitated. Lily's heart was pounding, but she kept her eyes demurely down. The moment of silence stretched out, until she thought her nerves would shatter.

'I shall ask my dear daughter Corinne to help with the girl,' Lady Ashford said. 'You know that she and her husband are familiar with the right people. Although she is too far along in her confinement to take the girl herself, they will know just the events that a girl like Lilith will do well at.'

'Yes, of course, nothing fast or too *tonnish*,' said Lady Dayle in reassuring tones. 'Perhaps a literary or musical evening.'

Her mother heaved a great sigh. 'Very well,' she said ungraciously.

'Oh,' breathed Lily. 'Thank you, Mother.'

Lady Dayle was positively gleeful. 'Oh, we shall have a grand time getting to know one another, my dear.'

Lady Ashford knew when to call a retreat. She stood. 'Well, it has been a long and tiring day and I must still see to the tally of the day's profits. I'm sure that Mrs Beecham and her daughter will both do better for a good night's rest.' She inclined her head. 'Thank you, Elenor, for the tea and for your interest.'

The farewells were made. Lily returned the viscountess's embrace and agreed to meet to make plans on the morrow. She approached her son with a cautious step and a wary glance. 'Mr Alden, I scarcely know what to say to you.'

She flinched a little at the disapproval she glimpsed in his expression. But then she squared her shoulders. She had faced disapprobation nearly every day for years. Why should his stab any deeper?

'Thank you for everything that you have done for me today,' she said with a smile, 'Even though I'm sure some of it was quite unintentional.'

He bowed. 'I am very happy to have met you, Miss Beecham. It has been an…interesting experience.'

Once again he had donned that impenetrable mask. It saddened her, this barrier that she could not breach. Earlier today he had handled a difficult situation with humour and ease. But now he only looked worldly and cynical. How disappointing. He obviously possessed a great mind. She suspected he also possessed a sense of justice, perhaps even a thoughtful nature, but how could she know for sure?

This was her chance. Lily knew there would still be restrictions, but she could not suppress this glorious feeling of *freedom*. For a few weeks she would be able to relax, to give her true nature free rein. Perhaps if she was very lucky she might even find a position, or, she blushed, a suitor. Anything to supplant her mother's idea for her future.

Lily knew she owed Mr Alden for this chance, and, indeed, she was grateful. But staring into his closed countenance, she knew she had no time to waste on him.

'Goodbye,' she whispered. She turned wistfully away and followed her mother out the door.

Lady Dayle chattered happily for a few minutes after her guests had left. Jack listened to her, content to see her so excited about the coming weeks. When the servants came in to clear, he rose, kissed her goodbye and let the butler show him out. The door clicked closed behind him. Jack stood for a long moment on the step, breathing deep in the cold evening air.

The girl was from Dorset. He was going to do it—he was going to find Matthew Beecham, who would lead him to Batiste. He no longer knew if it was truly justice he sought, or some twisted sort of redemption. He no longer cared. He was going to quiet the roiling furore that had turned his existence upside down.

It would take some delicate manoeuvring, he was sure. He was going to have to proceed very carefully. He was more than a little disturbed by his own actions. Right now he stood, evaluating his options with reason and purpose. That had not been the case in there.

He'd done what he could to manipulate the situation in his favour. And he'd succeeded. But one minute he'd been speaking like a man of sense and the next Lily Beecham had been glaring at him with accusation in her lovely face.

It had done something to him. His brain had shut down with a nearly audible *click*. He had spoken up to fix the situation with her goal in mind as much as his, and with an overwhelming desire to remove the wealth of hurt in her eyes.

It was a very dangerous precedent. It had been an unthinking response, an action dictated by *emotion*. Clearly this was a very dangerous girl.

Yet having recognised his weakness, he was armed against it. He would proceed, as he always did, with logic and reason as his weapons. And a healthy dose of caution as his shield.

Chapter Four

Lily closed her eyes and let her heart soar with the music. Happiness filled her and she didn't even try to stem it—the ascending harmonies matched her mood so perfectly.

The last several days spent with Lady Dayle had been full—and incredibly fulfilling. The pair of them had shopped a little, and explored much of what the city had to offer. Lily had lost herself in fine art and turned her skin brown picnicking in the parks. They had encountered Miss Dawson again and Lily had struck up a fast friendship with the young lady, and she'd coaxed her into showing her all the fashionable—and safe—areas of the city.

Lily had laughed at the raucous prints lining the shop windows and lusted after the huge selections in the bookstores. Best of all, she had spent endless hours talking and talking with the viscountess. Seven years of questions, comments and contemplations had bubbled up and out of her and Lady Dayle had matched her word for word. And though she did not share in it completely, the viscountess had not once chastised her for her boundless energy or curiosity.

Lily had not forgotten her end of the bargain either. She'd

taken Lady Dayle along to several meetings of charitable societies and introduced her to the hard-working, generous people who ran them. The viscountess appeared happy to be wading into these new waters, getting her feet wet and judging which of the endless charitable opportunities interested her most.

Tonight, though, came Lily's first society outing. Lady Dayle had indeed chosen a musical evening. All about her sat people who took pleasure in each other and in the beauty of the music, and finally Lily felt the last of her restraints fall away. Her spirits flew free to follow the intricate melodies of the string quartet. Even the gradual darkening of the piece could not shake her enjoyment. The beauty of the mournful finish echoed within her and when the last haunting chord faded away she sat silent a moment, relishing it, and ignoring the silent stream of tears down her face.

'Oh, my dear,' Lady Dayle said kindly. She pressed Lily's hand and passed her a linen handkerchief.

Lily smiled her thanks and dried her eyes. She was attracting attention. Two ladies behind the viscountess smiled indulgently at her, but further away she could see others watching with their heads together or talking behind their hands. She raised her chin. 'That was absolutely beautiful, was it not, my lady?'

'Indeed it was,' agreed Lady Dayle. She got to her feet as the rest of the guests rose.

'I'd forgotten that music could touch you so deeply.' Lily sighed, following. 'Will they be doing another piece?'

'Before the evening is over they will. There is an intermission now, with food and the chance to mingle with the others.' Lady Dayle flashed a smile over her shoulder. 'Mrs Montague has asked that her guests also take part in the entertainment. Should you like to play? You mentioned the pianoforte, I believe.'

'Oh, no.' Lily laughed. 'It has been so long since I played

anything other than hymns, and I doubt the company would be interested.'

'I think it would be very well received. This is the most fascinatingly diverse mix of people I've seen in a long time.' She gestured to a corner where a footman with a platter of hot oyster loaves stood surrounded by eager guests. 'Where else have you ever seen a bishop laughing genially with a patroness of Almack's and a banking magnate? Mrs Montague's acquaintances appear to come from nearly every walk of life.'

'I think it must be the extensive work she does for the Foundling Hospital,' Lily mused. 'It is easier to approach people when you do so for a good cause, and you quickly learn who is like-minded and who is not.' She took a glass of wine from a passing footman, and then stared at Lady Dayle. An odd smile had blossomed suddenly on the viscountess's face.

'There now, Lily, you must help me test my theory. Look over my shoulder towards the door and tell me if my son Jack has not just arrived?'

Lily started. A large part of her hoped that the viscountess would be proven wrong. She had not seen Jack Alden since the day of their first dramatic encounter. It was true that she had felt happier in the intervening days than in years, but too many times she had caught herself grinning at nothing, brought to a halt by a vivid recollection of that secret smile on his handsome face.

It still piqued her that this man—the first to awaken in her such an instant, physical response—should not also be the sort of man she could be comfortable with. She battled a sense of loss too, and a relentless curiosity. Why should Jack Alden—who appeared to have every advantage—have grown so closed? What could have happened, to cause him to retreat so far into himself?

She would likely never know. But even though she knew

that such a man was not for her, still she was plagued with sudden memories of the intensity of his hazel gaze, the heat of his touch upon her arm, the low rasp of his voice as he leaned close…

Stop, she ordered herself.

She took an unobtrusive step to the side and let her gaze drift towards the door. 'Yes,' she said. 'It is Mr Alden.' Her pulse tripped, stumbled and then resumed at a ridiculously frantic rate.

He stood framed in the doorway, casually elegant and annoyingly handsome. Though he focused on greeting their hostess, even from here she could see the cool remoteness in his gaze. He was the only man of her acquaintance who could manage to look both intense and aloof in the same moment. It irritated her beyond reason.

She stepped back, placing his mother between them so he was no longer in her line of vision. She cast a curious look at Lady Dayle. 'You are facing away from the door. How ever did you know that he had arrived?'

Lady Dayle laughed. 'A tell-tale gust of wind.' She nodded to the guests grouped behind Lily. 'Jack walks in and we are treated to a phalanx of fluttering fans, flittering eyelashes and swishing skirts. It is a sure sign when I feel a breeze tugging on my coiffure.'

'Is Mr Alden considered such a good match, then?' Lily asked. She grinned. 'I don't mean to offend; it is just that Lady Ashford indicated otherwise—and in quite certain terms.'

'Warned you off, did she? It's to be expected. She had hopes once, you see… Well, never mind, that's all ancient history.' She leaned closer. 'Jack is not approaching, is he?'

Lily carefully glanced over her shoulder. 'No. He's just moved past Mrs Montague. He doesn't look at all happy to be here, I must say.'

He looked across and met her gaze right at that moment. Her composure abruptly deserted her. Face flaming, she nearly took a step backwards just from physical shock. Reminding herself to breathe, she wrenched her gaze from his, concentrating on his mother once more.

'Good. Look at them.' Lady Dayle indicated the gaggle of girls who were focused subtly, and in some cases downright overtly, on her son. 'It's because he's so elusive, I suppose.' She sighed. 'It's a rare enough occasion that his brother or I can convince him to attend an event such as this. And with his name being bandied about lately after that contretemps at the Egyptian Hall, he seems to have become even more interesting.'

Lily stared thoughtfully at the hopeful girls. 'I assume Mr Alden enjoys the attention,' she mused.

'I wish he did,' Lady Dayle said flatly. 'Truthfully, I don't think he has the faintest notion of their interest. A fact that I believe sometimes spurs the young ladies on.' She sighed. 'He presents something of a challenge.'

Lily glanced carefully back in Mr Alden's direction. She might feel a bit of sympathy for him, if she could believe him to be as unmindful of them all as his mother thought. But her own experience had shown him to be intelligent and a keen observer.

She shook her head. She did not believe it. Mr Alden simply could not be oblivious to the fervent interest directed his way. Not even he could be so selfishly unaware.

Only consider their last encounter. Her desire to accompany her mother and Lady Ashford on their trip had been obvious, yet he had not hesitated to thwart her. The thought that he might toy with these girls in a similar fashion only fuelled her aggravation with him.

Lady Dayle had turned to glance behind her. 'Ah,' she said. 'Here he comes now.'

'Good evening, Mother. Miss Beecham.' Mr Alden bowed

low. Her heart thundering in her ears, Lily made her curtsy and tried not to notice the way the candlelight glinted off his thick dark hair.

'I do not have to ask if you ladies are enjoying yourselves,' he continued. 'Our hostess has already informed me and anyone else who would listen that Miss Beecham found herself transported by the music tonight. She is touting it as a sure sign of the success of the evening.'

Lily raised her eyebrows. 'Mrs Montague has no need of my approval, but I should be happy to provide it. The music tonight has been stunningly beautiful—I am sure I am not the only one to be so moved.'

'You were the only one moved to tears, it would seem.' He spoke politely, but Lily thought she caught the hint of disapproval in Mr Alden's tone. He looked to the viscountess. 'I hope that you warned her, Mother—'

'Warned me?' Lily interrupted.

He glanced about as if to be sure no one listened. 'I understand that you have been little in society, Miss Beecham—'

He got no further before Lily interrupted him. 'Pray do not concern yourself, Mr Alden.' She tossed her head. 'I believe we established your inexperience with women of my stamp during our last conversation.'

His mouth quirked. 'Your stamp, Miss Beecham?'

She glared at him over her drink. 'Yes, sir. My stamp. My education has not been limited to embroidering samplers and learning a smattering of French. Besides charitable work, my mother and I have duties to the lands my father left and the families upon it.'

'Very commendable, I am sure—' he began.

'Thank you,' she interrupted. 'Though you may smirk, you would be shocked at the lists of tasks that must be seen to on a daily basis, all while attempting to persuade the land steward that there is no shame in consulting a woman on crop rotation and field drainage. In the same vein, I have occasionally had to cajole proud but hungry tenants into taking a loan so that they may feed their families. I've been called to coax the sick into taking their medicine, persuade duelling matrons into working together on a charity drive and I have even spoken publicly against the evils of slavery. I think you can trust me to keep my foot out of my mouth at a musical evening.'

Mr Alden did not appear to be impressed. 'All quite admirable, Miss Beecham, but you've never before encountered London society, and that is a different animal altogether.'

'People are people, Mr Alden.'

'Unfortunately not. In society you will encounter mind-numbingly bored people—arguably the most dangerous sort. You must understand, they are looking for something, anything, to divert them. I would not wish to see you targeted as a new plaything. Ridiculing a new arrival, painting her as a hopeless rustic, ruining her chances of acceptance—for many this is naught but an amusing pastime.'

Lily stared. Fate, chance and the heavens had finally conspired to set her free—at least for a few fleeting weeks—and he thought to tell her how to go on? It was the last straw. Jack Alden needed to be taught a lesson, and without a doubt Lily had enough of her old spirit left to be the one to give it to him.

She straightened her shoulders. When she had been young and in the grip of this determined mood, her mother had told her that she was worse than a wilful nag. Well, she had the bit in her teeth now. Jack Alden was a fraud. He showed the world a mask, exhibiting nothing but dispassion and uninterest, but worse lay underneath. He was as quick to condemn as the most judgemental of society's scandalmongers. Well, Lily would give him a taste of his own, and she highly doubted he would enjoy the flavour of either uninterest or censure.

'Jack, dear,' the viscountess spoke before Lily could. 'Do you really think I would allow Lily to do herself harm?' She cocked her head at her son. 'And in any case, I do not think you are in a position to speak to anyone about calm and rational conduct, not when you consider your own erratic temper over the last few weeks.'

He had the grace to redden a bit, but he ignored the jab at his own behaviour. 'Well, there is that old Eastern philosophy—the one in which a person who saves a life becomes responsible for it thereafter.'

'Let us not forget that you were driving the vehicle that threatened me,' Lily said. 'In fact, you saved me from yourself.' She raised a challenging eyebrow. 'What does your philosophy say about that?'

'Oh, dear,' Lady Dayle intervened. 'If you two are going to squabble like cats, then I am off to speak with Lord Dearham. He is a great lover of music...' she cast her son a speaking look '...unlike others I could name.' Patting Lily affectionately, she said, 'I shall meet you back at our seats when the music begins again, shall I?'

Lily watched her go before turning back to her victim. 'If you do not enjoy music, Mr Alden, then I confess I am curious to hear why you would attend a musical evening.'

He rolled his eyes. 'In fact, I do like music. But my mother will not forgive me for eschewing the operas that she so admires. I find that sort of entertainment too...tempestuous.'

'I see,' Lily said reflectively. 'Not having experienced the opera myself, I must reserve judgement. Still, one wonders if something other than the music drew your interest here tonight.'

He stiffened, obviously a little puzzled by her hostility. 'You are very perceptive, Miss Beecham.' He glanced after Lady Dayle. 'I find that I'm quite interested in the Evangelicals. I would like to know more about them.'

Lily lifted her chin. 'We are not specimens to be examined, Mr Alden.'

'Nor do I think so,' he replied easily. 'My brother mentioned their works and their intriguing notions on how to reform society.' He shrugged. 'I am here to learn.'

'You chose well, then. There are several influential Evangelicals here tonight.' She nodded across the room. 'Mr Macaulay, in fact, would be an ideal person for you to speak with. I dare say he can tell you everything you need to know.' She smiled ingratiatingly. 'He looks to be free right now.'

'Yes, he does indeed.' He smiled and she received the distinct impression that he was trying to win her over. 'But I came over here seeking a restful companion.' His gaze wandered briefly over her. As if he had physically touched her, Lily felt her skin twitch and tingle in its wake. She had to fight to keep him from seeing how he affected her. 'May I say,' he continued with an incline of his head, 'that I could not have found a lovelier one.'

'Thank you.' She kept her tone absent, as if his compliment had not set off a warm glow in her chest. 'I should think that this line of inquiry is very different from your usual research. Your mother tells me that you are a notable scholar.'

He nodded.

'You mentioned the ancients at our late supper a few days ago. Is that your area of specialty?'

'Yes, ancient civilisations.'

She eyed him shrewdly. 'I imagine you find it much easier to shut yourself up and study people of long ago than to deal with them in person. Real people can be so…tempestuous.'

That sardonic smile appeared. Lily's heart jumped at the sight of it. 'I do get out and amongst people on occasion, Miss Beecham. Thank goodness for it, too; I would not have missed making your acquaintance for the world.'

She ignored the good humour in his voice and let her gaze drop to his injured arm. 'Yes, but I do hope you did not strain your arm in doing so.'

'No, it is fine, thank you. I should be able to remove the sling in a week or two.'

'When your mother told me of your profession, I asked her if you had sustained your injury in a fall from a library stepstool.'

Mr Alden choked on a sip of his wine. Lily saw his jaw tighten and when he spoke, his light tone had been replaced with something altogether darker.

'No. Actually I was shot—while helping to prevent a group of thieves from making off with some valuable antiquities.'

'So Lady Dayle tells me! I was quite amazed, and a little thrilled, actually.' She smiled brightly at his reddening countenance. 'You give me hope, you see.'

'Hope?' he asked, and his voice sounded only slightly strangled.

'Indeed. For if a quiet scholar like you can find himself embroiled in such an adventure, then perhaps there is hope for a simple girl like me as well.'

It was a struggle, she could tell, but still he retained his expression of bland interest. Curse him.

'Do you crave adventure, Miss Beecham?' he asked.

'Not adventure, precisely.'

'Travel, perhaps? A flock of admirers?' He was regaining his equilibrium, fast. 'Or perhaps you simply wish for dessert?' He flagged down a passing footman with a tray of pastries.

Lily had to suppress a smile. This oh-so-polite battle of wit and words was by far the most fun she had had in ages. She eyed the footman and decided to take the battle to the next level. She selected a particularly rich-looking fruit-filled tart. 'Travel,' she mused. 'That would be delightful. But since I have it on good authority that I am of no age or situation conducive to easy arrangements, I suppose I must wait until I am older.' She raised her tart in salute. 'And stouter.'

Her eyes locked with his while she took a large bite, only to gradually close in ecstasy. She chewed, sighed and savoured. 'Oh, I must tell your mother to try one—the burnt-orange cream topping is divine!' Breathing deep, she held her breath for several long seconds before slowly exhaling. She opened languid eyes, taking care to keep them half-hooded as she glanced again at Mr Alden.

And promptly forgot to take a second bite. That had done it. At last she had cracked his polite façade. He stared, the green of his eyes nearly obliterated by pupils dilated with hunger. It wasn't the tart that he hungered for, either. His gaze was fixed very definitely on the modest neckline of her gown.

'So if travel must be a delayed gratification...' he said hoarsely, then paused to clear his throat '...what will you sub-stitute, Miss Beecham?'

'This,' replied Lily instantly, waving her free hand. 'De-lightful company with warm and open-minded people. The chance to exchange ideas, enjoy music and good conver-sation.'

'I hear that Mrs Montague has opened her gallery to her visitors tonight,' he returned. 'She has several noteworthy pieces. Perhaps you will enjoy some good conversation with me while we explore it?'

Lily smiled at him. She popped the last bit of tart into her mouth and dusted the crumbs from her gloves. 'Thank you, Mr Alden...' she shook her head as he offered her his arm '...but I must decline. I see an acquaintance from the Foreign Bible Society and I simply must go and congratulate her on her gown.' She dipped a curtsy and, fighting to keep a trium-phant smile from her face, turned and set off.

* * *

Flummoxed, Jack watched Lily Beecham walk away. This was not at all going the way he had planned. He'd mapped his strategy so carefully, too, and the troublesome chit had derailed him completely.

Aberrant—that's what she was. If it wasn't against all the laws of nature for one female to inspire so many conflicting reactions in a man, then it should be. She acted in a manner completely unpredictable. Her sharp wit and quirky humour kept him perpetually unbalanced—just as he desperately sought an even keel.

His nightmares had grown worse over the last few days. He couldn't sleep and had no wish to eat. Worse—he couldn't concentrate on his work. The ability to form a coherent written thought appeared to have deserted him.

Things had grown so bad that scenes from his youth— memories of his father's disdain for his third son—had begun to haunt him even while he was awake. But Jack had not allowed his father's casual cruelty to touch him while he'd been alive, and he would be damned before he let the old codger torment him from the grave.

He'd focused all of his energies instead on the thought of capturing Batiste. One advantage Lord Dayle's 'damned bookish' son possessed was a wide correspondence. Jack had contacts all over the world and, though it had been a painfully slow process, he had been for several weeks laboriously writing and put them all on notice. If Batiste put in to port near any of them, Jack would hear of it.

His next step was to track down Matthew Beecham. The shipbuilder had had extensive dealings with Batiste, and he might just be able to lead him straight to him. But first Jack had to get through Lily Beecham.

He circulated amongst Mrs Montague's guests and tried

not to be obvious in his observation of the girl. He'd taken note of her altered appearance straight away. She had a number of new freckles sprinkled across her nose, if he was not mistaken, and her red-gold mane had been tamed into a sleek and shining coiffure.

He thought he detected his mother's hand in the new style of gown she wore. She still dressed conservatively, but the gown of deep blue poplin represented a vast difference from the shapeless sack she'd worn when they met. The white collar, though high, served to draw the eye unerringly to her substantially fine bosom, and the soft and sturdy fabric snuggled tight both there and down the long, shapely length of her arms.

She looked quiet, constrained, the veritable picture of re-straint—until she spoke. Then a man found himself either cut by the razor edge of her tongue or riveted by her marvellously expressive face. Nor was he the only one affected. She made the rounds of the room, talking easily with everyone she en-countered, and laughing with uninhibited abandon. Clearly she had a gift. Every person she spoke with ended up smiling right along with her. The ladies gazed fondly after her and the gentlemen stared, agape and entranced.

Jack hovered across the room, in complete sympathy with the lot of them. Like a naturalist who had discovered a new species, he could not look away. The girl appeared perfectly comfortable conversing with strangers and seemed to be on the best of terms with Minerva Dawson, too. He'd heard some nonsense about those two being distantly related. They flitted about the room like a couple of smiling butterflies, one darkly handsome, the other shining like a crimson flame. Jack saw Miss Dawson's mother gazing fondly on the pair, but her companion—her sister, he thought—observed them with a frown. Well. Perhaps not everyone in the family was enamoured of their new connection.

Jack, watching closely as well, failed to see why. To his relief and chagrin, Miss Beecham never made a mis-step—until an elderly couple, arriving late, paused on the threshold of the room.

Obviously, she knew them. Mrs Montague had begun to herd her guests back to their seats in preparation for the music to begin again, but Miss Beecham struggled against the flow of people to fight her way to the newcomers. Her eyes shone and her sparkling smile grew wider still as she embraced them both with enthusiasm.

It looked to be a happy reunion. Jack watched surreptitiously as they talked. A few of the other guests had glanced over at the chattering threesome, but he thought he was the only one still paying attention when the older lady sobered, laid a gentle hand on Lily's arm and said something in a soft voice.

Jack stood too far away to hear the words she spoke, but he could see that they were not welcome to Miss Beecham. She paled, instantly and noticeably. All of the joy faded from her face and her hand trembled as she grasped the other woman's.

Mrs Montague chose that moment to notice her new arrivals. The little tableau broke apart as she greeted the couple heartily and began to pull them forwards towards the seating. Miss Beecham did not follow. Blank disbelief coloured her expression as she stared after the couple. She flashed a glance his way and Jack averted his eyes, pretending to be scanning for a seat. He looked back just in time to see her slipping away into the hall.

Jack's heart began to pound. She was clearly distressed and probably sought a quiet moment to herself, but this was it—his chance to get her alone and talking about her family. He had to take it. He edged towards the door and followed.

The tinkling and tootling of tuning instruments followed him into the hall. The few people left out there began to move past him, into the music room. Jack could see no sign of the girl. He glanced up the stairs. Several women still moved up and down, seeking or leaving the ladies' retiring room. No, not there. Instinct pointed him instead down the dimly lit hallway leading towards the back of the house.

He found her in the bookroom. Only a small pair of lamps fought the dark shadows here. Her head bowed, she stood, poised in graceful profile at the window. One hand stretched, holding the heavy curtain aside, but she did not look out. Jack's breathing quickened. Flickering light, reflected from the torches set up outside, danced like living flames in her hair. He stopped just inside the door. 'Miss Beecham? Are you all right?'

For a long, silent moment, she did not respond. Then she simply drew a breath and looked back at him, over her shoulder.

Jack, about to step closer, froze. There it was again, in her eyes. Pain, sorrow, loss. It had been the first expression he had seen on her face and it had struck him hard then. Now, when he could so closely contrast it with the joy and animation that had shone from her all evening, it hit him a staggering blow.

'Good God,' he said involuntarily. 'What's happened?'

She dropped the curtain. 'I…that is… Nothing, thank you. I am fine.'

The urge to know, the compulsion to help her, fluttered in his breast. He realised that it happened every time he was with her. She forged in him a disturbing and unfamiliar yearning for a connection. He had to ignore it, to find a way to remember his purpose. To regain control.

'Come, Miss Beecham, I'm not a fool. I can see that something has upset you.'

A china shepherdess graced the table next to the window. She avoided his gaze and touched the delicate thing with the lightest touch of her fingertips. Jack watched them glide over the smooth surface and swallowed.

'It's just…some disturbing news from a friend, I'm afraid,' she said, still not looking at him.

'I'm sorry to hear it.'

Now she looked up. She set the figurine aside. Her chin rose and the icy coldness of her glare held him fast. 'I should think you'd be happy to find that I am following your advice.'

'Advice?' Once again she had him at a loss. Ancient Sumerian was easier to translate than this girl's fits and starts.

'Yes. You see—here I am, hiding away, keeping my unsuitable emotions private.'

Stunned, Jack stared at her. Was this the reason for her hostility? Had *he* hurt her? He considered stepping closer, taking her hand, but he felt inept, clumsy. 'I do apologise. If you thought I meant to criticise… I hope you will understand, I only meant to help you.'

She crossed her arms defensively in front of her. 'Help me what?'

He took a moment to answer. 'Protect yourself, I suppose.'

Her arms dropped. Her eyes grew huge and some emotion that looked dangerously like pity crossed her face. 'Protect myself from what, Mr Alden?' She gestured towards the door. 'In there is a roomful of people come to pass a pleasant evening and enjoy some good music. It is not a den of monsters.'

She was so young. So naïve. Jack wanted to wrap her in swaddling and spirit her away, to somehow keep her safe in this pristine, happy state.

He took a step back. He was doing it again. *She* was doing it again. This was not why he had come here. He sketched a quick bow. 'I'm sorry. I did not mean to insult you.'

She inclined her head a little. He took what he could get and forged ahead. 'Your mother, she is well? I hope that was not the nature of your news?'

'Oh. No. Mother is fine. I had a letter from her yesterday.

She and Lady Ashford appear to be enjoying themselves. They have met many new people and even approve of a few of them.'

'And the rest of your family?' he persisted. 'I hope they are well, also?'

'Thank you, but I have no other family. Mother and I have been alone since my father died.'

Jack's fist clenched. His breath caught. It could not be. Please. He did not want to have been wrong about her connection to Matthew Beecham. 'Just the two of you alone in the world?' he asked past the constriction in his throat. 'That is sad enough, in and of itself.'

'Just the two of us,' she said. 'Unless you count my cousin Matthew—but he lives in America now.'

Jack almost slumped in relief. Almost. He grinned at her. 'An American cousin? My brother's wife boasts such a connection. I hope yours is not so, ah, vibrant a character as hers.'

He'd actually drawn an answering smile. 'Oh, Matthew is a character, without a doubt.' She laughed. 'You would never believe me if I shared half the antics we used to get up to.'

'Are you close, then?' He held his breath.

She sighed. 'We were. Matthew lived with us for several years after his parents died. I was just a girl and I thought the sun rose and set with him.'

'I hope he returned the sentiment.'

'He did, or close enough to please me.' She smiled. 'He taught me the most unsuitable things! And I loved him for it.'

'Hmm, now he sounds like my brother Charles.'

'Oh, I've already heard a few of the tales about Charles.' She laughed. 'I don't think we could have kept up with him, even on our best days.'

'Nor could I.'

She glanced sharply at him and Jack wondered if he'd revealed too much.

'Matthew was special to me. Other than my father, I would say that he may be the only person in the world who has ever truly known me.'

Jack fought a twinge of conscience. He was too close to back down now. 'Was special? Do you not keep in touch any longer?'

'We exchange the occasional letter.' She grinned sheepishly. 'I confess, although I have altogether less to write about, I am far more likely to write him than vice versa. And though his correspondence has always been irregular and infrequent, it is always a delight when it comes.' She grinned again. 'American life has some rather droll differences from ours, based on his descriptions.' Jack watched, hopeful and more than a little enchanted, as a tiny frown of concentration creased her brow. 'But it has been months and months since last I heard from him. I don't think I realised until now just how long it has been.'

'And how does he find America, besides droll? Does he not miss his home?'

'Not at all, as far as I can tell. He's quite happy there. He's a shipbuilder and doing tolerably well.' She cocked her head. 'Perhaps his business has increased and that is what keeps him from writing.'

Disappointment and hope warred in Jack's chest. For a moment he considered telling her the truth, but cast the thought quickly aside. She obviously knew nothing of the trouble her cousin had tangled himself in. Matthew Beecham might just contact his cousin and ask for help. It would behoove Jack to stay close as well.

It was a sobering thought. She was damned perplexing. He didn't know if he could win her confidence, and, more importantly, he didn't know if he could keep a rein on his own unfortunate reactions to her.

He'd been quiet too long. She watched him, curiosity etched

in her clear, fresh face. 'Well,' she said, 'thank you for distracting me from my sombre thoughts. I had best return to the music room.' She glanced at him again and made to move away.

'Wait,' he asked. His conscience still pricked him. He could not forget the earlier hurt in her voice.

She paused.

'About what I said earlier,' he began, stumbling a little over the words. 'I have no authority to dictate to you, or even advise you. Truly, I meant my words, as I said, as a warning. A friendly warning.' She'd stopped on her way out and stood very close now. The darkened room contracted around them. 'Perhaps you do not know, but my own family has shown a disregard for society's expectations in the past—and been persecuted for it. I just wish to spare you that sort of pain.'

Her face softened. Jack's gaze locked with hers. Her colour heightened and he noticed that those adorable freckles disappeared when she flushed. 'I begin to understand,' she said softly. Jack had the impression that she spoke as much to herself as to him. 'Perhaps you will scoff—' she spoke in nearly a whisper '—but we are very alike.'

A frown furrowed her lovely brow, and she caught that enticingly plump bottom lip with her teeth. Jack could not look away. Somehow the chit had turned the tables and was now worried for *him*. It was an intoxicating thought. Yet he was here with a purpose. He drew a deep breath and tried to clear his mind of anything else.

Her hand rose between them. Jack's pulse began to race. Small and uncertain, that hovering hand drove all thought of his objective from his head. For a moment, he felt sure she meant to draw it back. His gut twisted inside out as part of him longed to jerk away—and the other waited in breathless anticipation for her to touch him.

She did touch him. He saw the resolution in her eyes as she

extended her arm and then he felt the butterfly touch of her fingers tracing a path along his jaw. His eyes closed. Her warm little hand slid over his shoulder and came to rest on his chest.

'When my father died, I thought just as you do,' she whispered. 'It is a very hard thing, to feel alone in a room full of people.'

But Jack's eyes were open again, and her words did not register. He could not think past the mix of empathy and desire swimming in the cool blue of her gaze, could not focus on anything but the movement of that tempting lower lip. Logic, his close companion all these years, screamed at him to stop, shouted a warning that, for the first time ever, he ignored. Her mouth beckoned. He had to taste it, mark it as his.

His gaze fixed, he mimicked her earlier movement, raising his hand and brushing the silky skin of her jaw. She gasped. He did not let it deter him. He ran his fingers into the smooth knot of hair at her nape and cupped her jaw. He leaned in, intent on his purpose—

'Miss Beecham?'

She jerked back, her eyes wide. Jack blinked. Then he cursed. Ever so slowly, awareness began to return. She stepped quickly towards the door, but the alarm in his head did not fade.

'Miss Beecham, there you are!'

It was one of the young pups who had drooled over her in the music room. He gave an extravagant bow and offered her his arm and a friendly grin. 'Miss Beecham, I've been sent to fetch you. Our hostess hopes you will entertain us all with a song on the pianoforte.'

She glanced uncertainly over her shoulder. The boy's gaze followed. His engaging smile faded.

Jack managed a grim nod. 'There, Miss Beecham,' he said, keeping his tone brisk. 'Perhaps this young man will take you back to my mother while I find the footman seeking me? Thank you for informing me of the message awaiting me.'

The boy's grin returned at the welcome request. 'I would be happy to escort you, Miss Beecham. Mr Bartleigh is but newly arrived, but he tells us you have more than a passing knowledge of many of the older broadsheet ballads. He's hoping you'll share your rendition of "Ballynamony".'

She hesitated. 'Perhaps I should not.' She glanced at Jack again, and this time there was a challenge glittering in her eyes. 'So many of the ballads are sentimental. I should not wish to expose myself to ridicule.'

'Never say such a thing! A lovely young lady such as yourself, in genial company such as this? Impossible,' he scoffed. 'And should anyone dare to suggest otherwise, I will deal with them myself.'

Jack's jaw clenched. Miss Beecham smiled up at her young admirer.

He had to escape. Logic whispered fervently in his ear again and this time he paid heed. Logic stood correct and un-assailable as always. He should feel grateful for the boy's interruption, not ready and willing to strangle both him and the baiting chit.

'Miss Beecham—' he could not look directly at her '—thank you for your kindness in coming for me. Please convey my farewells to my mother?'

'Of course. Goodnight, Mr Alden.'

He ignored the thread of steel in her voice and brushed past them into the hall. He did indeed go searching for a footman and sent the man off after his coat and hat.

He should be thrilled. He'd accomplished the first step and verified Miss Beecham's connection to his target. Now he only had to wait for him to communicate with her, or he might even prod her into discovering her cousin's whereabouts. She might even know more, such as where the shipbuilder might have gone when he disappeared.

He was not thrilled. The vague restlessness that had been plaguing him roiled in his gut, transformed into something altogether uglier. He'd had a narrow escape tonight, on several levels. This could not continue. He must control himself around the girl, no matter what tender emotions lived in her blue eyes and in spite of that damned tempting mouth of hers.

Control. Restraint. They were his allies, his support, as necessary to his existence as air. He breathed deep. He could do this. Hell, he'd already spent a lifetime doing this.

The footman brought his things. As he shrugged into his coat, the first few strains of a sprightly song began in the music room. Miss Beecham's bright, lilting voice wafted out and over him.

> *Wherever I'm going, and all the day long,*
> *At home and abroad, or alone in a Throng,*
> *I find that my Passion's so lively and strong,*
> *That your Name when I'm silent still runs in my Song.*

Jack placed his hat firmly on his head and walked out.

Chapter Five

Lady Dayle's morning room shone bright and airy, as warm and welcoming as the viscountess herself. Unfortunately, Lily's mood did not reflect the serenity of her surroundings. She sat at the dainty writing desk, trying to compose a letter to her land steward.

Last night's conversation had triggered the idea. She'd spoken of her cousin Matthew to Mr Alden and she'd woken this morning with a sudden longing for one of his breezy, affectionate letters. She'd realised that it had been quite some time since she'd last heard from him and resolved to ask Mr Albright to forward any personal mail on to London. Perhaps a light-hearted, teasing missive from America awaited her even now.

She hoped it was so. She could use a bolster to her confidence. She'd thought she'd come to London to find culture and learning and to broaden her experience. She'd begun to realise, however, that what she was truly looking for was acceptance, the casual sort of recognition and approval that most people experienced on a daily basis. She had found it, too, and from some truly amazing and worthy people.

But she had not found it in Jack Alden. She had seen flashes of approval from him, to be sure, and flares of something altogether darker, more dangerous and intriguing. But there had also been wariness and reserve and something that might be suspicion. And it was driving her mad.

The why of it eluded her. Perhaps because she had spoken truly last night—they were alike in some deeply elemental way. They both stood slightly apart from the rest of the world. The difference between them was that he seemed perfectly content with his situation. But her reaction made not a whit of sense. She both wished to achieve such serenity and, for some reason, wished whole-heartedly to shake him from his.

She sighed. She very much feared that it was for an altogether more common reason that she found herself fixating on him. He had been on the verge of kissing her last night. She'd guessed his intent and her heart had soared, her pulse had ratcheted and she had waited, breathless, for the touch of his mouth on hers. When they had been interrupted she had been frightened, and wildly disappointed.

Later, though, in the privacy of her own room, she had been appalled at her own behaviour and angry at his. Was he so far removed from the world that kissing a young woman in a public venue meant nothing? But, no, then she had remembered how brilliantly—and smoothly—he had covered their almost-transgression. And when she thought further on it, she realised that in actuality she had goaded him into it. He wore his cynicism and reserve like a protective shell and she had not been able to curb her desire to pierce it. She knew she should have shown more restraint, but she'd been left vulnerable by Mrs Bartleigh's news. When he'd shown a bit of his own vulnerability she had overreacted. She'd taken the conversation to too intimate a level, pushed too far, got too close.

And he'd pushed back, struck out with his heated gaze and warm, wandering hands. Even now she couldn't help wishing she had discovered a few more of the weapons in his sensual arsenal.

'Good morning, cousin!' a voice rang out.

Lily started nearly out of her chair, an instant flush rising. She turned to find Miss Dawson advancing across the room towards her.

'Oh, goodness! Good morning, Minerva.' She took up her still-blank sheet of paper and began to fan herself with it. 'You look lovely today!'

Minerva Dawson laughed, her eyebrow cocked as she clasped Lily's hand in her own. 'As do you, my dear. Something has put a beautiful hue to your cheeks. Do tell!'

'Oh, no, I am merely writing a note for my land steward.'

'So I see,' her friend said, glancing at the empty sheets in her hand and in front of her. 'Well, are you ready to shop? Mother gave me firm instructions. I am to find the perfect pair of gloves to wear to my engagement ball—elbow length and ivory. Not white, not ecru, but ivory.'

'I shall be ready to go in just a moment—if you would wait while I finish?'

Minerva rolled her eyes. 'Oh, if I must.'

Lily laughed. 'You know, Minerva, that I am thrilled that you found a familial connection between us, even if it is a distant relationship through marriage and largely born of your imagination—' she grinned to take the sting from her words '—but I do not think everyone in your family is as well pleased with such a link.' She gestured for her friend to sit and joined her in the comfortable grouping of chairs near the window. 'In fact, I think your aunt disapproves of me.'

'Oh, yes, she does,' Minerva returned cheerily. 'But Aunt Lucinda disapproves of nearly everyone without a title—including her husband.'

'Well, that does make me feel a little more sympathetic towards your uncle.'

'Don't let it,' her friend said flatly. She began to remove her gloves in a brisk manner. Leaning towards Lily, she lowered her voice. 'The man gives me chills. I don't care if he *is* my uncle.'

'I know just what you mean.' Lily shuddered.

'Well, you don't have to worry about them. I told dear Aunt Lucinda all about your vast lands in Dorset and the vaster amount of money you stand to inherit and that went a long way towards reconciling her to our friendship.'

'You are incorrigible.' Lily laughed.

'It is true.' Minerva sighed. 'But a little incorrigibility makes life ever so much more fun!' She waggled a stern finger in Lily's direction. 'And happily, there's a bit of it in you, too. Now don't try to bam me—you were mooning over some young man when I came in. Which one? That Mr Brookins, who waxed eloquent over your skills on the pianoforte?'

'No.' Lily abruptly decided to tell the truth. 'Actually, I was trying to decipher Mr Alden's puzzling behaviour.'

Minerva stilled. Much of the light faded from her smiling face. 'Oh? Do your thoughts lean in that direction, then?'

'No,' Lily said with a grimace. 'In fact, they travel in another direction entirely. I'm afraid Mr Alden does not like me much, and I was merely trying to work out why that is.'

'Hmm.' Her 'cousin' examined her closely. 'Lily, I am a very observant person, have I told you that?'

'Not that I've observed.' Lily smiled to defuse the serious tone Minerva had adopted.

'Ha. Well, I observed something interesting last night.'

'A sudden gust of wind?' asked Lily facetiously.

'No.' Her friend's brow furrowed. 'Whatever do you mean?'

'Nothing. Is this a game? Let me guess again. You

observed...the immense number of prawns devoured by the bishop during the intermission?'

'Well, I did notice that. Shocking, wasn't it? I'd wager that he's not feeling quite the thing today.' The stern finger appeared again. 'But that was not what I meant. I observed Mr Alden and he was watching you very closely last night.'

'Probably because we quarrelled and I got the best of him,' Lily said sourly.

Minerva drew back, surprised. 'You bested him in an argument? Well, I dare say that was a first for him. No wonder he looked so torn.'

'Torn?'

'Definitely torn. I swear, he alternately looked as he meant to devour *you*, or perhaps to bash you over the head.'

'No doubt he would prefer the latter.' She sighed, then got to her feet and wandered over to gaze out of the window.

Minerva pursed her lips. She sat back, levelling a stare in Lily's direction and drumming her fingers on the arm of her chair. 'Lily,' she began at last, 'you know that I only want what is best for you.'

Lily had to suppress an ironic chuckle. Minerva could have no notion how many times she'd heard *that* particular phrase in her life.

'Jack Alden is a very handsome man, in an intense and yet disarmingly rumpled way.'

'I know,' agreed Lily. 'Don't you have to stop yourself from straightening his cravat and smoothing out the line of his coat every time you meet him?'

Her friend stared at her. 'Well, no. But it is rather speaking that you do, my dear.' A gentle smile belied the slight crease in her brow. 'Just be careful,' she pleaded, her tone low and serious. 'Some men are amenable to having their neckcloths straightened and some are in no way ready to contemplate such a thing.'

'I understand what you are saying, Minerva, and I appreciate your concern beyond words.' Lily focused on the traffic outside in the street for a long moment. 'He's hiding,' she said abruptly.

Minerva heaved a great sigh. 'Yes, I know.'

'You do?' She spun around in surprise.

The corner of her friend's mouth twitched. 'I recognised the symptoms from personal experience.' She raised a questioning brow. 'As do you, I assume.'

Lily nodded.

'Well, then we both know that you cannot force him to stop. He will battle his own demons in his own time—just as everyone else must, sooner or later.'

Lily met her friend's gaze squarely. 'Would you consider me insane if I told you that I have been wondering…if perhaps I am meant to help Mr Alden?'

'No,' Minerva replied promptly. 'I would consider you the most generous girl with the grandest heart in all of England. But I would also warn you that Jack Alden is a man grown. He can help himself. You can go on enjoying your all-too-brief stay in London—as you were meant to do.'

Lily regarded her with affection. 'You are a very dear friend.'

'I know,' Minerva responded comfortably, 'but you deserve me.'

For several long moments Lily sat, silent. Her thoughts swirled while her conscience struggled to find a balance between her wants and her needs. At last she sighed. She knew what she wanted, but she also knew what she must do.

'Minerva,' she said slowly, 'we will likely be seeing much of Mr Alden over the next weeks.' She grimaced. 'Tomorrow, for instance, Lady Dayle and I are to accompany him on a day trip to a friend's country villa.' She gestured helplessly about them, at his family's house which sheltered them. 'But I think it is best that I keep my distance—for all of our sakes.' Lily reached for her friend's hand and clasped it tightly when it came. 'Will you help me?'

'Yes,' Minerva responded slowly. 'I rather think I will.'

Whistling, Jack swept a brush down the muscled flank of one of his sturdy greys. 'Now this is a job for a one-handed man,' he said aloud. The doctor had agreed to let him leave off with the splint, but his arm still felt a long way from fully recovered. 'Let's finish it up, boys!' he called to the men polishing his brother's landau. 'Our ladies will be ready shortly. Let's be sure to give them a beautiful ride!'

He could see the vehicle, shining already in the early morning sun, and the grooms scrambling over the cobbled yard of the mews. His brother's voice rang out just then and Jack turned as Charles entered the stable.

Charles called for his mount and joined his brother, running a critical eye over the horse he laboured over. 'Morning, Jack. Your greys look to be in fine fettle today.'

'Perhaps not so flashy as Pettigrew's bays,' Jack answered, grinning, 'but they suit me well. Thank you again,' he added, 'for the loan of your landau. It looks to be a good day for our drive. I'm sure Mother and Miss Beecham will prefer the open air to a carriage and none of us would be comfortable squeezing into my cabriolet.'

'Remind me again where you are all off to?'

'Chester House. Lord Bradington has invited a select group to view his Anglo-Saxon collection and he's invited some scholars interested in the period to speak. I'm to read my paper on King Alfred's system of justice.' He shrugged. 'I had originally declined, but the day is fine and I thought the ladies might enjoy it. Miss Beecham seems to go in for that sort of thing.'

Jack grinned as his brother gave him the same sort of once over he'd just given his horse.

'You do seem to be in remarkably good spirits,' said Charles. 'I don't think I've seen you looking so relaxed in weeks.'

'Remarkable what a good night's sleep will do for a man,' said Jack, continuing on with his brushing. He was in good spirits. In fact, he was vastly relieved and gloriously happy. 'It's all due to a grand bit of news, Charles. Do you recall Benjamin Racci, the fellow who had the apartments next to me at All Souls?'

He watched Charles grimace and search his memory. 'Vaguely. His area of interest had something to do with Muslims, yes?'

'Oh, you are good,' Jack said admiringly. 'No wonder you do so well in the Lords. Yes, in any case, Racci's obsession is Muslim influence on Western development. He's currently in Gibraltar, going over Moorish structures and mosques.' He paused, leaned on the back of his grey and smirked at his brother. 'And guess what he caught sight of in Catelan Bay?'

Charles's eyes narrowed as he stared at Jack a moment, then realisation dawned. 'Not Batiste?'

'Batiste, big brother!' Jack crowed. 'Racci got my letter, asking that he keep an eye and ear out, and then, wham! One morning he spots the *Lady Vengeance* riding at anchor in the bay. Racci sent a message off to the British Naval Commander, but she was gone before they got there.'

'So he's not been caught?' asked Charles.

'No, but neither did he re-supply. He's on the run, Charles, and for the first time I feel as if we truly might catch up with the bastard.'

His brother grinned. 'So that's why you are in such a good mood. Triumph of logic and reason over tyranny and villainy?'

'Perhaps not triumph, yet, but definitely a step in the right direction. And it was due to sound thinking and determination,' Jack corrected. 'As well as good contacts, of course.'

'Nice job, little brother.' Charles stepped back as his groom led his mount forwards. Another man came to take the grey and Jack savoured the feeling of his brother's approbation as he handed him over to be harnessed with his mate.

'I'm surprised you are bothering with poor Miss Beecham now that you've got Batiste on the run,' Charles teased as he swung up. 'Why bother taking her and Mother out if you no longer need to pursue her connection with Matthew Beecham?'

A small, cowardly piece of his soul had already whispered the same message in Jack's ear. He rebuffed his brother in the same way he had sternly talked to himself.

'The girl is Mother's guest, Charles, not a pawn in some game I'm playing,' Jack said reproachfully. He waved the groom away and checked his brother's girth strap himself.

'I know, I know, it was just a brotherly jibe.' Charles did not sound in the least repentant. 'I can't help thinking of what happened to me, though, last time Mother adopted a protégée.'

Jack froze. 'The situations are not at all similar.'

Charles laughed. 'I know. Just watch yourself.'

'Don't even joke about such things,' Jack said with shudder. 'What a wretched husband I should make, holed up in my rooms, losing myself for days on end in my papers and books.' He eyed Charles soberly. 'And we both know what a wretched husband does to a family. I have no plans to inflict such a fate on anyone.'

'You never know, Jack. Some day you might just meet a young lady who interests you more than your stale ancients.'

'Miss Beecham does interest me. She's a lovely girl, but I have no intention of making her miserable for the rest of her life. I give her the respect she is due as a friend of the family, but I'm not about to give up any other possible leads to Batiste.'

'Do you think the girl will co-operate, then?'

Jack shrugged. 'I won't know until I ask.'

'Best of luck to you.' Charles nudged his mount forwards. 'The vote on this bill comes soon, and then I'll be back to Sevenoaks for a few days.'

'I'm sure I'll see you before then.' Jack waved his brother off.

The landau stood ready, polished surfaces gleaming, the horses prancing in anticipation. Dissatisfied, Jack climbed in. He much preferred to do his own driving. But he gave a nod of readiness to the groom and the team went wheeling after his brother. As the man eased them into the flow of traffic in the street, Jack steeled his nerves against the coming confrontation.

Despite his fine words to Charles, he knew his last encounter with Miss Beecham had been a disaster, start to finish. His shoulders hunched involuntarily. Especially the finish. He'd been sick at the thought of what he'd almost done and horrified at his own complete loss of control.

So close. His hand had buried itself in the glowing softness of her hair. Her breath had mingled, hot and sweet, with his. He'd stood mere seconds away from locking her within his embrace and ending her disturbingly empathetic conversation with a searing kiss.

After his escape he had waged a silent war with himself, wavering between his wish to stay as far away as possible from the dangerous chit and his need to ask for her co-operation in finding her cousin. She had every right to refuse him—to slap his face and order him to keep his distance. But he hoped fervently that she would not.

He felt better, more like himself, now. His success in finding a first trace of Batiste's whereabouts had taken the edge off of his desperation. He'd slept at last without being haunted by taunting visions of the captain and his father. He'd clamped down hard on his wayward emotions and taken a step back towards the equilibrium he craved.

This exhibition should be the perfect venue to help him get back in Miss Beecham's good graces. A gorgeous house, intellectual stimulation, fascinating antiquities, beautiful gardens—what more could he ask for? He could deal with her in his own milieu, impress her, charm her and get her alone where he could offer up his proposition and in no way act again like a weak-willed fool.

She was just a woman. One endowed with wit and beauty and a good deal of spirit, to be sure, but no longer a match for his discipline and determination. He could do this. If only she gave him the chance.

Traffic quieted as they made the turn on to Bruton Street. Jack stared as the landau slowed, approaching his brother's house. What was this? At first he tried mightily to hide his dismay. Then he gave up, gave in and simply laughed out loud. He had not granted the wily Miss Beecham enough credit. Give him the chance? Clearly she meant to leave nothing to chance.

Instead of a pair of ladies waiting patiently inside, a large group of people milled on the steps and on the pavement in front of the town house. Several vehicles waited empty in the street. He spotted Minerva Dawson and her betrothed, Lord Lindley. There stood Mrs Montague and—Lord, was that Sally Jersey? In the midst of them stood Miss Beecham. He caught sight of her as she gave a little jump and a wave.

'Good morning, Mr Alden!' she called. 'I hope you won't mind a few additions to your party!'

Chapter Six

L ily had succeeded in her ploy. She'd been unable to deny
the twinge of satisfaction she'd felt when she'd glimpsed the
surprise on Jack Alden's face this morning, but, she had to
admit, he'd succeeded in surprising her, too.

A country villa? She turned round and round inside the incredible central hall of Chester House. Awestruck, she let her
eye rove from the stone floor, over the magnificent plaster or-
namentation and on to the high windows and the lofty dome
overheard. Her jaw had dropped when they had pulled up to
this gleaming neo-Palladian villa, but with her first step inside
she'd fallen instantly in love.

Oh, how her mother would despise the place. A wealthy
gentleman's playhouse. A hedonist's dream, replete with everything fanciful, ornate and overblown.

But so much more, as well. Like a light and airy treasure
box, it showcased art and antiquities flanked by and con-
tained within the most exquisite architecture. It stood testimony to man's capability for beauty, celebrated his sense of
ingenuity and wonder. It spoke directly to Lily's soul.

Guests, laughing and boisterous, began to spill in bchind

her. Lily was swept along to an elaborate, tripartite gallery where, en masse, they were met by their host. In the midst of all the splendour, Lord Bradington looked short and somewhat ordinary, yet he stepped up to a lavishly inlaid marble podium and welcomed them with generous and open arms.

'The best way to properly see the collection is in small groups,' he announced. 'We will split up. Besides myself, we are fortunate to have several experts among us. They will be happy, I am sure, to share their knowledge and thus enhance your own enjoyment of the treasures on display. There will be plenty of time to see everything before we gather back here…' he gestured '…in the gallery, to hear our notable speakers and enjoy a light repast.'

Good-natured chaos ensued as people began to separate into groups. Lily took advantage of the confusion. She slipped behind a gilded pillar, anxious for a quiet moment to recover and take it all in.

This was it—what she had been anticipating, hoping for, when she came to London. Not the riches that surrounded her, but the happy exuberance and simple joy to be found in sharing them, their history and the grand idea that they somehow connected every single person here.

Heart pounding, she leaned against the cool marble and peeked out into the crowd. Her eye unerringly went to Jack Alden, as it had done foolishly, repeatedly, all morning.

Why now? she wanted to cry at him. Why now, when she had reached her decision to stay away, made her resolution to avoid him, did he abruptly turn himself into the exact thing she hadn't acknowledged that she was looking for?

He'd had every right to be angry at her perfidy in inviting along Minerva and her fiancé, the Bartleighs, and a few others besides, to his outing. But he'd acted quite the opposite. He had taken off his hat, thrown back his head and laughed heartily at the sight of her entourage and she had been captivated by the sight of the breeze wafting through his dark hair and the green sparkle of amusement in his eyes. Even as she'd stared, he'd replaced his hat, and given her a jaunty salute, making her wonder if he'd guessed at the reason behind her strategy.

Nor had he objected when she had climbed up with Minerva to ride in Mr Brookin's flashy demi-landau. Instead, he had welcomed the Bartleighs into his own vehicle and, from what she could see, had spent the drive out chatting and charming them completely.

Now he gathered her friends into a group and then he raised his head and ran a scarching gaze about the room.

'Lily Beecham?' he called. 'Miss Beecham must join us as well.'

The others echoed his cry. Lily breathed deep. There was no help for it. All she could do was join the group and avoid Jack Alden as best she could.

This, it turned out, was no easy task. In fact, she thought at one point that it just might be the hardest thing she had ever tried to do.

Gone was Jack Alden's veneer of cool reserve. Not once did she catch even a hint of worldly cynicism. Instead, he led their group on a private, informative, highly entertaining tour. The Anglo-Saxon antiquities on display throughout the house were fascinating and it seemed he knew something about every piece. He explained the incised decorations on a disc brooch, and pointed out the faint remains of tinning on a Saxon wrist clasp. He spoke at length and with enthusiasm about the theories regarding the Alfred jewel and the possibility that more might exist. He showed himself to be knowledgeable and passionate.

And nigh irresistible.

Lily was unceasingly aware of him all day. She felt attuncd

to his every clever remark and deep, husky laugh. She grew warmer every time she noticed that his relaxed manner only emphasised the strength of his form and his long-limbed grace. All day she watched him and her body hummed, head to toe, with a heated, shivering awareness.

And yet she forced herself to behave with complete indifference. She did not meet his eye, kept at least two others between them at all times, permitted herself only a distant smile so many times when what she really wished was to laugh out loud.

It was torture.

By the time the papers were read, the speeches given and the lavish spread of food consumed, Lily's head was aching. She was tired of fighting to keep her gaze from straying to wherever Jack Alden stood. When Mr Keller, another of the scholars invited to speak today, asked her to stroll with him through the famous gardens, she allowed herself one last fleeting glimpse, and then she took the other man's arm and allowed him to lead her away.

Jack Alden stood poised on the brink of madness. Ahead loomed naught but the chaotic pit and behind him lurked Lily Beecham, one tiny hand placed squarely at his back, urging him forwards to his doom.

He could not believe that it had happened again. He'd come with a plan and a purpose. He'd visualised how he would proceed. He'd anticipated and prepared for her every response. Except, it appeared, for this one.

She blended right in to the atmosphere of Chester House, as if she was meant to stroll amongst the beauties of the ages and enrich them with her own special appeal. He'd half-expected that. He'd expected her to be lively and vivacious. He'd hoped she'd be caught up in his own attempt at charm and charisma.

He'd been at least partly right. Good God—her allure was a nearly palpable thing. She had every man here in her thrall. But something had gone missing. She seemed interested, happy—and utterly indifferent to him.

Jack knew that he did not possess the renowned charm of his brother, but he exerted himself powerfully and did his best to channel Charles's effortless likeability—to no avail.

And just like that, all of his careful planning, and reason and logic, too, flew right out of the proverbial window. He could swear he heard his father's mocking laughter mixed in with the gaiety of the company. Her complete lack of interest triggered something alarming inside of him. He felt hot and reckless, and uncertain as well, as if he would do anything to get her to look at him the way she had at their first, eventful meeting.

He had a limited supply of self-control left, and it took every ounce of it to stay calm, act the perfect host, and exude amiability and unconcern. When he saw Keller take her into the gardens he breathed deep, squelched the urge to roar like an enraged bull, politely excused himself from his companions and followed.

He found them in the middle of the gardens, where a large, flat lawn had been created. The two of them strolled slowly along the western edge, admiring the border of alternating stone urns and cypress trees. At least, the girl appeared to be admiring them. Keller's attention was focused somewhere else altogether.

'There you are, Keller,' he called. 'Lord Bradington is looking for you, old man.'

'How nice,' Keller responded. His eyes never strayed from Lily Beecham's lithe shape.

'Yes, he's debating the dating on that collection of gold, die-struck belt mounts in the library. Apparently someone is arguing that they might be Viking-made.'

'What?' Now Keller's head came up and he looked back towards the house. 'That cannot be right. No, no. Those were clearly manufactured by early Saxons.'

'Someone's convinced Bradington otherwise. He's already talking of changing the placard and moving them in with the other Viking artefacts.'

'That will not do!' Keller exclaimed. He looked with regret at the girl. 'I'm so sorry, Miss Beecham, but I will have to go back and remedy this. Shall you accompany me?'

'No, you go in,' Jack interjected. 'Miss Beecham has hardly seen any of the grounds. I shall take her on. You can join us again once you have cleared up this travesty.'

'Perhaps I should go back,' she demurred. 'My friends…'

'Are all already strolling the gardens,' Jack said smoothly. 'I will help you find them.'

She said nothing further. Keller hurried back towards the house and Jack decided it would be prudent to move on.

'Have you seen the stone gateway?' He inclined his head at her. 'It is quite renowned as a place of good fortune.'

'No…' she gazed up at him with something that looked like exasperation '…I have not. Perhaps we should walk that way before poor Mr Keller discovers your ruse?'

Jack laughed. 'Was I that obvious?'

'Perhaps only to those already familiar with your machinations,' she said sourly.

He indicated the direction and offered up his arm. After a long searching look, she sighed and laid her hand lightly on his.

'A gate of good fortune, you said?' she asked. 'How does it work?'

'I couldn't say how the tales originated, but the legend says that you must pause on the threshold, thinking very hard on the difficulties of your life. You must concentrate and count to three silently while you swing open the gate and cross through.'

'And then?'

'And then your troubles are over.' He shrugged. 'The hardships you focused on will have disappeared.'

'Would that it were that easy,' she said wistfully. 'But I shall definitely write and tell my old nurse of it. She adores tales of superstition and fancy.'

The sun rode low in the afternoon sky. Its rays, filtered through spring leaves, painted the ancient statuary with a forgiving brush. Miss Beecham paused to admire the figure of Palladio. The soft light erased the harsh wear of time on his stern-faced visage, but Jack could not look away from the little fires it lit in the fall of her hair.

'I tried to get away earlier and ask you to tour the gardens,' he said. 'I noticed that you looked a little pale and thought perhaps you'd welcome a quiet stroll with a restful companion.'

An ironic snort was her only answer.

Jack clenched his teeth. Even her sarcasm attracted him. When they resumed their stroll he allowed his gaze to run down the turquoise-and-ivory dress she wore and he briefly mourned the bosom-enhancing high waists that had lately fallen out of fashion.

He breathed deep and forced himself to focus. All of his work today had been leading to this.

'Hmm. I left myself wide open with that remark and you failed to take advantage of it. Forgive me, but you have not seemed yourself today, Miss Beecham,' he said. They'd reached a paved circular area from which three avenues radiated outwards. He ignored them all and instead led her on to a smaller, gravelled pathway through a copse. 'I'm sorry if the day has not been to your liking.'

'Of course the day has been to my liking, Mr Alden.' Had she been any younger he would have sworn she would have rolled her eyes at him. 'I found a peacock feather on the drive as soon as we arrived, so I knew it was certain to be a good day.'

He blinked at that, but she did not pause.

'But you are right, I have not been acting myself and it has taken some of the shine from what might have been a perfect day—and given me a dreadful headache besides.'

'Not acting yourself? Well, then, whose role have you been enacting?'

She cast him an arch look. 'Couldn't you tell? I would have thought you found it a familiar picture.'

They'd intersected the larger walk that would lead them to the gate. Jack stopped abruptly as his feet hit the smooth surface and stared incredulously at her. 'Me? You thought to act like me?'

Was that how he looked to her? Aloof, uninterested, distant? Was that how everyone else viewed him as well? The idea astounded him. He'd thought himself reserved, yes, but not so determinedly remote.

Suddenly he began to laugh. He allowed her hand to drop away from his arm, walked over to lean on a sturdy horse-chestnut tree and proceeded to shake with amusement, long and hard.

'It's not funny, I assure you.' Miss Beecham sniffed. 'I have no idea how you go about like that every day. It's too much work.'

'No, no.' He chuckled. 'You did an admirable imitation of me. I dare say I should have enjoyed it more had I known what to look for.' He straightened away from the massive trunk and grinned at her. 'And, in truth, it was only fair. Now you must return the critique, for I've been doing my damnedest to act more like you!'

'Were you?' She looked diverted. 'Well, without a doubt, you should continue.'

'No! As you say, it's too much work. I've fair exhausted myself.' He wiped his eye and returned to her side. Reaching down, he took both of her hands in his. 'Shall we strike a bargain? Let us just be honest with each other. It's far easier and we got on well enough before.'

She shot him an incredulous look.

'Well, perhaps I should rephrase. I, in any case, quite enjoyed your company. I would like to continue to do so.'

'Honesty?' she asked.

'Honesty,' he vowed solemnly.

'Well, I did enjoy your company before, when you were not being a sanctimonious bore.'

Another burst of laughter escaped him. 'Well, I cannot promise that it won't happen again, but if it does, I beg you to let me know and I will attempt to rein myself in.'

She ran a dubious eye over him. Jack felt the heat of her innocent gaze rush from the top of his head down to the shining tips of his boots. Well, perhaps there were a few things he would have to hold back.

This time when he offered his arm she tucked her hand in the crook of his elbow with a smile. They strolled companionably for a few minutes before he spoke again.

'So tell me, Miss Beecham, how are you feeling about your sojourn into society?'

She wrinkled her brow at him. 'How am I feeling about it? That's an odd question. Most people just ask me if I am enjoying myself.'

Jack carefully kept his tone neutral. 'Excepting today, of course, it is obvious to anyone who lays an eye on you that you are enjoying yourself.'

She watched him closely, and then smiled. 'How do I feel?' she mused. She took a moment to consider the question, her brow furrowed becomingly. 'Well, I am enjoying myself, of course. No one spending any amount of time with your mother could do otherwise. But...' she sighed '...I admit to a little anxiety as well. To be honest, I hadn't expected everything to feel so alien.'

'Alien?' he repeated, surprised. 'How so?'

'I was born to this world...' she gestured about them '...just as surely as you were, Mr Alden. My father was a wealthy gentleman landowner. My mother's family has multiple connections to the nobility.' She shrugged. 'But the last years of my life have been so drastically different from all of this, and I find that those years have altered the way that I view certain things.'

She fascinated him more every second. 'Would you share some specifics?' he asked.

'Well, all this, for example. Chester House.' She glanced back towards the house and at the guests they could glimpse wandering through the vast and varied gardens. 'It's fascinating and beautiful and educational. I'm very grateful that Lord Bradington invited us to experience it all, but I can't help but think of all the people who will never view anything like this. I walk through here and I imagine the pleasure these things would bring, the awe they might inspire, if it were all open to the public—in a museum or a pleasure garden, perhaps.'

'Would not most Evangelicals disagree?' he asked. 'I thought they wish to educate the masses only so far as it will help them do their duty and accept their lot in life?'

'I suppose you are right about that,' Lily admitted. 'But to stimulate the mind, to expose it to the greatness that might be achieved by man and perhaps invite it to travel along the same paths—that can never be a mistake, in my opinion.'

Her words set off a burning deep in his chest. She was lovely and generous. *And you are a fool,* whispered some dark and no doubt perfectly correct part of his soul. He shushed it and struggled to speak in a normal tone. 'You interest me more by the second, Miss Beecham,' he said. 'You also remind me a great deal of a friend of mine.'

'Really?' she asked with a half-smile.

'Truly,' he affirmed. 'Though you could not be more opposite on the outside,' he said with amusement. 'Chione is half-Egyptian. She is newly betrothed to a gentleman who spends his time searching out antiquities. He has always in the past sold them to collectors. Dragons, Chione calls them.'

Her blue eyes lit up in delight. 'That is it exactly! Dragons, sitting atop their hordes, jealously guarding it from all but the most distinguished visitors.'

'I shan't tell Lord Bradington you said that.' Jack laughed. 'Trey, Chione's betrothed, says that dragons pay best, though.'

'And his fiancée says…?'

'Oh, she's convinced him to commit to the British Museum instead. Now everyone will be able to see the treasures he finds in his travels.'

'I think I should quite like your friends,' she said decisively.

Like a bolt from out of the sky, Jack suffered a moment of blinding insight. He recalled the turmoil and frustration he'd endured all day and he knew that he'd felt something similar before. It had crept up on him as Trey and Chione had grown naturally closer. Their intensifying fascination with each other and the mission they were to set out on had left him feeling shut out. Extraneous.

Was that when all this unwanted emotion had begun leaking past the barriers of his internal dams? No, he thought with a twist of gut-wrenching honesty—perhaps it might have begun even earlier, when Charles and Sophie had become so wrapped up in each other and their new family. But no matter when it had begun, there was no doubt that his every encounter with Lily Beecham intensified the problem and left a bigger breach in his internal bulwarks.

Well, he would just have to do some shoring up—and fast. He had a job to do here. He must force himself to forget such nonsense and focus on his objective.

'I am very glad that you are not a dragon, Mr Alden.'

Her words startled him. 'What?'

'You have a vast deal of knowledge. You have obviously spent a great deal of time in research. Yet you don't hide away in a study somewhere, hoarding your knowledge and expertise like artefacts or jewels. You share it. As you did today. As you do with your journal articles and speeches.'

She looked at him with something he hadn't seen in her eyes before: respect. Esteem. Jack's gut clenched in a visceral reaction. He'd seen a beggar child once, standing outside a bake shop, his face a picture of longing and need. God, but he felt just the same way right now. He'd been starving for that look of respect his whole life.

'It is just as I spoke about earlier,' she continued. 'Your passion infects others with the urge to learn, the wish to expand their own horizons. It is a very great gift that you give to the world, and I, for one, am thankful.'

Her words were a surprise and a pleasure. And perhaps a torment. It had been as nothing to take that hungry child inside and gift him with the largest, meatiest pastry the baker had on display. Jack had even left coins in an account so the boy could return. He feared it would be a much more difficult thing to accomplish his aim and still bask in the warm glow of her regard.

A sudden image flashed in his mind's eye—an ugly picture of his father raging, sweeping a day's work from his desk, parchment and paper and ink scattering like dust motes through the air.

He blinked. And he hardened his heart and clenched his fist in resolve.

'We promised honesty, Miss Beecham, did we not?'

'We did.'

'Then I wish to be honest with you. Chione is actually part of the reason I wanted to walk with you. I hoped to tell you a little more about her.'

Her brow furrowed in question, but she gave an encouraging nod.

'When we spoke of my injury, I told you that my friends and I had foiled a robbery.'

'Yes, I recall.'

'Well, there was more to it. We were lucky to have stopped a kidnapping plot as well.'

Her eyes widened, but she did not speak.

'Chione's grandfather was kidnapped and held for months. The night I was shot, Trey and I and a few others only just prevented the scoundrels from taking her as well.'

She gasped. 'Thank goodness you were there, then, and able to stop them.'

'In fact, we were not able to stop them all. One of the villains got away. A very evil man, I'm afraid. A slaver.'

Her expression grew serious. 'That is unfortunate. I know something of the terrible things such men do to their fellow humans. Mother and I have worked hard to educate our corner of Dorset against the evils of slavery.'

'It is a shame that a woman like you must be familiar with the depths to which these men will sink. But I think you will understand when I tell you how worried I am. This man is obsessed with vengeance. Chione and her family may still be in grave danger from him.'

'How horrible,' she breathed.

They had reached the stone gate. Neither of them paid it a bit of attention. Jack steeled himself and spoke again.

'I believe that you might be in a position to help.'

Shock widened her eyes and hitched her breath. 'Me?'

'Yes. You—and your cousin, Matthew Beecham.'

'Matthew? What can he have to do with any of this? He is in America!'

'Actually, he has gone missing.'

Now suspicion darkened her eyes and clouded her features. 'How could you possibly know such a thing?'

'Miss Beecham—Lily,' Jack said, half-pleading. 'You appear to be well aware that slavery remains a reality in America, just as it does in the British colonies. It is the *trade* in slaves that has been made illegal in our country and the import of new slaves that has been outlawed in theirs. But apparently Captain Batiste, the slaver we spoke of, misses the days of putting his ship into port and selling poor souls like cattle right off his deck.'

'But what has any of that to do with *Matthew*?'

'I'm nearly there. From what I can gather, your cousin got into some kind of trouble with Batiste. A debt of some sort. Batiste demanded repayment—in the form of some adjustments made to a few of his ships. False compartments, secret holds, that sort of thing. All to enable him to resume his illegal trafficking in people, with those slaveholders unscrupulous enough to deal with him.'

Jack walked away from her horrified stare. The old gateway beckoned. If only the legends were true. He could pass through the archway and his problems would be solved. Well, hell, he would take help where he could get it. He tried the iron gateway set into the stone arch. His arm protested the effort, but it was to no avail anyway. The gate was locked. He should have known.

'The American government caught on to Batiste's tricks,' he continued. 'But the man is as slippery as an eel. They next went to speak to your cousin, but found he had fled. They want him for questioning.'

'I don't believe it,' she said flatly.

'I don't care about any of that, Lily. I just want Batiste. And your cousin may be able to tell me where to find him.'

Her expression hardened. 'And that is what all of this has been about, has it not?' Her slate eyes turned to chill, blue ice as she gestured about them, to the park and the house and the carefree revellers grouped in the distance. 'Or has it been only that from nearly the very beginning?'

He shook his head.

'What a lucky coincidence that it was I who you nearly ran down in the street, no?' she whispered.

'No. It's not like that,' Jack protested.

'I think it is. You think that I, in turn, will be able to tell you where Matthew is?' She gave an ugly, bitter laugh. 'Well I am destined to disappoint you once again, Mr Alden, because you know far more about all of this than I! I knew nothing about any of this. Nothing! I did not even know that Matthew had left his home. And I refuse to believe that he could be mixed up in something so foul as slavery.'

She whirled around and walked away from him and the gate. Before Jack could call out, she let out a sudden gasp and turned back. 'Does your mother know all of this as well?'

'No! Of course not,' he said.

Her shoulders slumped in relief.

'She knows nothing about it and she won't unless you choose to tell her. Please, just listen to me,' Jack asked quietly. 'You said you were close with your cousin, that you still correspond. All I ask is that you tell me if you hear from him.'

He'd thought her indifference was painful. The contempt that shone from her now cut deep and was nearly unbearable.

He winced and sighed. 'I can help Matthew. I want to help him. All I need to do is ask him some questions about likely spots where Batiste would hide away. He's spent a considerable amount of time with the man; he might know something that will enable us to find him.' He took a step towards her, held out a beseeching hand. 'My brother has a great deal of influence. He will use it to help your cousin.'

She turned her back on him once more. 'And if he does not possess the information you want? What will you do then?'

Jack did not even wish to contemplate such a thing. 'Charles and I will still help him, even if he does not. I swear.'

Her head dropped and she began to pace. Jack watched her graceful form and sent out a silent plea to the heavens. He needed her help. God help him, he was beginning to fear he needed *her*.

Avoiding his gaze, she passed him and approached the gate. She ran a hand along the elaborately carved stone until she came to the middle. There she ceased her restless motion and gripped the iron railings of the inset door.

'You don't know what you are asking!' She spoke not to Jack, but to the empty park beyond. In the distance people chatted and laughed, but Jack's world had shrunk alarmingly. Naught mattered save her and him and this gateway to their future.

'I simply cannot believe my cousin would be mixed up in this. Matthew is a good person. He's the only person left alive who knows me. Really, truly, deep down inside, he knows me. When we were young he never cared that I preferred a good gallop to gossip, that I would always choose to climb a tree over embroidering a sampler.' She sent a pleading look over her shoulder. 'Even now, when he writes, he doesn't ask me the same inane, irrelevant questions that the rest of the world seems to focus on. He asks me about the crops, and my tenants, and whether I've convinced my mother that attendance at a local assembly will not taint my soul.' She turned to face him again and he saw that her gaze had grown distant and unfocused. 'He even occasionally remembers to ask if I've seen two blackbirds sitting together on a fence post.'

'Blackbirds?' Jack began to feel as if they were carrying on two separate conversations.

'Blackbirds,' she answered firmly. 'You see—he understands me and all my foibles and still he cares for me. That is the person you think could stoop so low, the one you are asking me to betray.'

'It would not be a betrayal. You can trust me, Lily.'

'Trust you?' Her voice fairly dripped scorn. 'I do not even know you, Jack Alden.'

'Don't be absurd. You know me well enough to trust my word.'

'Not I! In fact, I question whether anyone in your life can claim to truly know you. I thought you hid behind your books, but today I begin to wonder if perhaps it is only in your intellectual pursuits that you are open and accessible. At all other times you've shown yourself to be distant and cold—closed behind walls that you only think are protecting you.' She crossed her arms in front of her. 'I cannot know you or trust you, Mr Alden, until you learn to know and trust yourself.'

With her every word Jack could feel the intelligent, rational man he knew himself to be fading away. She was an innocent, naïve little fool, but he felt wild, frenzied, like a child on the verge of a temper tantrum. She did this to him. Every time he got near her she shone a light on his every flaw, magnified his every emotion until he thought he would go mad with it.

He thought of Batiste, a malevolent threat hovering over Trey and Chione and their family—in just the same way his father had hovered contemptuously, dangerously in the background for most of his life—and he knew he would indeed go mad if Lily Beecham did not co-operate.

'You don't know as much as you think you do, Lily. Of a certainty you don't know what you are asking of me. But perhaps you are right,' he said, moving closer, his heart pounding, his blood surging. 'There are also many things that I do not know—including why you feel such antagonism towards me.'

'I…I don't,' she whispered, suddenly flustered.

'You do.' He was glad to see her unbalanced. It was only fair. She stirred him up until he felt as if he must prove his manhood or die trying. He approached her stealthily, a hunter prowling forwards with soft, light steps. And she, she was his prey. 'You lecture me, but I think you must follow your own advice. Everything I see and hear of you tells me that you are a warm person, giving to others. But you will not consider my request—even though it might benefit your cousin and will help save a family from a dangerous and unscrupulous man. And why not? Because the request comes from me?'

'No.' Her freckles disappeared again in the flush that rose from beneath her gown.

'It's true.' He advanced further, trapping her between him and the iron bars of the gate. 'Look deep, as you've asked me to do. You are allowing your dislike of me to influence your judgement.'

Her breathing quickened. He could see the flutter of her pulse in her throat, the quick casting about of her gaze as she searched for an escape. 'I don't dislike you.'

Discipline had gone. Reason and judgement had disappeared. The other, darker side of Jack's soul ruled now. It roared to life inside of him, loosing a great whirl of longing and want and more than a bit of anger too. The small bit of sanity he had left knew that anger had no place in this, and urged control. But it was too late for restraint. He held Lily's gaze prisoner with his own and asked the question to which he must have the answer. 'Then what do you feel, Lily, when you look at me?'

'I…'

'Honesty, remember? Tell me the truth.' Their lips were but a whisper apart.

She shook her head, looked away, breaking the hypnotic link between them. 'Not dislike,' she said to the ground.

He knew that she meant to hide the desire in her eyes—the same desire that flowed molten through him even now. Did it burn like fire through her veins—as it did his? He reached out to trace a fiery path, drawing a fingertip over her collarbone, along the smooth and shimmering nape of her neck. He lifted her chin and forced her to confront him, herself and the truth.

'Something else entirely,' was all she said.

The darkness inside of him rejoiced. She was caught—pressed up against the cold iron bars at her back. Jack's erection bulged hot and leaden between them, and he suffered a brief, stabbing need to press it against her, to trap her between hot and cold, hard and harder. Yet he didn't do it. Not yet.

Logic and reason put forth one last try, tossing a fleeting image of Batiste at his mind's eye. Jack ignored it. He'd gone beyond the reach of logic, into a place where pure emotion and hot, liquid lust held sway. Batiste could go to hell. Jack had given himself over to animal need and he revelled in it, sucking in the clean scent of her, gazing with wonder at the flushed expectation on her lovely face.

Then his eye fixed on her mouth. She stared back. That gorgeous, plump lower lip beckoned. As if she knew what it would do to him, she caught it suddenly between her teeth. The startling contrast of soft lush pink and hard white enamel made him want to howl. And then, ever so slowly, her bottom lip slid free, and the tip of her hot tongue traced a soft, wet trail along it.

His heart thumped. His cock surged. He slid his fingers into her curls of red-gold, cradled the back of her head for one long, tender second, and then let go to grasp the bars on either side of her. Pain flashed in his arm, but she made no protest, and only anticipation showed on her face. Jack slipped loose from the last vestige of reason and control, leaned in and branded her with his hot, searing kiss.

Honesty. That's what Jack gave her with his wild, insistent mouth. It was not what he'd set out to do. Lily had seen the calculation in his eye when he took his first step towards her. But she'd seen it disappear, too. Driven further away as he grew physically closer, supplanted by longing, and need and pure, undiluted want.

Almost from the first moment they met, Lily had asked, pes-tered, demanded that he come out of hiding and show her his true self. Now at last he'd taken the first step and opened a crack in the protective barriers around him. Her arms crept up, across the expanse of his chest and over his shoulders, locking behind his neck and pulling him close. No matter what he said, and despite his unreasonable request, she knew she had an obligation, a responsibility to meet him halfway.

He deepened the kiss, tempting and coaxing with lips and tongue and mouth, while a cascade of voices clamoured an alarm in her head. They threw accusations at her, ugly words like *immoral* and *shame* and *sin.*

She ignored them. This entire trip to London, she realised, had truly been about shutting out other voices and distractions, and learning to hear her own.

So she listened. At first she could only hear the clear and happy note that was born of his kiss. *Jack*, it hummed. *Jack, Jack, Jack.* But she forced herself to concentrate further. And what she heard was music, learning and debate. Camaraderie and intercourse with other people with similar interests. And a great clamouring for *more*. More of all of that, but above all, more of Jack Alden.

Joy erupted within her, stretching and growing until she had to give it voice. She moaned her approval and happiness and relief. And he answered in kind, emanating a low, appreciative rumble that originated in the back of his throat, but somehow ended up pooling hot and deep in her belly. Neither of them could deny the reality and the truth of this moment, just the two of them coming together with nothing else between.

Their kiss changed in the moment when her lips parted and her mouth opened under his. Suddenly he was inside, and the hot, slick slide of his tongue made her wild with need. Passion poured out of him and into her. She took it, honoured by the enormity of his gift, and gave it back to him twice over.

Slowly he coached her, taught her tongue how to play. An eager student, she met him thrust for thrust and pressed herself closer against him. His hands came off the bars and settled into the curve of her neck and shoulder, steadying her while he kissed her with long and languid strokes.

He drew back a fraction and Lily gasped, her breath coming fast and rough. It nearly ceased altogether when he buried his face in the curve of her throat. Her pulse tripped and pounded against him as he made his way down her throat with alternate hard, biting nips and soft, teasing kisses.

But honesty is a rare and fragile thing, and Lily should not have expected Jack's first foray into the light to be a lengthy one. He gradually slowed and stilled, until they stood clasped unmoving in each other's arms, his face still buried in the crook of her neck and her cheek pressed hard against his shoulder.

He was the first to disengage. Their hot breath mingled as their gazes met. His chest heaved as desire and need faded.

Lily knew how difficult this must be for him, and yet she had not expected to see regret loom so quickly, nor so strongly that it almost resembled despair. She shook her head. 'Jack, don't,' she whispered.

But the breach was repaired and he had already retreated behind his walls and into safety. His head was shaking, too, in constant small movements that nevertheless signalled a large degree of denial.

'No,' he said. 'This isn't right. It isn't *me*.'

'Jack…'

'No! I'm sorry—you ask for something I just don't have in me to give.' His brow furrowed, his lips compressed. 'All I want is to speak with your cousin. I'll do everything in my power to help him, I swear. If you hear from him, tell him that.'

He spun on his heel and walked away.

Lily could not bear to watch him go. She turned and gazed through the gate once more. For the first time in a long time, she felt she truly knew what she wanted. And it was not the iron bars in front of her blocking her path to good fortune.

Chapter Seven

Jack did not wait for the gathering to officially end. He took a terse leave of his mother, a more polite one of his host, and then he traded a spot in the landau next to Lily for Keller's mount. Within thirty minutes he was on his way back to London, cursing himself for an uncontrolled idiot and Lily Beecham for a damnably tempting vixen.

Why? He pondered his ridiculous dilemma as the miles passed. Why did the one time he *needed* to maintain his usual calm and rational focus become the one time he found it impossible to do so? The thought of how badly he'd botched nearly every moment with Lily Beecham sickened him.

He needed to think. Traffic entering London forced him to slow his pace and he cursed under his breath. He longed for the peace and serenity of his rooms. He would refocus, forget the taste of her, the incredible feel of her under his hands, and try to figure out what the hell his next move should be.

Fractious fate intervened, however. When Jack finally made his way home, he sprinted up the stairs—and froze at the sight of his door standing partially open. Wariness, confusion, and finally white-hot anger blossomed in his chest. Silent, he crept forwards. Tense, on alert for any sound or movement from within, he eased the door open. Nothing stirred. Amidst a rising, ever-more-familiar rush of rage, he stepped inside.

Whoever the intruders had been, they'd done a thorough job of it. Every drawer, book, stack of papers, even the clothes in his wardrobe had been torn apart and tossed asunder. Speechless, he stood in the midst of the devastation.

What in hell was this all about? He couldn't explain this ransacking of his rooms, any more than he could stem his rising tide of temper.

Already weakened by his encounter with Lily Beecham, surrounded by the wreckage of his life, discipline stood not a chance. Jack reached down to pick up a book, sorely tempted to throw it against the wall himself. A whisper of a sound outside gave him pause.

He waited. It came again. The steady, slow sound resolved itself into a set of footsteps on the stairs and only served to fuel his fury. He sunk into a crouch and let it wash over him. Rational thought ceased and blind, pure instinct took hold.

His brain fought back, trying desperately to send the message that something about the approaching threat rang peculiar. But Jack was in thrall to his jangled nerves. The enemy approached, stood just beyond the still-open doorway, set a cautious step over the threshold.

And at his next rational thought, Jack discovered he held a man pressed to the wall. His uninjured forearm pressed tight and cruel into the man's throat, even as he desperately wished for his knife.

'Effendi.' The soft voice in his ear cut through the angry red haze. 'I do not think you wish to be doing this.'

Startled, Jack glanced to his right. That accent, the silent approach, it could only be… 'Aswan?' He looked back, then, to the man he'd pinned. He stepped abruptly away. 'Oh, God. Eli!'

'Aye,' the old sailor-turned-groom grunted, rubbing his throat. 'And I'll thank ye for leaving my head attached. Bad enough that I'll be crossin' to the other side without my leg. I don't think the good Lord'll be so understanding, should I lose my head as well.'

'I'm sorry.' He turned to Aswan. 'But what the hell are you doing here?' Jack had to admit, he'd felt a surge of satisfaction at the sight of them. These two had been as deeply embroiled in Trey and Mervyn's search for the Lost Jewel as he had. Jack knew all too well just what this enigmatic Egyptian and peg-legged former sea captain were capable of.

'There's news.' Eli glanced about at the mess. 'Though I can see we left it a bit too late.'

'What in blazes is going on? Is Trey with you?' Jack had jerked suddenly to attention. 'And who the hell is looking after Chione and Mervyn and the children?'

'Treyford watches over the family. The slave-taker is still abroad,' Aswan said. 'But still he holds sway over many evil men in this country.'

'Aye, Mervyn's offices in Bristol and Portsmouth have both been broken into, and both on the same day, it looks like.' Eli tossed aside a pile of jumbled shirts and settled himself into a chair. 'I been stayin' in Wapping, but when I heard, we went up to Mayfair to find the town house looking just like this. We came straight over to warn ye to be on the lookout for trouble.'

Jack laughed bitterly, but not for long. 'Portsmouth and Bristol both?' he'd asked. 'And a synchronised effort? That's significant manpower.'

'It's clear enough now that Batiste is still after the Lost Jewel. Trey cannot hide the fact that he is preparing for a large expedition. He thinks word has leaked to Batiste and that's why he's searching the offices.' Eli glanced about. 'I s'pose it's why he'd do your rooms. The bastard wants to know jest where Trey's headin'—and he's thinkin' ye might know.'

Aswan spoke up. 'This man has a demon in him. He will not stop until he has what he wants.'

The three of them stared at each other in silence. They all knew what Batiste was after did not really exist—and that he would never be convinced of that truth.

'We've got to get our hands on him,' Jack breathed. 'He'll always be there, otherwise. Hanging in the background, waiting for his chance.'

'Trey's working on it. He says as you're to be careful. He feels bad enough about the trouble he's caused ye.' Eli exchanged glances with the Egyptian and they both headed for the door. 'You concentrate on finding Beecham. We'll uncover what we can about this mess.' He gestured. 'We'll be back to fill ye in before long.'

Dismayed, Jack watched his unlikely allies disappear. He hadn't the heart to call them back and tell them how badly he'd bungled his search for Matthew Beecham. His anger returned as he stared at the chaos of his rooms. But this time his brain remained engaged. Frantically he began to rifle through the mess, searching for older, sturdier clothing.

There was more than one way to skin a cat, his mother had always told him. Surely there must also be more than one way to catch a scoundrel like Batiste.

Thunk. The tankard hit the table hard, sloshing a wave of dark ale over the brim.

'Ye'll need to be drinkin' a mite more, if ye'll be taking up the table for the whole of the night,' the bleary-eyed barman grunted.

'I'll order the whole damned place a round when the man you spoke of shows up,' Jack shot back.

The tapster shrugged and wiped the spill with his stained and dirty apron. 'Told ye—I'm no man's keeper. The sod'll show up, or he won't. Plenty of other pubs to find 'is grog in, ain't there?'

God knew that was the truth, and it felt as if Jack had been in nearly every squalid dockside tavern and low riverside inn in London over the last few nights. 'I'll wait just the same,' he replied and slid a coin across the scarred wood of the table.

The barman eyed the gold, then Jack for a long moment. Finally he scooped up the money, turned and pushed his way back through the low-hung smoke to the tap.

Jack settled in to nurse another pint. The Water Horse might be the seediest, most disreputable pub on the river, but it was the only one that held a promise of a lead to Batiste.

Of all the sailors, dockyard labourers, whores and wharf rats Jack had questioned over the last few days, only the tapster here had flinched at Batiste's name. A very large purse had bought him the information that one of Batiste's former crew sometimes drank here.

It was a long shot at best, a fast route to a watery grave at worst. Yet what was the alternative? Pestering Lily Beecham until she heard from her cousin again? Torturing them both and allowing her to goad him into forgetting himself again? He'd rather spend a thousand nights in this sinkhole.

Jack took a drink of the warm ale and grimaced. He'd need an ocean of the stuff to drown his frustration with that girl. Her image hovered in his head, beautiful and lovely and all too tempting. He fought to ignore it, to forget the mad embrace they had shared in Bradington's gardens. Even the thought of her stirred the emotional turmoil he fought so hard to control.

And perhaps at last he'd come to the real reason he sat at the Horse again tonight. Here he had no attention or emotional energy to spare. Here he had no choice but to focus on his surroundings, on getting the information he sought and on getting himself out alive.

As the hour grew later the likelihood of the latter began to come into doubt. All manner of transactions took place around him, both above board, and by the furtive look of some of the participants, below. The crowd ebbed and flowed like the tide, but through it all someone besides Jack remained constant.

A high-backed booth flanked the door, and two men occupied it most of the night. A massive bull of a man, whose short dingy blond hair peeked from beneath a seaman's cap, sat silent and watchful with a smaller, swarthier man. They were not drinking either, Jack noted, but the tapster didn't stir himself to chide them. Not once did Jack see a word spoken between them, but as the taproom grew emptier, the smaller man began to flick an occasional, tell-tale glance his way.

He rose. Better to take his chances in the open than to risk events coming to a head here, where those two might have allies and Jack certainly did not.

He left the pub and strode quickly out into Flow Alley. The fog hung thick and rife with the stench of the river. It swirled and clung to him, making him feel as if he had to swim through it instead of walk.

A lamp hanging outside a pub cast an eerie pool of wavering light as he passed. From the mist floated an occasional snatch of disembodied conversation. It was not drunken revelry or ribald negotiations he strained to hear, but it was not until he reached the wide, empty intersection with Great Hermitage Street that he caught a hint of it—the faint echo of a footstep on cobblestones.

Jack ducked instantly into the doorway of a chandler's shop. If luck was with him, then whoever it was behind him would walk right on by. If it was not, then at least his back was covered.

Much as he'd expected—Lady Luck had abandoned him. First one figure emerged from out of the gloom, then another. The men from the Water Horse.

Jack drew his knife. Nobody spoke. The shorter man hung back, the larger pulled a stout cudgel from his bulky seaman's sweater and advanced with a menacing stride.

'Are you here at Batiste's bidding?' asked Jack.

The smaller man spat on to the rough stones of the street. 'Questions like that is what got ye into this mess.'

'I just meant to ask if you knew what sort of man you were taking orders from,' Jack said, never taking his eyes off of the big lout.

'The sort with gold in his pockets,' snickered the first man. 'And before ye ask, no, I don't care how he come by it—as long as he's forkin' over my share.' He thrust his chin towards Jack. 'Do it, Post.'

The big sailor moved in. Jack braced himself and waited…waited…until the cudgel swung at him in a potentially devastating blow. Quickly he jumped forwards, thrusting his knife, point up and aiming for the vulnerable juncture under the man's arm.

But the goliath possessed surprisingly swift reflexes. He shifted his aim and blocked the driving thrust of the knife with the cudgel. The point buried itself in the rough wood. With a grin and a sudden, practised jerk, he yanked the blade right from Jack's grip.

His gut twisting, Jack knew he was finished. But he'd be damned if he went down without a fight. He ducked low and aimed a powerful blow right into that massive midsection.

He swore his wrist cracked. His fingers grew numb. But the giant just grinned. He reached for Jack. Those thick fingers closed around his neckcloth—and suddenly the great ham-hand spasmed open.

Jack looked up into the broad face so close to his. He met a pair of bulging eyes and flinched at the sight of a mouth wide open in a wordless grunt of pain. From this vantage point, the reason for his silence was clear. Some time, somewhere in this man's violent past, his tongue had been cut out.

Jack strained, trying to slide out from against the door as the brute turned half-away, reaching behind him. His gaze following, Jack saw the hilt of a knife protruding from the man's meaty thigh.

The giant grasped the knife. With a thick grunt, he pulled it free. Jack acted instantly, kicking the blade out of the oaf's hand. Never too proud to take advantage of an opponent's misfortune, Jack aimed another hard kick at his wounded limb. As the leg began to buckle, he reached up and, yanking hard, pulled his knife free from the cudgel. In a flash, he had it at the man's throat. The point pricked, drawing blood, before his opponent realised his predicament.

The giant froze. Jack looked over at his companion. 'Back away,' he snarled. 'I'll cut his throat if I have to.'

A curious, regular tapping sounded out of the mist. Jack tensed, waiting to see what new threat would emerge. Someone had thrown that knife. But which combatant had it been meant for?

His mouth dropped and a wave of surprise and relief swept over him as the fog gave up another figure, wiry, grizzled and wearing an elaborately carved peg below one knee.

'Eli!' Jack grinned. 'You're like a bad penny, always turning up where you're least expected.'

The diminutive groom brandished another wickedly long knife. 'Fun's over for tonight, mates,' he said.

The swarthy man let out an ugly laugh. 'Says you.' He gestured to his partner. 'Kill 'em bo—' His sentence ended abruptly as his legs flew out from beneath him. He flailed briefly and hit the cobblestones hard. In a second's time, the dark-skinned man in a turban kneeled over him and rested a pistol nonchalantly against his chest.

'Good evening to you, Aswan.' This time a dose of humiliation mixed with Jack's relief. How many times would the Egyptian have to snatch him from the jaws of death?

'The pair of ye got nowhere to go, 'cept to hell,' Eli told the villains with a nod. He gestured for Aswan to release his captive. 'Unless you're in a hurry to get there, get up and off wi' ye both.'

'Aye, and you keep your friend where he belongs,' snarled the small man. 'If we see him again we won't be giving him his chance—it'll be a knife in the back from out of the dark.' He glared at Jack. 'Understand? Keep to your own lot, bookworm.'

The pair faded into the fog.

'Come on.' Eli clapped Jack on the shoulder. 'This damp is makin' me leg ache.'

The three of them walked to Leman Street, where they hailed a hackney and had it convey them to a still-open coffee house in the Strand.

The place was empty. The shopkeeper had thrown the chairs up on the tables to sweep, but he was thrilled to stir up a cheery fire and arrange three of his best seats in front of it. He bustled off to fetch coffee and Eli groaned as he settled in and rubbed his leg. 'Well, which is it, man?' he asked Jack.

'Which is what?' Jack gazed, puzzled, from one of his rescuers to the other.

The groom exchanged a glance with the Egyptian. 'We told ye we'd deal with this lot. And then we hear tell of a Mayfair toff askin' questions all over the riverside.' He shrugged. 'A man don't get hisself into a situation like that unless he's got either a death wish or woman trouble. So which is it?'

Jack groaned and hung his head in his hands.

'Woman trouble.' Eli sighed.

Jack peered up at the pair of them. 'Well, I suppose I should thank you, at any rate.' He grimaced. 'What do you hear from Devonshire?'

'We heard from Trey today. He's got everything well in hand.'

'Well in hand?' Jack scoffed. 'Batiste's got his fingers in every pie from here to there and Trey's got it well in hand?'

'What I want to know,' Eli demanded, 'is why you were at the Horse tonight.'

Jack explained, but Eli just shook his head. 'It's more likely that tapster's in league with Batiste's men. He probably lured you there and tipped them off.'

'Well, I had to take the chance, didn't I?'

The coffee came then, and Eli sighed as he wrapped his hands around his hot cup. Aswan glanced at his mug with distaste.

'*Effendi*, why do you feel as if you must take this chance?' the Egyptian asked.

Jack stared blankly. 'You just said it, Aswan. Batiste is a dangerous man.' He glanced around at the empty room, but still lowered his voice to a whisper. 'Chione is your family. Trey and the rest will be soon enough. Can you stomach the thought of him out there, hovering, just waiting for his chance to hurt them? They deserve to live their lives free, without fear and without a constant nagging threat in the background.'

'Batiste's more'n dangerous. He's obsessed, I'd say,' Eli

replied. 'Treyford wants him taken jest as bad as ye. He's not above throwin' his title around, neither. Aswan says as how they've had the Navy in Devonshire, and the Foreign Office, too. Even had a couple of Americans in.' He took a long swallow and grinned in satisfaction. 'Damned good coffee here.'

'Treyford sends a message. He has a favour to ask of you,' Aswan said abruptly. 'He says you have done well with your cors—corres—?' He looked to Eli for help.

'Correspondence. Damned good idea, that. But he's got someone he'd like you to talk to, as well.'

'Who is it?'

'Broken-down seaman, as used to sail with Batiste.'

'Yes, I've heard that one before.' Jack grinned.

'No, this one should be no threat. Mervyn's had word of him. Name o' Crump. He's poorly and been set up in the new Seamen's Hospital. Mervyn says as it's unlikely he'll be coming out.'

'Why me? Wouldn't he be more likely to speak with you, someone who knows the life he's led?'

'No.' Eli shook his head. 'He'll know of my relationship with Mervyn and there's a risk he won't want anything to do with me. Crump crewed with Batiste when the bastard still worked for Latimer Shipping. He went with Batiste when the pair o' them fought and Batiste struck out on his own. He'll know much about where Batiste hides his head when the chips start to stack against him.'

'But why would he want to share any of it with me?'

Eli looked him over, considering. 'Well, Trey says as how yer brother has a title, too—mayhap he wouldn't mind using it in the name of a good cause?'

'Oh, well, I'm sure he would not mind, if I asked him.'

'That ain't all, though. Trey says ye'll have been mucking about a bit with some Evangelicals?'

Jack started. 'Where the hell does Trey get his information? If I didn't know him better, I'd suspect him to be near as bad as Batiste.'

Eli laughed. 'Treyford does have his ways. And when ye pair him with Mervyn...' he shuddered '...I don't think there's nothing the two o' them couldn't tackle.'

'And just how do they think to use my Evangelical connections?'

'Crump's converted. Mervyn thinks he left Batiste when he saw how bad things get on a slave ship. If you could let on that you were of a like mind...'

'I have friends among the Evangelicals. I'm not one myself,' Jack said.

'Crump don't need to know that, do he?'

Jack sighed. He thought he'd rather take his chances back in the East End, rather than lie to a sickly old sailor. But he'd said he'd do anything that would lead to Batiste's capture, hadn't he? An image flashed in his head—Lily, her lips red and flushed full from his kiss, an unuttered plea in her eyes. Immediately, he pushed it away.

'I suppose not,' he said.

'Would you be needin' anything else, miss?'

Lady Dayle's footman did not look at Lily as he spoke. His gaze was very firmly locked on the pump house at the centre of the garden in Berkeley Square, where several giggling maids had gathered.

'No, thank you, Thomas, I am fine here,' she said, settling on to a bench situated under a shady plane tree. She'd come seeking solitude, and would not have brought the footman at all, had Lady Dayle not insisted. 'I shall call you when I am ready to return.'

'Very good, miss.' He turned away with an eager step, but

then paused a moment, looking back. 'You're sure you're all right, Miss Lily?'

She was touched by the concern in his tone. 'I'm fine, Thomas.' She smiled. 'But thank you for asking.'

He pivoted back to face her again, but kept a respectful distance. 'I don't mean to overstep, miss, but I hope you don't mind if I tell you: I think you've adjusted—to London and the fancy, I mean—right well.'

'Thank you,' she said again.

'It's just that I was new here, too,' he said earnestly, 'a few years back. I think your world, your old one, I mean, it was…different?'

'Oh, yes, vastly different,' she agreed with fervour.

'Mine, too. I was green as grass—and I made mistakes, some real whoppers. But I got used to it, and you will, too, and, like I said, I think you're doing fine.'

'Thank you,' she whispered past the growing tightness in her throat. Kindness from such an unexpected source cheered her—and made her realise how unskilled she must be at hiding her emotions.

'I shall wait for your summons, then,' he said, but his cheery grin negated the formality of his words.

Lily nodded and watched him join the knot of maidservants at the centre of the square. They welcomed him with enthusiasm and more than one flirtatious smile. Clearly Thomas had made a successful transition from his old world to his new.

She sighed, fearing her own task would turn out to be more difficult. For she did not seek to leave one sphere for another. She meant to somehow meld two very different worlds into a new one. All she wanted was to carve out a place of her own, a space of comfort and acceptance, where she could thrive and grow. But she had begun to fear that Jack Alden was right, she was asking for more than *anyone* was ready to give.

No. Jack was a spike in her heart and every thought of him ripped her open a little wider. She'd spent the last days in a restless state of anxiety and indecision. Over and over she played in her mind's eye those exciting moments, that soul-searing kiss. At every private moment, she relived the passion and the nearly magical sense of spiralling desire. She'd touched his lips, his body, his heart and mind.

And he had turned on his heel and coldly abandoned her.

Incredibly, Lily had understood. Not only did they come from different worlds, but different perspectives as well. She felt more than a little torn herself, and when she was not reliving the excitement of their embrace, then she was wavering helplessly between agony and joy. Joy because she'd reached him. She'd peeked inside him and seen that this indefinable pull, this attraction between them, was real and it ran deep. Agony because *he* had also asked too much of *her*.

She could never believe that Matthew had gotten mixed up with slavers. It was not possible, as anyone acquainted with him would know. He could not be capable of such cruelty.

Jack was a scholar. His brother did have political ties, and had seen more than a little success. But she knew from Lady Dayle that none of it had come in the area of diplomacy. According to the viscountess, Viscount Dayle's area of interest lay in economics and reform. He'd never, to his mother's knowledge, had dealings with the Foreign Office or contact with anyone in the American government.

Lily did not doubt Jack's wish to help Matthew. But she very much doubted his ability to do so. He wanted to see this Batiste captured so badly that he'd turned a blind eye to the likely consequences to her cousin. Even the suspicion of such a thing could ruin him.

She glanced up, wanting to make certain that Thomas was fully occupied. And sent up a prayer of thanks. Another man in livery had joined the group and Thomas had entered a full-scale war for feminine attention. While every eye locked on to the thrilling sight of a grown man in full livery and powder scaling the mounted statue of George III, Lily slipped away towards a more private corner of the garden.

The paths here, like the garden itself, lay in an elliptical shape. It did not take long to turn a curve and find herself alone. She breathed deep. This morning a parcel of forwarded mail had arrived from home. And in it had been a letter— slanted across with Matthew's familiar bold handwriting.

Lily's hand shook as she reached into her pocket to pull it out. Quickly, furtively, she broke the seal.

Dearest Lily,

In that moment, she knew the tidings could not be good. Every other letter she'd ever had from Matthew had been ad-dressed irreverently to Lilikins, his childhood name for her. Her eyes filled, making it difficult to read on.

I don't know what you might have heard, if indeed you would have heard anything at all. But I want you to know—a good reason lies behind my actions. I cannot explain now, but all will be clear when next we meet. I've only just left Le Havre, and I know not just where we will go. Please don't believe the worst of me. I will contact you again when I can.
Yours,
Matthew

Lily raised shaking fingers to her mouth. Jack could not have been right. She would not believe it.

But wait a moment. His story coloured her interpretation.

This told her nothing, really. She braced herself against a tree, sucking in air. She could not tell Jack about this letter.

Would he understand? She suffered a pang of doubt. The intensity with which he spoke of the danger to his friends suggested otherwise. She drew away from the tree, folded the note and stood upright. She would make him understand. Surely he was not so insulated behind his walls of intellect and scorn that he could not understand loyalty.

Suddenly a voice rang behind her, calling her name. 'Thomas?' she answered. 'Here, I'm just here, around the bend!'

It was not Thomas who came hurrying down the path, though.

'Fisher?' What was Lady Dayle's staid butler doing in the garden square?

'Miss? Oh, Miss Beecham, thank goodness. Please, come! You are needed in Bruton Street!'

Lily's heart stopped. She reached out and clutched the man's arm. 'Lady Dayle?' she breathed.

'Is in urgent need of you, miss. No, she's well, in the physical sense,' he rushed to reassure her. 'But more than that I cannot say. Just please, come with me, won't you?'

'Of course!' The situation must be dire indeed, if Fisher had come for her himself. Lily lifted her skirts and hurried after him, her own troubles forgotten. Fortunately, Bruton Street lay just outside the Square. In a matter of minutes they'd reached the town house. She followed the butler across the front hall and into the family parlour.

The viscountess stood inside, bent over her desk, scribbling furiously. Her hair hung in filthy strands; her hands, arms and the front of her gown were covered in thick, black soot.

'Martha, you go up to the attics; Susan, you can take care of the still room.' She clipped out orders like a military sergeant to a cluster of frightened maids. 'Linens, towels, soap, ointments... Oh, lord—' she coughed violently, then sagged suddenly and moaned aloud '—I cannot think!'

'My lady!' gasped Lily. 'What has happened?'

'Oh, Lily!' Lady Dayle looked up. Her face crumpled, and Lily saw a large red scrape across her forehead. 'You can't imagine—the most terrible thing!' Dirty tears began to track down her face. All the maids began to wail and the butler stepped forwards, wringing his hands.

But Lily was a country girl. She knew how to handle herself in a crisis. Her father's training kicked in and she crossed the room with a determined step. 'It's all right, my lady,' she said firmly. 'Out now, the rest of you!' she ordered. 'We will give the viscountess a moment to collect herself. You know what to do.' She paused a moment to gather her thoughts. 'Fisher, I think we'll need a tea tray in here,' she said. 'Send for his lordship, and gather as many of the staff as you can and ready them to send messages.' She waved the gawking footmen away from the door and shooed the maids out. The butler nodded, casting a look of profound thanks in her direction as he closed the door behind him.

As if the closed door were a signal, Lady Dayle sank into a chair and began to cough. The dry, hacking sound quickly deteriorated into heartrending sobs. Without a word, Lily enfolded her in a tight embrace and let her cry. She crooned softly and her mind raced while the viscountess cried herself out. When the storm had passed she took both of the dear lady's hands in her own and said, 'Tell me.'

'I'd been to that linen draper's in Long Acre, the one that had that roll of blocked dimity? I had it in mind to have it made into clothes for baby Maria.' The viscountess's voice was rough and strained as she spoke.

A soft knock on the door signalled the arrival of the tea.

Lily took the tray from the butler and quickly poured, encouraging Lady Dayle to drink and go on with her story.

'It was a fire, of course.' The viscountess spoke more easily after she'd finished her first cup of tea. 'It began in an engraver's shop, but quickly spread to the orphanage next door. Traffic stopped. I was stuck in the carriage down the street, but I could see what was happening. The flames, and the heat.' A massive shudder tore through her. 'But the screams! I had to help!'

She looked up as if needing validation and Lily nodded encouragingly. 'You absolutely did! As would any person of feeling.'

'At least ten of the children are dead,' Lady Dayle said. Another sob broke through, but she got herself quickly back under control. 'As many are severely injured. Fifteen or so are frightened out of their wits and suddenly homeless.' A single tear welled up and over, the sight breaking Lily's heart. 'We have to do something, Lily. I can't bear it, otherwise.'

'Of course we will,' affirmed Lily. Her heart began to pound. A vision arose in her mind—a glorious image of two worlds uniting. 'And we won't have to do it alone. Just think!' She smiled at the staring viscountess. 'Between your connections and mine, my lady, we will raise an army to help your orphans.'

Chapter Eight

It was only a few days later that Mrs Bartleigh's carriage splashed round the corner at Devonshire House, though so much had happened that it felt like many more. Rain spattered down from a desolate sky and back up as it was thrown from the rumbling wheels. Lily sat back away from the window and smiled gently at her friend. 'What a dreary day!'

The elder lady nodded her agreement. Lily feared she was too tired for small talk.

'I'm afraid that we've done too much. We're already on Berkeley Street now, though. Soon enough you can drop me off and go home for a nice, long nap.'

'Mmm, that does sound nice,' Mrs Bartleigh said wistfully.

'Mr Bartleigh will be furious if you overdo things.' She reached over and tried to rub some warmth into the older woman's cold hand. 'I do so much appreciate all of your help. We've made a good start. And just think—if Minerva Dawson's ball goes as it should, we may well be able to build the orphans a bigger and better home than they had before.'

Mrs Bartleigh heaved a sigh. 'I pray it will be so.'

Lily pursed her lips and reached for the right words to say.

'Perhaps, ma'am, it would be better if you were to forgo Miss Dawson's ball?' She grinned to take some of the sting from her suggestion. 'It would not do for you to fall ill on my watch, for you know that Mother would never forgive me. She relies so heavily on your support at home.'

The serene smile that had soothed so many of Lily's anxieties over the years failed to do so now. 'I'm already ill, and well you know it, Lily Beecham. I'll ask the same of you that I have of my husband—let me do some good with the time I have remaining.'

Beyond words, Lily squeezed her hand again and merely nodded.

She sighed. So many people had worked so hard the last few days. She and the viscountess had worked nonstop to recruit those acquaintances of Lily's likely to lend a hand in an emergency and those of Lady Dayle's who might be convinced to do so. Together they had indeed raised an army, or at least an entire squadron of kind and generous people willing to help the group of poor children who'd lost their home.

Already they had seen the tragic dead laid to rest with proper ceremony, the severely injured accepted into beds in various foundling hospitals and the rest welcomed into temporary homes. Still, there was much to do—and Lily welcomed the workload. It kept her from dwelling on more disturbing issues, such as Mrs Bartleigh's failing health and the fact that her mother would soon be returning. But, most of all, it gave her precious minutes, sometimes even hours, in which she fixed her mind on something other than Jack Alden.

The carriage pulled up to the Dayle town home. Lily kissed her friend goodbye and allowed the footman to assist her down. She waved, unmindful of the drizzle, as her friend pulled away, but her mind had already gone right back where it did not need to be.

No one had heard from Jack Alden since the expedition to Chester House. She heaved a sigh as she headed in. She couldn't help but wonder if she had driven him into hiding behind his books once more.

Fisher opened the door. 'Good afternoon, miss. I hope your errands went well.'

'They did, thank you,' Lily said with a smile. She handed him her bonnet and he in turn handed it over to a waiting footman. 'Several dozen lengths of the finest linen and softest flannel are being rolled into bandages as we speak, and eleven little girls have at last learned the lyrics of "The Well of St. Keyne".' She paused at the foot of the stairs. 'Lady Dayle and Miss Dawson went on to discuss arrangements with the musicians for the ball, Fisher. They should be arriving shortly.'

'I'll have Cook prepare a tray.'

'Thank you.' She turned to go, but stopped once more. 'Has his lordship arrived from Sevenoaks yet?'

'He has indeed, miss. The viscount is currently closeted in the library with Mr Alden.'

Lily froze. Here? Jack was here?

'I shall announce you, should you like to join them,' Fisher continued, moving towards the library door, just a few steps into the hall.

'No!' She didn't want to face Jack for the first time since their…encounter…in company with his all-too-observant brother. 'I mean, perhaps not just yet. I really should…' She did not stay to finish the sentence, but started quickly up the stairs.

Too late. The library door opened and Jack came backing into the hall. 'Fisher,' he called softly as he turned towards the foyer, 'my brother has fallen asleep over his brandy. I do believe the rigours of fatherhood are more strenuous than those of government.' He stopped as he reached the entry hall and caught sight of her on the stairs.

'Oh,' he said lamely. 'Hello, Lily.'

'Mr Alden.' His gaze shone far more intent than his tone. She glanced away from it, trying to slow the sudden hitch in her breathing, and hide the skittering beat of her pulse.

Fisher looked from one to the other. 'I shall just fetch a blanket to throw over his lordship.' He retreated to safety behind the green baize door.

Lily followed suit and started again for the safety of her chamber, but she was stalled as Jack awkwardly cleared his throat.

'Er, how have you been, then?' he asked.

'Fine, Jack. And you?' Perversely, much as she wished to speak with him, she was not about to make it easy for him.

He did not answer, just watched her with an uneasy sort of yearning. Or perhaps it was only solemnity in his expression, and she was endowing him with her own mental tumult. She hoped not. She would hate to be the only one in an emotional uproar.

'I heard that Charles was due back, and thought I'd ask him to accompany me...' he paused '...on an errand.'

'I'm sorry that he is too tired to be of use to you, then.' She hated this awkwardness. And the letter hidden away upstairs weighed heavy on her mind. All she wanted was to get away, lock herself in her room before she did something foolish— like blurt out Matthew's last known location or, worse, barrel down the stairs and beg him to stir to life once more the embers of desire he'd left smouldering inside her.

Suddenly his features hardened. 'Charles told me all about the fire and the work you and my mother have been doing,' he said.

'Yes,' she managed to reply with satisfaction. 'We've made a remarkable amount of progress in just a short while.' She paused. 'We've wondered where you've been.'

He shifted on his feet. 'I've had a...special project to attend to. I'm sorry I was not here to help, but I hear that Sophie has sent along a cartload of supplies for you to use with the orphans.'

She looked up at that. 'How kind of her. We shall certainly put them to good use.'

The entryway grew silent again. From the back of the house came the clang of a pan and a muffled shout of laughter. Lily could bear the tension no more. She turned to go.

Jack put his foot on the first step and called up, 'Charles also told me about the scheme you've cooked up for Miss Dawson's engagement ball. Some sort of performance?'

'Yes, we thought we would involve some of the orphans. They would like the chance to thank all of those who have been so generous.'

'Not to mention that seeing the pitiful victims firsthand might stir others to help with their plight?' he said with sarcasm.

Lily shrugged. 'If it does, the help will not go amiss. We've still much work to do. It was Minerva's idea. Apparently she recalled that Lady Ashford and her daughter did something along those lines a few years back.'

'I thought Charles counselled against it?'

'Yes, he did. But I confess, I don't understand his objections.'

'Charles has a great deal of experience in dealing with society's fickleness. If he doesn't feel it will go over well, then you should heed him.'

Lily hardly knew what to say to that. She spread her arms in a helpless gesture. 'It really is not my decision to make.'

'I hope you will at least try to talk some sense into them.' He watched her with half-closed eyes, yet still she could see the trouble glittering there. 'I recall the event you mentioned very well,' he continued. 'Sophie suffered a devastating setback at that charity ball. It was an extremely painful time.' He paused, and then said awkwardly, 'I would not wish the same to happen to you.'

She was touched and more than a little encouraged. 'But from what I understand, what we have planned is a very different matter altogether. Much more subdued and discreet. So you see, there is no need to worry.'

'I can't help but worry.' His voice had gone low and urgent again and he took another step up towards her. Briefly, she considered descending to meet him, but then the import of his words began to sink in.

'I've only just had a rather devastating lesson myself on straying outside my own sphere.' He gave a bitter laugh. 'And then Charles tells me that you have a plan elevating it to an art form. He says that besides performing orphans, you intend to invite moralists and reformers to mix with the *beau monde*?'

'Why do you speak with such scorn?' Lily asked, exasperated. 'Are you dreaming up more obstacles to throw in our path?'

'I don't have to—you insist on creating your own.' Frustration throbbed in his voice as well. 'Have any of you truly thought this out? I don't think you've yet been exposed to the sort of people who will attend this ball. I know the *ton*, Lily. I've been subjected to them for years. Most of the people there will be shallow, vapid, self-absorbed fools. Is this who you want to introduce your friends to?'

She raised her chin. 'Why don't you try for a little optimism, Jack? Perhaps the two groups will have something to teach each other.'

He snorted. 'Do you comfort yourself that it is only your Evangelical friends, then, that you have invited? Lily, you are a lovely, tolerant and open-minded girl, and even you confessed to feeling alienated in society. How will the more conservative—the Mr Cooperages—of your set react? He and others like him view the aristocracy either as a necessary evil or as a corrupt assemblage waiting to be led to the righteous path. In turn the *ton* will look at them as hopeless provincials or utter bores. It's a recipe for disaster.'

Disappointment swamped her. Her spirits, already agitated, slid further down into dark depths. 'Your mother and Minerva and I—and so many other people as well—we have all been working day and night. We have brought people together to help these children and we've been forging new relationships as we've gone. There is nothing wrong with that! And yet you seem determined to wrench it all apart!' She gazed at him in despair. 'Why, Jack? Why must you always believe the worst of people?'

He drew back. 'I don't do any such thing.'

'You do. You create walls. You hold people at a distance. Why?' Tears welled in her eyes. 'You speak of not wanting to see me hurt, but I think there is something more selfish going on here. I think you are afraid that *I* will hurt *you*.' She had to stop a moment. 'I don't want to hurt you, Jack.'

He retreated to the bottom step. 'Don't be ridiculous. I don't know what you are talking about. I've never said anything to make you think so.'

'Yes, you most certainly have,' she said with heated anger. 'You've held me at arm's length and held yourself back as if I were poisonous. Oh, perhaps you have not said it with words. But you've told me so over and over again with your eyes and your body.' She gestured contemptuously to his position of retreat. 'You're doing it now.' She narrowed her eyes. 'But the worst came the other day. You kissed me, Jack, but you only did it to push me away.'

Lily turned her back on him, sending her skirts flaring. She gathered them up, and raced up the stairs and away from Jack's shocked reaction.

'Lily,' he said, and in his tone lived a wealth of sadness and regret.

They both jumped when the door opened and his mother and Minerva Dawson spilled in.

'Oh, my, the wind is picking up! What good is an umbrella when the rain insists on coming in sideways?' Lady Dayle asked no one in particular. 'Minerva, do come in and get dry. We'll have tea and perhaps the rain will have gone by the time we finish.'

Wrestling her soaking bonnet off, the viscountess caught sight of her son. 'Jack! We've been wondering where you've been!' She grasped her son by the shoulders and kissed him wetly on the cheek. 'You look worn to a frazzle. What's been keeping you so busy?'

'This and that, Mother,' he said and returned her embrace. If his answer was falsely jovial, the viscountess did not appear to notice. 'But I must be going. Charles is back, though, and sound asleep in the library.' He walked towards the front door without glancing up at Lily.

'Wait, dear. I haven't seen you in days. Don't rush off!'

'Apologies, but I must. I've got an important errand to run.'

'Will we see you at my engagement ball, Mr Alden?' Minerva asked. 'It's nearly upon us, now.'

This time he did cast a neutral glance at the top of the stairs. 'Miss Beecham was only just telling me about it. I wouldn't miss it, Miss Dawson, and let me take the opportunity now to wish you very happy.'

He bowed over Minerva's hand, kissed his mother once more and walked out.

'Well,' Lady Dayle breathed. 'To be young again.' She looked up at Lily. 'Whatever is Charles doing sleeping in the library?'

'I'm sorry, I have no idea, my lady. I've only just arrived myself.'

The viscountess gestured imperiously. 'Well, do come down and take some tea with us, my dear. I wish to hear all about your afternoon.'

Lily could think of no polite way to refuse. She descended the stairs yet again, tired and feeling foolishly like a child's plaything.

Minerva took her arm as she reached the bottom. 'Come, let's forget our cares for a bit. We've been so busy planning for the ball, we've scarce discussed what we'll wear!' She exchanged a significant glance with Lady Dayle. 'Mother has had my gown planned for ages, but, you know, we need to decide what we are going to do with you.'

With effort, Lily was able to keep her eyes from straying to the door Jack had just walked through. 'I would like to wear something special,' she said slowly. 'But I'm afraid I don't own a ballgown. And I've just been too busy to worry about it. Now, I suppose it's too late.'

Minerva nearly glowed with triumph. 'Not at all, my dear, for Lady Dayle and I have made time to worry about it. We've been working with the *modiste* who altered your gowns.'

'We have something truly special ready for you, my dear—and I don't want to hear even a peep of protest out of you.' Lady Dayle's smile shone almost feral. 'The gentlemen—*tonnish* and Evangelical alike—are not going to know what's hit them!'

The sky above Jack's head hung heavy and grey as gunmetal. The Thames ran nearby, slate-coloured and sluggish as well. He blinked away the fine drizzle doing its best to diminish his vision and cut him off from the rest of the world. Even the pretty Greenwich gardens were reduced to a mere muddle of drab greens.

He hardly noticed. The weather only reflected his own bleak, inner landscape. The sharp repeat of Lily Beecham's harangue gnawed at him as he strode towards the river.

Hell, yes, he absolutely held people at a distance—and nearly every day he was convinced of the extreme wisdom of such a course. *Distance.* He even liked the sound of the word. A solid, secure word, and a perfectly sound principle on which to base the doctrine of one's life. Certainly it had served him long and well.

Walls, she'd said. And damned if she hadn't got that right, too. In fact, Jack thought it was safe to say that his walls were amongst his most cherished possessions. Right up there with his books and maps, and that rare note of approval from the Oxford don who had encouraged him in his studies of the ancients. Of course, there were a few people allowed into his inner sanctum, his family and even Trey and Chione, to some extent. But the rest of humanity he kept firmly on the outside, where he could observe them with interest and impunity.

Impunity? He stopped short. Damn Lily Beecham and her cursed perception to hell. By God, perhaps he was afraid to let people close. *Afraid?* He never thought of it in those exact terms, but still, admitting that Lily had been at least partly right did not change the prudence of it. The longer he considered the matter, the more convinced he became. Most people were thoughtless and self-absorbed at best, spiteful and malicious at worst. Then there were the truly deranged like Batiste. He was far better off keeping them all at a *distance*.

All of which begged an answer to the real question. Why the hell could he not keep Lily Beecham safely beyond his walls? Every time he turned around, metaphorically speaking, he ran smack up against her. Inside. In his way. On his heels. Always right there.

He stepped lightly down the stairs leading to the river. The marshes of the Isle of Dogs loomed out there, a greenish-brown blur in the mist. His eye fixed on the floating hulk of the HMS *Grampus*, the vessel that housed the newly founded Seamen's Hospital. As he drew near, he read the words painted on to the side: 'For Seamen of All Nations.'

A harried-looking man stepped forwards as Jack stepped across the gangplank. He appeared to relax slightly as he took in Jack's well-tailored appearance. 'Good morning,' he called as he made his way across the scrupulously clean deck. 'Can I help you with something?'

'I hope so,' Jack replied pleasantly. 'My name is Jack Alden,' he said, sketching a polite bow.

'David Arnott. I am the doctor here.'

'Then perhaps you can help me. I'm looking for someone. A former seaman by name of Crump.'

'Ah…' The doctor eyed him with a slightly arched brow. 'Would you be family?'

'No. I've had his name from a mutual friend. I'm just here for a visit—and to ask a few questions.'

Doctor Arnott looked him over carefully and said nothing.

Jack drew a deep breath. 'I've heard that the man is not likely…to set sail again. My visit just might offer him a little comfort.'

Still, the doctor paused. 'All right, then,' he said at last, 'but I don't want him upset.'

'I'll do my best.' He nodded as the man raised a brow in his direction. 'I give you my word.'

They went below deck. Here Jack could see that the normal fittings had been removed to make room for rows of beds. Most of them stood unmade and empty. Their footsteps echoed in off the close wooden walls.

'We are still recruiting staff and laying in supplies. Really, we are not yet ready to take on patients.' He shrugged. 'But we do not mean to turn away anybody if we don't have to, and Crump…' He gestured. 'Well, you'll see for yourself.'

All Jack could see was a small form huddled in the furthest bed, trembling violently. Even as he stared, another man pushed by them, carrying a large leather bladder, long as a man's torso. He took it straight to the shivering man in the bed.

'Here, now. Nice and warm,' he said gently as he pulled the covers back and tucked the bladder in quickly.

Crump, for Jack presumed it was he, curled gratefully around what must be a homemade warmer and gradually his trembling subsided.

'Now, by the time that's gone cold, I'll have the bed-warming pan nice and hot for you,' the caretaker said in a re-assuring voice.

'Thank ye,' croaked his patient.

The man nodded at Jack and the doctor as he passed. Arnott waved Jack in, but he shot an all-too-clear warning look as he did.

As Jack approached the bed, the reason for the doctor's caution became clear. The man in the bed was old and ema-ciated beyond anything Jack had ever seen. Beyond what seemed capable of supporting life, he would have guessed. But though the man's skin appeared to be as thin as paper over his bones and the tone of it shone a horrifying shade of greenish-yellow, still his eyes burned bright and intelligent from the wreck of a face.

'Mister Crump?' Jack asked as he drew near.

The small man let loose with a wheeze of laughter. It quickly turned into a cough. 'B'ain't no mister, jest Crump. Who are ye?'

'My name is Jack Alden.'

The seaman shot him a skeletal grin. 'Neptune's eye, but I hope that ain't s'posed to mean anythin' to me. I been com-fortin' myself that at least my mind's still shipshape. Be a shame to find out I was wrong now.'

Jack returned the grin. 'I'd say your mind is in good enough working order. We've not met before.'

'Ah.' The old sailor waved towards a chair sitting at the end of the row of beds. Jack pulled it over and sat close to Crump. He watched as the old man settled himself on his side, curled up around the warmer and eyed Jack steadily.

'Tropical fever,' he said conversationally. 'Been stalkin' me for years. Goin' to get me this time.'

'I sincerely hope not.' Jack strove for the same nonchalance.

'Wotch'er here for?' Crump said, suddenly abrupt.

'I'm learning what I can about the Evangelical branch of the Church of England: their accomplishments, their beliefs, their wish to reform society. I understand you are familiar with them?'

'Oh, aye.' His inquisitive gaze had gone shuttered.

Jack asked several innocuous questions until the seaman began to relax. Crump remained curt, however, until Jack began to ask him about the role of Evangelical women.

'Weel, now, I knows as how some folk dinna like to see a woman working for summat like abolition, but they's no denying the good they do. On t'other hand, look at Hannah More—fine, upstanding woman that she be—she's ruined her health working for Evangelical causes.' He shrugged. 'P'raps them as say that a woman b'ain't made for such things is right?'

'Perhaps.'

Crump chuckled, but it rapidly turned into a wheeze. He shook a moment with a hard cough, before he recovered himself. 'They can say all they like, but I don't see them Evangelical women givin' up the fight any time soon. Abolitionists will press on 'til slavery itself is outlawed, and womenfolk are a sight better 'bout confronting the evil in this world than us men.'

Jack sat, distracted by this train of thought, until the sharp edge of the seaman's voice cut into his reverie.

'Ye goin' to tell me wotch'er really here for?'

Jack met his gaze squarely. 'I truly am collecting such information. You've actually been quite helpful.' He paused and watched Crump closely. 'But I would also like to ask you a few questions about one of your former captains.'

'Which one?' The sailor's tone rang with suspicion.

'Batiste.'

Crump sighed and turned slightly away. 'Should ha' known that without asking.' He sat silent a moment. 'Why?'

'Why what?'

'Why do ye want to know anythin' about that devil?'

Jack thought carefully before he answered. 'He means to hurt someone I care about.'

Crump closed his eyes. 'That do sound like 'im.' He shifted position and, with his eyes still closed, said simply, 'Will ye tell me about 'em?'

'Them?' Jack asked.

'Those ye care about, as ye said.'

So Jack did. Sitting there in the chill, empty deck, with the sound of the river in his ears and the ship rocking slightly against the tidal pull, he talked. He told Crump about Trey, his daring friend who'd had adventures all over the world, but found his greatest treasure when he'd been reluctantly forced back home. He spoke of Chione, describing her tenacity and her commitment to keeping her family together against all odds. He spoke of Will and Olivia, the resilient children who never gave up the hope of getting their missing father back. He lost himself in the telling, but at the same time he felt a tightening around his chest at the thought of them all in danger.

Suddenly he realised that Crump's eyes were open and he sat watching him with canny intent.

'Tell me, what does she look like—this girl ye speak of?'

'She is beautiful, of course. What sort of tale would it be if she were not?' Jack answered with a smile. 'Actually, she is as lovely outside as she is inside. Long ebony hair, exotic skin and dark eyes with the most wonderfully thick lashes.'

'I knew it,' Crump whispered. 'Mervyn's girl. Isn't it? 'Tis Mervyn Latimer's granddaughter ye talk of?'

Jack hesitated—but he had to tell the truth. 'Yes,' he said, 'it is.'

''Tis Mervyn's family Batiste is going after?' His gaze was troubled.

'Yes,' answered Jack, and he fervently hoped he had not just ruined his chance of finding anything of use from the man.

'And is Mervyn Latimer still gone missing?'

'No—he is home. It turns out Batiste had him all those months he was lost—locked up in a slave hold of one of his ships.'

'God in his heaven,' breathed Crump. 'Batiste's finally gone stark, ravin' over.' The seaman looked stricken. 'Is he back to takin' up slaves, then?'

'Apparently so. Not in the same volume as before the trade was abolished, of course, but there are still those who wish to cling to the old ways.'

'Aye. So's I've told 'em all. There's still a battle to fight. It won't end 'til slavery is driven from the face o' the earth.'

'I fear you are right. And the battle is far from over for Mervyn's family as well. Batiste's men have only recently broken into the Latimer shipping offices, and Mervyn's home.' Jack paused. 'And my home as well.'

The seaman watched him with a shrewd eye. 'Ye'll be knowin' what he's after, then.'

'I do.' Jack leaned forwards and spoke low. 'And I can tell you unequivocally that he will never find it. The Pharaoh's Lost Jewel doesn't exist—not in the way that he thinks.'

For a moment, Crump's face burned with a bright curiosity. But then he shook his head as if to clear it. 'No, I don't want to know. I'll have answers to the biggest mystery soon enough, lad.' He lay back, looking exhausted.

'I can see you are tiring. I'm sorry.'

'Aye. Fever'll be next. It always comes on the heels o' the tremors.'

'I won't keep you long, Mr Crump, but I need to know where Batiste might be hiding. I thought you might know some of the likely places he would hole up in.' He let all the urgency he felt leak into his voice. 'He has to be stopped.'

'And ye think I'll turn on 'im, do ye?' Crump's voice was bitter.

'I hope you will. The man has caused so much suffering and pain. We must stop him before he can cause even more.'

Crump lay back and closed his eyes once more. He stayed still and quiet for so long that Jack began to wonder if the old sailor had fallen asleep. And then he wondered if the man would still be alive were he forced to come back tomorrow.

Jack nearly jumped out of his skin when Crump suddenly asked, 'Where was he seen last?'

'Gibraltar,' Jack answered, his chest suddenly filled with a fierce hope.

Silence reigned for a time again.

'Tazacorte,' Crump whispered eventually.

'Excuse me?' Jack leaned closer.

The seaman opened one eye. 'Ever been to Islas Canarias, lad?'

Jack shook his head.

'Go, then, do you get the chance. Each one o' them islands is a whole 'nuther world. Each different from t'other, but all beautiful.' He sighed. The other eye opened. 'They's Spanish, ye ken. Safe harbour if Batiste be running from the King's Navy.'

He sighed. 'Tazacorte—on the island of La Palma. Sheerest cliffs, then they suddenly open up to the sweetest little harbour. Not much, just a fishing harbour, with a village and a black sand beach. One long promenade filled with the prettiest girls this side o' the Atlantic.' His words trailed away and his eyes slid closed again, this time in remembrance, rather than exhaustion, Jack thought.

He shifted over from the chair to sit on the side of the man's bed and grasped his arm gently. 'Thank you, Mr Crump,' he said quietly.

The old man nodded. 'Oh, aye. Done a lot of things in this life I wisht I hadn't. Goin' to meet my maker soon enough— be as well to have a little more credit with 'im.'

Suddenly his arm lifted and his bony fingers gripped Jack with surprising strength. 'I give ye what ye needed, lad, and now I'll be givin' ye something ye didn't ask for—some advice.' He breathed deep and looked earnestly into Jack's face.

'Greed is the devil's friend, man—don't let it be your'n. It'll blacken yer heart and sour yer soul 'til ye don't even know the monster ye've become.' Tears welled in his eyes.

Stricken, Jack nodded.

'And don't let fear into yer heart neither. Life is short, lad. So short.' He managed a trembling grin. 'Find yerself a girl like yer friend did, spend yer life makin' her happy. Then p'raps when ycr lyin' on yer deathbed, ye won't feel the weight of so many regrets.'

Jack said nothing at first, just squeezed his hand. Slowly the skeletal hand relaxed its grip.

'Thank you,' Jack whispered again.

Crump didn't answer. After a moment, Jack realised the old sailor was asleep.

He didn't leave right away. He sat there, watching the slight rise and fall of the seaman's chest, absorbing the impact of the old man's words. All of his words. Finally, when the dim light from the passage beyond had faded away, Jack rose. He'd head to Whitehall and the Admiralty House tonight. Someone there would hear him, if he had to wait all night.

He gazed one last time at the frail form in the bed. Crump's words echoed in his head.

There were still battles to fight.

Chapter Nine

Lily pressed close behind Lady Dayle as they made their way through the crowd to the receiving line. It would seem that Mrs Dawson had achieved her heart's desire. Minerva's engagement ball could only be deemed that most coveted of appellations: a sad crush.

But it was not the crowd that had Lily's heart pounding and her knees shaking. Nor was the sense of anticipation in the air the reason behind her smile. No, that was partly the result of nerves—and part pure, wicked satisfaction at the chance to live out one of her own girlish fancies.

She felt as if she had stepped out of reality and straight into one of the stories her father had used to spin for her. A sigh of anticipation escaped her. Now if she could only craft a happy ending as easily as her father had.

Lady Dayle and Minerva Dawson had done their bit. They'd primped and pinched and powdered until Lily had cried out in protest. Their answer had been to drag her over to the full-length mirror, where her complaint had died a quick death.

She had not recognised the creature staring back at her.

Never had she dreamed she could look like this. The evening gown flattered her with shades of creamy ivory and the softest, shimmering green. Embroidery of darker green and a pale rose colour trimmed the round neckline and the low-cut bodice. The same colours echoed in short, slashed sleeves. A broad ribbon tied round the mid-level waist, and the ends trailed down behind her. They fluttered in her wake now as she moved forwards to embrace her friend.

'Is it not the most exciting thing?' Minerva asked with a smile. She looked exquisite and very mature in a magnificent, rust-coloured frock.

'So many people!' Lily whispered in awe.

'I know. Mama is over the moon!' She pulled Lily in close again. 'Word has spread that we have something special planned for tonight—everyone has been asking about it.'

'Where are the girls?'

'Upstairs. My Aunt Lucinda is, as usual, all doom and gloom, but you are not to mind her,' she admonished. 'My niece Claudette is simply smitten with the children. She's up there dressing and coiffing them as if they were dolls come to life purely for her amusement.'

Lily smiled. 'How are the children feeling about it?'

'Well, they were nervous as cats, but I think they are enjoying the attention.' She grinned and gripped Lily's hand. 'How are you?'

'Nervous as a cat.'

Minerva laughed. 'Don't be! I want you to enjoy yourself tonight.' Next in line, Lord Lindley smiled at Lily and tried to pull her away, but Minerva would not let go of Lily's hand. 'This is your night as much as ours, Lily dear,' she whispered. 'I'm so glad we are able to share this.' She released her over to Lord Lindley. 'Now, go and make this a night to remember.'

Lily smiled back at her as Lord Lindley swept her off her

feet and into an embrace. 'You look nearly as ravishing as Minerva,' he said into her ear before passing her along to Mrs Dawson. And within moments she was through the line and on the other side. Lady Dayle stood just a few steps ahead. She had stopped to greet Mrs Montague and it sounded as if their conversation had quickly turned to the hospitalised orphans and all the supplies the foundling hospitals found themselves in need of.

Lily nodded and smiled a greeting and moved past. Ahead lay the ballroom, and she faced it with both anticipation and anxiety. So much was at stake tonight. Over that threshold lay her first step into a new world—neither her father's or her mother's, but one of her own making. *Please*, she sent out a silent plea with all the yearning in her heart. *Please let this work—for all our sakes.*

And then she stood there on the brink, transfixed by the beauty of it all. Mrs Dawson had truly outdone herself. Lush potted plants lined the dance floor and graced every flat surface while garlands of fresh blooms draped the walls and twined gracefully up the pillars. Hundreds of glittering candles shone in three stunning crystal chandeliers. They cast their glow over a vast number of people—and they were all in motion. Even the air seemed to flow with the swell of the music and in time with the diaphanous drift of the ladies' gowns.

It looked a faerie world, unreal, like a glimpse into a shining, shimmering bubble. Such a fragile and delicate thing, to hold all her hopes and dreams.

'It is beautiful, isn't it?' Lady Dayle's tone was all admiration.

'Unbelievably so.' Lily met her gaze and tried to convey all the warmth and gratitude in her heart. 'Thank you so much, my lady,' she said fervently. 'I can't tell you what this has all meant to me…your friendship, all that I've experienced, the opportunity…' she made a helpless gesture '…everything.'

Lady Dayle smiled and took her arm. 'No, my dear, it is I who must thank you. I've thoroughly enjoyed our time together and you've shared something infinitely precious with me—yourself. Spending time with you, watching your uninhibited joy, learning the generosity of your spirit, it has been all my pleasure.' Her smile wavered a little, but she pressed on. 'You've reminded me of the great capacity for good that lies in all of us.' She waved at the throng of people ahead. 'Just take a look at the company assembled here. We've taken a tragedy and salvaged something good from it. We've worked hard and done well.'

And it appeared that they had indeed. As Lily moved through the ballroom she greeted many familiar faces—and they were all wreathed in smiles. Around every corner she found a new and gratifying scene. Dignified men of the church stood in casual conversation with society's leading ladies. Moralist matrons giggled at the bucks of the *beau monde*. She found Mrs Bartleigh at one end of the ballroom, exchanging stillroom receipts with a marchioness. Her husband stood nearby, eagerly absorbing horrifying stories from a half-pay naval officer. Even Mr Wilberforce had come. He sat enthroned in a comfortable chair in a corner and radiated good will on the crowd of admirers ebbing and flowing about him.

Taking it all in, Lily's heart overflowed. Hope flared high and lit her from within. Perhaps it had not been just a foolish dream. Her eye wandered, searching for Jack. She longed for him to see the success of their venture.

Suddenly the music ceased. Every eye turned to the dance floor where a proud Lord Lindley led a flushed Minerva to the centre. He nodded at the musicians and they struck up a waltz with a flourish as the betrothed pair opened the dancing.

For the first set they danced in solitary, happy splendour, but when the second began there was flurry of movement as people paired off and joined them. Lily ducked behind a pillar. All she wanted was a moment alone to absorb the grandeur and fix it firmly in her mind.

She was not to get it. A spark of awareness sizzled down her spine. Her pulse ratcheted up a little faster. Slowly she turned her head—and found Jack Alden watching her intently from just a few feet away.

Her breath caught. For once he looked as neat as a pin. His hair tamed into a smooth and shining crop of curls, in spotless linen and a dark coat that moulded splendidly to his athletic build, he looked the very picture of dark, masculine elegance. But it was his expression that sent a dark heat spiralling inside of her.

He looked shocked. Not the most flattering of reactions, she realised, but there was something else there, too, something primal and hot. There could be no mistaking the heat in his stunned gaze as it travelled up and down the length of her. She straightened her shoulders. The thrill of turning a man's head with her beauty might be a new one, but this bone-deep recognition of her own power must be as old as womankind.

She lifted her chin. Now she would discover just how solid Jack Alden's walls really were.

It had taken Jack a long time to find Lily in the congested ballroom. Tonight, pockets of sober-hued, conservative dress punctuated the usual gaily-coloured throng and he instinctively sought her there. She was not to be found. He did bump into his mother and ask her if she could tell him where to find Lily, but she only shot him an enigmatic smile and informed him he would have to search her out himself.

He wandered through the crowd, feeling foolish and impatient, but also unexpectedly carefree. He had indeed had to camp out at Admiralty House after he spoke with Crump. In fact, he'd been kept waiting in a sterile antechamber all night and into a day, and been asked to return the next. He'd returned all right, but not until he'd gone to the Foreign Office and the American Embassy and dragged a delegation back with him. This time, they'd only had to wait an hour before they spoke with the First Lord of the Admiralty himself. Jack had shared the information that he'd had from Crump, and the orders had gone out. The Royal Navy had a ship in Porto Santo and it could be at La Palma in a matter of days. A matter of days, Jack had breathed, and Batiste might be in custody. It had left him feeling lightweight and free.

Free of any real reason to attend tonight. And yet here he stood. Tonight he could concentrate on Lily Beecham without any ulterior motive or need to worry about her cousin. He was surprised—and a little uneasy—at how much he looked forward to it.

Finally, just as he was wondering if the tiresome girl had not come tonight at all, a gleam of red-gold in the candlelight caught his eye. He stepped forwards eagerly. But disappointment soon had him stumbling to a halt. Merely another débutante, although this one had the good sense to stay half-hidden behind a pillar rather than put her empty-headed charms on full and painful display. Impatient, he turned away to continue his search.

He had not got far before the information picked up by his senses finally connected into a startling conclusion in his brain. Very slowly he spun on his heel. He examined the girl again, in surprise, disbelief and, finally, wonder.

He had not expected this. Jack had come with an apology ready. Now it simply…disappeared, slid away, forgotten, as he stared at Lily Beecham, his jaw slack. When would he learn? Every time they came together she found a new and inventive way to knock him off kilter.

This...this vision before him must be the most shocking one yet. Gone was his conservative, young idealist dressed in necklines up to here and sleeves down to there. In her place stood a flame-haired siren.

No, not a siren, not in this lush, green environment. She must be a dryad—a spirit of the forest, dressed in the colours of spring.

Every such nymph represented in art and architecture put on a generous exhibition of flesh. Lily was not nude, of course, but her low-cut bodice clung tight to her curves and she most definitively had a glorious expanse of creamy skin on display.

Lord, and her hair! He gazed, spellbound, at her glorious tresses, dressed elaborately and with tiny, cream rosebuds anchored throughout. It shocked him that those delicate flowers were not incinerated amidst those fiery curls—for Jack certainly felt inclined to burst into flame.

His palms itched. He clenched his fists and slowly approached her. She'd caught sight of him, too, and she stood straight and proud. He stopped, inches away. She held out a hand, encased in long, ivory kid. He took it and bent low. As he straightened he lost himself in the endless blue of her eyes, unable to look away, forgetting even to speak.

A nearby giggle recalled him to his senses. He dropped her hand. 'Good evening.'

She inclined her head. 'Mr Alden.'

'I'd thought we'd got past the need for formality, Lily.'

'Given everything that has occurred, I think perhaps it best if we retreat back into it,' she said firmly.

'I'm sorry, but I'm afraid it's too late. You are fixed firmly in my head as Lily now.' He made a sweeping gesture that took her in from head to toe. 'And I'm sorry, but you look so formidably splendid tonight, that if I cannot call you Lily I might not muster up the courage to speak at all.'

She rolled her eyes. 'Someone is full of nonsense tonight.'

'Didn't you know? That's what all these events are about—nonsense.'

She watched him closely. Never would he let her know how that look unnerved him. 'Your mother warned me,' she said ruefully.

'Warned you? Now, just a minute, she's *my* mother— surely she should be on my side?'

She lifted her chin. 'Your mother is too great a woman to take sides,' she said loftily. 'And if she did, she'd take mine.'

Her playfulness enchanted him. 'Unfair,' he returned. 'You've had undue influence over her. You'd best cease, or I'll be forced to tell your mother—' he grew suddenly serious '—how incredible you look tonight.'

She grew flushed. 'I hope I haven't said anything to lower your estimation of my mother,' she said, her tone serious. 'Truly, she's a good person, and she's had to bear more than her share of hardship.' She shot him a wry grin. 'Not the least of which is a wilful and boisterous daughter.'

'I wouldn't dream of thinking ill of her,' Jack said. 'Unless she fails to value the treasure she has in you.'

'Of course she values me,' Lily declared. She stilled a moment. 'She just misses what she's never had.'

'What is that?' Jack asked quietly.

'A son.'

Silence fell between them. She rushed to fill it. 'You see, my mother was always the more serious of my parents and over the years, as she endured one failed pregnancy after another, she grew even more unhappy. It was very hard on her, not being able to give my father a son. I think she felt unwomanly, unworthy.'

'That's ridiculous,' Jack stated.

'You and I might not agree, but you cannot tell another how to feel.' Lily sighed. 'When I was ten years old, though, she did give birth to a son. My baby brother,' she said tenderly. 'My parents were ecstatic. But that winter the influenza swept through the countryside. He died when he was only months old.' She sighed again. 'It was nearly more than she could handle. She grew even more reserved and withdrawn. Then, when my father died...' Her voice trailed off. 'I know how lucky I am to have her at all.'

'As she is lucky to have you,' Jack said bracingly. 'And I know my mother feels lucky to have you, even for a short time. Now, are you going to tell me why she felt the need to warn you about me?'

She took a deep breath and glanced at him with a smile. 'Well, I admit that I found it difficult to believe, but she said you hate these sort of events. You really didn't want to be here tonight?'

'Not until now,' he said, and the truly frightful thing was that he meant it. 'Will you dance with me?'

Her air of queenly confidence abruptly dissipated. Her face fell and she visibly withdrew. 'I'm sorry. I cannot.'

Jack wanted to kick himself. Of course, she'd likely been forbidden to dance, if ever she was even taught. Even after the story she'd just told him, he'd forgotten her upbringing. The sight of her—so beautiful and proud of it—had stirred his blood and scrambled his senses. He spoke quickly to allow them both to recover. 'Forgive me. I should have realised. It's just that you've fair taken my breath away and knocked every sensible thought out of my head.'

She blushed and, encouraged, he pressed on. 'Would you take a stroll with me instead?' He couldn't seem to keep the tone of low urgency from his voice. 'Mr Dawson is a learned man and he keeps a very fine library. I would be happy to show it to you.'

She hesitated.

'If you don't intend to dance, no one will think it amiss if you sit out a set with me.'

'I know that, Mr Alden.' Her ire was obvious.

'Jack, please,' he reminded her.

She squared her shoulders. Her puffed sleeves were so tiny that they were nearly bare. 'This may be my first ball, *Jack*, but I do know how to conduct myself.'

He tried to look contrite. 'You must forgive me—and since I already owe you a rather large apology, you must consider this one a practice run.' He grinned. 'If you'll come along to the library, I will offer it up in proper fashion, on my knees and in sackcloth and ashes.'

She laughed. 'I don't think we have to go that far.'

She allowed him to take her arm and they made their way into the hall. A few people still mingled here and Jack nodded to those he knew. A stout dowager in brilliant yellow curtsied low as they passed and her companion leaned in to whisper something to her.

'Her?' the dowager answered, *sotto voce*. 'She's only another one of these endless Evangelicals here tonight.' She gave a nasty laugh. 'You've heard of mutton dressed as lamb? Well, now you've seen a reformer dressed as a débutante.'

Jack stiffened. They'd been intended to hear the insult, and he was greatly tempted to return the favour, but Lily gently shook her head and tugged him along. He raised his brow at her.

'Oh, don't look at me that way,' she said, her voice low.

'Which way?'

'The one that says loud and clear that you told me so and I didn't listen. The one that says I left myself open to such an insult.'

Though it was difficult, he kept quiet and smiled at a passing acquaintance.

'Well, I know you are right. There are others, too, that are not happy about what we've planned for tonight—Minerva's aunt and uncle have been quite vocal about their discontent. But I don't care, Jack. I've hidden myself away from life for too long. I can't go back. I'd rather tolerate an honest snub. At least with that lady, and the others, I know where I stand.'

They reached the library. The doors stood open and Jack bowed her inside with a flourish and then followed her in. He'd been in the large and comfortable room several times before. In fact, he'd dare say that he'd been in most of the libraries and book rooms in Mayfair. Invariably, he ended up there whenever he was convinced to attend a society event.

This, he had to admit, was one of the best. It was obviously in frequent use. Hundreds of books lined the walls and most of them had indeed been cut and read. A massive mahogany desk dominated the centre of the room, but scattered about were also a large, standing globe, a capped telescope and even a large embroidery frame pulled next to a comfortable chair.

Lily, however, went straight to the large glass doors leading outside to the back garden.

'I'm afraid there is not much to see out there. I don't believe Mrs Dawson is much of a gardener. Her tastes run to embroidery and fashion—and marrying off her daughters, of course.' He watched her peer outside and up towards the darkened sky.

'I know,' she said, 'but this evening is one of those rare London nights when you can actually glimpse the stars overhead.'

'Ah, a country girl at heart?' he asked, caught by the sight of her long, slender neck.

'More than even I knew,' she answered with a smile. 'I find

I do miss my long walks in open spaces and most especially I miss the green of the fields and forests.' She left the doors and walked further away, trailing her fingers along the spines of the books in their cases. 'I suppose I owe you an apology as well. Neither of us behaved well at our last encounter. But since our two apologies will cancel each other out, let's just call it even, shall we?'

'A fine idea, but I have an even better one,' Jack said. Curiosity had been eating at him. 'I propose a substitution. Instead of an apology, I will accept an answer to a question that has been plaguing me.'

She looked puzzled, and a little wary. 'I'm inclined to agree, as long as I get a question as a substitute as well.'

He shrugged. 'It's only fair, I suppose.' He crossed to a grouping of low, leather chairs in the opposite corner of the library and took one. The long table between them held a large selection of periodicals. He picked one up and idly flipped the pages without looking at it. Instead he watched her, half-hidden in shadows across the room.

'What is your question?' she asked across the expanse of the room.

He cleared his throat. 'Yes, well…'

His hesitation clearly intrigued her. She came closer and perched herself on the edge of the big desk. She was so small that her feet did not touch the floor. Captivated, he watched her legs swinging. She looked like a goddess, but acted as unconcerned as a girl. The incongruity of it had him starting to sweat.

'Yes?' She cocked her head at him, her brows raised in question. A heavy curl fell forwards and draped the extended curve of her neck.

He strategically placed the periodical over his lap.

'What in hell,' he enunciated clearly, 'do two blackbirds on a fence post have to do with *anything*?'

'Oh.' She gave an involuntary laugh and hopped down off the desk. 'Promise you won't laugh,' she ordered.

'I promise I'll try not to.'

'I suppose that will have to do.' She leaned back against the desk and grinned at him. 'It begins with my nurse. She was Cornish, and she had the greatest respect and fear for all things supernatural.'

Jack lifted a brow in disbelief. 'Such as?'

'Oh, all of it. She knew hundreds of ghostly tales and something about every sort of other-worldly being.'

'How many could there be?' he asked.

'Hundreds,' she said with conviction. 'And Nurse knew them all—marsh spirits, banshees, hags, trolls, all of them. She left tiny bits of food and milk on the windowsill every night—for the pixies. But her real speciality was at reading signs.'

'Signs?' Jack's logical mind was becoming more muddled by the minute.

'Yes, you know the sort of thing? Portents of good fortune or ill luck?'

'I swear, I've never heard of such a thing outside of a text book,' he said with a shake of his head. 'The Etruscan priests, you know, were famous for scrying the future in animal livers, but I thought we left oracles behind with the ancients.'

'Indeed not. Signs are all about if you know what to look for.' She smiled at him. 'For example, I'm sure you did not know that finding nine peas in a pea pod means good luck, but three butterflies together means bad?'

He stared at her, aghast. 'Surely you don't mean to say that you believe in such things?'

She hitched one shoulder up in answer.

'But…those superstitions are hardly in line with the teachings of the Church. Your mother must be appalled to think you would pay attention to such nonsense.'

She crossed her arms defensively in front of her. '"There are more things in heaven and earth, Horatio…"' She let the quote trail off. 'Perhaps Shakespeare had it right and there are things we just aren't meant to understand? Then maybe those logical thinkers like you are correct and most mysteries can be explained away by coincidence? But I've often wondered…' She abruptly stood straight and walked away to the other side of the desk. 'And in any case, that's only one of many things about me that appal my mother.'

'Come now, it can't be that bad.'

She shrugged again. The large piece of furniture between them appeared to bolster her courage. 'There. I've given a thorough explanation. Now, I believe it is my turn to ask a question?'

Jack was still shaken by her admission of belief in such rubbish. 'I suppose so,' he replied absently. 'What do you wish to know?'

'I want you to tell me about your childhood.'

The statement jolted him suddenly to awareness. 'That's not a question.'

'Come now, no semantics,' she chided. 'You must play fair.' She breathed deep. 'It's just that I've so enjoyed my time with your mother. She is so cheerful and generous and giving—'

'And you were wondering how she could have raised a curmudgeon like me?' he interrupted.

She laughed helplessly. 'Something like that.'

Her request unnerved him. It had never been a conscious decision, but he didn't talk about his childhood. He did his damnedest to never think about it. But he doubted she would give up easily on this, and he had no wish to raise further questions in her mind.

He sighed. 'What do you expect me to say, Lily? I am the son of a viscount. I had a privileged upbringing. I lived in a large house, and had plenty of food to eat. I had my family, lots of servants, a pony and a fine education. If you are thinking to find a reason for my character deficiencies in my past, you are barking up the wrong tree. The blame for any defects must lay squarely with me.' He blinked. 'Maybe I was just born this way.'

'What way?' she asked, looking intrigued.

Damn. He shot her a sharp look.

'I answered your question thoroughly. You must do the same,' she insisted.

'You did, but now I almost wish I hadn't asked. Perhaps you will feel the same.'

'Jack—'

'Very well.' He glared at her. 'What way, you want to know—but I think you already answered that question yourself. What was your word? Distant? It's a damned good word. I find I quite like it. It fits.'

'I'm sorry, Jack.' Her expression had gone sober. 'I did not mean to make you angry.'

'I'm not angry. You asked. I'm answering. It does fit—and it fit even as a child. My brothers were older, you see. They were closer in age to each other than they were to me.'

She had come out from behind the desk, though she still lingered near it. 'But I'm sure they still cared for you, no matter the age difference. You were their brother.'

He laughed at her, and it came out sounding bitter. 'Words of wisdom from an only child.'

She cringed.

Jack immediately pulled on the reins of his temper. *Control*, he reminded himself. 'I'm sorry. Yes, you are right. Of course, they loved me, as I did them. They just cared for each other more.' He shifted a little on the chair. 'I was occasionally jealous, especially when they were gambolling about the countryside on their mounts or romping in the forest. Sometimes I trailed after them and they would usually let me in on their games.' He hesitated before continuing. 'But most of the time I remember being relieved.'

She blinked in surprise. 'Relieved? I find that hard to believe.'

'You should not. What did their closeness get them, really, except a heartache?' He could see that she did not understand. 'My father, you see, had high expectations for his first son. He required much of Phillip and none of it had anything to do with running about with his unruly younger brother. Charles was hurt terribly when Phillip was forced to spend more and more time training to take over the estate and the title. Phillip was, too, though he did not show it in the same way.'

She'd crept closer now and he forced himself to breathe. 'The whole notion of love has always seemed completely arbitrary to me. Father loved Phillip, and he nearly suffocated him because of it. He didn't love Charles and that nearly destroyed him, too.'

He had no wish to reveal how all of that misplaced emotion between father and sons had twisted itself into something ugly and tragic. Or how he had congratulated himself on avoiding the pain, and realised how much better it was to stick with his books and regard such sentiment as just another subject to study. How he far preferred never to be touched by such feelings at all.

'I think I see,' she said and he was afraid that she did. She stood right next to his chair now, her eyes huge and her face troubled and all of her concern centred on him. He reached up and took her hand. Her mouth trembled at the corners. Lord, her mouth.

He could feel her pulse racing at her wrist. It echoed the pounding of his heart and the sudden throbbing of his shaft. He was far beyond rational thought, had been since he'd first glimpsed her in the ballroom. So he listened to his instincts instead. He pulled, gently but inexorably, on her arm and dragged her on to his lap.

She landed on the periodical. Harsh and impatient, he ripped it out from under her and settled her more comfortably across his legs and the yearning bulge at his crotch. He grasped her head with one hand and rubbed a thumb over her open, gasping mouth.

'You do see, don't you?' he asked in a rough whisper. 'Now you know where and why it all began—why I started the laborious process of building my walls. I built them tall and strong, and they've served me well and kept me safe— except from you.'

He moved in to kiss her, but she drew back and ran a finger gently down the side of his face. 'Why me?' she asked.

He groaned. 'I wish I knew.' He kissed her gently on the mouth, and then moved to her nose. He nipped her there, then brushed a fluttery kiss across her forehead and on her lovely, stubborn little chin. 'Because you are open and warm and kind?' His hands gripped her tight. 'And yet an infuriating, irresistibly wicked minx at the same time. It's a heady combination.' He pressed another soft kiss on her mouth, capturing her lush lower lip between his. 'Or perhaps it is just that I am a fool.'

He took her then, in a fierce, hard kiss. Desire surged in him and through him, burst past his restraints as he strained towards her. And she answered, opening at the urging of his lips and tongue and pressing herself closer against him. Her hands roamed over his chest, then curled round his shoulders and buried themselves in his hair. The softness of her breasts pushed against his chest, their hard little peaks teasing him right through the heavy fabric of his waistcoat.

Music swelled from the ballroom, and the echo of laughter

drifted in from the open door to the hall, but Jack couldn't give a damn. Lily was in his arms, and they were alone, tucked away into the dim corner of the room and it might as well have been a continent away from the rest of the party.

He tightened his hold on her, drifted his hand down to her bottom and settled her firmly against his arousal. She stilled, but for just a moment. Then, with a moan, she deepened their kiss, touched his tongue with hers, arched her back and rode down, hot and eager, against him.

With nearly an audible crack, something broke inside of him. How did she do it? She was like a beacon, illuminating all the dark and shadowy corners of his soul—and incredibly, she did not cringe from what she found there. Instead she acknowledged and accepted all the parts of him—even those hidden in his deepest, unplumbed depths.

He was vulnerable, helpless against her power. Up and out of him she drew a great, terrifying mixture of lust and longing and dreadful need. She pulled at him and it washed over him, his every defence swept away before it.

He had to catch his breath. Yet stopping was out of the question. He dragged his mouth from hers while his hands busied themselves at the neck of her gown. In a moment her bodice was loosened, her stays pushed aside and his hand was inside, cupping the glorious weight of her breast, lifting it high.

She gasped.

'God, but you are beautiful,' he moaned. He kissed her in soft reassurance, while he smoothed soft caresses over the eager peak of her nipple. She began to move, writhing eagerly in time with his touch, setting him on fire with the motion.

He was lost, and oh, God, but she was sweet. He needed more. He ran questing fingers down her leg, but as he reached the embroidered hem of her gown, an unwelcome sound penetrated the thick haze of his lust.

'Lily?' The voice sounded heavy with annoyance in the darkness. Whoever it was, they must be at the library door.

Pleasure and longing and lust disappeared. Lily pulled away and sucked in a fearful breath, but he placed a finger on her lips and quickly eased her back inside her bodice. He lifted her up and clambered to his feet beside her. He would have to trust to the low light to hide the massive bulge in his breeches.

'Lily—are you in here?' the voice came again.

'Minerva,' Lily whispered in relief. She shot him a questioning look and he nodded.

She stepped away, towards the centre of the library. 'Minerva? I'm here.' Her words emerged thick with residual desire. She looked dazed and thoroughly mussed—and utterly irresistible.

'What are you doing in here?' came the exasperated reply. 'It's nearly time for the performance! Claudette wants her turn at dolling you up, too.' Her words faded as Lily drew near the door. 'Well, I can see her services will be needed.' She pursed her lips. Then she reached behind her and shut the door.

'Jack Alden, you can come out from skulking in the corner,' Minerva called. 'For if it was any other gentleman in here, you can be sure I'd have a bone to pick with him.'

Horrified and embarrassed, Jack stepped into the light. He winced as Minerva marched forwards and pulled Lily protectively to her side.

'Minerva…' Lily began, in a clear warning tone.

'Yes, I know, dear.' But the young woman was not looking at her friend. She glared at Jack, admonition clear on her face.

'I'd like to strangle the both of you! Could you have picked a worse time and place for this?' She rubbed a hand across her brow. 'We have a very delicate balance to maintain tonight.' She stood straight and made a sweeping gesture towards the door. 'The entire world is outside there—*my aunt* is outside there, looking for any reason to pronounce this evening a disaster and the two of you…' She shook her head. 'I'm not going to say anything about what's been going on in here. But I want you to *think*, Jack Alden. That is what you do best, isn't it?'

'Usually,' Jack answered. He glanced at Lily, but her worried gaze was focused on Miss Dawson.

'Well, start thinking. Clearly. Here and now. Lily's situation is not ideal. I will not have you making things more difficult for her, Jack.'

Jack nodded. He had no words. No excuse, either.

'Let's go,' Minerva said. She took Lily by the hand, opened the door and led her out.

Jack watched them go. It took every ounce of will power he could muster not to follow. God, but he wanted to. They could all go to hell; every one of them out there with a viable reason why he should not. He wanted to run those two down, snatch Lily up and lay claim to her in the most primitive and basic way.

He could not. He stood rooted instead, the barrenness of the room a pale reflection of the inescapable emptiness of his soul.

Chapter Ten

Lily sat silent in front of the mirror while Minerva's niece fussed with her hair and dress. Her gaze was fixed on her mussed reflection, but she felt strangely calm. Absently, she examined herself. By rights she should look drastically different than she had just a short time ago. She did not. She supposed it was only her outlook that had been so radically altered, not her outward appearance.

She had to stifle a laugh at that thought. Surely she was becoming unhinged. The orphaned girls chattered in excitement all around her. She had to hold herself together for their sake. And really, what did she expect? That a scarlet W—for wanton— would appear on her forehead to make known her sins?

Except that it had not felt like sin. Instead, it had only felt…right. So perhaps wanton was the wrong word. What, then, was the correct terminology for someone who had just indulged in…what she had?

Lily very much feared the correct words were *in love*.

No. She was not ready to commit herself to such an extent, not even in her own thoughts. It had been wonderful beyond her expectations, and it was true that Jack had shared something of himself, but whatever was happening in his head right now would tell the tale. Would he discover that he had lightened his burden by sharing it with her? Would he understand that exposing himself a little would only make him stronger? Or would he react in fear? Would he shut down and shut her out?

There was no way for her to know.

So Lily did what she must. She ignored the hollow place inside of her and fought to keep fear and anxiety from rushing in to fill it. She summoned words of reassurance and praise for the young performers and tried hard to believe they applied to her as well.

When it was time, she and Minerva took the girls down to the music room. A raised dais had been placed at the front of the room and a partition taken out at the back to enlarge it. They arranged the girls on the little stage and Lily gazed over them with affection and pride.

'You look lovely,' she told them. 'Like a group of angels come down from the heavens.'

Guests began to enter the room. Minerva went to direct them in and help them find their seats. A couple of the girls shifted nervously and Lily smiled. 'Do not worry about a thing. I've performed in front of others many times and people are always kind, even if you hit a sour note.'

A couple of the girls giggled. Another one called out, 'But, Miss Beecham, you said you mostly played in church.'

'This ain't church,' someone whispered.

Lily laughed. 'No, it is not. But everyone here is curious and happy to see you perform. They want to see you do well as much as you wish to.' She looked over her shoulder. The seats were beginning to fill. 'It is a little nerve-racking to watch them all shuffle in, isn't it? But as soon as the music begins, you will all know just what to do.'

She chatted with them quietly a few minutes longer, hoping to distract them from their nerves. When Minerva came and took the stage, Lily went and sat quietly at the pianoforte.

Minerva began to speak. 'Thank you all so much for coming to my engagement ball.' She smiled at the quieting audience. 'My mother urges you all to drink freely of the champagne, as I am the last of my sisters to marry and she swears she will never, ever undertake an event of this size again.'

Good-natured laughter swept through the crowd. Minerva's face grew more sober. 'I would also like to thank you all for allowing me to share something more unusual and undoubtedly special.' She gestured to the girls standing behind her.

In a quiet, unassuming tone, Minerva spoke of the fire at the orphanage. With reverence she read the names and ages of the children who had died. Lily could see tears gathered in more than one lady's eye as she went down the list.

'Now you understand how fortunate indeed we are to have these girls with us here today.' She introduced each girl and if a pair of singed eyebrows here and a bandage there elicited a little more sympathy, then so much the better, Lily thought.

Minerva explained all that had already been done to help the remaining orphans. 'Still there is much work to be done, but these girls would like to take the chance tonight to thank those who have already worked so hard on their behalf. In that spirit we have prepared a short programme to sing for you.'

Minerva stepped down and Lily stood for a moment. 'My father had a great passion for music of all kinds. He kept a large collection of broadside ballads. The girls have chosen a few to share with you tonight.'

She sat and began to play. The girls did a marvellous job. Before long they had established a rapport with their responsive audience. Several listeners were visibly moved; one or two openly wept. After each of their songs, the girls were treated to a rousing round of applause and when they were finished and the audience called for an encore, Lily had reason to be glad she'd included 'The True Lover's Farewell' in their instruction.

> *The river never will run dry,*
> *Nor the rocks melt with the sun;*
> *And I'll never prove false to the girl that I love*
> *Till all these things be done, my dear,*
> *Till all these things be done.*

The last notes died away to a moment of silence, and then another long, heart-warming roll of applause. Lily stood with the girls, flushed with relief at their warm reception. They had done it. People approached the stage, offering congratulations, well wishes and their help.

Lady Dayle was there, and Minerva and Mrs Dawson and Mrs Bartleigh as well. They all exchanged glances of triumph and success. Lily's heart swelled with happiness for all that they had achieved, and her gaze swept the crowd, hoping against hope that Jack was here to see.

Jack stayed in the library for a very long time. Pacing back and forth, he tried to adjust to feeling raw, vulnerable and exposed.

What had he done? He'd spoken to Lily of things he'd never shared with anyone. He'd hinted at things he never wanted to even consider himself. He'd ignored all the tenets of good behaviour, cast aside any thought of consequence and run his hands and his mouth all over her. He was so far beyond his normal boundaries that he might never get back. He'd lowered his fortifications and let emotion run havoc. Now he was paying the price.

He could not think. It was as if he'd so long neglected reason and rational thought that now they had abandoned him in turn. Desperately, he tried to organise his thoughts, gather himself into some semblance of normalcy. A futile effort.

He made his way back to the party and sought out a footman for a drink. Then he sought out another. But the alcohol did not help. The small, cold knot of anger at his centre was missing. Oddly, he did not feel better without it. He felt adrift, unrestrained. He felt dangerous, as if he were capable of anything.

Charles found him eventually. His brother clapped him on the back, spoke to him at length and with enthusiasm about…something. Jack couldn't rouse himself enough to discover what it was. He stared unseeing at his drink.

Others joined them. He didn't care who. His breath started to come in ragged gasps. Did most people go about in this way, continually feeling so unprotected? It was insupportable. He felt at the mercy of whatever punishing wind might blow through. He had no defences. He'd let them all go.

He needed an anchor. Lily. He looked up and realised that a stream of guests was moving out of the ballroom. Oh, yes. The performance. She would be there. He followed, wandering away from his brother and the others without a word.

A huge sigh of relief whooshed out of him when he caught sight of her up on the dais, behind the girls who were to perform tonight. She looked beautiful and serene at the pianoforte. He needed her help, or perhaps he just needed her. She'd destroyed his barriers and then she'd left. He didn't know how to deal with the loss. Tucking himself into the shadows near the back of the room, he decided to bide his time. When the performance had finished, he would whisk her away again, beg her to shore up the crumbling remnants of his soul.

The little concert they put on surprised him. The girls were quite good and obviously well rehearsed. The innocent picture they presented contrasted dramatically with the tragic tale of their plight and genuinely touched the audience. Lily played well and when she joined the girls in the chorus of their songs, her rich soprano soothed Jack's frayed nerves.

The only sour note of the presentation came not from the performers, but from a member of the audience. Seated to the side of the dais, but close to the front, a heavy-set man encased in clothes too tight for his well-padded frame watched in avid fascination. The hunger in his eyes disturbed Jack, but as the man sat quietly and applauded enthusiastically, there seemed little he could do.

Jack relaxed as the set ended to accolades. In front of him the audience rose to their feet and milled about, waiting their turn to reach the performers and convey their enthusiasm. Triumph and relief shone on Lily's face and were echoed in the girls' expressions and in those of his mother and Minerva Dawson, too. The warm reception and the rush of well-wishers had Minerva's mother practically glowing in ecstasy. More than just empty praise came their way as well. Many enthusiastic listeners were offering their help along with their congratulations.

Jack recalled the passion with which Lily had defended this idea, and her belief in their ability to both forge new relation-ships and stir sympathy for their cause. And she had been right. She had believed in the best of people while he had expected the worst.

Chagrin engulfed him, but he also recognised the rise of other sentiments: pride and perhaps even fledgling hope. It would seem, he thought wryly, that having given way to lust, he would now be forced to endure the whole spectrum of emotion.

He suffered a healthy dose of annoyance in the next moment as Lucinda Whitcomb, Minerva's disapproving aunt, rushed into the room, dragging their beleaguered host behind her. She made her way to the dais, pushing aside guests and children alike in her hurry.

'There now, brother,' she said, hauling Mr Dawson along like a disgraced urchin. 'Tell them. Tell them I've been right all along!'

Mrs Dawson retrieved her husband from his overwrought sister. 'Whatever are you about now, Lucinda dear?'

'I told you this would happen, but would you listen? I knew you would not be happy until you dipped our family name into the scandal broth!'

Mrs Dawson obviously had experience dealing with her sister-in-law's histrionics. She turned her back on the woman. 'Is everything all right, dear?' she asked her husband earnestly.

Mister Dawson scrubbed a nervous hand through his hair and glanced about at their keen audience. 'Er, perhaps you'd better come.' He shot a glance at his daughter, too. 'You, too, Minerva. Shouldn't leave your betrothed to handle this sort of thing alone.'

'What sort of thing?' Minerva asked, suddenly concerned.

'The sort of thing more suited to Sadler's Wells than a betrothal ball, you reckless girl!' Mrs Whitcomb's strident tones grated even at the back of the crowd. 'Your ridiculous insistence on ruining this evening is likely to ruin our family right along with it.'

Jack's heart jumped into his throat. He didn't like the sound of this. He began to quietly push his way through the crowd.

'Do be quiet, Lucinda,' Mrs Dawson begged. 'Dearest,' she said, already starting for the door and bringing her husband along with her, albeit more gently than his sister had, 'do tell me what's happening?' They were out the door and on their way before her husband could respond.

'What is it?' Minerva asked her aunt.

'It's a disaster, that is what it is.' Jack could hear the satisfaction in the harridan's voice. 'There is a crone in the card room lecturing on the evils of gambling! Your betrothed is even now trying to disengage Lord Danley's second son from a bout of fisticuffs. He's out there, sparring with a man who refused to concede the necessity of slave labour on his West Indian plantation! Of course, it was difficult to hear the cause of their quarrel over the vulgar sea ditties being sung by the two drunken men at the punch table.'

'Oh, no,' moaned Minerva. She shot an apologetic look at Lily. 'Can you handle the girls? I'll go see what I can do.'

'Of course,' Lily responded to her friend's fleeing back. 'Come, girls! You did marvellously!' There was a chorus of agreement from those in the still sizeable crowd who had not rushed off after the Dawsons. 'Let us go upstairs. We promised you all an ice, did we not? We will have them sent up.'

'Hold there, young lady!' Mrs Whitcomb had not spent all of her venom yet, it would seem. 'This fiasco will be in every paper tomorrow. We will be laughing stocks—and I know where to lay the blame!'

She shook her finger in Lily's shocked, white face. Jack let out a bark of protest. He tried to move faster through the densely packed mass ahead of him.

'You! You have been pushing yourself and your agenda forwards all this time! This night was supposed to be about the joining of two respectable families, not your ragged urchins and radical notions.'

The crowd had a bird's eye view on the most fascinating incident of the Season. None of them wished to give way willingly. Frantic, Jack began to indiscriminately thrust people aside. Then he saw that he was not the only one trying to break through. The jowly man with the troubling look in his eye suddenly broke through the cluster of gentlemen he'd been skulking behind.

'There you are, my dear,' he said to Lucinda Whitcomb. His wife didn't turn from her target to greet him. 'Is this the impertinent little baggage you told me about?' The words were malicious, but the look he raked over Lily held more than a hint of foul craving.

'Will you *move*? Let me through!' Jack demanded of the portly lady ahead of him. Frantic and frustrated, he nearly picked the woman up and set her aside in his effort to get to Lily's side. He shouldn't have worried, though. His mother had no intention of tolerating such an attack on one of her own.

'Lucinda Whitcomb!' Lady Dayle scolded. 'You are the only one stirring the scandal broth tonight. I should think you've done enough damage for one evening. Take yourself off and leave this girl alone.'

'You have no say here, Elenor,' Mrs Whitcomb retorted.

'Everyone wants to know, Lady Dayle, why you've picked up another stray?' The heavy man—Mr Whitcomb, one assumed—cast a contemptuous glance on Jack's mother. 'Cannot your sons manage to get themselves wives on their own?'

A collective gasp went up.

'*Enough!*' Jack shouted. He broke his way through the last ranks of spectators. 'That is enough!'

'You are right! I've had enough. I don't care that this social-climbing chit has got her clutches into your family—just keep her away from mine!' screeched Mrs Whitcomb.

Jack drew a furious breath, but never got the chance to retort. Into the breach stepped a new defender.

'That will be all!' Jack recognised the thin woman as Lily's elderly friend, Mrs Bartleigh. Her face shone bright red and she was trembling from head to foot with the force of her anger. 'You will not enact such a scene in front of these children!'

'Perhaps the old woman is right, dear,' Mr Whitcomb said

with a lascivious glance at the group of rapt young faces. 'These innocents should not be left in the care of such an obvious opportunist.'

'Don't you take one step near those children, Whitcomb.' Jack tensed with fury. Anger and disgust suffused him, until he thought they must be leaking from his very pores.

'Mr Alden is right,' Mrs Bartleigh said, still in her quiet but forceful tone. 'These children will go with the girl who has laboured so hard for them. I don't know you,' she said with a flick of her eyes over the Whitcombs. 'But I've known Miss Beecham from the cradle and I couldn't be prouder of her, were she my own. She is a good girl, one who puts others before herself. Instead of haranguing her, you would do better to strive to be more like her.'

'Thank you all the same, but I haven't the dramatic skill to cover such a greedy, grasping nature behind a cloak of virtue,' Mrs Whitcomb said nastily.

'No, Lucinda,' Lady Dayle shot back, 'your ugly nature is all right here in the open.'

Jack strained for control. Hatred for these petty, spiteful people ran hot in his veins, urging him to action. They'd taken something beautiful that Lily had created and tainted it. The need to defend and revenge her nearly overwhelmed him. But that would make him no better than they. He longed for the return of his walls, the security of his old emotional ramparts even as he struggled against the tide of emotion that threatened to swamp him.

'Mrs Bartleigh,' Lily suddenly gasped.

Briefly startled out of his anger, Jack saw that the elderly woman did indeed seem to be in distress. All of her bright colour had drained away, leaving her pale and breathless. Suddenly her knees seemed to give way. Lily caught her and called her name frantically once more.

'Mrs Bartleigh!'

'Come, my dear,' said Mr Whitcomb with an unsympathetic glance at the poor woman's plight. 'Let us go back to the party. It seems as if there will be one less irritating reformer for you to worry about soon enough.'

Rage exploded out of the top of Jack's head. There were not enough walls in all of Christendom to restrain him at that moment. He grabbed Whitcomb by one fleshy arm and spun him around. The despoiler of innocent goodwill whimpered in fright. His sudden pitiful fear was no deterrent to Jack. He hauled back an arm and, pouring every drop of hatred into his swing, smashed his fist into the man's face.

'No!' someone cried. 'No, Jack! Stop!'

He ignored the voice, would have shouted his defiance, had he not needed his breath for another vicious hit. Anger sang in his veins, altered his very being, until he was not himself any more, but someone else entirely, someone with a lust for blood and a bitter satisfaction at the solid thud of his fist into flesh.

'Jack, stop! Control yourself!'

The desperation in the voice finally penetrated. He unclenched his fist, dropped the scoundrel and turned slowly around.

It was Lily. She sat on the ground with her friend cradled in her lap. 'Her husband,' she whispered. 'Go, please, fetch her husband.'

Ignoring the blubbering, bleeding idiot at his feet, Jack stepped over him and went to do her bidding.

Chapter Eleven

A hard, uncomfortable chair sat outside Mrs Bartleigh's sickroom. As she had so often over the last few days, Lily perched on it, waiting for the doctor inside to finish his examination. The gruff physician had not expected the lady to live through the night after her collapse, but somehow she had rallied, and had even appeared to have grown a little stronger since.

A fact for which Lily was profoundly grateful. All of her hopes and her grand plans for forging a new place for herself might have disintegrated along with the success of Minerva's betrothal ball, but her old and dear friend lived still, and that was a trade Lily would gladly make again.

Minerva had escaped the disastrous ball unscathed, thank goodness. The whole affair had been caricaturised in every London paper and on multiple broadsheets, but Minerva had only laughed. Her engagement would go down in history, she said, and the new orphanage already being planned would stand testament for years to come. For although Mrs Whitcomb had been busy blackening both Lily's and Jack's names all over town, the notoriety only served to bring the orphans' quandary to even broader attention.

A scandal? A fire? Penniless children in need? The tale touched the heart of everyone in London. It became the perfect cause to distract the bored *ton* from their end-of-Season *ennui*, and the perfect chance for cits and mushrooms to involve themselves with noble interests. Bank drafts, volunteers and pledges had poured in. The Duchess of Charmouth granted a lease on a large parcel of land in Kensington, a charter was in the process of being drawn up and Lady Dayle was assembling a board of directors.

Lily had gaped at how swiftly things had begun to move and then quietly stepped into the background. Thank goodness, their plan had been a triumph overall, but the personal price had been very high indeed. Lily had nearly lost a friend, and she had lost her chance at a future with Jack. He had fetched Mr Bartleigh as she had asked, that fateful night, then he had disappeared into the crowd and not been seen in public since. His brother, Lord Dayle, reported that he was shut up in his rooms once more. Lily knew what that meant. He meant to withdraw again, from the world and from her. His walls would go back up and he would live behind them in splendid isolation and safety.

His reversion to his old way of living had come as a blow. It had also acted as the jolt she needed to force herself to step back and look at the situation without the heady filter of desire. What she had seen had shocked her. It was the same old pattern that she had been endlessly repeating with her mother. Once more she found herself striving to please someone emotionally incapable of returning her affection.

She'd wished to come to London specifically for a chance to escape such a fate, and she'd let the intensity of her response to Jack blind her to the fact that he only represented more of the same.

The door opened beside her, preventing another futile round of regret. Lily stood as Mr Bartleigh escorted the doctor out.

'Oh, Lily, I'm glad you are still here.' Mr Bartleigh breathed his relief. 'Doctor Olmer says that she is strong enough to travel, if we go slowly and by private coach.'

'I also said I do not recommend such a course of action,' the sour physician said. 'Your wife has made more progress than I would have thought possible, but a trip would likely negate it.'

Mr Bartleigh's features set in determination. 'You told us when we first came to London and sought you out, sir, that my wife had not long left among us.'

'And less time does she have now,' grumped the doctor.

'I believe you, sir, but if my Anna says she wants to breathe fresh Dorset air again before she breathes her last, then I'm going to make sure that happens.'

'You'll do as you will, and I can't stop you, but just be sure to take it slow and in short stages.' The doctor reached out and gripped Mr Bartleigh's arm. 'Her spirit is strong, but her body is frail—remember to take that into consideration.'

Tears blurred Lily's vision, but not before she glimpsed the pain in Mr Bartleigh's face.

'Lily, would you be a good girl and stay with my Anna while I go and find us a well-sprung carriage?' he asked. 'We'll want to set off as soon as possible, and she does find you a comfort, dear child.'

'Of course. When will you leave, sir?'

'In the morning, if possible.' Mr Bartleigh waved a hand for the doctor to precede him and the pair departed. Lily wiped her tears and stood for a moment, gathering calm and summoning a smile before she opened the door.

There was no chance to do the same later as she arrived back at Lady Dayle's home. Fisher opened the door to greet her the minute she stepped down from the carriage.

Lily thanked the butler. She'd been trying to decide, on the way over, if she should have asked to accompany the Bartleighs back home to Weymouth. Lady Dayle had plenty to keep her busy with the orphanage now; she would hardly miss her. Minerva had a wedding to plan. Mr Bartleigh could likely use the help and there was nothing else keeping her here. She fought back tears; she'd done enough crying in the last days.

No, her mother would be arriving back in London shortly. Lily would do best to wait for her. She sighed. Never would she have thought to find herself wishing to go back home.

'I hope the good lady is recovering,' the butler said as he took her pelisse.

'As well as can be expected, thank you, Fisher.'

'A message has come for you, miss,' he said. 'The bearer said it was urgent.'

'Oh? Perhaps it is from Mother. She said she would write with the day we could expect her.' Lily took the letter, glanced casually at it, then stopped. It was thin, probably only one sheet, and she recognised the bold hand.

'Thank you, Fisher,' she said again, and rushed upstairs. She closed the door behind her and broke the seal. There was no date and no signature, and it was composed of only two short sentences.

I need your help. I'm coming home.

Lily clutched the parchment to her breast. The decision had been taken out of her hands. One might even call it a sign, she thought wryly. She threw the letter down on the vanity, crossed to the wardrobe and pulled out a portmanteau.

For the first time in his life, Jack had grown weary of hiding away. Over the last days he had slowly restored order to the neglected mess of his rooms, all the while attempting to do the same for his disordered mind.

An agony of guilt and shame and indecision racked him. Not that he was ashamed of hitting Whitcomb. The beating he'd given that worm might be the only good that had come out of this fiasco. No, the man had deserved it. Jack was more than a little tempted to do it again, in fact, because the lecherous mushroom kept coming around demanding satisfaction, insisting that Jack duel with him, or at least pay his medical bills. He was persistent, irritating and generally making a nuisance of himself.

Jack ignored him. Eventually the man had gone away, but only to begin harassing Jack's family instead of him. Charles had shown up to complain, but Jack had only shrugged. He'd told his brother what he'd observed of the man.

'Oho,' Charles had said. 'I know just how to handle that.' He'd left, but the next day he returned, a satisfied smirk on his face as he dropped into a chair.

'Well, Whitcomb's taken care of,' he said.

'Oh?' All of Jack's attention was focused inwards. He forced himself to look at his brother and concentrate on his words.

'I introduced him to Mills.'

'Mills?' Jack vaguely knew the name. 'Wait—the newspaper editor? At *The Augur*?'

'The very one. I took Mills to Whitcomb's house and we had a very interesting afternoon.'

'What did you do? Threaten to have Mills write an editorial about lecherous asses?'

'No, there was no mention of any of lechery, at least out loud. I merely told the bastard all about the new feature Mills is working on.'

'And what feature is that?'

'Oh, just a piece about the poor souls in service, the harshness of their life and the mistreatment they suffer at the hands of their wealthy masters.'

Jack raised a brow.

'Whitcomb did pale a little, but he tried to bluff through. But I told him that unless he wanted to be featured on the front page of *The Augur*, he'd best leave our family alone. All of our family,' Charles said with emphasis, 'and our friends and acquaintances, too.'

Jack did not respond. He knew what Charles wanted to hear. He just wasn't ready to talk about it yet.

But Charles wasn't done yet. 'Then I asked Whitcomb to assemble all of his staff, just so Mills could do a little research. He didn't want to. Turns out they have an unusually large contingent of very young maidservants. I promptly hired them all away.'

Jack laughed.

'And I told Mrs Whitcomb to replace them all with strapping footmen if she hopes to have any sort of social standing left in this town. The bounder's too cowardly to try anything with someone who can hit back.'

'Well, you wrapped him up nice and tight, didn't you?' Jack felt vaguely ashamed. 'All I could think to do was pummel the worm. What good does it do a man to possess an intellect if it is so easily overcome by temper?'

'Sometimes a man's passion is greater than his intellect, Jack,' said his brother. 'And that is no bad thing.'

Jack snorted. He watched as his brother stood. Charles went to the bookshelves and spent a few moments examining the titles there. When at last he spoke, he kept his face turned towards the well-worn tomes.

'It wasn't so long ago that I was in the same state as you, little brother—although it does feel like an eon has passed since then.' He sighed and it sounded more reminiscent than troubled. 'We stood in this same room and you gave me some remarkably good advice. Do you recall what it was?'

Jack grimaced. 'Lord, no.'

'You told me to stop, to take the time to look around and decide what it was that I wanted.' He left the bookshelf then and crossed the room, gripping Jack's shoulder in camaraderie. 'Now it's time you followed your own advice, Jack. Decide what it is you want. And I'll make the same offer you made me—whatever it is, I'll help you to get it.'

It was too much. Jack could not meet his brother's gaze. Silent, he nodded and dropped his head. But he reached up and grasped the hand on his shoulder, trying to convey with the pressure of his grip, everything that was in his heart.

'Thank you, Charles.' There was nothing more to say. How could he tell his brother that he'd been too preoccupied with his own ugliness to deal with Whitcomb's? That weightier than the question of what he wanted was the question of what he had the ability to cope with?

'You know where to find me, should you need me.'

Jack nodded again, and his brother turned and left.

He turned his gaze to the fire once more. Getting shot had somehow affected his head as much as his arm. It had cracked his defences. Anger and lust and myriad other unsightly emotions had been leaking out of him regularly since then.

But Lily Beecham had finished the job. She'd opened the locked door inside of him. Jack suspected that it had best been left closed. But now it was far too late. The portal had been thrown open, his barriers knocked down. For so long Jack had thought that those walls had only protected him from what lay outside. Now he discovered that they had also been keeping something locked in. Something not meant to see the light of day.

The idea haunted him, as did relentless images of his father. The man's negligent disdain had poisoned Jack's childhood. He had been able to draw blood with only a casual barb. The rare occasions when he had been moved to use his fist, a crop or a belt had counted as the worst days of Jack's life. But the thing that had always unnerved him the most had been the ugly satisfaction in his father's eyes—the same despicable feeling that had flooded through Jack as he pummelled that vile Whitcomb.

Was this, then, the true reason for his walls? Had he known all along—deep down and unacknowledged—that such a monster lurked inside of him? Had he been as eager to keep himself in as he had been to keep the world out?

He didn't know. He wasn't sure that he wanted to know.

Everyone eventually came to a crossroads in their life. Jack knew that he'd arrived at a defining moment in his. Lily had knocked him off his established path. He'd been forced to look at himself with new eyes and the sight was not pretty.

He had a choice to make now. Should he step back on where he'd left off? He could rebuild his ramparts, lock himself away again. He—and everyone else in his vicinity—would likely be the safer for it.

Or should he summon his courage and blaze a new trail? Could he learn to open himself to the people around him? Life seemed to exist part and parcel with a tidal surge of emotion. Everyone else appeared able to handle it. Could he do it, too, and without inadvertently following in his father's footsteps?

A month ago logic would have supplied the answers to such questions. No doubt it would have urged him towards the former. It seemed the easier and safer decision all around. But logic had deserted him. He was on his own. He looked around, but his rooms, finally in order again, were sterile and empty. He felt miserable and lonely.

It appeared, then, that the choice had been made for him. After days of indecision he was forced to acknowledge it. He could not go back.

Somewhat irritably, Jack readied himself to go out. By God, Lily had got him into this mess. He might have to forge a new path, but he was not going to begin until he had her as his guide. Finally presentable, he yanked open the door and stepped out.

Straight into a uniformed messenger, standing poised to knock.

'Message from the Admiralty, sir,' the man said smartly.

Eagerly, Jack took it. Surely this was the news of Batiste's capture? He laughed as he tore it open. Lily would say this was a sign that he'd made the right decision.

He read the words quickly. Shocked, he read it again, fighting not to drop the vellum from suddenly nerveless fingers.

The *Lady Vengeance* had indeed been holed up in Tazacorte, but the Navy had failed to take her. Batiste had slipped away again.

Jack burst into the drawing room unexpected and unannounced.

'Good heavens, Jack!' Minerva Dawson exclaimed, dropping the pen she was using. 'You scared the wits out of me!' She sounded distinctly annoyed. 'Now I'll have to begin on this invitation again.'

'Where is she, Minerva?' Jack demanded. 'Fisher says that my mother is spending all of her time in Kensington working on the orphanage, but that Lily has left?' He came to a halt in front of Minerva's writing desk. 'Left my mother's house? Left town? Where is she?'

She set down the pen. 'You took your own sweet time deciding you needed to know,' she grumbled.

'Minerva!'

She sighed. 'She's left London.'

'When?'

'Yesterday. Really, Jack, are you going to break out the thumbscrews? I feel like I'm being subjected to the Inquisition.'

He ignored her attempt at humour. 'Has her mother returned? Have they gone back to Dorset?'

'No—although her mother is expected back any day now. Lily left with the Bartleighs. They were travelling back home to Weymouth and she decided to accompany them.'

'Why?' Jack was pacing through the parlour now. 'Has something happened? Has Whitcomb or someone else bothered her?'

Minerva stared at him, and disgust coloured her expression. 'You have to ask why she left?' She shook her head. 'I suppose she felt she had no reason to stay.' She bit her lip. 'Mrs Bartleigh, it seems, has been ill for a while now. It pains me to think…' She paused. 'The excitement of the ball overset her. She's very unwell, Jack.'

Jack bowed his head. Here was yet another burden he was not sure he could handle. 'I'm sorry,' he rasped.

He paced up and down Minerva's parlour for a moment. Abruptly he stopped. 'But Fisher said Lily received a disturbing message.'

'Yes, I badgered the same information out of him, except that I thought the message had come from you.' He met her gaze and she tapped her fingers together thoughtfully. 'I can see now that it did not.'

Suddenly she shrugged and got to her feet. 'I suppose it must have been from her cousin. I did notice before that she appeared to be a little subdued after she heard from him, but she never said why.'

But Jack had frozen at her first sentence. An instantaneous, icy sweat broke over him. 'What did you say?' he asked and his tone echoed the cold.

She stared. 'I don't know, what did I say?'

'A letter from her cousin?'

'Well, I'm only surmising, after all, but based on how she's acted in the past—'

'She's had others?' he interrupted. 'Other letters from her cousin in America?'

'Yes. Is there something wrong with that?'

But Jack was already heading for the door.

'Jack, where are you going?'

He didn't turn back.

'To Weymouth!'

Chapter Twelve

Reason might have deserted Jack, but necessity could not be got around. Arrangements had to be made, and therefore he was obliged to wait until the next morning to start out after Lily. Two days' lead time that gave her and the Bartleighs. They could easily be in Weymouth already, but Minerva had sent around a note saying that they had meant to travel slowly and at an easy pace, in deference to Mrs Bartleigh's condition. Jack thought that he would begin to watch for them as he neared Dorset.

He didn't yet know just what he was going to do when he caught the infuriating girl. The scenarios in his head were continually alternating. One moment he imagined himself grabbing her up and kissing her senseless, the next all he wanted to do was shake her hard and demand she share the information she'd been withholding.

Either way, he ached for her. He'd agonised over his decision and now that it was made, he found himself burning for her with a desperation that had him driving himself hard and his mounts to the edge of their endurance.

He broke off to change horses often and asked after Lily

and her friends at each stop. Yet he could find no word of them. As the day wore on it began to worry and frustrate him. There was a very real chance that he could unknowingly overtake them, and then what would he do? He sighed. Continue on to Weymouth, he supposed, and wait for them there. Lord, but he hoped it didn't come to that. He'd waited too long already.

He made it all the way to Basingstoke, in Hampshire, before he uncovered a hint of them. Evening was coming on as Jack spoke to the ostlers at the Brown Bear. They recognised his description and said Lily and the Bartleighs had stopped here for a leisurely lunch.

'Aye, that'd be them,' the head groom said, rubbing his jaw with dirt-stained fingers. 'They rested here a long spell. One o' the ladies looked to be in a right bad way. The lads were taking bets that they'd end up stayin', but they left and I heard the coachman say they'd only be going as far as Winchester today.'

Overwhelmed with relief, Jack clapped the man on the back. 'Give me your fastest horse, man,' Jack told him. 'And I'll make it worth your while.'

'Yes, sir!'

Moments later, the groom led out a spirited chestnut, easily handling the hack as he pranced and tossed his head. 'This here's a good 'un and he's eager to be away, sir,' the man said. 'Just let him go flat out at first. He knows the way to Winchester in his sleep and he'll settle right out, soon as he's had a good run.'

'My thanks,' Jack said, swinging up and tossing down a purse that had the man's eyes bulging.

'Well, I'm gormed,' the man said in wonder.

Jack laughed and nodded for him to open the yard gate and, with a clatter of hooves, they were off.

* * *

Darkness had fallen before he reached the outskirts of Winchester, and rolling mist rose from the fields, spooking his mount. But Jack had pushed them both and the animal couldn't summon the spirit to do more than snort uneasily.

His hopes rising, Jack spoke soothingly and reached down to give the gelding a reassuring thump. He knew Winchester well. It had been King Alfred's capital city and Jack had spent a good deal of time here, researching one of his favourite subjects. He had several colleagues who lived here, in fact, and he'd visited often. He made his way easily to a livery in the centre of town, left the chestnut to be bedded down, and began to search the inns and taverns.

They were not to be found at the first two he visited. Disappointed, Jack stepped out of the Old Vine and stood a moment, gazing at the Cathedral silhouetted against the night sky. He forced himself to breathe deep. He had to stop rushing around and *think*.

What was it that Minerva's note had said? He cursed himself now for not bringing it along. Something about fresh country air? His heart began to pound a little faster. Could it be? He knew just the place he'd go if he were here and in search of a little serenity. Hesitant, he glanced back in the direction of the livery. No, it would take as long to rouse someone and hire another horse as to walk. Praying his instincts were right, Jack set out purposefully for the far edge of the town.

The Wood Grove Inn was aptly named, sprawled as it was in a lovely copse just outside of the bustle of the town. Timbered, thatched and rustic, the buildings and the beautiful gardens behind were well maintained and wonderfully enhanced by the nearby winding stream and the low, ancient granite wall that ran beside it. Jack had stayed here several times when he was here on extended research trips. There was a lovely private cottage at the back of the gardens that he liked to take when he was here. It was quiet and wonderfully conducive to work.

Tense and hopeful, Jack stepped into the familiar old building. Warm kitchen smells welcomed him and mixed with the yeasty tang of home brew. The door to the taproom swung open and the innkeeper stepped out.

'Good evening, sir,' the broad, comfortably padded woman spoke with formality. Then she stopped short and a great smile wreathed her red cheeks. 'Why, and it is Mr Alden, is it not? Bless me, but it's been an age since we saw you last! Come in, come in!'

'Good evening, Mrs Babbit.' Jack returned her smile. 'It is good to be back. I'm hoping most desperately that you can help me.'

'But of course I can! Are you here to consult with the deacon again?' She arched a coy look at him and did not wait for an answer. 'Would you be wishing to take the cottage again? We've had no bridal couples or anyone else, for that matter, in the longest time to take it. The place might be a tiny bit musty, but I swear, I shall have it aired out before the cat can lick its ear.'

'Thank you, no, I don't wish to be any trouble. Truly, I'm not here to do research this time, ma'am. I'm looking for someone, and hoped they had the good sense to stay here.'

She chuckled. 'And I'm havin' the same hope. Who is it you're looking for, sir?'

'An older couple by the name of Bartleigh. They are travelling also with a young woman, Miss Beecham.'

Mrs Babbit's good-natured smile faded. 'Ah, yes. They are here, indeed, Mr Alden.'

Jack's fist clenched as elation pounded through his veins,

yet he struggled to keep his expression sober, to match the innkeeper's. She glanced towards the taproom door, then reached out to pull him towards the hallway nook where she kept the guest log.

'You've likely made it just in time, lad,' she said in a low voice. 'The lady appears to be in a bad way.'

'Yes, I'm aware.' He realised she was trying to tell him something with her lowered brow and pursed lips. 'Do you mean…?'

'Aye, I do. But I'll be asking you to keep it quiet, if you please.' She nodded towards the taproom. 'A death in the house is never good for business.'

'Death?' The sense of urgency inside of him surged. 'Where are they, Mrs Babbit?'

'Upstairs, in the garden wing. I'll make you up a room there as well, if you won't want the cottage.' For the first time she looked at his empty hands and then behind him. 'Have you any bags, then, sir? Or shall I send a boy out to fetch them?'

'I've only a couple of saddlebags I left at the livery in town; if you could send a man there to fetch them, I'd appreciate it. I'd really like to go up,' he said, edging towards the stairs.

'Go on with you, then, and let me know if they're needing anything, will you, please?'

Jack was already halfway up the narrow staircase before she finished.

'You'll find them in the last door on the right,' she called.

Mrs Babbit's news set Jack on edge and thwarted the urgency with which he had rushed to find Lily. He could neither embrace her with relief nor question her about her cousin in this situation. Frustration ate at him, and then shame.

The air up here lay close and silent, and together with the sad tidings, formed a forcible reminder of the tense atmosphere in his home when his father lay dying. Those dark days had seemed nothing but a jumble of grief and scurrying feet, sobbing and bitter recriminations. Suddenly Jack found his feet dragging a little over the squeaking floorboards. How difficult this must be for her. In his mind Jack knew that this situation bore little similarity, yet his reluctance grew.

He reached the door at last and stood a moment, gathering strength. The soft murmur of voices reached his ears. Perhaps this was not a good time? He wavered, and then decided not to knock, but turned the knob slowly and edged open the door a bit.

He saw Lily first and his heart jumped. She sat facing slightly away from him, in a chair at the edge of a bed centred on the left-hand wall. As he watched, she leaned in towards the frail figure lying there and laid a gentle hand upon her brow. Mrs Bartleigh murmured something, but Jack did not hear the words. His gaze remained fixed on Lily.

Even from here he could see that she wore one of her shapeless gowns again. Her sleeves were rolled up and damp spots trailed down the front of her. Several heavy locks of her hair had slipped loose on one side and he could see her fingers tremble a little as she wrung out a cloth and pressed it to the dying woman's forehead.

Jack thought he'd never seen her look more beautiful. The tender light in her eyes moved him, and she exuded such a calm strength that it touched him from here. Her caring and warmth were not even directed at him and yet he felt their soothing effect.

The sick woman spoke again in a whisper and Jack realised that she was asking for something. Her thin hand reached out and grasped Lily's, but she only had the strength for a moment's grip. Her hand fell away again and Lily stroked it where it lay.

'Do sing it, please.' Another voice emanated from a dark corner of the room. Jack looked and saw the lady's husband lying on a cot, an arm draped over his eyes. The window above him was thrown open to the night air. 'You've a lovely voice, dear girl. It will do us both good to hear it.' The man's voice quivered with emotion and fatigue.

Lily nodded. She grasped Mrs Bartleigh's hand, gave her a tremulous smile and began to sing.

Jack stood rooted, listening. The song was vaguely hymn-like, but he had never heard it. Not a song of lament, it spoke instead of peace and joy and homecoming. Mrs Bartleigh's eyes closed, but her face was turned towards Lily and there was a small smile of contentment on her thin face. Her husband did not stir, but Jack saw the wet track of tears slipping from beneath his arm. Jack knew a sudden, fervent hope that the song could bring the man a measure of peace.

Lily's voice, sweet and clear, trailed through the room, weaving a spell of acceptance, of love unending and unbroken. Almost palpable, her sweet spirit touched them all, washed over Jack and through him, bringing him comfort, and in some mysterious way, transferring some of the peace in her soul into his.

He swallowed. This scene could not be more different than he had expected. He could not bring himself to interrupt the tableau. Very slowly he backed up and eased the door closed again.

For a long time he stood alone in the hallway, staring at the portal before him. This, then, was what he had missed out on, shutting himself away from the world. This girl had stirred and shaken him from the first moment they met. Now, without a word, she shattered some of his most entrenched beliefs. All of the standards on which he had built his life and moulded his character lay shattered at his feet.

Lily had burst into his life like a comet, a shining example of a strong woman and a truly giving spirit. His polar opposite.

She lent out pieces of herself endlessly, sharing her joy and enthusiasm and her will to make things better. He hid away among his books, hoarding himself and his feelings as if they were gold. She gave of herself freely and emerged ever stronger. He secreted himself away and only dwindled, growing colder and more distant.

The shock of self-awareness left him feeling deeply weary and on the verge of breaking. He stumbled away from the door, turned blindly towards the stairs, seeking solitude and peace.

Mrs Babbit lay in wait. She took one look at his face and, nodding her understanding, she pulled open the front door. Grateful, Jack stepped out into the darkness.

He headed for the gardens at the back of the inn. The sky was clear tonight and the moon rode high and half-full, casting just enough light to illuminate the path ahead. He strolled slowly, breathing deep and allowing the peace of the night to soothe him. An occasional rustle sounded as his passage disturbed a sleeping bird or roving night creature, but he didn't stop. The gurgling stream at the back was calling him. He scooped up a handful of pebbles and perched beside it on the low granite wall.

Surprisingly, perhaps, his brother loomed at the forefront of his thoughts. He'd lied to Charles when his brother had asked if he remembered giving him advice. He did recall the occasion, vividly. Charles had been beleaguered then, and in a state of turmoil—just the state Jack sat in now. *Decide what it is that you want.* It was excellent advice, but Jack had thought that it did not apply. He already knew what he wanted, had known almost since the first moment that he saw Lily Beecham. The question was: did he have the ability—the courage, really—to seize it?

He'd thought he'd finally found the courage. Yet now he found himself hesitating, and for a totally different reason. He realised that the entirety of his focus had been on himself and his own conflicted needs and desires. Lily spent so much of her time thinking of others. It was past time he took a page from her book and thought about what was good for her. The stunning, terrifying truth was that that might not be him.

Open, generous, loving—Lily represented everything good in this benighted world. She could find someone so much better than a surly, stunted scholar. He'd already hurt her, would undoubtedly do so again. Would she think him even worth the pain and effort?

Jack took a pebble and tossed it into the stream. It hit with a satisfying plop and sent out a wave of ripples to catch the scant light. He needed answers to his questions.

A faint step sounded on the path behind him. He turned and she was there, a gorgeous figure lined in softest moonlight. He sighed. Now would be the perfect time to get them.

'Jack!' Lily stared in stunned disbelief. 'It is you. When Mrs Babbit said you'd come, I did not quite believe it.' She took a step closer. 'What are you doing here?'

He rose and beckoned her closer. 'Come and sit.'

Her heart pounded, but she did not heed him. She could never keep her head when she was too close to him, and she needed to know. 'Why, Jack?'

He stared at her. The darkness made it difficult to see where he directed his gaze, but she could feel its caress, could follow its path by the heating of her blood.

'I came to find you,' he said simply. 'But instead, I think I've lost myself.'

Lily snorted. 'That is exactly the sort of answer I should have expected from you,' she said, piqued.

'You don't sound happy to see me,' he said. She could tell he was trying to sound meek.

He failed miserably.

She gave up. She chuckled and stepped towards the ancient wall where he'd been sitting. 'I am glad to see you, I'm just…I'm feeling too many things to sort out right now.' She sighed.

He swept a hand towards the stream. 'There's a nice selection of rocks here. Perhaps you'd like to throw one at me? It might make you feel better and there's a slim chance that it will knock some sense into me.'

She tsked at him and allowed him to help her over the wall so she could sit. 'Whatever it is that you are lacking, it isn't sense. In fact, I've come to think that you set entirely too great a store by it.'

'Do you?' He opened his hand. She had to look close to see that he held a handful of tiny smooth stones. 'Have some,' he said. He demonstrated by plunking one into the water. 'It helps you think.'

They sat pitching rocks in companionable silence for a while. He was right. It did help restore her balance after a long and heartbreakingly difficult day. The night lay quiet about them and the peace gradually helped calm her frayed nerves. But he sat too close for her to feel truly settled. She could feel the heat rising from him and smell the comfortably masculine mix of soap, smoke and horse.

The silence stretched out between them until, suddenly, Lily felt it had gone on too long. 'The truth, Jack,' she demanded. 'Why are you here?'

At the exact same moment he spoke into the silence. 'How is Mrs Bartleigh?' he asked.

They laughed together. A dangerous moment—she did not want to get too comfortable with him—yet.

'Your friend, how is she?' he asked again, gently.

'Asleep now, but not as strong as we'd hoped. Mr Bartleigh is resting as well. I left a maid to sit in with them.' She threw her last stone and dusted her hands together. 'It will be no more than a day or two, the local doctor said, when we asked him for advice.' She drew a deep breath. 'The worst part is not being able to make it home. But this inn is lovely and the air is sweet. I think it helps.'

'I'm very sorry.'

She looked up into his eyes. 'Tell me, Jack. Why are you here? I need to know.'

He dumped his remaining pebbles and wiped his hand on his thigh. Then he reached for her hand and entwined his fingers tenderly with hers. 'Come, will you walk with me a little? I can express myself a little better if I am moving, I think.'

She nodded and they set off. The gardens were extensive, reaching from the stream, past the main building of the inn and on nearly to the stables on the other side. Plenty of room for pacing and explanations.

'When I left that ball, Lily, I was appalled at myself,' he began. 'The intensity and violence of my feelings—it was unnerving. All of my feelings,' he emphasised. 'Not just the anger I felt towards that bounder Whitcomb, but everything I felt about what…we had done, too. I don't think you can imagine how unsettling it was for me.'

'Then tell me,' she said.

'For so long I've dampened my emotions, ignored them or tucked them away, and suddenly so much was exploding out of me.' He shrugged. 'I don't know how to control the intensity of what I feel. Because I've never really let myself feel much of anything at all.'

She smiled. 'All you need is practice.'

'I need you, too, Lily,' he said, his voice lowering. 'I meant at first to go back, to suppress everything you'd set free and return to the safety of my isolation. But for the first time solitude felt all wrong. I was miserable. It's too late to turn back. I want to learn. I'll do what it takes, but I'll need help.'

'You have it,' she whispered, stepping close.

'Lily,' he said abruptly. 'I watched you tonight. With the Bartleighs. In there.' He jerked his head towards the inn.

'You did?' She felt puzzled and slightly alarmed at the strange vehemence of his tone. 'What did you see?'

He laughed, but there was no humour in it—only pain. 'What did I see?' He drew to a halt and dropped her hand. 'I saw an angel come to earth.' He walked a few steps away, but then spun on his heel and stalked slowly back towards her. 'An angel with eyes the colour of the sky and red-gold hair like the setting sun.' His voice lowered to a rasp. 'An angel with a devil's mouth, continuously tempting me to sin.'

She started as he reached for her, cupped her face in both of his powerful hands. 'I saw exactly what I've been lacking all my life, everything I want to lay claim to—and everything I should not.'

Tears welled in her eyes. She lifted her own hands up to grasp his wrists. The frantic beat of his pulse singed her fingertips. 'Why shouldn't you?'

Abruptly he let go. The absence of his touch was worse than pain. 'Because you give all that you have and I give nothing. You are a tower of strength and I…' He stepped away into the shadow of a tree's spreading branches. 'I am broken.'

Lily dashed away the tears in her eyes. 'Stop it,' she said fiercely. 'First, stop making me out to be so perfect. I am not. I'm human just like everyone else, with all the same faults and foibles. And if you need a reminder, then I will tell you that when I came out here I heard an owl calling twice, and I've been anxiously listening, because if he calls a third time it will mean bad luck!'

He made a dismissive noise and she followed him into the

darker shelter of the tree. 'Second, you are not broken.' Sure of herself now, she stepped between his legs and pressed against him, forcing him to lean back into the tree to support them both. Arching into him, she reached up and stroked lightly along his jaw.

'And third, there is only one thing that you lack—and that is a tiny piece of information. It's not a secret, but it's something that few enough ever truly understand.'

She stood on her toes and brushed a light kiss across his lips. 'Whatever you give in this life—that is what you get back. You are right—I do lend my help, my strength, where I see a need for it. But it all comes back to me and makes me stronger.' He started to speak, but she pressed a finger to his mouth to stop him. 'Listen well, for I hope you will take this to heart. If you give nothing to the world, how can you expect to get anything back?'

She removed her hand and pressed closer still. Softly she kissed him again, then ran a line of tender kisses along the strong line of his jaw and into the vulnerable spot beneath his ear. 'One last thing I mean to tell you,' she whispered. 'There is no need for you to lay claim to me. For I am giving myself to you.' She drew back and looked him full in the eye, allowed him to see all the longing in her soul. 'I would appreciate it if you would follow my advice and return the favour.'

He responded at last with a low moan, then he dipped his head and returned her kiss, taking possession of her with lips and mouth and tongue and lifting her hard against him.

Joyfully, Lily gave herself over to him and to the flare of passion sweeping through her. She twined her arms about his neck and her fingers into his dark, unruly hair. He made a sound of approval into her mouth and she felt the reverberation of it slide down into her, settling deep and hot in the pit of her belly.

Boldly he stroked her with his tongue, while his hands moved lightly over her body. The juxtaposition of his hot, possessive mouth and the slow, tantalising dance of his fingers down her back and over the curves of her bottom forced her hunger higher, until she wanted to laugh with the delight of it. Yes, she thought, this is what she'd been waiting for.

We were not put on earth to enjoy life.

The words echoing in her head were Mr Cooperage's, but the ringing tones sounded suspiciously like her mother's. Or perhaps it was just the outraged voice of some deeply buried part of her conscience. She ignored them all.

They were wrong. All of them were so sadly mistaken. Lily knew without a doubt that people were meant to enjoy life. We were all meant to *live* life, and how could one survive without joy? Lily could not. She'd tried. Oh, how hard she'd tried, for her mother's sake, but duty and virtue turned dry as dust when it was not leavened with love and happiness.

Jack was her chance for both. Perhaps some would call her unwise—gambling on Jack Alden could not be called a sure bet. But she had set out to find just who Lily Beecham was, and now she'd discovered a large part of the answer. Neither her mother's daughter nor her father's, but a person in her own right, with her own moral sense of right and wrong. The sort of person who knew the right thing to do was to take a chance on love.

Chapter Thirteen

Jack tore his mouth away from Lily's, but only long enough to press a burning kiss to her sweet nape. She hummed her approval and let her head tilt back, granting him access to the slender column of her neck. He paused to let his appreciative gaze wander over her flushed cheeks and closed eyes. He drank in the enchanting sight, and then buried his face in the lush curve of her neck and shoulder and breathed deep. If only he could inhale some of her strength along with the clean and heady scent of her.

Greedily he covered her mouth once more, rejoicing when she echoed the urgency of his kiss. He pulled her closer, marvelling that she should feel so small, when the force of her personality and the beauty of her soul loomed so large.

He pulled away, suddenly impatient that he could not see the excitement in her eyes. Stepping back, he lifted her hand, kissed it soundly and began to lead her down the path.

'Where are we going?' she asked, breathless.

'I know the perfect place.'

He kept her tucked close as they moved through the gardens, relishing all the points of contact with her from shoulder to thigh and craving a hundred more intimate touches. Even in the moonlight, the gardens loomed luxurious and fragrant, but Jack had more important things on his mind. He led Lily ever further back, until they passed through a marching line of tall yews and she halted suddenly, caught up in the beautiful scene before them.

Jack could understand her awe. The little cottage nestled in the last stand of the wooded grove. Beyond it lay another low granite wall and a pasture awash in moonlight. The moon hung just above, in fact, as if placed there for the sole purpose of illuminating this secret hideaway.

'What is it?' she breathed.

'It used to be a dairy, I believe, but Mrs Babbit transformed it into a cottage. She lets it to those who are staying longer than a night or two.' He pulled her in close for a lingering kiss. 'Or occasionally a bridal couple takes it.'

She heaved a sigh of wonder. 'You're right. It is perfect.'

It was hard to tell, but he thought she was blushing. Jack had to kiss her again, then, because she was so adorable. He pressed his lips to hers once, twice, and then he picked her up and swung her around. He ignored the sudden protest of his arm. Buoyant with happiness, he swept her off her feet and carried her to the door.

Once there Jack grew suddenly sober. He set her down on her feet and pulled her close. 'There is no reason we have to…' He paused. Feebly, he gestured back towards the inn. 'We could just…'

She smiled, though he failed to see the humour here. Grabbing his hand, she repeated his earlier gesture and kissed it, but softly. Then she held it close to her bosom. He could feel her heart pounding with excitement and need.

'Don't be absurd, Jack. What we've found, what we feel for each other—it is a gift. How many people are so fortunate?' Slowly she opened his hand, spread his fingers, and kissed each one. Then she took his hand, slid it down and across until she placed it squarely on her bottom once more.

Jack let out an incoherent moan. No man had ever been this fortunate, he was sure. She was such an intoxicating mix of innocence, wisdom and desire. 'Not nearly enough,' he answered.

'Exactly. And that is why we shall not squander this honour. We will accept it,' she whispered. 'Celebrate it. With all of our hearts.'

'And our bodies,' he said huskily.

'Yes. Our only shame would be in refusing such a gift.'

Her words set his heart to pounding. He bent to her again. A whispered sigh escaped her and she melted against him, all the tension draining from her body. She opened her mouth beneath his, inviting him in once more, tempting him, setting fire to his blood. He strove mightily to pull back. 'This is an irrevocable step, Lily. I made my choice back in London. I chose you. Your decision comes here and now.'

She shook her head. Her eyes remained half-lidded. 'Yes. No. Of course.' Her lips brushed gently along his jaw. 'All I want is you.'

'No, I mean it, Lily. God knows, I'm a bad bargain at best, and I want you to be sure of what you are getting. If we do this, we will be bound.'

She stood on tiptoe and pressed herself tight against him. 'I can think of nothing I would like more.'

His heart in his mouth, Jack reached behind her and tried the door. It swung wide and he silently blessed Mrs Babbit. Just as he remembered, a lamp lay on a table close to the door. He lit it quickly, and then moved further into the room to ignite a pair of candles on the mantel.

The cottage was all one room, with a handsome, stone fireplace on one end, flanked by a pair of chairs and an all-purpose table. On the other side of the room loomed a wide, four-posted bed, done up in faded, once-rich silk. Lily trailed across the room, examining everything, but Jack noticed that her eye shied repeatedly away from the bed.

'Have you stayed here before?' she asked faintly.

'Yes.' He wanted to put her at ease. Ignoring the existence of the bed, he sat in one of the wide, well-cushioned chairs by the fireplace. 'Come here,' he said, low and urgent.

Relief showing in her face, she came. She obviously recalled their embrace in the Dawson's library as vividly as he did. She turned to sit sideways on his lap as she had then.

'Wait,' Jack commanded. He positioned her so that they were knee to knee, and then with a wicked smile he leaned down to grasp the ends of her skirts. She began to breathe heavily as he allowed his fingers to trail a circuitous route up the length of her legs.

'Like this,' he whispered once her skirts had reached her knees. He urged her forwards until she straddled him in the chair.

'Oh, my.' She sank down and Jack swallowed hard as her moist heat settled right over the growing bulge in his breeches.

'I do so enjoy your way with words.' He grinned up at her, fighting for control. His head settled on the back of the chair. 'But don't you want to kiss me?'

She smiled back, a look full of mischief and longing. 'I want to kiss you…' she leaned down and her breath was a hot caress under his ear '…more than you can possibly imagine.' She hovered enticingly over his lips.

'I beg to differ,' he said breathlessly. 'I have quite an active imagination.' God, it was killing him, but he held still, kept his hands at his sides and allowed her the lead.

A wise move on his part, for Lily made it entirely worth the wait. She spread her legs further apart and settled herself more firmly over his erection. Her bosom pressed close against him, tempting him with the promise of more and then she leaned in and kissed him, sweet and deep. Her tongue stroked his with slow and languid strokes and her soft, yielding lips drove him wild.

Jack could take no more. He was at her mercy and in the grip of a vortex of lust. It surged through him, urging him on as he reached for her and buried his hands in her hair, tearing pins away and loosing a glorious fall of red-gold hair. It spilled down and over them both, teasing Jack's jaw and neck. He suffered a sudden vision of her curls spread across his bare chest as she kissed her way down towards his ramrod-stiff shaft.

Almost fierce with impatience, he tore his mouth from hers and submerged his face in her sweetly scented mass of curls. All the while, he kept his hands busy at her back, searching out the fastenings of her gown. At long last the final button on her bodice popped free and the last tie of her stays came undone. He pushed it all down to her waist.

Only her shift was left, a simple cotton garment that exposed more than it covered and rose and fell with her rapid breath. The magnificent outline of her high, full breasts showed clear. Enthralled, Jack encircled them with his hands, tested their weight, and thumbed her searching, straining nipples until she gasped with pleasure.

He had to see her. A thousand tiny buttons marched down the front of her shift and Jack had to fight the urge to tear them all open. He took his time instead, popping them off one by one and revelling in the sensation of her shifting restlessly over his straining body.

At last it was done. Jack spread her shift apart and pulled it down her arms. Then he lay his head back and let the sight of her drive the breath from his lungs.

She looked unreal, otherworldly with the dim candlelight sparking in her hair and lining her curving figure with gold.

Round, high and tipped with rose, her breasts called to him. He answered with lips, fingers and fervent caresses. A sound emerged from deep inside her and her back arched, inarticulately asking for more. He answered again, setting his mouth to one breast, teasing it with his lips and tongue while he gently pinched the nipple of the other.

For long moments he pleasured her, licking one nipple with slow thoroughness and then moving to the other. Lily's breathing grew ragged and she began to rock her hips against him in quick, untutored motions. He could feel the hot, wet heat growing at her centre.

With a growl, Jack came off the chair. She whooped in surprise and locked her legs around him. Laughing, he carried her to the bed and set her square in the centre.

'I think we're both wearing entirely too many clothes,' he said with a smile.

She nodded and he worked the rest of her clothes up and over, down and off. Standing back, he gazed at her perfect form with reverence. Elation filled him. Tonight, for the first time, he would be free to let go, to loose all holds and let his emotions roam free—because for the first time he did not have to fear their heavy weight. Lily was strong. Beautiful, yes, and so amazingly formed that he itched to run his hands over her again. But it was her tenacious hardiness that made her so perfect for him. She knew her own mind and somehow she managed to bolster his own strength with her own.

Impatient, wanting to touch her again, he began peeling his clothes off. Propping herself up on her elbows, she watched him with unabashed curiosity. As the layers fell away, a sensual smile lurked on her face, igniting another erotic vision, a picture of those full, luscious lips locked around him. When at last he sprang free he was as hard as stone. Her eyes widened. The look of utter fascination she wore had him swelling impossibly huge.

He crawled up next to her on the bed. 'You are so incredibly beautiful,' he breathed in her ear.

'As are you,' she whispered back.

Jack laid a hand on her breast, stroking it with idle caresses as he gazed seriously into her eyes. 'You were right all along, you know. I had built walls around myself. And then you came along and reduced them all to rubble.' He kissed her softly. 'But now I find I am tempted to build them up again, just to keep you inside.'

She lifted a hand to his face. 'You don't need walls to keep me close,' she said. 'I'm not going anywhere.'

He kissed her then, in gratitude and something more. He might have worked out what that more was, but she trailed a hand over his shoulder, down his chest and poised it over him. She pulled back and there was a question in her eyes.

'Yes,' he moaned. 'Touch me.'

She touched her index finger to the tip of him and Jack fought hard to keep from thrusting further into her hand. He held back and let her explore. It was the most exquisite torture. Lightly caressing fingers ran all over him, from crown to sac, until at last he could not wait. He took her hand and wrapped her fingers firmly around him.

'Ah,' she said. 'Like this?' She gave an experimental stroke.

'Yes, just like that,' he begged. 'More.'

She grinned her triumph, but only until his hand left her breast, trailed down her body and burrowed into her nest of copper curls. Beneath them she was hot, slick and wetter than he could have dreamed.

'Ohh,' she said, loudly. The sound echoed through the small room.

'Lie back.'

She complied and he spread her wide, and bent to suckle her breast again as his fingers stroked, teased and circled her into a frenzy.

'Like this?' he asked, his voice heavy with humour and lust.

'More,' she demanded.

He laughed low and kissed her hard. 'As my lady pleases.'

He rolled above her and nudged her legs apart. She hissed long and low as he reached down and parted her. Gritting his teeth to hold on to the shreds of his control, he fondled her again, letting his fingers roam in her slick heat until she squirmed beneath him once more.

Now. He had to have her now. He sucked in his breath when he encountered the wet evidence of her desire. Slowly, carefully, he pushed in, easing his way into the hot, tight core of her.

Good God. He could feel her body stretching, giving way, but still surrounding him with a snug embrace. He'd had bed partners aplenty, but never had he experienced this blinding sense of intimacy. Never had he felt so close, so connected with another person, body and soul. It was exhilarating, and a little frightening.

Lily wiggled beneath him, a frown of concentration on her lovely face.

'Are you all right?' he asked. He eased further and held his breath, sure he would die if he had to stop now.

'Yes. No. Just a moment.' She shifted again and suddenly opened wider. 'Yes. That's it.' She sighed. She threw her head back and gripped him tight.

He needed no further encouragement. He rocked his hips and began to move, slow and sure. Gradually, she caught on, caught his rhythm and began to move with him. Incredibly, his shaft flexed and stretched again.

'Oh, Lord.' Jack gripped her bottom and braced her for a series of long, hard strokes. She met him thrust for thrust. Her hands roamed, restless, until they finally settled on his buttocks and urged him on. Together in breath, body and rising hunger, they climbed. Jack could feel the mounting tension in her body. He swore as her passage tightened again.

'It's coming for us, Lily,' he murmured. 'Let it take you.'

'I don't know how,' she cried, desperation in her voice.

Jack could not wait much longer. She was too perfect in every way. He slid his hand between them and found the aching centre of her pleasure. She keened her response and the reaction of her sex was instantaneous as it began to flutter around his surging shaft. Lightly he stroked her, coaxed her along, until suddenly, without warning she broke apart, pulling him in even deeper.

It was too sweet, too much. A great swell of emotion grew inside him, a rushing tangle of affection, gratitude and, God help him, it was true—love. It swamped him so he thought he would drown in it. Harder and faster he thrust, mounting ever higher. With a roar, he went over, abandoning himself to the flood, letting it drag him through shattering need and gusts of pleasure. For endless moments he arched into her and no longer was he a lonely, flawed being, but one part of a glorious whole. He crested, riding high, reaching new heights never possible without Lily's support. He shuddered, poised in tight ecstasy above her until gradually the emotional tide receded, and he drifted home, wrapped in the contentment of Lily's arms.

Afterwards they sat together in the chair once more. The hour grew late and the little cottage filled with caring words, affectionate banter and soft laughter. It was perfect, just as Lily had always dreamed. She rejoiced in the simple pleasure of acceptance, the immense thrill of just being herself and finding that he neither expected nor wished for anything else.

But gradually Jack's mood grew sombre, his hesitation

more obvious. With a sigh, Lily snuggled against him and prayed he wouldn't end their idyll so soon.

He shifted in the chair beneath her and cleared his throat. A smile tugged at the corner of her mouth and she gazed up at him. 'What is it, Jack?' She traced a tender line across his brow and down the strong plane of his face to his jaw and tried to lighten his mood again. 'You're not regretting the loss of your virtue, are you?'

His chest heaved as he choked with surprised laughter. 'No, you saucy chit.' A frown creased his brow and he looked down at her with concern. 'I hope you are not, either.'

'Not in the least,' she said, planting a kiss on his lips.

But he was not to be distracted. He took her hand and spoke earnestly. 'I want you to understand, I consider tonight the greatest gift, the highest honour of my life.'

'As you should,' she said with a smile.

'I'm perfectly serious.' His brow furrowed even further. 'We've both been through so much lately and death can act as a powerful influence. I would hate to think that your grief has led to something that you would regret later.'

She sat up straighter in his lap and gripped his hand tight. 'You need to understand as well, I will never regret spending this night with you.' She imbued her voice with all the earnestness and fervour in her heart. 'Everything we feel tonight is true and beautiful. You are right, my friend is dying, but her passing will be easy. Do you know why?'

He shook his head.

'Because she's lived a good and full life. None of us is perfect, but she's done her best. She's done what good she may and she has no regrets to weigh her down or mar the peacefulness of her last moments.' She breathed deep and softened her tone. 'If we had *not* done this, I would have regretted it for the rest of my life, and I would have carried that disappointment with me to *my* death bed.' She gave him a gentle smile. 'We will take the future as it comes, but rest easy knowing that tonight was meant to be.'

She thought his eyes filled, but he only nodded and gathered her close. She sighed and enjoyed his embrace for a moment, but something of what he'd just said nagged at her.

'You know, you were right about death being a powerful influence on the living,' she said. 'I've learned that lesson in hard school.'

'Your father?'

'Yes, his death was so hard for me and it certainly changed the path of my life.' She looked up at him. 'As I'm sure your father's death did for you.'

She saw his jaw clench, and the hated, empty look stole back into his eyes. And right then she knew. 'What is it, Jack? Is there something about your father I don't know?'

Jack let out a bitter laugh. 'Undoubtedly there is—nearly as many things about him that I never knew.' He stood abruptly, carrying her off his lap and setting her on her feet. 'I'm sorry, it's just that he was a hard man. We were not close. He wasn't close to anyone, really, not even my mother.' He began to putter about the room, straightening the already made bed and other things that had not been disturbed.

'How sad, for all of you.' Lily sighed.

'I think he tried with Phillip, my eldest brother, but in the end he only pushed him away. And then Phillip died and my father followed, not long after.' He glanced over at her. 'They both had a heavy load of regrets, I would imagine.'

Pieces of the puzzle were rapidly joining in Lily's head. He never mentioned his father. He had not been close with him. Their relationship had been distant, one might say.

'I truly am sorry, Jack. At least while I had him, my father was loving, open and warm. I still miss him so much.'

He didn't respond. Lily watched as he went to the door and opened it a crack. 'It will be dawn soon,' he said. 'We should get back.'

'I never told you how my father died.'

That got his attention. He came back and gathered her in his arms. 'It's not necessary, Lily. I'm fine.'

'I've never talked about it with anyone,' she whispered. 'But I'd like to tell you.' She tried to ease his discomfort with a smile. 'And as you are fond of saying, it's only fair.'

'Let's go outside, then, into the garden.'

She nodded and they closed up the little cottage and found a bench near a bank of sweet-smelling roses.

'I told you how I bewildered my mother as a child,' she said, snuggling up close to him. 'She didn't know quite what to do with me. But that changed when I turned fifteen. She took a sudden interest in me and decided to rectify the lack of ladylike refinements in my education.'

He chuckled. 'Was it horrid?'

'No, not really.' She smiled. 'I was just so happy to find a way to please her. I applied myself to learning about fashion and decorum and whom to sit where at the dinner table.' She shot him a grin. 'Of course, I did not give up my horses or my rounds about the estate with my father, but still, she was thrilled. I think she had got it in her head that even if she couldn't have a son, she was going to make sure I made the finest marriage in the county.'

'What happened?'

'There was an assembly being held in Weymouth. It was to be my first. Mother was determined I should go, get my feet wet, so to speak, and begin to polish my manners locally before she took me to London to bring me out.'

She sat silent a moment, preparing herself to speak aloud things that she had never spoken of to anyone before. Jack did not push her; he just held her close and drifted his fingers through her hair.

'It began to cloud up, but Mother was adamant. Nurse muttered and moaned about weather signs, but Father just laughed and said he could wait no longer to dance with me.' She sighed. 'The storm broke while we were on the road, nearly halfway there. It was a terrible thing to see, with the trees bent nearly sideways and the rain coming down so hard you could not see from one end of the carriage to the next.'

'You must have been frightened half to death.'

'We all were, I think. The road turned into a quagmire in an instant. The horses were in a panic. The coachman climbed down to try to calm them, and promptly slipped in the mud and broke his leg. Papa said there was no help for it. He bundled the coachman into the carriage with Mother and me, cut the horses loose and set out on foot to find help.'

'What happened to him?' Jack's voice was heavy with empathy.

'Oh, it took hours, and by then the storm had passed, but he made it back with a farmer's dray heavy enough to navigate the mud. It wasn't until the next day that he started to feel ill. He caught a putrid sore throat and died a few weeks later.'

'Oh, my dear, I am so sorry,' he said. He wrapped her in a comforting embrace.

'It was bad,' she said quietly. 'Grief was a heavy burden, but the guilt and the fear were worse.'

'You had nothing to feel guilty about!' he protested.

'I know that now. But I was fifteen and I thought the world began and ended with me,' she said with a sad smile. 'Nurse rumbled that we had ignored her and all the signs. I worried that if I had not wished to go to the assembly, we wouldn't have been caught in the storm. My self-recriminations were endless—and then my mother...'

'I cannot begin to imagine her pain,' Jack murmured.

'I told you she was reserved before, but after my father died— Well, you've seen what she has become. She is so dour, and refuses to take any pleasure in life. I worried that her transformation was my fault, too.'

He kissed her temple. 'My poor girl.'

'It was Mrs Bartleigh who saved me. We got to know her as Mother became more involved with the Evangelicals and their charitable efforts. She and Mother grew close and she saw how terribly hurt we both were. Eventually she helped me to see that none of it had been my fault. She showed me that my job was to grieve and move on. Never to forget—but not to let it ruin me either.'

'She sounds a wise woman.'

'She is, and a very dear friend. I wish, though, that she had been able to help my mother. It was a long time before I realised that Mother is frantically trying to do good to somehow balance out what she thinks of as her fault. I wonder when, if ever, she will realise that her guilt exists only in her own mind.'

Lily pulled away and looked into Jack's eyes, so hard to read in the dwindling moonlight. 'I've watched you, Jack, and thought I would never begin to understand what drives you. But now I wonder if you might not share some of my mother's burdens.'

He looked as if he'd been kicked in the gut. 'What?' he asked in shock.

'No one in your family speaks of your father much. You, on the other hand, have never mentioned him at all. When I do, or someone else does, then you look exceedingly uncomfortable and you invariably change the subject.'

'That does not mean I have anything to feel guilty about.' He was beginning to sound outraged.

'No, of course not. And if I am wrong, then I am sorry. I

just wanted you to know that it's possible that I once felt similarly. If ever you wish to talk about…anything, then I am always ready to listen.'

He shook his head and smiled down at her, but she could tell it was forced. 'I told you I was broken—now you are trying to fix me?'

'I'm just trying to help,' she said, worried that she had perhaps spoken before he was ready to hear her.

He rose and pulled her to her feet. 'Thank you. It isn't necessary, but it makes me feel good just to hear it.'

It was a lie. Her questions had clearly disturbed him, set his nerves on edge.

He pressed a soft kiss to her mouth. 'Come, it's time we went in. If we go in the servants' entrance, we can get upstairs without anyone knowing.'

Her heart falling, she nodded her agreement. The sense of contentment and peace imbuing the night had flown. What else could she do to win his trust? He claimed his walls were down, but still he would not open his heart and mind to her.

Chiding herself, she tried to rally. She'd had tonight, and they had a chance at tomorrow. She could move at as slow a pace as he needed. Clasping his hand tight, she followed him in.

Chapter Fourteen

Jack spent a few restless hours trying to sleep, but his mind was awhirl and what little sleep he managed was racked with disturbing images. He tossed and turned until he had his bed-clothes as muddled as his head. When he finally got his foot so entangled that he nearly cut off the circulation, he put a period to the attempt.

His saddlebags had been delivered. He rose, exchanged one rumpled set of clothes for another and went in search of breakfast.

'There's precious little to be had, I'm afraid,' Mrs Babbit said in answer to his enquiry. She huffed as she carried linens up the stairs. 'There's a fair in Winchester today. Half the servants have the day off, the other half are sulking because they don't. Even the cook's gone in search of some fancy spice or other, much good it'll do in a place like this where folks expect good, plain English fare,' she grumbled. 'There's bread and cheese and cold meat in the larder, Mr Alden. Help yourself. Your friends are occupied now, in any case, as the young lady is helping me to change the linen on Mrs Bartleigh's bed.'

'Thank you, Mrs Babbit.' Jack watched her climb the rest of the stairs. Lily's talk of her father—and his—had set him on edge. It had also reminded him forcibly of his other reason for searching her out. But it did not look as if he'd be able to question her about her contact with her cousin any time soon.

'Oh, ma'am, just a minute,' he called after the innkeeper. 'Do you have room for my mount in your stables?'

'Aye, should be plenty of room,' she called back. 'Just check with one of the grooms.'

The single groom left behind confirmed that there was an empty stall. 'And plenty o' good feed, too,' he assured Jack. 'Not like the half-rotten stuff the livery in town'll be givin' your mount.' He looked almost hopeful. 'Do you want me to go in and fetch him for you, sir?'

'Thank you, no,' replied Jack. 'I think I'll go myself.' He could get a hot breakfast while he waited, as long as Lily was busy in any case.

The long night had taken its toll and Jack's pace slowed as he entered the town proper. A savoury meat pie from a cart vendor revived him a bit. Feeling better, he began to make his way through the crowds, in the direction of the livery.

A coldly familiar sound brought him up short. Definitely that was the echo of leather slapping against flesh. He cast about until he discovered the sound bouncing eerily from the high walls of a nearby lane.

A poorly dressed man, a farmer by the looks of his work-stained hands and the contents of his cart, stood at the mouth of the small space, smacking his thin belt against his palm. A young boy cowered in front of him.

'What good do ye think ye'll do me, boy, if ye land yer arse in gaol for thievin'?'

The boy bowed his head and didn't answer.

'Ye've whacked him once,' a feminine voice said. Jack

saw a woman in worn but clean clothes at the back of the cart. 'He's learned his lesson. Haven't ye, Tommy?'

The boy nodded vigorously and wiped his nose.

'Aye, and he'll be spendin' his fair day workin' for the man he thought to steal from,' the farmer growled.

Dismay bloomed in the boy's face and Jack moved on. But the image of the man's anger conspired with his fatigue and the unease brought on by last night's conversations. Together they called forth an uncomfortable vision from his own childhood.

'What good is he?' his angry father had demanded. Perhaps ten years old he'd been that time? He vividly remembered emerging from the library to hear his father's shout echoing through the hall. 'Your indulgence has ruined him! He's soft and weak.'

'He's got a brilliant mind.' He'd heard his mother defending him. 'And a devastating wit, as you'd discover if you spent any time with him.'

'And so I would if the boy would begin to show an interest in worthwhile pursuits. As it is, I've got no time to waste on babes and books!'

The words echoed painfully even through so many years. And stirred up the same roiling sense of resentment and determination. Jack shook his head and set off purposefully for the livery. He had not let his father's disdain sway him from his course then. In the same vein, he could not let either Lily's misguided loyalty or his own feelings for her deter him now.

The livery was as crowded as the streets and they were glad to see him free up an empty stall.

'I'll have your mount saddled right up, sir,' the owner said. He started to say something further, but the precipitous arrival of an obviously blown team ahead of a carriage full of merrymakers had him striding out into the yard, shouting orders as he went.

Jack waiting impatiently, ignoring the noise and bustle until a youngster brought his rented hack. He tossed the fees to the boy and mounted with resolve. It was time he got back to the inn and back on the trail of both Matthew Beecham and Gustavo Batiste.

'Oy!' the livery owner came back on a run, shouting as Jack left the yard in a flurry of hooves. 'Hold a moment, sir!'

His bellow blended into the racket in the yard.

'Did ye tell him about the men who come by lookin' for him?' the owner demanded of the boy.

The young groom shook his head.

'Ah, well, then.' The owner turned back to his business with a sigh. 'They'll find each other, if 'tis important enough.'

Mrs Babbit thrust a tray into his hands as soon as he burst in the door. 'Thank God, you're back,' she said urgently. 'Take this up with you, please? The poor lady's time is nigh and the two of them won't leave her side for a minute.'

'Oh, no.' A host of conflicting reactions hit Jack at this sad news. Ruthlessly he suppressed the impatience that surged to the forefront.

'Go on, then! Hurry on up.'

'Oh, yes, of course.' For the second time in two days he trod with high-running emotion and reluctant feet to the dying woman's chamber. This time he knocked before swinging the door gently open.

It was a wasted effort. Neither occupant of the room heard him. Lily sat in the same spot as she had yesterday, but now she cried quietly into a handkerchief. Mr Bartleigh was leaning over his wife. Gently he closed her eyes and kissed her lips. 'Goodbye, my love,' he whispered.

For a long moment Lily's soft weeping was the only sound in the room. No one moved. Then the gentleman stood straight.

'I'll take her home,' Mr Bartleigh said in a rough voice. 'We are near enough to make it in a day's journey.' He looked over at Lily. 'I'll see to a cart and a bo—' He stopped and swallowed. 'A co—'

And right before Jack's horrified gaze, the man crumpled. Harsh, broken sobs tore their way out of him. He sank to his knees beside the bed. Jack's chest burned just hearing the horrible evidence of this man's grief and his eyes welled alarmingly.

'I can't do it,' Mr Bartleigh sobbed wretchedly. 'How am I supposed to face each day without her?'

Tears streaming down her face, Lily dropped down beside him. Crooning wordless sounds of comfort, she enfolded him in her arms.

'You know, Lily,' the older man rasped. He gazed at her with stricken eyes. 'You know—she's my light, the greatest joy in my life.' His voice broke. 'She was my heart,' he said on a thin, piteous cry. 'How am I supposed to survive without my heart?'

He went limp, his body curled around his pain. His entire form shook with the force of his sobs.

Jack ached with crippling compassion and grief. His hands trembled, setting the tea service on the tray he still carried to clattering. The sound caught Lily's attention and she looked up. Her face was flushed, her nose red. Relief flashed briefly in her eyes as she caught sight of him. She raised her arm and beckoned.

In that moment, Jack could not have moved if his life depended on it. Terror reached down his throat and choked him. All thoughts of Batiste, of his father, disappeared. With sudden, terrible certainty, he knew. He'd made a mistake.

Almost against his will, he had fallen in love with Lily Beecham—and he had wondered if he was strong enough to bear the emotional burden of it. Last night he'd told himself that he could do it. He no longer had to be impenetrable or impervious to emotion. He could allow himself to be vulnerable for her sake and the rewards would be more than worth the risk.

But he had never considered this. Watching that wretched old man bent double with grief, Jack felt his own heart crack open. Sheer, utter panic gripped him hard and shook him to his core. If he opened himself to her love, then he would be equally susceptible to pain as well. And pain such as this he had never witnessed, did not even know existed. It was more than he could handle, more than he could even contemplate. He would never survive such a loss.

He shook his head. He stared at a future that he could not face and he knew. This moment would remain with him for ever, imprinted indelibly in his mind. It would fester there, and grow. It would taint their life, their love. It would ruin their chance at happiness.

He needed to go. Needed to think. He cast a last, imploring look at Lily, begging silently for her forgiveness, and then he set down the tray with trembling hands and walked out.

Chapter Fifteen

A good deal of time passed before Lily could leave Mr
Bartleigh and go in search of Jack. Evening was falling again
as she searched fruitlessly through the inn and the gardens.
Her anxiety growing, she even peeked into the cottage, but he
was not there. Finally, she found him in the stables. A pair of
saddlebags lay propped against the wall and he was lugging
a saddle from the tack room.

'Jack?' she said sharply. 'What are you doing?'

Sadness etched in his face, he stared at her. 'I'm sorry, Lily.
I'm leaving.'

'Leaving? But—' She stopped herself. Her burden of grief
grew heavier as a sudden flood of anger added to it. 'Where
are you going?'

'Back to London.'

All of her pain and disappointment must have shown, for
he turned away. She struggled to find calm. 'It's too late to
shut me out, Jack. You're going to have to talk to me.'

'I'm sorry,' he repeated. 'I know that after last night you
must have expected me to stay, and that we have not had a
chance to talk.'

'No, we have not. I've been preoccupied,' she said with bitter irony.

He did not meet her gaze. 'While I have had plenty of time to think,' he said as he tightened his cinch. 'You spoke so eloquently last night of regrets and it was timelier than you knew.' He crossed back to retrieve a bridle. 'I haven't been able to get it out of my head.'

He regretted last night? Lily drew a deep, shuddering breath. This was what she had feared when she glimpsed the icy, carefully blank expression on his face earlier.

But he had seen her flash of emotion and at least partially interpreted it. 'No, I don't regret last night,' he said in a rush. He left the stall and crossed to take her hand. 'We were so... absorbed with each other and then today...' His voice trailed off. 'I did not get the chance to mention it to you, but we nearly caught Batiste. We had a good lead and he only just slipped away. Today I realised that for me—he is unfinished business. If I don't see this through, see him caught and punished and prevented from harming more people, then that would be my greatest regret.' He stopped and pulled her close. 'I'm sorry, but I can't—I won't feel free to pursue my own happiness until this job is done.'

Her anger was growing, solidifying into a solid, steadying mass. She glared and watched him hasten to throw up a wall of words between them.

'I know about your letters from Matthew, Lily.'

She stepped back, out of his arms. 'How?' she asked. She felt quiet, calm and quite deadly.

'Minerva let it slip. Don't hold it against her—she did not mean to do it. But I want you to know, I'm not going to ask you to betray your cousin. I'll find another way. I'll comb through every ship's log in the Latimer Shipping offices, I'll camp out in front of the First Lord of the Admiralty's doorstep, by God I'll beg a ship off of Mervyn, if I have to, and track him down and bring him in myself.' He heaved a sigh. 'And then I'll be back.'

Disappointment rose up from the deepest pits of Lily's soul. Wrath came close behind. He was doing it again. Jack was creating barriers, telling lies. Except this time, she could not tell if he lied only to himself or to her too. 'You've got it all worked out, don't you?' she asked quietly. 'All wrapped up tight and neat in a logical little package.'

'Lily?'

'I don't believe you, Jack.' Her voice rang out, harsh sounding. She hardly recognised it as her own.

'You don't believe me?' He sounded as if he could hardly believe her.

'You *are* just like my mother—just as I suspected. You are using the world's ills to keep from confronting your own.'

'Lily, I—'

But she stopped him with an abrupt gesture. Eyeing him coldly, she said, 'Do you know? I think I am going to give you just what you deserve, Jack Alden. I'm going to give you exactly what you think you want.'

He took a step back. 'What do you mean?'

'I'm going to take you to my cousin, Matthew.'

Suddenly his entire demeanour shifted. 'You know where he is?' he asked eagerly. 'He's told you?'

'I do. But you must promise to keep him safe.' She waited a moment, and then huffed impatiently. 'Promise me, Jack!'

'I do promise. I will do my best to protect him.' He was all earnestness and anticipation now. 'They only wish to question him, you know. He should be fine.'

'Then I will take you to him,' she said with disdain. 'With any luck he will know where your Batiste is.'

'Thank you, Lily,' he breathed. His eyes were alight.

'I want you to find Batiste, Jack. Take him in, watch him hang. Do what you think is so very important to you. And when he is gone and you find that your demons still haunt you—I hope that then you will finally remember all that I've told you.' She spun on her heel and marched away. Without stopping she spat over her shoulder, 'Just know that by the time you finally reach that point, it may be too late.'

Against Jack's will and Mrs Babbit's protestations, Lily arranged to have one of the inn's mounts ready for her as well. 'If I don't go, you don't go,' she said stubbornly.

'But what of Mr Bartleigh?' Jack asked.

The exhausted, grief-stricken man had folded in the face of her vehemence. 'He does not need me to travel with him. His arrangements will be complete tomorrow and he can head home. I'll be back there in plenty of time for the services.'

Jack sighed and shot her a look of resignation. 'Where are we going?'

'I'll tell you when it is too late to turn back,' Lily said grimly.

She swung up, refusing to give way to her own weariness, allowing her anger and her determination to be done with this once and for all to keep her straight in her saddle.

Jack must have suspected when she took the road heading south and west, but they rode in dismal silence for several hours before he spoke.

'He's at your home, then?'

Lily merely nodded. 'If he's not there now, then he soon will be.'

'How long before we reach it?'

'We'll get there by daybreak.'

'You mean to ride all night?' He looked at her with disbelief.

She shot him a scornful glance. Her brow raised as she ran

a disparaging look down the length of him. 'If you cannot keep up, then I'll welcome you when you get there.'

There it was again—that smile. *Her* smile. The one that played around the edges of his mouth when she did something to amuse him. It made her want to weep.

'Let's go then,' he said. 'Totton is just ahead. We'll change horses there.'

It was a long and miserable ride, though Lily would have died before admitting it. Grief and sorrow made for dreadful travelling companions. Her dear friend was gone and Jack was running scared. He'd become spooked and closed himself off again and Lily wanted to scream her frustration to the universe.

Only her righteous sense of anger kept her on her horse and moving. Anger, and a heartfelt determination that she was done trying to please the unappeasable, convince the unconvincible. She'd determined to break that pattern with her mother and she did not plan to begin it with Jack. He would come to her with an open heart, ready to share all that life had to offer—both good and bad—or she would not have him.

Dawn had arrived, the sun heralded by a riotous sky, when they finally reached Weymouth. Any pleasure she might have felt at her homecoming had been muted. Instead she only felt empty and resentful. Jack, on the other hand, looked the picture of anticipation; he'd perked up further with every mile they'd ridden.

At last they reached her home—a sprawling, two-storeyed farmhouse constructed of ancient, weathered stone. Without waiting, Lily jumped down from her horse, leaving him for Jack to attend to, and hurried inside. The housekeeper met her in the wide entryway, her steps echoing on the flagstone floor, her keys jangling at her side as always.

'Miss Lily,' the woman exclaimed with surprise. 'I can

scarce believe it is you! We had no idea of your coming.' She bobbed a quick curtsy and, smiling, looked beyond Lily towards the door. 'Is your dear mother with you?'

'No, Mrs Tilbury,' Lily said wearily. 'Mother is still on her tour. She—' Before she could get any further she was tackled bodily from the side.

'Lilikins!' a shout rang out.

'Ohh,' she gasped. 'Matthew!' Her cousin lifted her up and began to spin her around, whirling her until her feet flew out behind her, just as her father used to do. 'Have you gone mad?' she croaked. 'Let me down!'

The housekeeper smiled at their antics. 'I'll just go on back to...' She paused and directed a look at Matthew. 'To the kitchen. I'll send one of the men out to fetch your things, Miss Lily. You just go and catch up with your cousin.'

'Thank you, Mrs Tilbury,' Matthew said. He turned to Lily with a huge smile on his face. 'I'm so glad you came. I was so afraid you would not make it before we had to...' His smile faded away and he let her slide to the floor. Lily followed his gaze and saw Jack framed in the front door. 'Who is this?' Matthew asked. She could feel the sudden tension in his arms.

'Matthew, this is my...friend, Mr Alden.'

Her cousin sketched a quick bow in Jack's direction. 'Forgive me,' he said. 'I didn't expect anyone other than my aunt to arrive with Lily.'

'Mother is still travelling, but she is due back in London any day now.' She laid a gentle hand upon her cousin's arm. 'I brought Jack because he knows about Batiste, Matthew.'

Her cousin recoiled in shock, before casting a look of resentment and betrayal on her. 'They got to you already? I'd hoped you'd keep my secret, if only for the sake of our old fondness for one another.'

'He wants to help you,' she responded quietly. 'I would not have brought him, otherwise.'

'I am not with the ministry, nor with the American government either.' Jack stepped in. 'I'm after Batiste. I want to see the bastard hang.'

Matthew sucked in a deep breath. 'Well, then, that's a different kettle of fish.' He grasped Lily's hand. 'I'm sorry, cousin, it's just that—well, can we sit somewhere and talk? I've a long story to tell.' He shot a curious look at Jack. 'And I think I'd like to hear yours.'

The three of them trooped to her front parlour, which Lily was glad to see sparkled and shone just as it always did. They each chose a seat somewhat equidistant from the others. Lily glanced uncomfortably from one of the men to the other.

Matthew leaned forwards and addressed Jack. 'Will you tell me how you got mixed up with that devil?' he asked. He raised a brow at Lily. 'Then I'll make my own explanations. A confession of my sins is the least I owe you.'

So Jack began by explaining his connection with Lord Treyford, his betrothed, Chione Latimer, and the rest of her family. Lily saw an immediate reaction from her cousin as he spoke.

'Latimer, you say?' He squirmed a little in his seat. 'I know the name. I heard Batiste ranting over a Mervyn Latimer more than once in my dealings with him. He's got a powerful grudge against the man.'

'Powerful indeed,' Jack agreed. 'He kidnapped Mervyn and held the old man captive for nearly a year and a half.'

Matthew scrubbed a hand over his mouth. 'Kept him locked up on his ship, did he?'

'Yes.' Jack stared at her cousin. 'How could you possibly know that?'

'Did he kill the man?'

'No,' Jack answered. 'But it was a near thing.'

With a sigh of relief, Matthew rose. He paced to the window and back again, one hand at his temple, the other braced on his hip. 'Oh, Lord,' was all he said.

'What is it?' Lily asked, fearing the answer.

Her cousin turned decisively. 'I built the prison cell the man was kept in.'

'Matthew!' Lily exclaimed in horror.

Jack, however, remained calm. 'Just how did that come about?'

Matthew sat again and hung his head in his hands. 'I was a damned fool, that's how.' He looked up at Jack. 'The bastard crimped me!'

'Ahh,' Jack said knowingly.

'What?' Lily asked. 'Crimped? What is it?' She looked at Jack in confusion.

'It used to be a common enough practice—back when slave-ship captains had difficulty finding a full crew for their ships. They would make an arrangement with a certain tavern, then they would lure in boys and men, get them roaring drunk, and then either cheat them at cards or in some other way convince them to sign an article of debt. To pay off the debt, the men would be forced to serve as crew on the slave ship.'

'How horrible!'

Jack looked thoughtfully at her cousin. 'I gather they did not want you as crew, though.'

'No.' Matthew sighed. 'Batiste wanted me to make alterations to his ships.'

'Prison cells? Did you not wonder at such a thing?'

'That was not what he asked for at first. The first job was on one of his merchant ships. He had me alter the cargo hold— disguise a section of it that he could use as a slave deck.

I had to build it small, and be sure it could be easily disguised and quickly hidden with supply casks.'

'But the slave trade has been abolished,' Lily said, bewildered.

'Yes, the trade of slaves has, in England and her empire,' Matthew said. 'The fine for slaves found on board is as high as one hundred pound per head. He was tired of risking his profits or losing any chance of them by tipping the poor people overboard.'

'What?' Lily suffered a childish urge to cover her ears, to block out the picture of such evil. 'He's a monster,' she breathed.

'The Americans have banned the import of new slaves. All that has done is raised their value. Plenty of them are still bought and sold in the slave markets over there,' Matthew explained. 'Men are getting rich growing cotton in the southern states. Batiste said there were plenty of planters willing to circumvent the law and pay a large price for able bodies.'

'And the prison cell?' urged Jack.

'That was a later job. On his own *Lady Vengeance*. A cell, he wanted, small, for one person. Well ventilated, as it might be used for some time, and watertight and secure. By that time, I knew what sort of man Batiste was and realised the trouble I'd got myself into. I knew I had to run. The villain was never going to forgive my debt. He'd wait until he was done with me and then I had no doubt he'd have one of his men slit my throat.'

Lily raised a shaking hand to her mouth.

'I bided my time and made my plans. I knew I was going to have to give up my business, start over somewhere with a new name, but it was my only hope. By this time, I had free run of the ship, coming and going as I needed to get tools and supplies.'

'The American government has already pieced together much of your story,' Jack said. 'But they said you did something to anger him greatly. He apparently ranted and raved about getting vengeance on you, but they could not discover what it was you had done. In fact, at first they thought you were dead. Later they heard different—someone let it spill that you had run.' He looked thoughtfully over at her cousin. 'What did you do, to anger him? It wasn't just that you skipped out on your debt, was it?'

'No.' Matthew glanced towards the door. 'Will you wait here? I have something to show you.' He left the room in a hurry.

Lily stood and began to pace the room. She could not believe that she'd been wrong, that Matthew truly had done the things Jack had inadvertently accused him of. She wanted to weep, to hide away from both of the men who had stripped her of her illusions. Finally stopping at the window seat where she'd loved to read as a child, she sank down and gazed out over the drive and the circular patch of garden in the middle. She stiffened a little as Jack approached her from behind.

'If it makes you feel any better,' he said, 'I think the Americans have sympathy with his plight. If he tells them his story and answers their questions, then I believe they will release him right away.'

Lily nodded her head and fought back tears. So much sadness. And temptation, too. Jack stood close behind her. She could almost feel his heat. She turned to drink in the sight of him. So beautiful, with his dark, earnest eyes and his unruly mop that begged for her taming fingers. All she wanted to do was hurl herself in his arms and beg him to stay with her. But she knew he would not.

She stood as the door opened behind them. Looking over his shoulder, she saw Matthew come just a step into the room. His face shone full of anticipation.

'You asked how I angered him?' he asked Jack. 'The answer is simple. I took something that belonged to him.' He opened the door and nodded encouragingly. A very lovely, obviously pregnant Negro lady stepped into view, her gaze darting nervously around the room.

'I'd like to present my wife.'

Lily's legs trembled. She sat down hard again on the window seat.

Chapter Sixteen

'This is Anele,' Matthew said after both Lily and her new cousin had been seated comfortably in the middle of the room again. Lily smiled at the girl and she shyly returned the gesture.

'Anele and her sister were captured by a rival tribe and sold as slaves. One of Batiste's captains bought them and brought them to Charleston. I'll spare you the more horrific details of the voyage,' Matthew said with a glance at Lily. 'But though the women were allowed to roam the decks free during the day, they were at the mercy of the crew. They had little food and no hope. Anele's sister did not fare well. She was weak when they arrived in the Carolinas and Batiste decided to keep them both for a while—for his own personal use.'

Lily shuddered. Jack sat beside her and took her hand.

'I found her one day, lying sobbing in a passage on the *Lady Vengeance*. She was chained, wrist and ankle, to her sister. Her dead sister. Batiste had been called away and had not bothered locking her up, because where was she going to go chained to a corpse?'

Tears started to flow and Lily was helpless to stop them.

She gestured for Matthew to continue and accepted the hand-kerchief that Jack offered.

'What could I do?' asked Matthew. 'You would not have wanted to see her then, Lily. She was wasted away, bruised. She could hardly stand, let alone walk. I was running anyway, I decided to get her away, too. I used my tools to break her shackles and I sneaked her off the ship.'

Jack nodded his approval. 'It could not have been easy.'

'No. It upset all my plans. But I went to a friend and he hid us in his warehouse for a few weeks, until Anele was stronger and able to travel. We've been in hiding and on the run ever since.'

'I'm so glad you saved her,' Lily said.

'I hired myself on as ship's carpenter to get us passage to France. I thought we could make a life there, where Anele would be more accepted. We were happy and settled in Le Havre for a while, but not long ago we spotted one of Batiste's men and I panicked. I didn't know where else to go, so we came here.'

'Just as you should have,' Lily told him. 'You will be safe here.'

'But Matthew should come with me,' Jack interrupted. 'It's more important than ever that we find Batiste. You two face the same sort of danger from his twisted outlook that Trey and Chione do. The man is sick. If he can harm you, he will.'

Matthew looked uncertain. 'What do you want me to do?'

'Talk to the Admiralty and the Americans. Tell them every-thing you can remember about Batiste and his men. Everything they ever said, every place they ever mentioned. I will speak for you. If you co-operate, I'm sure they will let you go in peace.'

Matthew shared a long glance with his wife. 'I suppose I'll have to do it,' he said slowly. He squeezed her hand. 'It's our only chance to live without fear.'

*   *   *

It was soon arranged. Lily lent them her father's travelling carriage and the two men were loading and preparing to leave the next morning. Lily hauled out a large basket of food that Mrs Tilbury had packed. Jack caught her as she set it in place. He locked her in a tight embrace and they stood, silent for several long moments.

'I will be back, Lily.'

She closed her eyes and did not answer.

'I hope you do not doubt me.'

She sighed. 'I'm not doubting your intentions, Jack. But I am wondering what will happen once Batiste is caught. Perhaps you will come straight back here. Or perhaps you will discover some other mission, something urgent and requiring all of your energy and focus. Something to enable you to avoid that with which you are not entirely comfortable.'

He winced. 'I suppose I deserved that.'

'You know I want you to return, more than I can say. But I am not willing to settle.' She looked up at him. 'These weeks since we met, they have been the best of my life, and the worst as well.'

He ran his hands up her back and pulled her a little closer. 'I understand.'

'I wanted a journey, and truly, I've had one. Though it has taken place in my head and my heart rather than on roads and highways, it has been the most important one of my life. And you helped set me on the path. Do you remember?'

His eyes narrowed, he shook his head.

'The day we met, you asked me what sort of woman I was. I didn't know the answer, and it frightened me more than I can say. But I've been thinking and learning and discovering that answer. What has been amazing and so wonderful is that each time I found a new piece of myself, I shared it with you.

Sometimes you laughed with delight, sometimes you frowned with concern, but each time you met it with acceptance and value. You've accepted and valued me. It's meant so much. You've been a catalyst and a help and the prize at the end, and for that I thank you.'

He laughed. 'You're the first to consider me a prize, Lily, but I'm glad to hear it.'

She did not return his smile. Indeed, she hoped that he could see the gravity and seriousness that had led her to take this step. 'You told me once that I did not know what it was that I asked of you, and I've discovered that you were right. One of the things I've discovered is that I need to share my life with someone whose heart is open, as well as his mind— I just had no idea what a rare commodity that is.'

His smile had faded. 'I'm trying, Lily.'

'I know you are, and I love you for it.' She snaked her arms around him and held him close, hoping he could feel all the love and longing in her heart. 'I've already spent too many years living with avoidance and silence, grief and guilt. I'm ready to leave all of that behind. I want to live my life with hope and joy and optimism. I want to share myself and I want someone who will share themselves as well.'

Her hands gripped his arms hard, and she swallowed against the most difficult words she'd ever had to speak. 'With all my heart and soul, I want that person to be you, Jack. But if you are not, then perhaps it is best that you don't come back.'

His face hardened. 'I think you are forgetting the pact we made several nights ago, Lily. You gave yourself to me, and in more than just the physical sense.'

'Yes, and you walked away. And now here you are, distancing yourself even farther. And I don't mean distance in miles. This trip is about more than Batiste and we both know it.'

'There might be consequences. If there are—'

'There will not be. It became certain this morning.' She sighed. She'd almost been disappointed, but it was better this way. 'It is for you to decide,' she whispered. 'You know I want you, I wish I could show you just how much. But I want all of you.'

He nodded. Something large and important loomed in his expression, but he didn't speak. Matthew approached from the house and they stepped away from each other. Lily ached as he walked away from her and climbed aboard. His face set, he sat silent, waiting as Lily said goodbye to her cousin.

'I explained it again to Anele, but she is emotional, as you can expect. Are you sure you will not mind her staying, Lily?' her cousin asked anxiously.

'Not at all. She is family, is she not?' Lily took Matthew's hand. 'You've chosen a difficult path. It won't be easy for Anele. Or for you.'

'I know,' he said, his voice hoarse. 'But I had no choice.'

'I'll do all I can to smooth the way for you both. I think Mother will, too. If naught else, you'll always have us.'

'Thank you.' He bowed his head.

'Now,' she said briskly. 'You go on. Mrs Tilbury and I will take care of your wife. The whole staff is already looking forward to the next addition to the family.'

Matthew kissed her cheek. 'Thank you. I'm sorry I involved you in all of this.'

'Don't be. It will all work out as it was meant to. You followed your heart and saved Anele's life. Now Jack will help you—and he is a paragon of logic and rationality. If the two of you combine your heart and head, then I believe that there is nothing that you cannot accomplish.'

Matthew climbed aboard and, without looking at her, Jack gave the signal for the driver to go.

A draining sense of fatigue crept over Lily as she watched

them drive off, stealing the breath from her lungs, the strength from her limbs. The thought that she might never see Jack Alden again paralysed her. She wanted to sink to the ground and cry out her despair and fear and loneliness. But she could not. She'd done the right thing, though it was no comfort to know it. She gathered the tattered shreds of her confidence and squared her shoulders. Then she slowly made her way inside and went to comfort her new cousin.

Chapter Seventeen

Sodden, Jack stood in the courtyard of the White Horse, trying to ignore the lowering notion that each drop of the pouring rain pounded him ever further into defeat. Before him, Matthew Beecham scrambled over the wet cobblestones, handing over his portmanteau to be loaded on to the Portsmouth-bound coach.

'I can't believe it, Jack,' Matthew called over the sound of the deluge. His manner was anything but defeated. 'Still, I just cannot believe my good luck.'

Jack forced a smile, trying to raise some enthusiasm. There were a few things he had difficulty believing, too, foremost being the fact that he was up and out at this ungodly early hour. Not far behind lay the sad fact that they'd been in London for nearly a fortnight and there had been no further news of Batiste.

Matthew had endured several days of close questioning in Whitehall. He'd been informed that he would be required to return to give testimony at Batiste's trial, but his name had been cleared. Mervyn Latimer had also come to town and talked at length. The Foreign Office now had quite a case built against Batiste; they just had no idea where he'd gone.

Matthew had manfully apologised for the part he had played in the old man's kidnapping.

'Ah, but I would consider you a victim of Batiste's greed as much as any of the rest of us,' Mervyn had said on hearing his story. 'And you more than made up for any mischief when you rescued your wife from his clutches.' The old adventurer had chuckled. 'I have to admit, you do good work. I tried to break out of there any number of times.'

Mervyn had been so impressed with Matthew, in fact, that he'd offered the man a job working for his shipping company. 'If you can outfit an entire ship as watertight and sound as that hellhole, then you'll save me hundreds of pounds per year,' he'd said, grinning.

Mervyn had left to return to Devonshire, taking Eli and Aswan with him. Matthew was heading to Portsmouth, happy to begin his new employment and planning to find a little house before fetching Anele to their new home.

'I can't believe my luck,' he said again.

Up on the top of the coach, the driver blew a blaring note on his horn, calling the passengers to embark.

'Time to load up,' Jack said.

Matthew held out his hand. 'Thank you, Jack. For everything.'

'It is I who should thank you, for having the courage to come forwards,' Jack said, shaking his hand. 'When you get to Weymouth, tell Lily I'll be there soon.'

'I will.'

Jack bid Matthew goodbye, then stood, staring after the coach long after it had gone, wondering if he'd spoken true. God in heaven, but he hoped so. His longing for Lily was a constant ache.

Around him men shouted and horses splashed through puddles. Dogs barked and women hurried through the rain, calling out in shrill, nervous tones. But jealous as he felt at the idea of Matthew returning to the woman he loved, still Jack did not move. Once he did, once he took a step away from this spot, he would be forced to face the awful truth; he would have to acknowledge the idea that Batiste might never be found.

He sighed and glanced towards the taproom. Perhaps a dram or two or ten would make that reality more palatable. He shook his head, knowing it would not even as he turned towards the door. Ah well, maybe a drink would warm his innards and ease the biting cut of frustration.

He noticed a gentleman standing to the side, under the inn's extended eaves. The man's gaze remained fixed on Jack as he approached and then he made a sweeping bow and moved to hold the door for him. Jack thanked him and noted the tall figure, the well-cut clothes and the fancy waistcoat with an elaborate fob. The man was older than he, his face brown and lined, his hair held back in an old-fashioned queue.

The gentleman fell in behind him and entered the taproom on his heels. As Jack headed for the scratched and scarred bar, the man stepped in close.

'Pardon the intrusion,' the stranger spoke with a slightly accented flair. 'But you have the appearance of a man who could do with a drink. I hope you will allow me?'

Jack shrugged and took a seat. His shadow perched beside him and called out for service. When the tapster shuffled from the back and slapped down two pints of ale, Jack raised his in thanks and drank deep of the bitter brew.

No one else occupied the room at this early hour. The pair of them sat in silence for several minutes.

'Was that the coach to Portsmouth that lately left?' the man asked companionably.

'It was. Did you mean to be aboard?'

'Not I. I do wish I had gotten here just a little earlier, though.'

'It's a daily run,' Jack said absently. 'You can have another go at it tomorrow.'

The gentleman smiled into his ale. 'I rather thought you were the one who meant to be on it. Forgive me for saying so, but you were staring after it as if it held your heart's most enduring desire.'

Jack flinched. The man hit uncomfortably close. He drank deep and tried to laugh the suggestion off. 'No, I merely stood there trying to decide if such a thing exists.'

'Oh, but of course it does.' The stranger's eyes glittered as he glanced over at Jack. 'Every man knows the thing his soul yearns for—even if he does not care to admit it.'

Jack set down his glass and stared at him. 'Do you truly believe that?'

'Without a doubt.'

'And do you have a secret yearning?'

The gentleman chuckled. 'Oh, I have many, and not one of them a secret.' He sighed. 'For a very long time I have known my greatest desire.' A hint of frustration crept into his tone. 'The difficulty is that I am not sure how to go about finding it.'

Jack brooded silently for several long moments. He could not imagine a more ridiculous conversation to be having with a complete stranger. And yet it fit so appropriately with the junction he'd reached in his life.

'Ahh,' the man breathed. He leaned in, oddly intent. 'I see that you have indeed discovered your greatest desire. But my question is—do you know where to find it?'

Jack stood. He tossed a coin on the counter and met the stranger's gaze. 'Weymouth,' he said simply. Shock blazed on the other man's face, and a bright flash of triumph, but Jack's eye was focused inwards. 'Yes,' he said, 'I rather think it is in Weymouth.'

He turned to go. The stranger reached out a restraining hand. He stared at Jack intently, his expression alight with an intensity as odd as the conversation they'd been having. His fingers dug into Jack's arm, and then abruptly, he let go. He nodded. Jack turned and walked out.

Jack stalked out of the courtyard and on to Piccadilly, heedless of both the steady rain and the relentless human traffic out in it. He'd reached new depths, sharing drinks and sentimental foolishness with strangers. And yet he had told the man nothing but the truth. His heart lay in Weymouth with Lily.

Then why the hell wasn't he there with her? That was the question, wasn't it? Why was he still here, worrying and fretting over a situation he'd done his best to resolve?

Because he was a damned fool. A damned childish fool. A passing carriage doused his boots with a splash of cold, murky water, but that was nothing next to the sudden dose of insight he was suffering.

He'd been shot—by a woman, no less—and the incident had triggered all of his old feelings of inadequacy. Jack knew he'd allowed the controlling, shadowy figure of Batiste to become mixed in his mind with his distant and disdainful father. But somehow he'd never understood that the idea of bringing Batiste to justice had become synonymous with justifying his choices, demonstrating his worth, proving himself a man.

Except that in trying to meet his father's standards, he'd betrayed his own. He'd forsaken logic and all rational thought. He'd acted like a volatile, scheming child, bent on achieving his own ends.

With a start, Jack realised that while his mind was treading new paths, his feet had taken him on the familiar route to Somerset House. On impulse he crossed the expansive courtyard and went in, travelling unerringly to the apartments of the Society for Antiquaries of London. He did not enter. Instead he stood in the corridor and delved even deeper into his soul, searching for the truth inside himself as he'd once sought knowledge inside those doors.

This place, together with his London rooms, had become his haven. Here he had come to find like minds, opportunities for intense study, and, most of all, respite from his father's contempt. But it was only more of the same, was it not? A place to build walls, to hide. He had arranged his entire adult life so carefully, manoeuvring neatly so he could avoid the harsh realities of his life.

Lily had opened his eyes, allowed him to see the extent to which he had secreted himself away. He had thought he had allowed himself to open up, but the truth was he had let her in and then slammed the door closed again. And at the first sign of trouble and heartache he had fallen right back into his old habits.

His quest to bring Batiste to justice had only been another barrier. He'd used it to keep from confronting his anger at his father and he'd used it to avoid the risks and fears that came with loving Lily too.

She'd been right. Oh, how Jack hated to admit it, but it was the truth. Even if Batiste had been in custody right now and on his way to the hangman's noose, all of his doubts and conflicts would still exist.

She was right about other things, too. It was time; time to grow up, time to let go. It was time and past that Jack Alden stopped hiding and fully entered the world.

Resolutely, he turned away. He left Somerset House, returned home and locked the door—and with blazing determination he did the single hardest thing he'd ever done in his life. He dropped his internal armour and let all of his suppressed feelings out. He allowed hurt, anger, fear and betrayal to wash over him. From childhood resentment, to his failure at the Egyptian Rooms, to the shameful way he'd left Lily Beecham, he examined scenes he'd laboured to forget and he faced his worst fears for the future. He ranted, railed and when he could contain himself no longer, he went back out into the streets and walked restlessly through the night.

With each step Jack beat his fury and frustration into the pavement. So long he had laboured to hide from the negative aspects of his life. But in reality all of those damaging emotions had burrowed inside him, fermenting, growing until there was no room for the affirmative, richer side of life. It was time he let them go. For hours he roamed the city, until his feet were tired and his soul felt empty and drained.

Then, at last, he returned home. He sat in front of the fire, watching the flames dance, and he tried to forgive, to allow peace and healing to take the place of hidden anger and thwarted longing. With all of his will and with the all of the yearning in his heart, Jack tried to become the man that Lily Beecham deserved.

Chapter Eighteen

'Enjoy your visit, dear.' Lily squeezed Anele's hand as they made their way up the short front walk. 'I've visits to make and these medicines to distribute. You'll have plenty of time for a proper goodbye.'

She smiled as Mr Bartleigh met them at the door and watched as Anele made her careful way inside. The separation from Matthew had been hard on the young woman. Lily's servants treated her kindly for Matthew's sake, but her tenants tended to view her with either awe or bland contempt. The local ladies had tut-tutted over the story of her ordeal, but had shown no inclination to invite her into their homes. Only with Mr Bartleigh had the girl struck up a friendship. Fresh from his own sorrow, he was sensitive to hers and he appeared grateful for the distraction. They had discovered that they shared a great love of music and spent hours teaching each other their native songs.

The first chords of the pianoforte followed Lily as she climbed back into her gig. She had several errands to run before they left for Portsmouth tomorrow. Matthew had written several times in the days since he and Jack had gone, but none of his letters had been more welcome to his wife than the one informing them of his new situation and asking her to join him there. There had been no word from Jack Alden at all.

Lily set off and told herself once more that it was best that way. A clean break was kinder, if Jack did not mean to return. Yet still she found herself fluctuating wildly between bleak despair and a vivid, uncontrolled hope. She tried not to pine as obviously as Anele, but she found herself eating little and sleeping less. As the days passed it became more difficult to keep from bursting into tears at odd moments. She sighed and sat straighter on the bench, eager to be done with the day's work. This trip to Portsmouth would be a welcome diversion.

It was evening before her visits were complete. Clouds gathered above, and the light was fading fast when Lily wearily turned the gig towards Weymouth once more. She had not travelled far when she came upon an abandoned farm cart alongside the road. Boxes and barrels were stacked in the cart, as well as other bulky goods covered by a large canvas, but she could see no sign of a driver. It wasn't until she carefully manoeuvred her gig past that she caught sight of the still form lying half in the ditch.

With a gasp she pulled to a stop and wrapped the reins. Looking helplessly up and down the quiet road, she scurried down and over to the fallen man. He breathed, thank goodness, but did not respond to her calling or nudging. Desperate, she shouted out, hoping someone would come to help.

No one appeared. She could see no sign of a wound or broken limb. He faced away from her, down into the ditch. It was impossible to tell who he was or how old he might be. Rather than roll his still, heavy form over, she scrambled around him, into the ditch. Her gown grew damp as she brushed his hair away from his face. To no avail. She had never seen him before.

She jumped as, without warning, his hand shot up and grasped her wrist where she touched him. Lily gasped in alarm and tried to withdraw, but the stranger reached over and captured her other wrist as well. 'I've got her,' he called, propping himself up on his elbows.

'Let go! What are you doing?' Lily struggled to get away. She hauled hard against him, twisting and trying to free herself, but the man's grip was iron, his expression implacable.

'Bring the rope,' he shouted.

There was a muffled response from the cart. Lily watched in horror as another man crawled from beneath the canvas and approached.

'Who are you?' she cried. 'What do you want?'

Neither answered. With grim efficiency the second man tied her wrists and hauled her from the ditch. He held her tight, despite her struggles, while the fallen man secured her ankles. No words were exchanged. Their unyielding silence and businesslike manner frightened Lily nearly out of her wits. Kicking, fighting, she screamed, as loud and long as she could, until her captor let loose the hand clamped over her stomach and clapped it over her mouth.

'Enough,' he growled.

'Where's the bottle?' the counterfeit victim asked.

'Still in the cart.'

'Dose her, then, and do it quick. You heard the orders. We've got to get back quick as we can.'

She panicked when the second man tossed her casually over his shoulder. She pitched and tried to throw herself off him, but he carried her to the cart as easily as he would a child. 'What are you doing?' she cried. 'What do you mean to do with me?'

And then she could see nothing as a thick white cloth came down over her face, covering her mouth and nose and eyes. A heavy, cloying scent stifled her until she was afraid she would choke on it. She strained, trying to rear back and away, but a hand held the fabric clamped firmly over her. Gradually her movements slowed, her limbs grew heavy and after a few minutes she had forgotten why she struggled.

Her mind drifted. Vaguely she felt a jolt as she was tossed into the cart and covered with the canvas. Shouldn't she be doing something? She concentrated. Oh, yes. She struggled to sit up, but the damp spots on her clothes distracted her. She felt the cold and discomfort intently, yet she felt strangely detached from everything else going on about her.

'She's a right tidy piece, that one,' she heard someone say, far away. 'Sure we can't delay the trip back a little?'

Someone else snorted. 'I busted a gut getting here in one day, and I'm turning about to make the same, damned miserable trip because Batiste said he wanted the girl in London before daybreak.'

Batiste, Lily thought idly. That name meant something… important. But her eyelids were so heavy.

'He didn't say nothing about leavin' her be,' came the sullen reply.

'Might be, but do you wanna mess about with a woman that he wants that quick and urgent? This is Batiste we're talking about. You do what you want, but leave me out of it. My bum might be swollen when we get back, but at least it'll be in one piece.'

The cart started up then, and the regular rocking motion lulled Lily, soothed her, until the blackness closed in and she drifted off to sleep.

'Be sure and tell the groom that I'm in a tearing hurry to leave. You know the address?' Jack passed his landlady's eldest son a coin and grinned at his eager expression. 'Tell him I'd like my rig here within the hour. Thirty minutes would better.'

The boy nodded and headed for the door. Jack watched him go, then turned to race back upstairs as quick as he'd come down. He'd slept the day nearly through, but he'd awakened feeling…light, eager. Perhaps even happy? More than ready, in any case, to get packed and on the way to Weymouth and to Lily.

'Mr Alden?' a hesitant voice called.

Jack turned and peered down over the railing. The street door had opened again and a man stood on the threshold.

'Mr Alden,' he said. 'Hello.'

'Yes?' The man looked vaguely familiar. Jack turned and started back down the stairs, but the gentleman had started up. They met on the first landing and Jack finally recognised him. 'Dr Arnott?'

'Yes,' the man said in relief. 'I'm glad you remember.'

'Of course! Please, come up and tell me what brings you from Greenwich.'

'No, sir, I do not mean to intrude and cannot stay. Two things, really, brought me.' The man carried a walking stick and nervously shifted it from hand to hand. 'I have to thank you so much for the donation that was made to our hospital. I know it came from your brother, but I also know you must have been behind it.' He reached out and shook Jack's hand. 'You must know we will put it to good use.'

'Of course, I expect no less. But tell me, how is Mr Crump? I hope he enjoyed the fruit I sent along?' Jack scrubbed a hand sheepishly through his hair. 'I confess, I've been meaning to come along for a visit before now…'

'That is the other reason I had to come. I'm sorry to tell you, sir, that Mr Crump passed on last night.'

Jack's heart fell. 'I'm very sorry indeed to hear that,' he said softly.

'I know he appreciated your kindness,' the doctor said.

'He thought of you, in the end. In fact, he asked me to pass a message on to you.'

'A message?'

'Yes.' The doctor frowned. 'He asked me to tell you that "He's back in London".'

Jack was puzzled. 'To be buried, you mean?'

'No, he was not referring to himself. That was the wording of the message. "He's back in London." I wondered if you would know who or what he meant.

Jack's heart stopped. 'Here?' he whispered.

'Mr Alden? Are you all right?'

Jack grasped the banister to steady himself. 'Batiste here? Now?' He'd finally unburdened himself, at long last let his past go, forced himself to recognise his obsession with Batiste as the avoidance it really was—and the man turned up now?

Frustration stabbed him, had him clenching his fists. He'd already kept Lily waiting too long. But this information could not be ignored. Batiste was still an evil, dangerous man and a real threat to Trey, Chione, Matthew, and who knew how many countless others. Jack's mind began to race. Much as he wished to, he could hardly leave London if Batiste was here.

Logic, long neglected, reared its head and kicked his grey matter into motion. He'd need to send the news to Devonshire straight off. Charles, he'd need Charles. The Admiralty should be notified straight away…

'Post!' A new voice, nasal and somehow familiar, interrupted his train of thought. The call echoed in the hallway and up the stairs. 'Did ye hear? This bloke's gone and ruined our surprise!'

From the shadows beneath the stairs stepped a familiar figure. Jack stared. The swarthy man he had fought in the East End grinned up at him, a pistol aimed squarely at his chest. 'And I was so looking forward to breaking the news to ye, Bookworm.'

'Mr Alden?' The doctor's voice wavered and Jack followed

his gaze almost directly upwards to the top landing. The giant Post glared down at them, a filthy bandage wrapped around one thick thigh, his cudgel in his hand.

'Don't ye worry none, guv. I'll forgive ye fer letting the cat out o' the bag,' the short one down below said. 'We been waitin' fer the chance to see yer friend again. It's him we want. Ye can just ease yer way down the stairs and out the door.' He gave a twisted grin, the pistol never wavering. 'Besides, I got me one more secret to tell.' He took a step closer to the bottom of the stairs, glanced about and spoke in a dramatic whisper. 'Batiste's got yer girl, Bookworm.'

A molten wave of fury twisted through Jack's gut. Logic died a final, painful death, swept away by raw hate and bleak determination. The thought of Anele and all that she had suffered ripped through him. By God, he'd almost ruined his relationship with Lily because of Batiste. There was no way in hell that he was going to let that bastard harm her further.

'Mr Alden?' Dr Arnott whispered again. He clutched Jack's arm and nodded his head towards Post. The man's massive form was gaining speed as he advanced towards them down the stairs.

The time for thinking and rationalisation was done. The situation called for decisive, immediate action. He cast about, looking for an advantage, anything to help. Hours of studying the ancients and their battle strategies had to count for something. But the Romans had touted the advantage of holding the high ground, and his opponent held that. He watched Post moving determinedly towards him and something clicked in his brain.

He braced himself against the railing in the middle of the narrow landing. As Post turned around the corner at a clip, Jack reached out, not for the cudgel, but for the giant's nearest arm. He gripped the man tight and swung him forwards, following the advice of ancient Oriental warriors and using the man's own momentum to propel him unexpectedly towards the next flight of stairs.

He'd caught Post by surprise. The man stumbled, continued forwards, but caught himself at the very edge of the top step. As he teetered there, on the brink of getting himself under control, Dr Arnott grasped the situation. He poked the behemoth sharply in the back with his walking stick.

Post went over. His feet flew out from beneath him and he went tumbling head over heels with a grunt and a great deal of thudding and thumping. He hit the hall floor hard and lay there in a great, sprawling heap.

'Post?' the swarthy man said with low urgency. 'Post!'

Jack heard a querulous cry from his landlady's rooms. In a moment his other opponent would collect himself and more innocent bystanders would arrive to complicate the situation. He had to act now. And now *he* held the high ground.

He reached out, snatched the doctor's cane and, turning, leaped on to the banister. Without pausing for even a breath, Jack launched himself straight down. The swarthy thug below still faced his fallen companion. He caught sight of Jack out of the corner of his eye, but it was too late. He fell beneath the outstretched walking stick and conveniently broke the worst of Jack's fall. His pistol skittered harmlessly across the hall.

'And I'll have you know,' said Jack as he straddled the villain and pressed the cane threateningly across his throat, 'I learned each one of those skills from a *book*.'

His only answer was an indistinct wheeze.

'My God, are you all right, Mr Alden?' Dr Arnott called over the railing.

'Fine, Doctor.' Jack had to fight down a panicked sense of urgency. 'Please come down here and retrieve that firearm before one of my landlady's children toddles out here and picks it up.' He did not wait for the doctor to comply, but turned to the man beneath him. 'Where is she?' Jack demanded.

The thug narrowed his eyes and grimaced through his pain.

Jack pressed the heavy stick tighter against his voice box. 'My brother is a viscount, did you know that, lowlife? Do you know what that means?' He leaned down to glare into his face. 'It means freedom. In short, I am free to do whatever it is I wish with you. I could shoot you now with your own pistol. I could cart you down to Brother Molly's and turn you over as the newest plaything for his particular clientele. No safe jail cell at the magistrate's office, no trial or chance for transportation. And no pesky questions or recriminations for me. Just you, and a permanent dunk in the Thames, should I so choose.'

The man's eyes had widened.

'Where?' Jack shouted. He eased up on the stick.

The thug snarled.

'Fine.' Jack gripped the staff with both hands and pressed it down mercilessly. 'Brother Molly's it is. But first I'm going to make damned sure you spend the rest of your short life as silent as your friend Post. Molly won't mind the mess. It's not the front of you his clients are interested in, in any case.'

Beneath the stick, the man choked and nodded his head. 'Little Bure Street,' he spat out when Jack raised it.

The need to hurry, to get to Lily, overwhelmed Jack. 'Come over here with that pistol, Doctor. And please see if the landlady can find you some stout rope. You'll want them both restrained before our friend over there wakes up.' He crawled off Batiste's lackey and strode for the door.

'But where are you going?' asked the doctor.

'My cabriolet will be along shortly. Please take it and fetch my brother. The boy accompanying it will know the address. Tell Lord Dayle I'll need him and any reinforcements he can round up in Little Bure Street. I cannot wait.'

'But I…' Dr Arnott protested.

Jack did not wait to hear. He was on the street and summoning a hackney before the doctor finished his sentence. He'd allowed the idea of Batiste to waste enough of his time, and Lily's. Batiste might have finally made his first mistake in returning to English shores. He'd made his last when he laid hands on Lily Beecham.

Chapter Nineteen

The ever-increasing clamour of aching bones and throbbing muscles pulled Lily awake. She moaned and forced her eyes open—and was tempted to close them again and pray for the return of oblivion.

She lay in an ungainly sprawl on a dusty, wooden floor. Slowly and with much effort, she rose to her knees, and after several joint-popping, agonising moments, she climbed to her feet.

They'd left her in the dark. The only light leaked from beneath a door just a few feet away. As her eyes slowly adjusted, Lily explored the room, hands outstretched, step by painful step.

It did not take many steps. She was in a small room, empty but for a rickety wooden chair along the back wall. She tried the door, but it was solid and firmly locked. She had no idea where she might be or how much time had passed while she slept. Thank heavens, though, she did not appear to be on board a ship.

Moving about eased her aches a little, and as her discomfort decreased, her thoughts began to churn. Her memory remained fuzzy, but she clearly recalled hearing her captors use Batiste's name. But what could he want of her? Perhaps to use her against Matthew? But if he had discovered enough to know of their connection, then surely he knew it was too late to prevent her cousin from bearing witness against him. Did he think to trade her for Anele? Or had he associated her with Jack Alden? Her head drooped in despair. Perhaps he only meant to kill her as an act of revenge against them both.

A scraping sound echoed in the small room, and with a start, Lily recognised the sound of a key in a little-used lock. Lily turned to face the door and tried to calm the frantic beating of her heart.

The door opened only wide enough for a head to poke in. It was the man who had lain in the ditch. Lily glared at him. He grinned and called out, 'She's awake.' Abruptly he shut the door once more.

Lily stood in the dark and fumed. She would *not* let her fear rule her. No matter what it was that Batiste and his lackeys wanted, she would thwart them in any way she could.

Mere minutes passed before the door swung open again. Light flooded the tiny room as the same man entered, this time carrying another chair and a large candelabrum. He ignored her complctcly as he set the chair down and placed the light upon it. He retreated once more, giving Lily only a moment to contemplate how she could make use of the heavy thing before he returned. This time he carried another chair, and this time he did not return alone.

Lily studied the man who strolled so casually into her prison. It must be Batiste, based on his air of supreme confidence alone. He was surprisingly small of stature, and looked a little older than she had expected. He had the grim, severe expression of a man who has lived hard and seen much. He returned her perusal, standing with his hands behind his back while his eye traced a leisurely path over her.

His minion withdrew. The sound of the door closing carried a finality that was reinforced by the reptilian smile on Batiste's face.

It struck Lily that he clearly expected her to be intimidated—and that he was looking forward to her reaction with some anticipation. She folded her arms. Fine, then. That would be the first thing she denied him.

'I'm afraid there has been a mistake,' she said, lifting her chin and getting the first word in. 'Please tell whoever might be behind this ridiculously botched manoeuvre that they have taken the wrong girl.'

Batiste's smile did not fade. 'You are Miss Lily Beecham, are you not?' he asked calmly.

'I am,' she replied in the same tone. 'And I have neither money nor jewels to offer you, nor a rich husband or family to ransom me.' She sighed. 'I'm afraid that you have all quite wasted your time. And mine.'

He pursed his lips. 'Oh, I think not,' he said softly. 'Do you know, I have heard that you are quite an intelligent girl, besides being a beauty?'

He waited, but she did not respond.

'Can you not hazard a guess as to who I am?' he asked with an ingratiating grin.

She raised a brow and let her gaze wander over him. She made sure to pause at the queue at his nape, and again at his elaborately embroidered waistcoat, set off by the slightly too-long cut of his coat. 'Someone too attached to the fashions of his youth? Other than that, I'm sure I could not say.'

His face remained blank. He circled around the extra chair and sat down. Carefully, his eyes fixed on her face, he spoke softly. 'I am Batiste.'

Lily raised her brows. 'Indeed?' she asked. She waited a long moment until impatience showed on his expressive face. 'Batiste?' She frowned in concentration. 'Oh, yes,' she said, glaring at him accusingly. 'You are the one! You caused my cousin Matthew to lose his business in America!'

He leaned back. 'On the contrary, Matthew Beecham stole something of great value from me.' He paused. 'I wonder, do you know where she is?'

Lily stared. 'She? She who?' She waited just a beat. 'I knew it! I knew you had taken the wrong woman! Who was it that you *meant* to abduct?'

Batiste gaped at her. Then he scowled ferociously. He stood and began to pace back and forth in the tiny room. 'No, this cannot be,' he said, low and furious. 'Jack Alden is by all accounts a brilliant man—he came close to besting me, for God's sake! Surely he would not waste his time on such a—'

He stopped and subjected her to another long examination. Suddenly his brow lightened. 'Oh, but you are good, my fair one.' He laughed. 'Almost, you convinced me that I had made a grave miscalculation.' His expression hardened. 'But I have matched wits with greedy tribal chiefs and wily Egyptian *kashifs*. You, my dear, don't stand a chance.'

Lily stared. 'I do not understand you at all,' she complained. 'You speak in riddles.'

'Then let me explain.' His voice had grown hard. 'Your cousin may have made himself into a thief and an informer, but for all that, he is a mere thorn in my side. I crush men like Matthew Beecham daily, without trouble or remorse. But your Mr Alden, he has become a larger problem altogether.'

Batiste ceased his pacing and approached her. Lily fought to keep from cringing as he reached out and stroked a stray lock of her hair. 'For nearly a score of years,' he said in a near whisper, 'I have sought information about a treasure of immense value. So close, I came, to obtaining the key, the last

clue I needed to find the Pharaoh's Lost Jewel. Mr Alden, it
turns out, played a large part in keeping it out of my hands.'

He spun away. 'And if that were not enough, now I find
that he was behind the ridiculously close call I recently had
with the Royal Navy. For years I have gone about my business
with my head down. A few coins paid to the right people here
and there and I have been free to carry on without worry. No
longer. Now I find my capture has become a top priority and
that I have Mr Alden to thank for this as well.' He turned back
to face her, his eyes filled with deadly intent. 'That is far
more insolence than I have had to face from any man in a very
long time. I have had enough. I have come back to England
to cut the head off this snake that threatens my every step. And
I shall at last obtain the information I need to seek out the Lost
Jewel.' He smiled at her, and Lily felt the malice contained in
him down to her toes. 'And you, my sweet, devious darling,
are exactly what I need to achieve both of these goals.'

Lily cringed inside. The man was truly insane. Jack had
been right all along. Batiste must be stopped. But how—

She stopped. A commotion sounded somewhere outside of
the room. Not close, but loud.

Batiste had heard it as well. 'Joss!' he called. He strode to
the door. 'Withers?' He opened the door, but Lily could see
nothing except a darkened hallway beyond. The madman
turned back to her and grinned. 'Come, my dear. The game
has begun.'

The large purse Jack had tossed to the hackney driver had
done the trick. The man broke every rule of traffic etiquette
and caused at least one accident, but he got Jack to the East
End in record time.

Jack asked to be let out a good way up Little Bure Street.
The busy day was ending in the dockside neighbourhood. Fat,

well-satisfied merchants strode along with burly stevedores and ink-fingered counting clerks, all eager to reach home or the local chop house or tavern. Jack brushed past them all. Unthinking, he'd carried the doctor's walking stick with him. He tightened his grip on the thing and wished he'd been carrying his knife when that pair of thugs had showed up. He vividly recalled his last trip to this destination, but this time a far greater danger than a wary Eli awaited him.

He approached the narrow alley with caution. The height of the surrounding buildings had cast it into near darkness already. Jack lingered a moment at the corner, straining to hear any hint of a sound.

There it was: footsteps, and a low murmur of voices. Jack braced himself, raised his stick—and slumped when two lightskirts emerged arm in arm into the light.

One of them, a garish redhead with a brightly painted mouth, eyed him and the cane up and down. 'If you're the business they turned us down to tend to, then we're well out of it,' she remarked.

Her companion, an older brunette with dark shadows under her eyes, sniffed. 'Still, they had no need to be hateful about it.'

'Sorry, ladies, I did not intend to frighten you,' Jack apologised.

The redhead glanced at him hopefully. He shook his head and she sighed. 'Come on, then,' she said to her friend. 'We got to find a bawdy house that'll take us.' She sighed. 'My feet hurt.'

'Just how many of them were in there?' Jack called quietly after them.

'Jest the two acid-tongued devils—leastaways, that's all that was in the front rooms.'

Jack watched as the pair turned towards the river. His mind ranged ahead, recalling the bare, cobbled courtyard that opened at the end of the alley. A diversion would be extremely helpful. What was it the ancient Chinese proverb said—something about starting a fire to rob a house? He shrugged. The ancients had not led him wrong yet today. He ran the few steps after the pair of prostitutes.

'Ladies!'

They turned around.

'I can't help you get into a bawdy house, but I'll give you each a fat purse and the chance to get your own back against those two, in exchange for a little help.'

The pair exchanged grins.

'It is not my fault!' screamed the redhead. She stumbled out of the dark alley and into the small open courtyard that housed Batiste's old offices.

''Tis, I tell ye!' yelled the brunette, following her. 'And that be my scarf ye've got wrapped round yer chicken neck—give it back!' She reached out and grabbed hold of the bright cloth.

'It's mine!' the redhead shrieked. She held on and the two of them engaged in a loud, raunchy tug of war. 'It's yer fault if 'tis anybody's—ye've got bags under yer eyes as big as rats—and twice as big as yer bubbies!'

'Oh, ye evil baggage!' A resounding slap echoed against the close walls. Jack, pressed up against the building that housed Batiste's old offices, tensed as the door opened and two men came out to watch the show. Laughing, they stepped out on to the small landing and leaned on the iron railing.

Jack flattened himself even further and crept up the stairs behind them. When he reached the landing, he swung the walking stick hard and knocked the closest man over the rail and on to the cobbled yard below. The two prostitutes screeched like harpies and fell on him, hauling his arms and legs behind him to be tied with the long scarf.

Jack was left to deal with the remaining lackey. This one did not seem the least perturbed by the fate of his comrade. He grinned evilly, and fists clenched, beckoned Jack to come on.

Jack obliged him. He gripped his stick tight and swung, trying to repeat his earlier success and knock his opponent down the stairs. But this adversary had more experience. He ducked under the swing and closed in, burying his fist in Jack's gut.

Jack dropped his stick. Bent double, he had no chance to acknowledge the pain. From inside the decrepit offices came a call, clear and heavy with a note of command. There was no time for any of this. Jack had to get to Lily.

But his opponent had heard the shout as well. It distracted him for the instant that Jack needed. Reaching deep, he drew on every lesson on fighting dirty his brothers had ever given him. He swung hard and true and delivered a crippling wallop to the man's kidney. The man gasped, and then turned just in time to meet Jack's next swing right on the jaw. His head jerked and he fell back, slumping slowly along the railing to the hard landing floor.

The lightskirts cheered. Jack flashed them a weak grin and shook out his hand. His newly healed arm screamed in protest of such abuse. 'Can you watch these two?' he asked, picking up the fallen cane.

'Aye, you go on.' The redhead nodded. Her mouth twisted bitterly. 'I'm good with knots.'

The last thing Jack heard, as he turned to enter the building, was her remark to her friend. 'Did ye know, in some houses they pay ye good to tie the blokes and beat them?'

Chapter Twenty

Batiste's grip bit cruelly into Lily's arm. He dragged her, slow and careful, into the hall. They travelled past several closed doors and turned left. Ahead, Lily could see dim light shining. The sounds of a scuffle grew louder as they approached the light at the end of the hall, and then the noise abruptly ceased.

'Quiet, girl,' Batiste said in a savage murmur. 'It would appear I am going to have to deal with this nuisance myself.'

He slowed as he approached the end of the hall, tugging her close as he edged into an anteroom at the front of the building. It was filled with only a broken table, a chair or two and the pervasive dust. But even as she gazed around the door opened and Jack Alden rushed in.

The sound of the cocking gun sounded eerily loud in the small room. Lily gasped as the cold muzzle dug into her jaw.

'Good afternoon, Mr Alden,' Batiste said in politely formal tones. 'How very resourceful you are. I admit I fully intended to meet you again before the day was out, but these were not the circumstances I envisioned.'

'My God…' Jack faltered, seemingly shocked. 'You! It was you at the White Horse, chattering on about hearts' desires.'

'Get rid of your weapon, Mr Alden.' He shifted the muzzle of his gun so it rested directly beneath Lily's chin. She stared, terrified, into Jack's eyes.

He cursed and tossed a stout cane aside. It clattered to the floor a few feet away.

'Ah, thank you,' Batiste said mildly. 'Yes, I must also thank you for your frankness the other day. What a stroke of luck that conversation proved to be. I fully intended to grab you then and there, but I confess, I had worried that you would prove stubborn as well as resourceful. You've shown such tenacity in your pursuit, I feared that not even my men would be able to persuade you to give me the information that I want from you.' He smiled affably. 'But things worked out so much better than I had hoped. You gave me the weapon I needed to convince you. And now here we are—I have what your heart desires most and you hold the information I need to find what mine desires most.' He ran the cold steel along Lily's jaw in a revolting caress. 'Shall we trade?'

'Don't listen to him, Jack,' Lily said tightly. 'He means to kill you.'

Batiste gave her a shake. 'I will kill *her* if you don't tell me what Mervyn Latimer found in that coffer. Where is Treyford travelling to? Damn it—where is the Lost Jewel?'

An indescribable weariness washed across Jack's expression. 'I cannot believe that I actually owe you anything resembling thanks, Batiste, but it is true. What you said at the White Horse held more truth than you realise. I thought all I needed was to bring you to justice, but I was wrong. There is only one thing I need.' His gaze held Lily's and she knew. Despite the dire circumstances, her heart swelled and great, unshed tears collected in her eyes. 'I nearly walked away from it to follow a twisted obsession,' Jack said. 'I nearly turned myself into you.'

Through her watery gaze, she saw his attention turn back to Batiste. 'Let her go now. The Jewel does not exist. It is over.'

Batiste laughed, but it was an ugly, desperate attempt. 'It is *nearly* over, boy. The Jewel does not exist,' he spat. 'God, I hate to say it, but Mervyn Latimer is a genius. He may have duped you, but I have laboured for nearly twenty years in search of the Jewel. Do you think I would give it up on the word of a besotted fool? It has been a long and difficult journey. I have been tested time and again. You—' He shook his head. 'You are the last obstacle I must breach.' He moved the gun to Lily's temple. 'Tell me!' he shouted.

Jack stared long and hard at Lily. His jaw clenched. In an agony of fear and longing, she stared back.

Jack sighed. 'It's in Devonshire,' he said simply.

'Jack, no!' Lily cried.

'Shut up, girl!' Batiste pushed her violently away. She struck the listing table, stumbled and fell.

Batiste turned the gun on Jack. 'Devonshire?' His voice had gone eager and unnervingly possessive. 'Do you mean that Mervyn has it already? It cannot be. Tell me what you mean!'

He advanced, but Jack merely spread his hands. 'The Jewel is not what you think. It is not a jewel at all, nor an ancient collar nor even a map, as has been theorised. It is something altogether different and unexpected.'

Batiste stepped closer. 'Yes, what—?'

He never finished his question. Jack's foot shot out and kicked the firearm from his grasp. Batiste's roar of rage was cut short as Jack's fist caught him in the nose.

The villain stepped back. He actually laughed. 'Fine, then, we'll do it the hard way. But rest assured that I will kill you slowly.' He pulled a curved blade from his waistcoat. 'I will carve you into pieces and there will be plenty of time for you to tell me what I want to know before you die.' Almost before he had finished speaking he rushed, his knife poised with deadly intent.

Jack danced back. On hands and knees, Lily crept along the wall, trying to reach the castaway pistol. Batiste must be stopped, before he harmed Jack, before he continued to destroy others in his self-serving madness. For all of their sakes, this had to end now—even if she had to shoot the bedlamite herself.

But Batiste had doubled his assault, fighting with the ease of long practice. Lily could scarcely credit how fast and cleverly he handled his blade. Jack was younger and quick on his feet, but unarmed and clearly at a disadvantage. Batiste surged suddenly forwards, delivering a vicious slash, low and quick. Jack staggered. Lily gasped as a thin red slice opened across his midriff.

Desperate, she turned again to find the gun. It had slid beneath an overturned chair. She strained to reach it, brushed the polished handle with her fingertips. There! She grasped it and pulled it free. With shaking hands, she held it tight and climbed to her feet.

But Jack had recovered. He stood his ground as Batiste pressed his next attack. He dodged a sharp thrust and feinted one of his own. Instinctively, Batiste lunged back, helped along with a well-timed swipe of Jack's boot. The villain lost his footing, tried frantically to regain it, and stepped squarely on the discarded walking stick. His feet flew out backwards; he crashed to the ground, automatically throwing his hands forwards to break his fall.

Batiste had not let go of his blade. Too late, he tried to rotate out of harm's way. Lily grimaced and closed her eyes against the sight as he fell straight on to his own knife, gave a massive jerk and died.

Jack's shoulders slumped. His breath came in ragged gasps and he struggled to regain control. It was over. Thank God, it was over at last. He pressed a hand against the cut on his belly and glanced over at Lily, hoping to share his elation and relief and sorrow. But her eyes were closed. She swayed on her feet, her complexion gone stark white against the subtle fire of her hair.

'Lily!' He leaped over to her, took the pistol from her shaky grasp and gathered her gently into his arms.

She clung to him. 'Oh, Jack—I am so sorry! You were right all along and I did not believe you, refused to understand—'

'No, no. All the apologies are mine to make. Hush now,' he soothed her as she trembled against him. 'Come, let's get you out of here and into the fresh air.'

Before they had taken a step a great noise rose up outside. Shouts and the echo of many footsteps rang loud in the court-yard. His heartrate ratcheting, Jack thrust Lily behind him as someone pounded up the steps and thrust open the door.

'Charles!' he exclaimed in relief.

'Fisher!' Lily exclaimed in surprise.

A multitude of footmen, groomsmen and a few men Jack had never seen before crowded behind the two. Charles took a good look around and then took instant command. 'Several of you search the back. Bring back anyone you find. The rest of you help the uh…ladies…outside with their burdens and keep anyone else from entering that damned alley.' He turned to his brother, 'You might have left us a sign. Do you know how many alleys there are off Little Bure Street?'

Jack scrubbed a hand through his hair. 'Sorry, this is not my area of expertise.'

Charles laughed. 'Little brother, judging by the trail of criminals you left in your wake, I'd say you were an expert.' He sobered and nudged the body on the floor with his foot. 'Batiste?' he asked.

Jack nodded.

'Then I'd say you were an expert who's done the world a

favour.' His voice gentled and he extended a hand towards Lily. 'Miss Beecham, our mother is waiting anxiously for you.' He chuckled. 'I nearly had to tie her down to keep her from coming along.' He took her hand and pulled her towards the door. 'I have a closed carriage waiting for you.'

'Thank you.' She sighed.

'I think I should warn you that word has come that your own mother is due in at any time.' He grinned. 'Let's just hope that you make it to Bruton Street before she does.'

'Oh, heavens, yes.' Lily took his brother's hand and allowed him to start to lead her away, but she cast a lingering glance back Jack's way.

'Wait,' he protested.

'Oh, I'll clean up your mess, Jack,' Charles said with exaggerated patience. 'You go along with her.' He shot Jack a pitying look. 'You've got some explaining to do.'

Jack stepped up to Lily's side. 'Truer words were never spoken.'

A considerable amount of time passed before Lily found herself settled into the carriage. There were a multitude of questions to be answered and assurances to be given. Hugs were exchanged, a few tears were shed, and she and Jack made a point to personally thank everyone who had been involved in Batiste's end and her rescue.

Now, at last, the two of them climbed into the coach. Fisher made a half-hearted protest, offering to send a footman along for propriety's sake, but Charles firmly shushed him and shut the door. With a clap on the side of the carriage and a shout to the driver, he sent them off.

It took only a moment for Jack to compose himself. Lily watched as he drew a deep breath. When he opened his mouth to speak, she held up a restraining hand.

'Wait. I have just one question.' She leaned forwards, suddenly terribly self-conscious of her dirty face, rumpled gown and dishevelled hair. But there was too much at stake to let such things stop her now. 'Is it true? Did you tell Batiste that I was your greatest desire?'

Jack laughed. 'Oh, Lord, Lily. Trust you to get to the heart of the matter.' He leaned in as well, until their faces nearly met in the centre. Lily breathed in the heady, masculine scent of him as his breath mingled with hers. 'Yes,' he said, looking a little sheepish. 'Yes, I did.'

Lily sighed happily. 'That's all I needed to hear.' She shuffled across to his side of the coach, burrowed under his arm and laid her head against his shoulder.

He lifted her chin. She was caught, mesmerised by the light, unburdened quality of his gaze. A great well of joy and gratitude swelled within her at the sight. Every moment of danger and fear, every tear and frustration—they had all been worth it. She would have endured far more to see such a shine in his hazel eyes.

He kissed her then, searing her with equal parts tenderness and fierce possession. She wrapped her arms tightly about him and abandoned herself to the slow, thorough pleasure of it.

She was not nearly ready to stop when Jack suddenly pulled back. 'God, that mouth of yours is irresistible,' he murmured, running a thumb along her lower lip. 'But resist I must, for, despite your generosity, there is more I find I need to say.'

Lily tried to draw him back down to her. 'Jack,' she protested. 'We'll be talking non-stop once we reach Bruton Street. Surely we can think of something better to do until then.'

Jack groaned. 'In a moment, minx.' He took her face in both of his hands, his expression grown serious. 'This is important. I want you to know I was on my way back to you when I found out that Batiste had taken you.'

She stilled, struck by what he had said, and then she smiled. He was right. It was a thrill to know that Jack had battled his enemy to save her, but the fact that he'd recognised his obsession for what it was and chosen life, love—and her—instead was infinitely more reassuring.

'Thank you,' she said with tears in her eyes. 'I know how incredibly difficult that choice must have been.' She gave him a tremulous smile. 'And it must have been doubly hard after the horrible lecture I read you when you left.'

'Horrible?' He gave an ironic chuckle. 'It was absolutely, in every way correct.' He settled back and pulled her in close. 'You were right all along. I harboured a seething mass of anger all those years, and a deal of sadness and resentment with it, but I couldn't acknowledge it.'

She placed her hand on his chest. 'So you built your walls to keep them out,' she said, trying to imbue her voice with all the sympathy in her heart.

'Yes. I used logic and rationality as bricks and mortar and I thought to keep myself safe. But instead of keeping the ugly emotions at bay, my walls only trapped them inside.' He squeezed her hand. 'Until you came along and demolished them.' He laughed ruefully. 'I thought I didn't know how to deal with so many feelings running amok, but the truth was, I was still clutching them tightly.'

'But you've let them go,' she said in wonder and absolute assurance. 'I can see it in your eyes.' She let her gaze drop to his mouth. 'And taste it in your kiss.'

'Yes, thanks to you, I saw that darkness for what it was, and I let it all go.'

She smiled. 'And how do you feel?'

'Empty,' he said, shifting beneath her. 'A little frightened. I nearly died when I heard that Batiste had you, Lily. Because I need you. I need you to fill me with light.' He turned towards her, holding her tightly. 'I thought I needed walls, but all I needed was you.'

The tears did fall then, as the enormity of all that he had done, for her sake, hit her. 'You've faced so much and shown such bravery,' she marvelled. 'But you've got something better than walls now, Jack. You've made a foundation.'

He wiped a tear from her cheek. 'Shall we build on it, then?'

Nodding emphatically, Lily pulled him down for a kiss. A kiss, and so much more. It was a promise, a vow, a vision of a future filled with contented days and passionate nights. For long moments they lingered, savouring passion, escalating desire, and the tantalising idea of a future faced together.

He broke the kiss and smiled down into her eyes. 'I'm afraid it'll be no easy job, being the keeper of my heart. It's not perfect. It's been neglected too long, and might still be subject to periods of surliness or need moments of solitude. But thanks to you, it is in better shape than it has ever been before.' His mouth quirked. 'Are you willing to take on such a heavy burden?'

'You know I will. You couldn't stop me if you wished to.' Lily reached up and ran a finger through his unruly hair, at long last taming it with her fingers. 'You should know, there was never any need for you to feel empty—for I gave my heart and soul over to you long ago.'

'That's all that has saved me,' he said simply.

She raised a brow at him. 'And you are already familiar with the burdens I represent. Along with me you'll get my opinionated mother, and assorted orphans, abolitionists and other charitable causes. Not to mention, I have a long list of requirements.'

He laughed. 'Requirements?'

'Yes, things that you will have to provide on a regular basis.'

He lowered his voice to a seductive whisper. 'Such as?'

Lily fought back a giggle as he buried his face in the nape of her neck. 'Oh, many things. Music, learning, travel.' She gasped as his hand climbed to cup her breast. 'Laughter,' she whispered, 'and kisses.'

'Like this?' He raised his head and brushed his lips, soft and clinging, across hers. His hands were busy with the line of buttons at her back.

'Oh, my, yes,' she breathed.

'And is that all of your requirements?'

She hunched a shoulder, helping him in his efforts to remove her bodice. 'No, I can think of so many more. More passionate interludes in libraries, for one.'

'And gardens?' he asked wickedly. He had her stays unfastened and pushed them wide.

'Definitely gardens.' She had to fight back a moan as his mouth traced a molten line down the column of her neck. 'And you must solemnly promise, Jack, that we will do this in the carriage, oh, at least once a week.'

'I promise,' he vowed right before he bent to suckle her through the thin fabric of her shift.

Lily closed her eyes and let her head fall back. 'So,' she eventually managed to bite out, 'will you agree to take me on, knowing me for the heavy burden I am?'

He raised his head and kissed her, long and hard. 'It's only fair,' he said.

Epilogue

The dining hall of the J. Crump School for Orphans had been transformed. Lord Dayle's wife Sophie had blown in like a whirlwind. In a matter of days what once had been a plain, serviceable room had magically become a beautiful desert city.

Actual sand covered the floor in strategic spots and ancient pillars created open-air rooms. Rich fabrics, earthy colours—it was a fitting setting for the first lecture and display on what was becoming internationally known as Lord Treyford's Lost City.

Scholars around the world had vied for tickets to tonight's event, along with a multitude of wealthy would-be patrons, but Lily made sure that tonight's festivities included those from every walk of life and level of society. Formal wear and gorgeous gowns rubbed up against brushed Sunday best, but no one made a peep of protest. They were all too caught up in the magic of the night and the wonderful array of artefacts and etchings that Lord Treyford's expedition had sent back to England.

'How long is Mr Alden goin' to talk?' a young boy whispered in Lily's ear.

'You know how he is,' answered another with a roll of his

eyes. 'He talked for the whole class about what ancient Egyptians planted in their kitchen gardens.'

'Your turn is coming soon,' Lily replied softly. While the guests were sitting enthralled by her husband's brilliantly stirring history of the lost city and its rediscovery, Lily sat in the hallway outside, surrounded by students, attending to last-minute adjustments to hair and costume. As all the profits from tonight's event were going to help the combined school and orphanage, it was only fitting that the children should be a part of it.

'Missus Alden!' The quiet wail came from a girl with a drooping coiffure and a handful of hairpins. 'My hair!'

'Come, Daisy, I'll fix you straight up,' Lily reassured the girl.

Daisy pushed through and thrust the hairpins in Lily's hand.

'Turn around, now.' The girl obeyed and Lily was left holding the pins. She glanced around, and then ruefully set them on her well-rounded belly. She just had Daisy's hair repaired when a thunderous round of applause broke out in the dining hall. 'That's our signal, children! Line up, now.'

They all waited several minutes until the applause died down. 'All right. In you go!' She smiled universal encouragement over her group of performers. 'You'll be marvellous, I know it!'

Lily waited until the children were safely onstage before she followed them into the atmospherically lit hall. She kept to the back, lurking behind a pillar, glad to find something in the display rounder than she. She leaned against it, closed her eyes and allowed the simple beauty of childish harmonies to soothe her.

A draught of cool air across her cheek alerted her. She opened her eyes to find several seated ladies fluttering their fans and lashes. Smiling, she followed the direction of their gazes to find the handsome form of her husband approaching down the side of the hall.

'Your mother says you must sit down, and put your feet up if it can be contrived,' he said, his eyes running over her in a nearly tangible caress.

'She worries, bless her heart,' Lily said with patience. Casting an impudent grin at Jack, she asked, 'And what did my new father have to say?'

He grimaced. 'Your mother has improved Mr Cooperage greatly, my dear, but some things never change. I don't care what he says about women in an advanced childbearing state, there is no way I would allow you to miss this evening.' He took her hand. 'But would you like me to find you a seat?'

She shook her head and leaned against him with a contented sigh. 'It was so generous of Lord Treyford to allow all of this.'

Jack laughed. 'Believe me, Trey is happy to miss all the uproar—especially since Chione finds herself in a condition similar to yours. There is no way they could travel home right now.'

'I know. I do not think it bothered her to miss this either, she sounded so completely happy in her last letter. I know just how she feels,' Lily said, gazing about at the spectacle. 'It's hard to believe, is it not?' she asked with a sweep of her hand. 'It feels as if we've built so much and come so far.'

Jack laid his hand on her belly, bent down and brushed her lips with his. 'It's easy to build, my darling wife, on a solid and beautiful foundation.'

* * * * *

Tall, Dark
and Disreputable

To the Biaggi's Bunch…
You all already know why—
and that's what makes it beautiful!

Chapter One

⸎

Berkshire, England—Summer 1821

Ribald laughter and drunken babble spilled out into the night. The owner of the Spread Eagle Inn took cheerful part in the bonhomie as he shooed his last customers into the dark. He stood a moment, listening as they scattered, secure in the knowledge that they would be back tomorrow and that the satisfying weight of coins in his apron pocket would only grow heavier.

Inside his taproom, quiet settled over the abandoned tables and peace wrapped itself around the place in lieu of the dissipating curtain of smoke. Mateo Cardea alone had not stirred when the innkeeper called. Here the fire burned warm, the ale was good and the accommodating wench in his lap ran soft fingers through his hair. He should have been blissfully content.

He was not.

The lightskirt slid a finger around his ear. She leaned in close, her brassy blond hair tickling his jaw, her other hand trailing a whisper-soft caress against his nape. Mateo could feel the tough calluses on her fingertips. He closed his eyes and imagined the touch of them against his other, more sensitive areas.

Arousing as the image might be, Mateo still could not summon the enthusiasm needed to climb out of his chair. Ridiculous. A few paltry coins and the girl was his for the taking, yet the thought did not dredge up more than a faint stir of desire.

The yawning innkeeper ambled back into the tap-room. He cast a glance at Mateo and crooked a finger at the girl. 'Get these chairs atop the tables, Etta, and I'll help you sweep up,' he said, not unkindly. The girl gave a soft groan of protest, but rose up and out of Mateo's lap. She trailed a finger over his shoulder and down the length of his arm as she went. Mateo recognised the gesture for the promise it was and briefly waited for an answering surge of interest.

It did not come. Inside him there was no room for such clean and simple things as peace and desire. *'Dio nel cielo,'* he breathed. Oh, but he was tired of the unfa-miliar burn of anger in his gut and the caustic flow of resentment in his veins. For weeks he'd been like this, since he'd first discovered his father's shocking betrayal.

All of it gone. Everything he'd spent his life work-ing for, planning towards, gone with the reading of a few cold words. Years of biting his tongue, of endless explanations, of patiently coaxing his father to more modern business practices, and still the old man had not trusted him in the end. Mateo was in disgrace and, for the first time in a hundred years, control of Cardea

Shipping had fallen outside the family. It was more than a man's pride could bear.

His indifference was more than the strumpet could bear. She had worked her way back over to his side of the room and into the dark corner behind him. Now she leaned against him, blocking the heat of the fire, but warming him none the less when she bent low to encircle him in her arms. Her impressive bosom pressed soft against his back.

'Are ye even here, tonight?' Etta asked, demanding the return of his attention. 'What are you thinkin' of, that's got your mind so far away?' She stiffened a little and drew back. 'Some other woman, p'raps?'

Mateo smiled. 'I am not so foolish, sweet.' With a sigh of regret he acknowledged the need to evade her interest and retire upstairs alone. Tomorrow held fair promise to be the worst day of his life and no amount of mindless distraction tonight would help ready him for it.

'What is it, then?' she demanded, circling round to the front of him again, her bottom lip forming a perfect pout. 'Something important, I hope,' she said low in his ear, 'to be distracting you from the bounties at hand.'

He disentangled himself and drew her around to his side. Taking the girl with him, Mateo crossed the small distance to the bar. Here the innkeeper tidied up, trimming the wicks on cheap tallow lamps and polishing the worn wooden counter with pride. Mateo took the furthest stool and gestured for the girl to perch next to him.

'No, tonight I have been lost indeed—thinking of fathers, and of sons. Do you know,' he continued in a conversational tone, 'that my father once caused a city-wide riot over a wh—' Etta straightened in her seat and he cleared his throat '—over a celebrated courtesan?'

She relaxed. 'He never!'

Mateo smiled at her obvious interest. Even the innkeeper sidled closer to listen. 'Oh, but he did. It happened in Naples, long ago. La Incandescent Clarisse, she was called, the greatest beauty in Europe. Endless poems were written to the soft pink of her lips, to the sweet curve of her hips. Playwrights named their heroines for her, artists worshipped her as their muse. Men followed her carriage in the street. My father was only one of many caught firmly in her spell.'

'What happened?' The girl's face shone bright and she had briefly forgotten her practised seduction.

'The inevitable.' Mateo shrugged. 'La Incandescent got with child. All of Naples held their breath, fascinated to hear who she would name as the father.'

'Who was it?' she breathed. 'Not your da?'

'After a fashion. You see, Clarisse could only narrow down the field. The father of her child was either *my* father, or Thomas Varnsworth.'

'No!' The innkeeper gasped.

'Him what's the Earl of Winbury?' Etta asked, amazed.

'The old Earl, rather,' Mateo replied.

The innkeeper could not contain his shock. 'But his daughter lives—'

'Yes, I know,' Mateo interrupted. 'Shall I continue?'

They both nodded.

'Upon hearing the news, Lord Thomas—for he was not the Earl yet—and my father got into a terrible row.

They fought long and hard, nearly destroying La Incandescent's apartments, and still they raged on, until the fight eventually spilled out into the streets. Spectators gathered. Someone spotted the tearful Clarisse and the rumour spread that La Incandescent had been harmed. The crowd grew furious, for Clarisse was a favourite of the people, and soon the two men found themselves fighting for their lives.'

'And all over a strumpet?' the innkeeper said in wonder.

'Hush, you,' the girl admonished. 'Let him finish.'

Mateo shifted. Too late he worried about raising the tavern wench's expectations, but that thought set off another surge of bitterness. It had been a woman's damned expectations that had ruined his life. Portia Varnsworth had once expected to marry him. Mateo's father had expected him to go along with the idea. Mateo might have expected somebody to consult him on the matter, but no one had bothered.

Etta, however, appeared to have taken the tale as a challenge. She raised a brow and tossed him a saucy grin. 'I'm summat well known, myself, in these parts,' she said.

'Indeed?'

'Oh, aye,' she purred. 'Would you like to know what I'm famous for?'

'He don't need to know now,' grumbled her employer, 'and not in front o' me. What ye do upstairs is yer own business. Down here, it's mine. Don't ye want him to finish his tale? And you've a taproom to straighten first, in any case.' He nodded for Mateo to continue.

'Ah, yes, well, my father and Lord Thomas were

arrested—for their own protection. They spent two days in a cell together and came out the best of friends.'

'And the lady? Clarisse?' Etta leaned closer.

'When they were released, she had gone. She left Naples and disappeared. No one ever knew where she went, although rumours abounded. My father and Lord Thomas made a vow to find her and searched for years.'

She stilled. 'Did they? Find her, that is?'

'No,' he said soberly. 'Not to my knowledge. But they never stopped looking, either, until their dying days.'

Her eyes shone in the dim light, bright with unshed tears. 'That's the most romantic thing I ever heard.' She sniffed.

The innkeeper snorted. 'Then I would say you were in sore need of a little romance.' He nodded towards Mateo. 'He might be the one to give it to ye, but first—'

'Aye, I know, I know, the taproom,' Etta grumbled. The weight of her gleaming gaze felt nearly solid on Mateo's skin. 'I just mean to give him a taste of what comes after.' She slid down from her stool and reached for him.

Mateo saw the stars in her eyes. The girl's mind tumbled with fancies and dreams and he knew that he had perhaps not been so wise in his choice of tales. It is no bad thing to create a vision of things that might be, but of a certainty he would not be the one to bring her grand ideas to fruition.

He stilled as her arms went around him. He had no wish to damage her feelings. A woman had brought his world to a crashing halt, but he would not take his revenge on this, her artless sister. He sent a swift plea to the heavens for something, anything to distract the girl and extract him from the awkward situation of his own making.

The knob on the taproom door rattled. A floorboard creaked in the passage outside. Mateo jerked to attention along with the others as the door opened swiftly and his name echoed through the empty room. He stared, speechless, at the figure framed in the shadowy entrance and he knew that in the future he would be more careful in what he wished for.

A breeze wafted over Portia Tofton's flushed cheeks as she approached the Eagle. The night air was cooler than she had expected. She didn't care. She had her indignation to keep her warm, her dead husband's pistol to keep her safe and a fervent desire to shock the wits out of Mateo Cardea to keep the purpose in her step.

Coming to a halt in front of the inn, she cast it a look of loathing. The beady eyes of the building's painted namesake returned her glare. The raptor's outstretched talons glittered in the moonlight, sending a shiver down her spine

Mateo had arrived in the village today; word was out and spreading fast across the county. Weeks it had taken for him to take ship and make his way here, but had he come to her? She snorted. Of course not. Apparently not even the loss of his family legacy was enough to tempt him to her side. Despite the urgent wording of her request he had holed up in the most disreputable tavern for miles around. No doubt he'd spent the day drinking, carousing, and who knows what else, while she had been left to twiddle her thumbs.

How utterly predictable.

No. Portia squared her shoulders and took a step forwards. Such treatment might be standard in her old life, perhaps, but it was not at all acceptable in the new. She was a widow now. Her husband's death had granted her a new freedom and independence that she meant to take full advantage of. Heaven knew—and everybody else did too—that it was more than he'd given her while he lived.

She raised a fist to knock loud and long upon the tavern door, but noticed it stood slightly ajar. She put her hand on the knob and paused. Gone were the days that Lady Portia Varnsworth—or even Mrs. James Talbot Tofton—meekly did as she was expected. She'd had enough of men ruling her life. Though her brothers might try, there was no one left with the authority to order, bully—or, worse, ignore her. And Portia meant to keep it that way. She wanted nothing more than her independence, the chance to be in charge of her own destiny. She'd thought she had it, too, until that wretched solicitor had come calling.

But no matter. She had a grasp on the situation. One even exchange with Mateo Cardea and she would have her freedom—and her home—safe again. It only wanted a little courage and a good deal of determination. Sternly she reminded herself that she had an ample supply of both. Boldly she pushed the outer door open and let herself in, steeled to face—

Empty darkness. Silence.

'Is anyone there?' Some of her bravado faded a little as she stepped forwards into the gloom. Portia paused to take a good look, curious to see the place servants and villagers whispered about. The ante-room appeared perfectly ordinary at least, certainly not like she'd imagined a reputed den of debauchery and iniquity. Disappointed, she continued forwards.

A doorway sat at an angle to the right. From beneath it shone the faintest glow of light—and from behind it she caught the low murmur of voices. She crept closer.

There. Faint but unmistakable: Mateo Cardea's wicked chuckle.

Portia stood helpless against the intense shiver of reaction that swept through her. As a young girl she'd spent hours tagging after Mateo and her brothers. She'd lurked in hallways and corners, listening for that infectious sound. Five years older than she, Mateo Cardea had been an ideal, the unsuspecting object of her first consuming love. An absent smile from him had held the power to light up her day, but it had been his rich laughter, full of mischief and exuberance, that had set her young body a-tremble.

Not that he had ever taken notice. Despite their friendship, she'd never been more than background scenery to him, a secondary character in the drama of his young life.

She was determined that things would be different now. All day she had sat, waiting for him to come, seething when he did not. Until—as the hour grew late and her temper grew short—she'd finally decided that this time she would begin with Mateo as she meant to go on. She would force him to look at her, to see her, to truly recognise her for the woman she was. Mateo, her brothers, indeed the whole world—it was time that they all took a second look at Portia Tofton.

With a purposeful and careful tread she approached

the door. But he was not alone. Feminine tones mixed with his, and then both faded away. Portia's face flamed. Etta was as notorious as the Eagle itself. Of course Mateo would be with her. Everyone else had been—including Portia's own husband.

She was a different woman, now, though. She would not sit idly by and be ignored. She turned the latch as quietly as she could and paused once more. The manner of her entrance must lend itself to the image she wished to convey. She wished to appear a woman of self-possession and authority. *A woman he could desire*, whispered some deeply buried part of her. She shushed it. Above all, she would not be a supplicant.

She shifted her weight, hoping for a strategic glimpse into the room before she entered. A board creaked loudly underneath her, but Portia did not heed it.

It was he. Her stomach fluttered in recognition. How well she knew that rogue's twist of a wry grin, the tangle of inky, wind-tousled curls, and the spark of wickedness dancing in a gaze as warm as her morning chocolate. Her pulse tumbled nearly to a stop, then rushed to a gallop as her mind made sense of the rest of the tableau before her.

Mateo Cardea at last—but perched on a stool, the infamous Etta entwined around him tighter than the Persian ivy Portia had coaxed up the walls of her arbour. She gripped the door handle until her knuckles whitened. God, but it was the old hurt all over again. How many times in a woman's life could she withstand such a whirlwind of pain and humiliation?

One too many times. But this would be the last. She breathed deeply and willed her spine straight and her voice steady. With a flourish she swept the door open and stepped into the taproom, trampling her heart underneath each tread of her foot. 'Ah, here you are, Mateo,' she called. 'As ever the scapegrace, I see, seeking pleasure when there is serious work to be done.'

A rush of anger pulled Mateo off of his stool and out of the circle of Etta's arms. In an instinctive reaction his knees braced, his toes flexed within his boots to grip the floor and his breath quickened to match the sudden racing of his pulse. It was an old impulse, standing fast to face his enemies—except this adversary was neither a ship of the line bent on impressing his men nor a fat merchant clipper ripe for the picking. Instead it was a slip of a girl in a sky-blue pelisse.

He stared as Portia Tofton sauntered into the taproom as if it belonged to her. But this was not the shy, round-shouldered girl he recalled from his youth. From her head to her curvy figure and on to her dainty little toe, this was a woman to be reckoned with. Her stylish bonnet beautifully framed the look of cool amusement fixed on her face. Mateo's jaw tightened even as she removed it, letting it swing by ribbons of shaded velvet.

For so long he had imagined this confrontation. In his mind he had rehearsed his collected entrance into her presence, practised the biting words with which he would consign her to the devil. Now it would seem she had connived to rob him even of that satisfaction.

His fists clenched. An air of assurance hung about her as she stepped into the candlelight. And why not? She thought she had him right where she wished. Heedless of propriety, unmindful of the great wrong she had done him or perhaps just without regard for his feelings, she stood there, all expectation, smiling up at him.

That smile made him wild. Fury set his temples to pounding, but he would be damned before he would let her see it. 'Peeve!' he called. 'It is you, is it not?'

Her expression of triumph dimmed at the use of the old nickname. Relentless, he pressed his advantage. 'But I see that much is the same with you, as well, my dear.' He shook his head sadly. 'Still, after all these years, you are pushing yourself in where you do not belong.'

If he had hit his mark, she hid it well with a toss of her head. 'Come, let's not be rude, Mateo,' she cajoled.

He nearly choked. 'Rude? You conniving little jade! You would count yourself fortunate should I stop myself at merely rude!'

'I don't think the occasion warrants it.' She cast a quick, curious gaze about them. 'This is a place of… conviviality, is it not?'

He had not thought it possible for his anger to grow hotter. But the roiling mass of resentment inside him ignited at her words—and his control slipped further as the flames licked higher. Incredulous, he gaped at her.

He pushed away from the bar, away from her. Retreating back to the dying fire, he glared at her. 'Conviviality,' he scoffed. 'Is that what you expected from me? Damn you English, and damn your deadly, dull-mannered ways,' he said thickly. 'And damn me if I will greet with equanimity the woman who has usurped my life's work, and then—as if I am but her lackey—calls me to her side with a damned insulting peremptory summons!'

Her eyes narrowed and she took a step towards him. 'Mateo—'

'Stop,' he ordered. 'By God, I am not one of your reserved English gentlemen! Come within an arm's reach of me and I won't trust myself.' He turned away from her and gripped the stone mantel over the fire. 'Never in my life have I struck a woman, but you, Portia Tofton, tempt me beyond reason.'

Perhaps he had gone too far. At the bar, the innkeeper made a slight sound of protest. Etta watched with avid interest. But Portia barely reacted.

'Ah, Mateo...' she sighed '...I'd forgotten how incredibly dramatic you become when you are angry.'

She could not keep the slight mockery from her tone—and that was all it took. The last of his restraint tore away. Everything this infuriating chit did and said only fuelled the blowing gale of his anger.

'Dramatic?' he ground out. 'I am betrayed. I am robbed of the future that I have laboured all my life for. I am a laughingstock where once I was a respected businessman. And I am *furious*. What I am not is *dramatic*.' He whirled around and advanced on her with menace alive in his step. His voice, gone rough and threatening, reinforced the truth in her words and the lie in his. But Mateo was beyond caring. Hell and damnation, but she pushed a man too far! And she was—at last!—a bit frightened. God help him, but he wished to frighten her.

She stood her ground, though her eyes widened, and her fingers crushed the velvet of her ribbons. 'I believe you have let the Cardea temper and your own imagination run away with you,' she said. 'I sent an *urgent* request for you to come and discuss this situation. There is a vast distance between urgent and peremptory.'

'Ah, it is my mistake,' Mateo growled. 'Yes, I am sure your urgent need of a long and thorough gloat required my presence. Well, I can assure you, I feel your triumph keenly enough without such a humiliation.'

'But I—'

He swung his arm in a sharp gesture and cut her off. He was close enough now to clearly see the puzzlement in her great brown eyes. Good, then. There was one question that had hung between them for years. He would answer it one last time and put an end to this entire farce. 'We've both trod this ground before, have we not? It was not enough that you and our fathers sought to manoeuvre me into marriage? But I won that battle—so now you must find a new way to steal my future. Once again you have played a game without informing me I was a participant—and just as before you will find that I refuse to act as the prize.'

She gaped up at him. 'What are you saying?'

'Do not play the innocent with me, Portia, not after you have conspired to steal all that I value,' he growled. 'Perhaps it is not so inappropriate for you to be here tonight, after all. It is a fitting setting for you to learn that I will not be bought like a whore, no matter the bait that you dangle in front of me.'

Portia gasped. Behind him, Etta echoed her. The innkeeper dropped his cloth and took a step towards the corner of the bar. 'That's enough, now.' He cast a conciliatory eye in Portia's direction as he came around and approached them. 'I don't claim to know what there is between the two of you, but the gentleman was right the first time, Mrs Tofton. You shouldn't be here, let alone at this hour. If word got out, your credit would suffer, and so would mine.'

All of Portia's colour had faded at Mateo's last heated words. As the innkeeper's objection penetrated, her flush returned with a vengeance. Her chest heaved as an angry red wave crept upwards from beneath the standing collar of her pelisse. 'I'm sorry for it, sir, but surely the damage is done.' She cast a neutral glance at Etta and then regarded Mateo with the sort of loathing his crews reserved for an empty rum casket. 'And well worth it, I must say, for suddenly I find several things have become clear.'

She looked away and this time it was she who took a step back. 'I never thought—I can scarcely believe—' She dropped her head, placed her hands on her hips and actually paced back and forth a few steps, seemingly lost in thought. Some of Mateo's ire began to fade as he took in her air of bewilderment and the forgotten bonnet swinging against her knee.

She stopped suddenly, caught at the apex of her trajectory. Her chin lifted and at last he caught a glimpse of answering anger in her gaze—but there was hurt there too, and something bleak and sad.

'I wished you to come because I needed your help.' She spoke low. 'I thought it possible that you might have some insight into why your father and mine would have acted so contrary to expectation and good sense. I know *nothing* of why your father made the choices he did. I'm sorry he died, but I was as shocked as you were to hear the contents of his will.' She paused. 'My father is dead, too, Mateo. And my husband, as well. Together they have left me in a dilemma as terrible as yours.'

Her words doused the burn of fury inside of him, but she was not done yet. At her side, her fists clenched. 'I came here tonight to chide *you*, for I was unable to fathom why I had to ask you to come to sort this mess out in the first place, and why you would dally so long once you set out, in the second. But now I see.'

He watched her pull her bonnet on with shaking fingers. 'I had no notion that your opinion of me had sunk so low, but truly, it matters naught. I *ask* you, please, to come to Stenbrooke tomorrow.' She tied the strings with short, jerky movements. 'You are both right. This is neither the time nor the place. But if you will come tomorrow, we will discuss this business.' She swept the room with a glare that included all three of them. 'Business, and nothing else. I trust I make myself clear?' With an all-encompassing nod, she turned on her heel and strode out of the taproom and into the night.

The towering heat of his anger had faded to mere embers. She had cut the legs out from under him. Still, Mateo managed an involuntary step after her. The tavern owner deliberately put himself in his path. 'Mayhap, sir, you don't have all the facts you need,' he said gently.

'Aye, I fear you're right in that.' Mateo stepped back, scrubbed a hand from brow to jaw, and cocked an enquiring eye to the man. 'She tells the truth, I think?'

The innkeeper shrugged. 'They do say as she's one for straight dealing, hereabouts.'

'I would say it is either truth she's given us,' Mateo paused, 'or a beautiful performance.' He sighed. 'I feel like the Mariner—discovering the world has shifted and the sun is rising in the west.'

'A woman'll do that to a man, eh?'

'I fear so.' Mateo glanced back at Etta. 'Look at me. Knocked off my pillar of righteous anger in the space of a few minutes—and damned if I'm not exhausted from the fall.' He reached beyond the man to grasp his ale and drained it in one long haul. 'I am for bed,' he declared. 'It seems I've a mess to straighten in the morning.'

The innkeeper nodded his approval. 'I'll see that you are not disturbed.'

Mateo shook his head. 'It's far too late for that, my friend, but I thank you just the same.'

Chapter Two

A glorious morning dawned the next day, spilling sunlight into the breakfast room at Stenbrooke. A breeze
drifted, rewarding early risers with the taste of heavy
dew and the fresh scent of green and growing things.
Never had Portia felt more out of harmony with the start
of a beautiful day.

For once immune to the call of her gardens, she stood
at the window while her breakfast grew cold behind her
and the light limned the fair hairs on her arm with gold.
The parchment in her hands glowed nearly transparent,
grown worn with time and tears and frequent handling.
And though she hid the letter when her elderly butler
came in to shake his head over her untouched plate,
he would have been hard pressed to read the faded ink
in any case. Portia, of course, had no need to read it;
its message had long ago been etched into the darkest
corner of her heart.

Philadelphia, 11 July 1812

Your curst brother has arrived safely, Peeve— it began without preamble—*bringing with him details of this preposterous scheme our fathers have hatched between them. I cannot believe they have risked him at such a time of conflict between our two countries, and I am inclined to agree with Freddy when he wonders what put such a maggoty idea as marriage in their brains. I know we spent a good deal of time in company together when last I was at Hempshaw, but surely they must realise that was years ago and we were only friends, besides?*

In fact, I feel that I owe you a most profound apology—for this must be my father's doing. He is grasping at straws because I mean to sign a letter-of-marque bond. It's a surety he'd rather see me occupied with a wife and marriage than a privateer's cruise. I am deeply sorry to have caught you up in such a muddle but what must we do to break free?

Stand firm, I suppose, is the only answer. I pledge to do my part here—for at last I have got my own ship and she is the fastest schooner, with the sweetest lay in the water that you've ever seen. I mean to make my fortune with her, Peeve, though I promise not to target any ship that carries your brother back to you. In any case, I'm sure you've your own plans you don't wish me to

disrupt. Stand fast, dear girl, as I mean to, and
there is little they can do to force us otherwise.

'What's this?'

Portia started as the door opened again behind her. Over her shoulder she watched as Dorinda Tofton, her cousin by marriage and companion, entered on the heels of the butler.

'Vickers tells me that you are neglecting your breakfast again, Portia,' Dorinda chided. 'He also suspects that you are mooning over a letter. Has *that woman* sent another of her hateful missives? I thought we'd seen an end to this nonsense! I won't have you harassed—'

'No, Dorrie,' Portia interjected before her companion could get herself too wound up. 'I was just going through some old correspondence.'

'Oh. Well. You're all right, then?'

Portia hesitated. 'Of course.'

'Good.' She shot a brief glance out of the window before focusing on the food spread out on the sideboard. 'Will you please come and have some breakfast then, dear? I can see that we are in for a beautiful day, but you know how I feel about you disappearing into the gardens without so much as a piece of toast in you.'

For a long moment, Portia did not answer. The letter she held was the last communication she'd had with Mateo Cardea until last night—and even after so many years it still held the echo of her youthful shock and dismay. With gentle fingers she folded it up and tucked it into her bodice. Right over her heart she placed it— where she would wear it as a reminder and a shield.

'Portia?' Dorinda paused in the process of making her own selections and eyed her curiously.

She turned. 'Yes, of course. I was just sitting down to finish.'

Dorinda took a seat and tucked into her coddled eggs with relish. 'What do you mean to tackle today, dear? The damaged bridge on the Cascade Walk?' She frowned. 'Or did I hear you say that the dahlias were in need of separating?'

Portia smiled. Only politeness led Dorrie to ask—she neither shared nor understood her charge's passion for landscaping. 'Actually, I mean to stay in this morning.'

Dorinda brightened noticeably. 'A wise choice. The sun is quite brilliant today. You know how harmful it can be to one's complexion.' Dorrie's own milky countenance was her pride and joy—and Portia's significantly browner one counted as a chief worry. She set down her fork and took up her teacup. 'Perhaps,' she began, her word choice seeming as delicate and deliberate as the stroke of her finger over the fine china, 'we might begin to pack some of our winter things? We might even consider starting on the books in the library.'

Portia set down her toast.

'It's only sensible to be prepared.' Dorinda sounded as if she were coaxing a reluctant child. Her voice lowered. 'We're running out of time, dear.'

Portia was a woman grown. She'd been married—and then widowed in spectacular fashion. She'd run this estate entirely on her own for years now. Never had she shown herself to be fragile or weak, and especially not since the day she'd first received the letter tucked into her bodice. Bad enough that her father and brothers had always treated her like a nursling—when Dorrie followed their example, it made Portia long to act like one.

But this was not the time for such indulgences. Instead of treating Dorinda to a screaming fit, she caught her gaze and held it. 'There is no need to pack, as I've told you repeatedly. We are going nowhere. We will proceed exactly as planned.' She leaned forwards. 'Even better, we begin today. Had you not heard? Mateo Cardea has arrived in the village. I expect he will call on us today.'

'He's here at last?' Dorinda nearly dropped her teacup. 'Oh, but will he co-operate?' she fretted. 'I know you recall him fondly, but there is this business with his...well, his business!' She reached over and laid her warm hand over Portia's. 'I want you to be prepared. I know you have not wished to consider it, but when you put this admittedly odd circumstance together with what you've told me about the marriage scheme your fathers tried to force on both of you... It's just that it's entirely within the realm of understanding...' She exhaled in exasperation. 'Portia, he's likely to formulate *ideas*. And none of them are likely to paint you in a favourable light.'

Portia felt the heat rising in her face. Dorrie had raised this concern before, and she had refused to believe such a thing of Mateo. Unfortunately, Mateo had been all too willing to believe such a thing of her. Bitterness churned in her belly. So much for the friendship she had valued so highly and for so long.

But admitting it also meant confessing her entirely improper, late-night visit to the Eagle, and that was a pot that Portia had no intention of stirring. 'If he is so disobliging as to think so of an old and dear friend,' she said with heat, 'then he is not the man I thought him to be.' She drew a deep breath and squared her shoulders. 'And I will just have to set him straight.'

'Oh, if only we'd bought that French muslin when we had the chance! The sage would have been so flattering on you, dear.'

Portia frowned. 'I begin to worry that you are the one with *ideas*, Dorrie. And if that is the case, then you can just rid yourself of them straight away.'

'Well, forgive me, but he's a man, is he not? And if you mean to ask for a man's help, then you've got to use every weapon in your arsenal—and give him every reason to agree.'

Portia rolled her eyes at the familiar refrain, but Dorinda had not even paused to take a breath. 'I confess, I'm so nervous about meeting him! I know you count him an old friend, but in all of these years there's been not so much as a letter between you. I—'

She stopped as Portia slapped both hands on the table and stood.

'Please, Dorrie! Stop or you'll have me tied in knots along with you.' She straightened. 'I have what Mateo wants. He can help me get what I want. It will be as simple as that.' She ignored her companion's huff of disagreement and stepped away from the table. 'I'll be in the library, settling the accounts, should you need me.'

It took only minutes at her books for Portia to regret her decision. A bundle of frayed nerves, she fidgeted constantly in her chair. She could scarcely believe that Mateo had laid the blame for his troubles at her door. They had always been at ease in each other's company, accepting of the other's foibles, keepers of the other's secrets. It should never have been so easy for him to believe the worst of her.

She put down her quill and rested her head in her hands. He'd casually crushed her fledgling feelings so long ago. It should come as no surprise that he did it again, and so easily. A conniving jade, he'd called her! Even her husband's betrayals had not cut so deep into the heart of her—perhaps because they had been expected.

She stared blankly at the housekeeper's note complaining of the rising cost of candles. A bitter laugh worked its way out of her chest. Beeswax could become as dear as diamonds and still not jolt her as deeply as the sight of Mateo Cardea's arms around the Eagle's Etta. The sight had been a jagged knife to her heart and to her faith in her friend. And Mateo had only twisted the blade deeper when he made his suspicions clear.

Abruptly, she pushed away from the desk and crossed to the window. Staring out over the beauty she had coaxed from the earth, Portia forced herself to acknowledge the truth. Through a span of years, a disastrous marriage, neglect and isolation, some part of her old schoolgirl self had survived—and she still suffered an infatuation for Mateo Cardea.

It must end here and now. Any lingering softness or longing must be locked tight away. She thought she might go a little mad if Mateo also thought of her as helpless and weak. So she would meet him as a woman—composed, controlled, in charge of her own life, and to some extent, his as well.

She could not suppress a smile at the thought. Of all the men in her life, Mateo might be the only one she had never been able to best or ignore, but she had the whip hand over him now. Keeping it might not be easy, but it could prove to be a great source of satisfaction.

With a flourish, Portia threw open the casement. Breathing deeply, she acknowledged the subtle siren's call of the gardens. Abruptly, she decided to answer. Turning, she strode out of the library, and headed for the stairs. 'Dorrie!' she called. 'I've changed my mind! I'm going out!'

In general, Mateo's mood suffered when he found himself landlocked for any length of time. It seemed some part of him always listened, yearning for the timeless thrum and endless animation of the sea.

Today, though, the beauty of the day and the peace of the country conspired to silence his craving. A wonderful mosaic of woodland and farmland comprised this part of Berkshire. His mount stretched out beneath him, light on his feet. The faintest breeze blew across his face. It all made for a pleasant enough morning, but not enough to distract him from his pensive musings.

Dramatic, Portia had called him. Hardly the worst label that had been handed him. Hell, he'd been called everything from rascal to reprobate. But through months of war and a longer struggle to keep a business literally afloat, he'd always maintained his reputation for cheerful roguery. Even through the heat of battle, his crew teased time and again, he'd kept a fearsome grin on his face and his wit as sharp as his blade.

That had not been true in the last months. He'd been on the verge of a major business coup when he'd been struck hard by the grief of his father's passing. That unexpected tragedy had been difficult enough to deal with, but swift on its heels had come the reading of the will, and, with it, the added afflictions of anger and betrayal. They made for unfamiliar burdens, but Mateo had embraced them with a vengeance—as anchors in a life gone suddenly adrift.

He and his father had always had their differences. Leandro Cardea had been a serious and driven man, determined to live up to the ancient merchant tradition of his family. Mateo's lighthearted manner had at times driven him mad, as had his ideas for the business. Their disagreements had been loud; their heated debates, on the future of shipping and how best to steer the business in the hard years after the 1812 war with England, had been legendary. Mateo had been constitutionally unable to submit to the yoke of authority his father wished to confine him in, but despite different temperaments and differing opinions, he had thought they always shared the same end goal: the success of Cardea Shipping.

He did not know who he was without it. His first steps had been made along the teeming Philadelphia docks. He'd spent his childhood in that busy, dizzy atmosphere, learning arithmetic in the counting houses and how to read from warehouse manifests. He'd grown to manhood on board his father's ships, learning every aspect of the shipping business with sweat and tears and honest labour. His adult life had been comprised of an endless search for new markets, new imports, new revenue. For years he had worked, struggled and prepared for the day that he would take the helm of the family business.

And now he never would. So, yes—he had grabbed on to his anger with both hands and held tight. But it was an unaccustomed affliction, and it had grown heavier and more burdensome with each passing week. It would be a relief indeed to set it aside, but was he ready?

Not quite. Portia had been convincing last night. Something inside him wished to believe her, but he had a need to question her closely, and a rising desire to compare stories.

I need your help, she'd said, and she'd mentioned something about her own dilemma. It set his mind awhirl, with curiosity and, worse, a growing sense of suspicion. His father's heavy-handed manipulation blared loud and obvious, but could Portia truly have been unaware of her part in it?

As he'd already done hundreds of times, Mateo dragged his memory for details of the thwarted marriage scheme Leandro Cardea and the Earl of Winbury had attempted nearly nine years ago. Their timing had been preposterous. Mateo had been completely occupied with his sleek new schooner, and the opportunity for fortune, glory and adventure that privateering would give him and his crew. The notion of a marriage had been his father's last, desperate attempt to steer him from that course. Ever the rebel, Mateo had laughed at the idea—and at his father's clumsy choice of a bride.

Portia Varnsworth? A girl-child she'd been, with

plenty of pluck, but no more appeal than a younger sister. At the time he'd hoped she'd been just as incredulous as he. He'd written to her with that assumption, and certainly her response had reassured him. She was far too young to contemplate such a thing, she'd replied, and entirely too caught up with a landscaping project on her father's estate. And there was the Season for her to look forward to the following year. Mateo had sighed in relief and promptly forgot the entire scheme.

But he had thought of her occasionally, over the years. He remembered her shy smile and her willingness to listen. He'd been surprised and curious at the news of her marriage, and sympathetic when he'd heard of her husband's death. Had anyone asked, he would have confessed to remembering her fondly.

Until the day he'd sat in the solicitor's office and heard that his father had left the controlling interest in Cardea Shipping to her. Instead of leading the family legacy into the future, he would be working for Portia Varnsworth.

Mateo's shock had been complete. Doubt and suspicion had sprouted like weeds in his mind. And if he hadn't been so angry, he would have laughed at the—once again—impeccable bad timing of the thing.

At the thought he urged his mount to a quicker pace. Whatever the outcome of this meeting, *someone* had to quickly take control of Cardea Shipping. Ahead must be the lane that would take him to Stenbrooke. He took the turning, but after only a few minutes' travel he found himself distracted. Gazing about him, Mateo realised that, of a certainty, there was one thing about his childhood friend that had not changed.

Portia Tofton, née Varnsworth, was a gardener. Digging, planting, pruning, cutting, Portia had never been happier than when she was covered in muck. Looking about, it became clear that she had continued to indulge her beloved pastime here at Stenbrooke.

The lane he followed led first through a wooded grove, immaculately kept and dotted with the occasional early-blooming clump of monk's hood. Eventually, though, the wood thinned, giving way to a sweeping vista of rolling hills. Ahead the path diverged. To the left, over the tops of a grouping of trees, he caught sight of a peaked roof. On the right nestled a jewel of a lake, edged with flowering shrubs and spanned by a rustic stone bridge.

Mateo marvelled at the beauty of the scene. Then he spared a moment's empathy for the hardship some sea captain had endured in transporting the obviously exotic specimens.

He shook his head. The landscaping work here was awe-inspiring. Surely Brown or Repton had had a hand in it. Had Portia kept this up herself after her husband's passing? But of course she had. Care and attention to detail were evident in every direction.

It was ongoing even now, he noted, catching sight of several labourers grouped on the far side of the bridge. Standing thigh-high in the lake, they were repairing one of the arches, judging from the steady ring of hammer against stone. He watched them idly until he reached the fork in the lane, and then he turned his mount's head in the direction of the house.

Until suddenly his brain processed what his eyes had just seen. He hauled on the reins, startling the animal, and spun him swiftly around. Raising a hand, he cast his best weather eye towards the lake again. Yes. One of the labourers had moved to the edge of the stone pedestal and into view. A labourer in skirts.

A sharp bark of laughter broke free. Yes, he mused, men did die. Enterprises failed, empires grew and nations were born. Mateo had learned that lesson the hard way. One had only to look about with an unjaundiced eye to know that change and upheaval were the only persevering truths in this life.

Perhaps that explained, then, why he should be struck with unexpected delight at the odd tableau before him. It was something of a relief to discover that some things never did change.

The ghost of a smile flitted about his mouth. It was even more of a relief to once again find pleasure in a simple, unexpected moment. He let the stranglehold on his anger slip—just a little—and spurred his mount towards the lake.

Chapter Three

'That's done it now, Mrs Tofton.'

Portia's ears still rang from the blow of the mallet. Her foreman's voice sounded tinny and distant, though he loomed close by her side.

'You can let go. That's the last one.'

She did, shaking out the strain in her arms and stepping back. The damaged pedestal of her stone arch bridge was nearly repaired, she saw with satisfaction.

'Aye, that does it,' Newman echoed her sentiment. 'A bit of mortar and it'll be right as rain.' He turned as another man splashed up. 'We'll not be needing another block after all, Billings. You can throw that one back in the cart. We're nearly done now.'

Billings turned, but cast a resentful eye back towards the bridge. 'Can I be gettin' back to the orchard now? New branches don't train themselves.'

'Yes, of course.' Portia grasped her water-logged skirts and started back towards shore, as well. 'Thank you, Billings. I am sorry I had to tear you away from your trees.' She sighed. 'Perhaps next year we shall be able to hire some more permanent labourers.'

'Aye, well, and if you do, let them waddle after Newman here. I'm fine alone in the orchard, but if you be wantin' a crop this year or next, you'll be lettin' me get on with me work.'

'Oh, go on, you old crosspatch,' she said, smiling over her shoulder at him. 'Newman, can you finish up on your own? I suppose I must get back to the house and change before our company arrives.'

'You've left it a bit late.' Billings shifted his burden and spat casually into the water. 'Leastaways, you did if your company's dark, broad as that yonder oak and near as tall.'

Portia's gaze followed the thrust of his chin towards the shore before the impact of his words truly hit her. With a gasp, she splashed to a halt and dropped her skirts. A horse stood tethered near the pony cart they had used to transport stone and supplies, and striding down the slight incline towards the water came Mateo Cardea.

Tall and strong, with sun glinting off his dark curls and shining boots, he advanced with a purposeful tread. Portia's mouth gaped open as he failed to stop at the shore's edge, but the chiselled lines of his face were set and determined. Without hesitation he strode right into the water and towards her. She stared, noting his furrowed brow and the large straw hat dangling from his fingers.

Water sloshed around her knees as he drew to a halt in front of her. Her breath caught.

And then he smiled.

Unfair! The cry emanated from the vulnerable part of Portia's soul, the one that she had spent just this morning locking away. It was a nonsensical notion, but the sudden pounding of her heart felt eerily like the bang of a fist on a closed door.

Where was the angry, brooding man who'd hurled insults at her last night? She searched his face, but the stormy countenance and dangerous gaze had fled like clouds before sunshine. And left only the visage that had fuelled her adolescent dreams for years.

The real irony was that it was a face that might have been made for anger and brooding. Bold, dark eyes flashed under arched brows and amidst a longish, angular face. The great Cardea nose might have overwhelmed any other man's features, but on Mateo was balanced beautifully by his wide, sensual mouth and irresistible tangle of curls. Masculine splendour shone down on her, warmer than the rays of the sun. And suddenly Portia wobbled, as weak in the knees as if she truly had spent too long in the heat.

Mateo stepped close and grasped her arm.

Billings snorted as he sloshed past them. 'Coming through, Mrs Tofton.'

Newman followed without comment, and without turning his gaze in their direction. Portia barely noticed. She watched, mesmerized, as Mateo's other hand lifted, rose and disappeared above her head. She jumped, startled at the gentle touch of his fingers moving in her hair.

'Forgive me,' he said softly. 'But—' Brown and capable, his hand hovered before her face, holding a large chip of stone. Comprehension dawned, along with a flush of embarrassment. She suppressed it and watched him toss the thing into the water. Grasping the straw hat where it dangled beneath their arms, he offered it up. 'You'll want your hat, Peeve,' he said quite casually. 'Your nose is turning red.'

She lost her fight with the advancing tide of warmth. And just the thought that he might notice turned a simple blush into a spiralling wave of heat. She tried calling herself to task. She'd meant to demonstrate her complete indifference to his anger, to present a picture of a woman occupied with her own pursuits, fully capable of commanding her own destiny. She had *not* meant to blush like a girl at his first words or to meet him standing knee-deep in the lake.

But this was the Mateo of her youth—and somehow their bizarre situation seemed fitting. He towered over her, one eyebrow elevated, a matching wry grin pulling at the opposite corner of his mouth. Portia drew a long, shuddering breath. It struck her hard—that oh-so-familiar gleam in his dark eyes, full of good-natured mischief and just the smallest hint of irony.

She pulled abruptly away from his touch and struck out on her own for the shore. 'Don't call me that, please.'

He followed, literally in her wake. 'I will not, of course, if you dislike it. But I assure you that today at least, I meant it only in affection.'

'Nevertheless.' Portia climbed the springy bank, bent down and grasped her shoes.

'Shall I call you Mrs Tofton, then?' he asked with a quizzically raised brow.

She heard the unasked question. He wondered why she did not use her hereditary title. And deliberately she did not answer. 'That is my name,' she answered in the same tone. 'But why don't you just call me Portia, as you used to?' She summoned a smile. 'I beg your pardon for meeting you in such disarray. My foreman said we had to act quickly to prevent further damage to the bridge, and I'm afraid I cast all other considerations aside.'

She lowered her gaze as he drew close, and caught sight of his ruined footwear. 'Oh,' she gasped, 'your boots!' She glared up at him. 'Whatever possessed you, Mateo? There was no need of that.'

'But it was necessary—after my display of spectacularly bad manners, I feared you would strike out for the opposite shore at the sight of me.' He still held her floppy hat. With delicate movements, he lifted it high. Moving slowly, as if he worked not to frighten her, he scttled it on her head.

She stood stiff and ram-rod straight. He followed the line of ribbons with his fingertips and began to tie them under her chin.

'I suppose I could not have blamed you if you had,' he spoke low and his jaw tensed. 'I owe you an apology, *cara*. No matter the situation, I should not have lashed out at you like that.'

She flinched at the old endearment. He was too close. She was too flustered. She'd wanted him to look at her, *see* her, but she'd imagined it at more of a distance. Portia's heart began to flit inside her chest like a bird in a cage.

She pushed his hands away and stepped back. 'I'm perfectly capable of tying my own ribbons, thank you,' she said irritably. She breathed deep, needing to regain control of her wayward emotions and the situation. *You aren't a love-struck young girl any more*, she reminded herself fiercely.

'There is no need for an apology.' There, that was better. Her tone, at least, sounded tightly controlled. 'The circumstances are highly unusual. I suppose anyone might have jumped to the conclusions you did.'

His dark gaze roved over her. He said nothing for a long minute, just watched her closely while she fiddled with half-tied ribbons. 'Ah, but I begin to see now,' he said. 'Anyone might have suspected the worst, but you didn't expect it of me.'

Some heavy emotion weighted his voice. Guilt? Sorrow? She wished she knew which she would have preferred it to be.

'And that changes much of what I thought would pass between us.' His brow furrowed as he stared down at her. 'And what do I do with you now, I wonder?'

Portia stiffened. 'Not a thing! It's not your place to *do* anything at all with me. In fact, I'd say the shoe was quite on the other foot.'

He winced. 'I deserved that, did I not?'

'And far more.' She raked her gaze down the length of him. 'Hard as you may find it to believe, Mateo, I've had important things on my mind—and not a one of them involved a scheme to trap you into marriage.'

He returned her speculative gaze. 'Do you know—I think it would have been better for me, had you been the villainess I suspected you to be.'

How was she supposed to answer that?

'Portia! Are you down here still?'

The shrill call saved her from the necessity. She glanced up and caught sight of a glimpse of colour through the trees. Many times over the years, she'd had reason to be grateful to Dorrie, but she could recall nothing like the great tide of relief that swept through her now.

'Portia?'

'Here, Dorinda!' she answered with a wave as Dorrie erupted from the trees at a trot.

'Portia,' Dorrie called, urgency alive in her expression, as well as in the unusual quickness of her step. 'Vickers tells me a rider was spotted…' Her gait faltered. 'Oh, yes. I see I'm too late.'

Portia fidgeted as the heavy weight of her companion's gaze fell on her.

Dorrie let out an audible moan. 'Oh, Portia, dear! How could you?'

From beside her came an unexpected, but completely familiar sound. From this broad-shouldered hulk of a sea captain came an almost boyish snort.

Portia's eyes widened. How many times had she heard that exact sound? Hundreds, if not thousands. It triggered a whirlwind of old emotion: exasperation, irritation and fleeting camaraderie. Visions danced in her head, of infuriating pranks, of whispered *risqué* stories she'd tried desperately to overhear, and of the pair of them united, usually to get one of her brothers either into or out of trouble.

It was a sound from her past. But today it ignited a great, yearning well of hope for the future. The old Mateo Cardea would have helped her in an instant. Perhaps he was still in there somewhere.

And perhaps he would enjoy getting to know the new Portia Tofton.

Her heart pounding, she moved forwards, beckoning Dorrie closer. 'It's just a little lake water, Dorrie,' she cajoled. 'And you're not late, but just in time to meet Mr Cardea. Come, and I will introduce you.'

Mateo watched Portia hurry away. A great wave of guilt and confusion had swamped him at her earlier words. He allowed it to fade a bit, allowed it, even, to be replaced with a wholly ungentlemanly sense of satisfaction. He'd rattled her. Good.

He had a sneaking suspicion that it would be in his interest to keep Portia unsettled. And a little rattling was no more than she deserved. After all, she'd rocked his moorings loose last night. And she'd done it again today, too, without even so much as trying. Ah, but the picture she had presented just now had been priceless! Pink-cheeked, covered in rock dust and knee-deep in water—*Dio*, but she'd been the most beautiful sight. He'd seen the contentment on her face and the glint of mischief shining brighter than the gold flecks in her eyes, and he'd forgotten his purpose.

What was he to do now? He closed his eyes. Exactly what he'd intended, he supposed. Her artless confusion and hesitant manner convinced him of her innocence, but changed nothing, really.

Mateo had arrived in England with a purpose. He'd meant to rebuff Portia Tofton, thwart any attempt at manipulation and get his company back. Failing that, he meant to say a last goodbye to his old life—and move on to the new. Old expectations were of no more use than a leaky skiff. A clever man knew when to abandon them and move on.

'Mateo, may I introduce my cousin and companion?' She approached again with the new arrival in tow. 'Miss Dorinda Tofton.'

'*Piacere*, Miss Tofton.' Mateo bowed respectfully over her hand. 'It is indeed a pleasure to make your acquaintance. My old friend is fortunate indeed to be surrounded by such beauty.'

'Oh, yes,' Miss Tofton agreed with a sweep of her hand towards the lake. 'Is it not the most charming prospect?'

'Nearly as charming as her companion.' He delivered the compliment smoothly, but with just the right touch of sincerity. A flush of pleasure pinked her pale cheeks, but she did not grow uneasy.

'And almost as pleasant as a reunion with an old acquaintance.' Miss Tofton knew how to play the game. She glanced over at Portia and her brow creased once more. 'Please do not allow the manner of our greeting to dishearten you, sir. Though it may not look it, we have been awaiting your arrival with the utmost anticipation.'

'Yes, yes, Dorrie.' Portia grew impatient with the fussing. 'I do thank you for coming today, Mateo. We must talk of your company, of course, and I have something of the utmost importance to discuss with you.'

She called out suddenly to the men preparing to leave in the pony cart. 'Billings, Newman! Just a moment, please!'

She turned back to Mateo. 'Dorinda is right, though; I really must change before we speak. Perhaps you would care for a stroll about the gardens?' Mateo caught the significant glance she shot towards her companion and wondered what it foretold. 'I would love you to see some of Stenbrooke before we discuss our...troubles.'

She smiled sweetly before he could protest. 'We'll bring your mount along to the stables, and you can get acquainted with Dorinda.' Her hand swept towards the bridge. 'It's quite safe now, and there are some lovely vistas on the Cascade Walk.'

Again, he was given no chance to respond. In a flash she was gone up the hill and climbing into the cart. One of the labourers hitched his hired horse to the cart and jumped on the back as it jerked to a start.

'Well...' Miss Tofton sighed as she waved them off '...it's an unorthodox reception you've had, to be sure, Mr Cardea, but as Portia tells me you've been acquainted since infancy, I gather you won't be too surprised by it.'

Curbing his impatience, Mateo laughed. 'Surprised that Portia let a landscaping project distract her from every other concern? Not at all, ma'am.'

She glanced askance at him. 'I see you do indeed know Portia well.'

He gestured towards the lake and they set off at an easy pace. 'Perhaps it surprises you that a half-Italian merchant sea captain should be on intimate terms with the family of an English earl?'

Her denial came quickly, and, if he were any judge, in sincere terms. 'Not at all,' she assured him. 'Portia has explained how close your fathers were. I have to say, I was more than a little jealous when she spoke of the visits back and forth your families undertook. It sounds infinitely more exciting than my own childhood.'

'I admit it was great fun, in most instances.' He

smiled down at her. 'And I will tell you, over the years, in all the months we spent together, there were always constants,' he said. He held three fingers up. 'During each and every visit, my father and Portia's would spend at least one evening drinking and recounting the story of La Incandescent Clarisse.' He folded down one finger and laughed at the sight of her rolled eyes. 'Yes, I see you are acquainted with the story.'

He ticked off another finger. 'At least one of Portia's brothers would rake up a scrape that I would be forced to rescue him from.' He raised a brow. 'Again, you do not look shocked.'

The last finger he wagged in her direction. 'And three—whenever Portia went missing, we all knew to look in the gardens.' He dropped his hand and sighed. 'I have only just finished telling myself that in a world of chaos, it is most comfortable to know that some things do not change.'

Miss Tofton tucked her hand a little more firmly into the crook of his arm. For a few moments they walked in silence and Mateo welcomed the cool comfort of the shade as the path led them through a grove of birches.

'I confess it is a relief to hear you speak fondly of Portia and her family,' her companion said after a few minutes. 'I realise that you have not had a chance to discuss…things, but I am very grateful to think that we might have your help.'

Curiosity quickened his pulse. But as so often happened with women, his silence had encouraged Miss Tofton to continue. 'One thing I know from experience, Mr Cardea, and I would ask you to remember, is that a woman alone does not have an easy path in this world.'

'None of us alone do, ma'am.'

'You are right, of course, but I profess that it is particularly hard for a woman; we have so many more
obstacles and fewer options, you see. A woman in such
a situation must display more courage, resilience and
determination than a man.' She let go of his arm and
crossed over to a pretty little bench. She ran her fingers
over the scrolled ironwork, but did not sit. 'Portia in
particular is strong in many ways, but vulnerable in
others. She's had a difficult time of it since her husband
died. Aside from the obvious repercussions, there's been
the unfortunate notoriety…' She shook her head. 'And
debt—you would not believe some of the indignities
she's been exposed to in settling James Talbot's debts.'

Debt Mateo could well believe. Even as a young man,
J. T. Tofton's tastes had run towards high stakes, fast
horses and loose women—tastes that a mere squire's
son could not often indulge. But notoriety, indignities?
The companion's words and manner suggested something more than a husband who lived a little beyond his
means. A sharp spike of curiosity peaked inside him,
followed by a faint sense of shame.

'You will be happy to hear, perhaps, that one area in
which she has stood fast is in her belief in you, sir.'

'Indeed?' Shame quickly outpaced any other reaction.

'Yes. You must excuse me, but with no personal
acquaintance of you, sir, I counselled her to proceed
cautiously. I thought you might naturally have wondered
if Portia had any prior knowledge of or design in your
father's actions.'

'Naturally,' he echoed weakly.

She pierced him with her stare. 'But Portia stood staunch in your defence and has claimed all these weeks that you knew her better than to suppose so.' Her expression darkened. 'I hope you will deserve her faith in you, sir.'

As a warning, it was most effective. Mateo fought back another surge of guilt and tried instead to focus on just what all this might mean: for him and for Cardea Shipping. 'I hope I will, too,' he said. He held out his arm once more. 'Shall we go back and find out?'

Portia changed quickly to dry stockings and her prettiest day gown of palest yellow, the one that Dorrie said made the most of the dreaded sun-kissed streaks in her hair. On the verge of leaving her room again, she gasped. Her hair! She'd nearly forgotten. Bending over to peer in the mirror, she moaned at the liberal coating of rock dust.

Well, she was not going to ring for her maid and wait an eternity to be re-coiffed. Instead, she took up a brush herself and stroked until her arm was tired and her plain brown locks were clean and shining. A quick high knot, a tuck of the wayward strands that would soon be working free in any case, and she was off, tripping down the stairs and rounding the turn at the bottom towards the back of the house.

Vickers stood outside the dining room, giving low-voiced instructions to a footman. Portia nodded and, trying not to give the appearance of hurrying, she headed straight for the morning room, where double doors led out to the veranda. They stood open, bathing the room in sunshine and warmth. Despite her urgency, she could not resist pausing on the threshold.

Here. This exact spot—her favourite. Her eyes closed. She loved to stand here, poised at the juncture of inside and out, balancing on the common point between untamed nature and domesticity. Beeswax and baking bread scented the air behind her, the earthy smell of the sun-soaked lawn in front. In between. Neither here nor there. The perfect metaphor for Portia Tofton.

Voices sounded ahead. Her eyes snapped open and she crossed to the stone balustrade. There. They had reached the ha-ha; Mateo was assisting Dorrie over the stile at the far end of the lawn. Portia watched closely as they approached. Could she do it? Could she make him understand what all of this meant to her?

Carefully, she tried to gauge Mateo's mood. Certainly he appeared relaxed as he talked easily with Dorinda. Portia stared, transfixed as the breeze tossed his curls and he laughed out loud. Their words were indistinct, lost in the crunch of gravel underneath their feet as they crossed the path, but as they approached her spot on the edge of the veranda, his tousled head rose. He looked up and met Portia's gaze.

They grew closer, and he continued in his steady regard, until gradually it turned into a slow survey, down the length of her and back up. Something shifted inside of her, a thrill of awakening excitement, long gone but not forgotten. She gripped the balustrade beside her.

'Portia,' he said gravely as they reached her, 'I was just telling Miss Tofton how impressed I am with your gardens.'

Dorrie smiled. 'And I was just about to tell Mr Cardea how much more impressed with Stenbrooke he would be, had he seen it before all of your hard work.'

Mateo's brow furrowed. Portia could see his mind working, remembering. 'It was not in good shape, then?' he asked, but he said it as if he already knew the answer.

Portia merely shook her head.

'You know,' he mused, 'at first, as I rode in, I could only think of harried crews of seamen struggling to keep your more exotic specimens alive to make it in to port.' He smiled. 'But I also thought to myself that one of the great landscapers must have had a hand in all of this.'

'Yes,' Dorinda said firmly. 'She did.'

'Oh, don't tease him, Dorrie.' Portia smiled and lifted her brows at the pair of them. She wanted Mateo at his ease for this interview. 'Thank you for giving me a moment to repair myself.'

His gaze travelled once more over the square neckline of her gown. 'It was my pleasure.'

Her pulse jumped. 'Come,' she said. She gestured to the elegant table and comfortably padded chairs set up in the shade. 'Please, join us for some refreshments. This is one of our loveliest spots.'

'Thank you.' After he had seated them, he took his own chair and cast a smile at Dorinda. 'When you mentioned the state of the place, I suddenly recalled the time when Portia's aunt passed on and we all discovered that she would inherit this estate. It wasn't until just now that I remembered that it was supposed to be a run-down old spot. Her brothers teased her unmercifully.'

He turned his gaze to Portia and she noticed tiny

lines at the corner of his dark eyes. 'Brothers do tend to believe in the right to cruelty towards their siblings, no? And in Portia's case, I believe they regarded it as a sacred duty. Especially when they heard the estate was to come to her on her marriage. They spent hours speculating how decrepit this place would become before Portia found someone to marry her.'

Dorrie choked back a laugh. 'Well, marry she did, and a good thing it was for me too,' she said staunchly. 'I've hardly been as comfortable and happy in my life as I have since Portia graciously took me in.'

Portia returned her fond smile, but Dorrie continued. 'And despite their meanness, her brothers were not that far off the mark. Of course, I was just a visitor then, but the house and grounds were both in a terrible condition when Portia and James Talbot moved in.'

Perhaps Portia should not be watching Mateo so closely. Tension throbbed through her until she thought he must be able to sense it. But if she had not been paying such close attention, she might have missed it. There. Just the smallest wince at the corners of Mateo's eyes. Not a smile line, either; it showed up at the mention of J.T.'s name. She had the fleeting thought that it resembled pain—or perhaps she only thought so because of the stabbing clench of her stomach that occurred for the same reason.

He hid it well, by turning his gaze about him. Despite her anxiety, Portia felt a thrill of pride. She could not be falsely modest about the beautiful prospect; she'd worked too hard to achieve it.

'Do you mean to say that this—' he gestured '—is all your design?'

'It is,' Dorrie answered for her. She glanced at Portia and then graced Mateo with a determined smile. 'And since there is yet no sign of the tea cart, why don't the two of you walk along the front of the house? Portia can tell you about the changes she's made.'

'A tempting notion, Miss Tofton, were this a social call. But it is not. Portia has stated that she had no notion of my father's intentions and I've offered my apology for jumping to conclusions, but I would like to hear the particulars, if you please.' Mateo paused, his lips pressed tightly together.

'Ah, the devil!' he finally exclaimed, pushing away from the table. 'This is a damnable snarl we've found ourselves in and whether it goes your way or mine in the end, we need to get it untangled—and the sooner, the better.' He sighed. 'But I suspect that first we must find out how we ended up here. To begin with, I'd like to hear more of the dilemma you mentioned last—'

Portia jumped to her feet. 'Please, Mateo?' she interrupted before Dorrie could catch a hint of her late-night activities. 'I promise your questions will be answered. And, in fact, there may be a solution to make both of us happy. But if you will bear with me, I'd like to start by showing you some of the history of this house.'

'Portia…' He sighed. '*Cara*, for me, this is already painful enough. I just wish to be done with it and truly there is some urgency…'

She turned a pleading gaze on him and he trailed to a stop. She thought he meant to balk—but then he heaved a sigh.

'For a moment,' he relented. 'And then, Portia, we talk.'

Grudgingly, he stood and offered his arm. She

took it, and then led him on a slow revolution about the house. She spoke ardently as they went, trying to convey her passion along with a picture of the estate as it used to be. And trying to subdue the hum of passion that coursed through her with every step.

But it was difficult. Her head might know how useless and more, how stupid, it was to fall into old patterns. Her heart might shrink, fearful of trusting the man who'd scorned her first, fledgling love and bruised her tender, young soul. But her body—her traitorous body didn't care. It lit up for him, surging with awareness, trembling with intense response to his nearness.

How could it not? He was Mateo, and he was beautiful. Not the right word, perhaps, for a sun-browned example of strong and robust manhood, but the one she chose none the less. It was the beauty of character that he possessed—stamped into his laughing dark eyes, moulded into the kindness, the confidence and the absolute assurance of his manner. It called to her, just as it always had. And she could not answer.

So she talked instead of the choking ivy that they'd had to tear down, the sagging columns that had barely supported the first-floor balcony, the gradual replacement of the casement windows and large sections of the slate roof. She used every excuse to pull away, to walk ahead and remove herself from danger.

To her relief, he paid close attention, questioning her about the house and grounds, and when they circled back to the veranda he took his seat once more with a shake of his head.

'I admit to being suitably impressed,' he said to Dorrie as he held Portia's chair. 'Portia's descriptions

are so vivid that I can nearly see the sad state of disre-
pair that she first encountered here. The enormity of
what you've accomplished is humbling.' He gazed about
at the tranquil scene. 'I can only imagine the hue and
cry and mess of reconstruction. It must have taken an
army of labourers.'

Dorrie chuckled. 'That's exactly the remark that all
visitors make.'

Conversation was interrupted by the arrival of the
refreshments. Portia poured: tea for Dorrie and coffee
for Mateo. Strong, hot and sweet—she recalled exactly
how he liked it. The quirk of his lips told her that he
noticed. He sat back with a sigh of satisfaction.

'I'm glad you realise the scope of the work we've
done here, Mateo,' Portia began, ignoring her own
tea. 'We started with the neglected fields first, and the
orchards and the dairy. Once we had an actual income,
we began on the house and the gardens.' She leaned forwards. 'But we've never had an army of hired workers.
Everything we've done has been through the effort of
our small staff and tenants. We've all worked hard and
made something useful and beautiful. I know that you,
of all people, understand what happens when people
share goals, work and rewards.'

He stared. She thought he looked curious and a little
resentful. 'I think I know what you are trying to say,
Portia. You've done an admirable job here.' He pressed
his lips together once more. 'I suspect you mean to
retain your control of Cardea Shipping, but before you
decide, I ask that you listen to me, please—'

She cut him off. 'No, what I'm trying to convey is
that we are a family, Mateo. All of us here at Sten-

brooke.' China clinked as she pushed her cup to the side. 'And that is why I need you to help me save it.'

Mateo sat upright, jolted out of his customary lounge by the startling unpredictability of Portia's words. In fact, that was not remotely what he'd been expecting her to say. He'd thought she'd been laying the groundwork, preparing him to accept her as the head of *his* company. Instead—

'Save Stenbrooke?' he asked. 'From what? Explain please.'

Her pretty face twisted with pain. 'You've complained that your father betrayed you. I find myself in complete sympathy, for mine failed me.'

'I'm going to require a more thorough explanation than that.'

'First I will tell you one last time—I have had no hand in your misfortune. I had no earthly idea of what your father was about, to will me controlling interest in your business.'

'It is true, Mr Cardea,' chimed in her companion. 'I was here when her brother's solicitor arrived bearing the news. I can testify to her utter shock.'

'I panicked, in fact,' Portia said. 'I thought something dreadful must have happened to you.'

Mateo saw sincerity in her eyes and an urgent need to be believed. 'I'll accept that—since we've met again, I already strongly suspected it. But what does it have to do with Stenbrooke?'

'Nothing yet.'

Mateo caught his first glimpse of hesitation. He leaned forwards.

'I was bewildered, but Anthony's man didn't have

any answers. I sent a letter with him back to Hempshaw, thinking my brother would have them—or at least have news of you.'

'And did he?'

She shook her head. Mateo watched several heavy strands of her honeyed hair fall from confinement and curl against the slender column of her neck. 'No, neither. So I immediately sent a message to you, asking you to come and help me decipher this mess.' Her gaze fell away. 'I realise it might have been short, and perhaps awkward. That was precisely how I felt, considering how long it had been...and especially considering the nature of our last contact.'

Her hand rose and hovered near the bodice of her gown. Mateo recognised her obvious unease and thought back to her letter. It had indeed been curt and cryptic—and it had helped fuel his rising fury and suspicion. He sighed. It didn't matter now, he supposed, but he was surprised at the intense relief that came with the knowledge that she had not conspired against him.

'It was only a day or so later that yet another solicitor came calling—but for a very different reason.' Portia exchanged a pained look with Miss Tofton. 'He carried with him a deed of conveyance and informed me that Stenbrooke was no longer mine.'

Mateo shook his head. His brain hurt from the sudden shifts in this conversation. 'How can that be?'

'That was exactly our reaction,' Miss Tofton said indignantly.

'It could be—' and now Portia's voice rang with bitterness '—because of my rotten blighter of a husband.'

'Portia!'

Mateo felt inclined to echo her companion's gasp of shock.

'I beg your pardon, Dorrie, but you are well aware of my feelings and Mateo might as well be, too.'

'But to speak so of the dead...' She shuddered.

'Will not bother him in the least,' Mateo assured her. He turned to Portia. 'Please, go on.'

She nodded. 'As you said, Stenbrooke came into my possession on my marriage. It was meant to be secured to me and my children in the marriage settlements. Somehow, my father failed to see it done.' She fought to keep her resentment from overpowering her. 'I have no notion how my father could have neglected to take care with the single most important thing in my life, but the fact remains that he didn't. Stenbrooke therefore became my husband's property, according to law.' She paused. 'And I had no idea. It was an oversight that no one saw fit to inform me of.'

Drawing a deep breath, she continued. 'J.T. knew of it, obviously. He used the estate as a stake in a card game. He lost my home over a hand of faro—another fact that he neglected to tell me before he went and got himself so ignominiously killed.'

There was not enough room in Mateo's head for all his myriad reactions to this conversation. A whirlwind of conflicting thoughts and feelings set his temples pounding. Ridiculous, then, that the one at the top was an ugly sense of satisfaction that perhaps Portia had not loved her husband.

'I am sorry to hear it,' he managed to say.

'Oh, but you don't even know the worst of it!' Miss Tofton exclaimed. 'This new owner is craven. He didn't even have the decency to face Portia; he merely sent along a newly hired solicitor to deliver the news. And that dreadful man was in turn evasive and cruel. He said that his employer is an experimental agriculturist who is always in search of new ground for his research. He said it was quite likely that all of this would be ploughed under if ever he got his hands on Stenbrooke!'

Mateo narrowed his focus, and watched Portia intensely.

'I want you to help me,' she said simply.

He exhaled sharply. 'And how do you expect me to do that? Portia, you must know why I've come. I want to make arrangements to buy back your interest in Cardea Shipping.'

She shook her head. 'I won't sell it to you.'

He closed his eyes and tried to ignore the twisting of his stomach. 'Perhaps just the Baltimore office, then. I started that branch myself, in the face of my father's opposition. I confess, I don't have enough ready capital of my own to buy you out completely, but I could likely manage just the one office.'

She shook her head again.

Now there was anger churning inside of him along with everything else. 'Portia—'

'No.' She interrupted him yet again. 'There will be no sale.' Tension shone apparent in the thin line of her mouth and in every stiff angle of her body. 'Instead I propose a simple trade. Stenbrooke for Cardea Shipping.' Her hands gripped the end of the table until her knuckles whitened. 'Buy Stenbrooke, Mateo, and sign it back over to me. Give me my life back, and I'll give you yours.'

* * *

Portia clenched her teeth, her fists, and every muscle at her command as she waited for Mateo's answer. He would agree. Of course he would. He had to.

His gaze, staring so boldly into hers, broke away. He exhaled sharply and pushed back from the table, crossing over to the stone balustrade. Leaning heavily, he stared out over the garden and beyond for several silent minutes. Portia's head began to ache with the strain.

'Why do you not go to your brother for assistance?' he asked at last.

'I have,' she said, helpless against the bitterness that coloured her tone again. 'Nothing there has changed since we were children. I am still the youngest, the baby of the family, and a woman besides. What need have I to live alone on my own estate?' She rose to her feet and crossed over to the potted *rosa rugosa*. With quick, sharp movements she began to pick fading leaves off it, keeping an eye on his bent, still form all the while.

'Anthony cannot spare the expense, and if he had that sort of ready income, he'd be honour bound to put it into his own estate. He sees no reason why I should not be happy to pack my things and move back to Hempshaw. His countess is overrun, you see, exhausted from birthing four boys in six years, and could use a bit of help with keeping them in hand.'

Mateo let loose a sharp bark of laughter, although there was little humour in it. 'That is Anthony all over.'

'Yes,' she said flatly. 'But I won't have it. I am tired of being let down by the men who are supposed to have my best interests at heart. I want my home, Mateo. I want my independence.'

'At the very least she should be allowed to use the London house,' Dorrie complained. That had been her favourite plan for their future. 'But her brother is adamant about saving expenses and has leased it out.'

Finally Mateo turned and looked at her.

'The rest of the world would no doubt agree with my brother,' she said. 'But I had hoped that once you were here, and saw what we've done, you would understand. We've both had everything we wanted in our grasp, only to have it snatched away.'

His expression was carefully blank, but she could see the tension in the stiff line of his jaw. 'I don't have enough to purchase an estate like this.' He gestured about him.

'Perhaps not, but between the two of us, together in possession of a company like Cardea Shipping, surely we could, ah, liquidate some assets?' Her spine had gone as rigid as stone, but she would not plead, even now. 'I realise that the prospect is not pleasant, but it must be better than the alternative.' She let the unspoken threat hover.

But Mateo's head had come up. 'I suppose it could be done. We've the *Lily Fair* just in at Portsmouth with a cargo of flax-seed and fine walnut. And the agent there is as good as any we have in the company. The cargo itself will fetch a fair price, but once she's unloaded, we could put it about that we'd like to sell her.' His hands clenched on the balustrade behind him. '*Dio*, but I hate to give her up. She once made the run from Philadelphia to Liverpool in sixteen days, just two off the record.'

He stared unseeing at the terrace. 'Her captain will be fair disappointed. I'll have to reshuffle, offer him something special to keep him and his crew content. I'll have to see her refitted, renegotiate with the insurers.' He sighed then, and met her gaze. 'But there's no doubt she'll fetch a fine price—perhaps enough so that with what I have set back, we won't need to sacrifice any others. I'll start the process.' He grimaced. 'And with both of our signatures upon the papers, there can be no questioning the order.'

He abandoned the balustrade and began to pace, his expression lighter than she'd yet seen. 'There'll be no need for me to linger, though. With her reputation, she'll sell quickly. Our agents can handle the rest. And all you really need is funds. My own ship is waiting. A few days to draft up the exchange, leave instructions for proceeds from the sale to be sent to you, and I can be on my way.'

'No,' Portia said yet again.

Mateo stopped. He pivoted on his heel and turned to face her.

'You must stay,' she explained. 'My brother is seriously annoyed that I will not let Stenbrooke go. He tells me there is nothing to be done and has forbidden his solicitors to aid me in this. After all the strife following his death, my husband's solicitor will not even admit me any longer.'

Now she was on her feet and moving. 'I have serious questions about the validity of this conveyance, but no one will give me any answers. I broached the subject of buying the estate back with the new owner's solicitor, but he would not even agree to present the idea to his employer. This whole transaction seems cloaked in mystery, and no one will see it.' She turned away, allowing sour frustration to leak into her words. 'I am shushed like a child, patted on the head and ordered to pack my things.' She spun back. 'I am sick to death of it.'

She watched Mateo draw a deep breath. The excitement drained from his face even as it began to settle into an expression of exaggerated patience.

'I'm afraid you don't understand,' he began. 'There are business matters—'

She fought back a gasp. 'Don't you dare!' She could not believe it. How did he dare to patronise her after all she'd told him? 'Do not even think to speak to me in that reasonable tone! I've reached my limit, Mateo. I tell you now that I do not care what pressing business awaits you in Philadelphia. It has become painfully obvious that no one will take me seriously in this matter. Well, I am done being bullied, silenced and ignored. Clearly I need a man to aid me in this—and *you* are the only viable candidate.'

Anger flashed in his dark eyes and his jaw clenched. He moved away from the balustrade and began to pace from one end of the veranda to the other.

'You will stay and help me with this matter until Stenbrooke's deed is in my possession. Only then will I give you Cardea Shipping.' Though she suffered a pang of guilt at his resentment, on that she must stand firm. 'I am sorry to have to insist, but every other avenue is blocked.' She tossed him a bitter glance. 'I suppose I should not have hoped for sympathy. I doubt you have any notion how it might feel to be left without choices.'

'Until now?' he ground out.

She raised her chin.

'And you would be wrong in any case,' he continued bitterly. 'You knew my father.' He heaved a sigh of resignation. 'He was a good man, as I know you will agree, but a hard one, as well, and one absolutely committed to his own path. You cannot imagine the frustration I have felt, the times I thought I must be crushed under his thumb. And now I find myself back in the same position.' He raised an eyebrow at her. 'Albeit, under a smaller, daintier thumb.'

Portia's breath hitched. She'd been a fool to hope that they could get through this without harming each other's feelings once again. But she *would* be free at last. She was determined. She was also fully aware of the great irony here; that the one man she must force to help her gain her independence was the only one she'd ever truly wished to give it up for.

She straightened her shoulders. 'I would not place you in such a position if I could think of another way. So I suppose it is you who must decide. In the end you will get your legacy back, but you will have to wait, and I am afraid you will have to adjust to the weight of my thumb.' She summoned her courage. 'So—what will it be? Will you allow my hand on the rudder? Or is it too great a price to pay?'

His eyes glittered. 'You may have the upper hand here, Portia, but I must insist that you keep your hands off my rudder.'

Careful. His pride had already been dealt a massive blow. She must handle this delicately, but the thought of surrendering her fate into the hands of another man made her reckless.

'This is a crucial point, Mateo. We act as equals, or we do not act at all. I will not blithely turn this over for you to handle, while I sit at home. If you cannot accept me as a partner in this, then you will not get Cardea Shipping back.'

It was incongruous, the sight of him and his restless energy and gathering ire. He drew the eye, demanded attention, and looked completely out of place here in the midst of her green and tranquil haven. She blanched as he spun on his heel and approached her. The storm clouds were back, gathering across his brow.

'So you do not trust me with your business, Portia?' he asked in an acid tone. 'No doubt you think I'll be distracted by a stray wench and forget the weighty matters at hand.' He frowned. 'Careful, *cara*, you begin to sound like my father.'

'Nevertheless.' Her chin thrust even higher. 'What is it to be, then? Will you accept my terms? Or is the price too dear?'

'Almost, it is,' he growled. 'Almost, you tempt me to fling your offer back in your teeth. But I will do it. As you knew I would. I've no choice, really, do I?'

His words cut the taut line of tension running up her spine. She collapsed, sinking back onto the support of the balustrade. Relief and a fierce, hot joy blossomed in her chest.

'Give me a name,' he demanded. 'Where do I find this man and his deed of conveyance?'

It took a moment for her to gather her thoughts. A great weight had been lifted from her. For the first time in months she felt...light. Hopeful. Happy. She sucked in a breath, wanting to smell and taste and wallow in it.

'Portia? Dear, are you all right?' Dorinda eyed her with concern.

She breathed out. 'Of course. Mr Rankin is his name,' she said to Mateo. 'He has offices in Newbury.'

'How far?'

'Less than an hour's ride.'

'I'll see him tomorrow. You can be sure that I will only ask questions, scope the lay of the land. I'll not make a single decision,' he said sourly, 'and I'll call when I return to tell you of the outcome.' He turned away from her and sketched a brief bow in Dorrie's direction. 'Miss Tofton, it was a great pleasure to make your acquaintance.' Without hesitation he turned and strode for the steps.

'But...Mateo, wait!' Portia crossed the veranda in a hurry and leaned over in the exact spot he had so recently vacated.

'No. By God, I have no patience for any more today.' He paused and looked up at her. She recoiled at the annoyance and frustration suddenly visible in the depth of his dark gaze. 'I do not know how you do it, Portia, but always you poke and stir in just the right spots to send my temper flaring. I leave now, before either of us gets burned.'

Abruptly silenced, she pursed her lips and watched him stride away.

Chapter Four

Better a serpent with two heads than a man with two minds. It was advice that his *nona* had always delivered earnestly to his female cousins. Mateo had suddenly developed a more perfect understanding of what she had meant.

He'd been horrified at Portia's flat refusal to sell him back her portion of Cardea Shipping, and then he'd nearly shouted out his pleasure and relief at her proposal. Of course he had. It was a good solution—one that he would likely have come up with, had he found himself thrust into her unenviable predicament.

Cardea Shipping would be his again. Soon enough he'd have the freedom of the open sea before him, and the streets of Philadelphia underfoot. And then, at last, the autonomy to steer the business where he believed it needed to go. He clenched his fists. The family's docks would be a hive of activity again, their warehouses full to bursting. And those who had long scorned his ideas and lately laughed at his misfortune would soon be eating their words. He would prove to the merchant community of Philadelphia at last that they must let go of their past to secure their future.

His elation would be complete—were it not for the delay. Time was of the essence. Cardea Shipping had been on the brink of their most important venture in years when his father had died, and Mateo was going to have to hurry to salvage what he could of it. He could only hope that this business with Stenbrooke would go quickly.

And truthfully, something else had him swallowing a bilious rush of anger, even as he left the gloom of the inn and stood blinking in the bright morning sun. In his head he understood and even empathised with Portia's position, but he could not completely subdue the small, ugly ball of resentment churning in him.

She didn't trust him—and, oh, how that stung. The wound of his father's mistrust still lay open and now she rubbed it raw.

Purposefully, Mateo breathed deep and brushed such small thoughts aside. Where was his mount? The sooner he set this devil's bargain in motion, the sooner he'd have his business back on course.

He turned back and opened the inn door. Impatient, he called for the innkeeper. Abbott, he'd discovered the man's name to be, an irony which he found to be humorous on several levels.

'Abbot!' he called. 'I thought you'd sent word to the stables?'

The man came from the kitchens, brushing his hands on a stained apron. 'Yes, sir, I did. It'll be just a minute, though. We had a late customer come in. He was up early and bespoke my last nag for hire. I've sent to the livery in town for another.'

'How long?' Mateo asked.

'Any minute. Lads could be saddling him up right now, even.'

'I'll wait outside.'

Cursing the delay, he stepped back through the door. A rider circled around the building from the direction of the stable. On *his* mount, no doubt. Mateo watched him pass, a man of roughly his own age, dressed in the universal buff breeches and long brown coat that served as the uniform of a country gentleman. Only his hair, dark and a good deal longer than fashion currently dictated, made him stand out. He tipped his hat and Mateo swore he saw the hint of a smile as he passed. Damned impudence.

He left the empty courtyard and headed for the stables. Dew lay heavy on the ground this morning, sparkling off the blades of grass and beading like diamonds on tiny spider webs stretched between them. It brought to mind the dazzle of light bouncing off the water of the lake yesterday and the vision of Portia—full of sunshine and mischief—emerging from it.

Hard to believe, but she'd looked more enticing in the full light of day than in the flattering shadows of the inn, and that was not a claim one woman in a hundred could make. A child of Apollo, that one, with the sun captured in streaks through her tawny hair and golden flecks glimmering from her dark eyes. The sight of her had been a blow low in his gut, stimulating both a stir of desire and another flare of heated anger. His reactions to her were bizarre. He couldn't explain them to himself, let alone to her.

So he decided to learn from her example instead. Look at what she'd done with that bridge. She'd pitched in and helped repair it with her own two hands, even knowing that it might shortly belong to some damned farmer with a gambling habit. Surely she'd been full of worry, doubt, and, yes, anger. But she'd set it all aside to attend to what needed to be done.

Just exactly as he was going to have to do.

He rounded a corner and came into sight of the stables—and stopped short.

Of course he would. Right after he finished wringing her neck.

The reason for his mount's delay became suddenly apparent—she sat perched on top of a restless bay mare, resplendent in a rich brown habit with golden frogging in a military style. The animal tossed its head, shifting in her eagerness to be away, but Portia controlled her easily, never losing her smile or pausing in her conversation with the inn's groom who stood dazzled, grinning doltishly up at her, holding in one hand the lead of Mateo's patient, and apparently forgotten, gelding.

Irritation blossomed yet again. Hadn't he told her he would go alone and report back to her? It should be enough of a concession that he had cast himself in the role of lackey. Hell, he'd agreed to her proposal and ignored her overbearing arrogance. He'd let her relegate him to a subordinate, though she had to know that it grated every nerve in his body to do it. And she couldn't summon enough patience to wait a couple of hours at home?

He unlocked his knees and started forwards again. 'What in the name of Triton's forked tail are you doing here?'

He'd used his captain's voice, authoritative and designed to scare the slack out of hardened sailors. It spooked her mare instead. The bay reared and tried to bolt. Though she'd been caught by surprise, Portia reacted smoothly, bending lithe and low over her mount's neck. Graceful and at every moment in control, she allowed the animal to dance, gradually gathering her in and soothing her to a trembling halt.

As the mare calmed, Portia straightened. Mateo expected her to snap back, or at least resort to the high-handed manner she'd adopted yesterday, but she only watched him with a clear gaze. 'I'm going with you,' she answered simply.

Mateo drew a deep breath. Her calm helped him to keep his. 'Why?'

Her steady gaze did not waver or retreat. 'Because I need to.'

An echo of her words rang in his head. *I am tired of being let down by the men who are supposed to have my best interests at heart.* They were a pair, weren't they? He—fighting the old, stifling sense of suffocation—and she—battling a well-deserved feeling of helplessness.

He sighed. 'You understand that I will do the talking,' he said.

The mask of anxiety about her eyes faded away. Mateo watched it disappear and was struck by a sudden thought. In their every encounter he'd wondered what had happened to the old Portia. Now he knew that those lines of worry were the first glimpse he'd got of her.

He didn't like it. He much preferred the bold, confident Portia over the shy, reserved version.

Frowning, he mounted quickly. 'Let's be off, then.'

They set out, Portia keeping her mare pulled in to his gelding's shorter stride. Neither spoke and Mateo was just as glad. He did not want to feel any sort of preference for Portia Tofton. It could only be dangerous, given the awkwardness in their past and the volatility of their present. The old ease that they'd felt together was gone. Long ago they had taken comfort in each other's company, had often ridden out together like this, in companionable silence. But everything had changed.

Everything about their current situation rang problematic, but it was more than that. He was acutely aware of her, in a manner he had not expected. Like a man was aware of a pretty, vibrant woman. Or like a man on top of a powder keg warily eyed a burning brand.

Mateo spurred his mount to a faster pace. He would set aside his emotions, make the necessary transactions and he would be gone. As she said, in this fashion they would both get what they wanted. And then they would move on.

Horatio Rankin kept them waiting. It had to be a calculated move on his part, for his dour clerk had at first assured them that Mr Rankin was free. When he'd come shuffling back from his master's office, though, the clerk had sourly informed them that they would have to wait. And wait they had, for nearly an hour.

Portia was not annoyed in the slightest. She was feeling quite in charity with the world, and most particularly with Mateo Cardea. It seemed nothing had changed between them, and everything had. Out of the pack of her brothers and their friends, he'd always been the one to treat her with consideration, the one who had taken her seriously. It was the reason why she'd pinned her hopes for Stenbrooke on him, and he had lived up to all of her expectations.

She watched him wander from one corner of the dingy office window to the other and back again, the embodiment of restless motion, and she knew that Mateo had not changed. Worse, she knew that the feelings she'd once harboured for him had.

She'd been a girl all those years ago, and she'd wanted him with a girl's vague yearnings for a boy. Now she was a woman, a widow. Her eyes followed him, alive and vibrant with suppressed energy and impatience, the only thing worth watching in this bleak and barren space, and this time she knew just what she yearned for.

It would not do. There was too much unsaid between them, and in any case she could feel the resentment simmering just under the surface of his calm civility. This situation might not be of her making, but she still stood as the figurehead of all that had befallen him. No. It would be better all the way around if they just finished their business and parted ways.

He sighed in exasperation and bent low, his hands on the window sill as he stared at the bustling activity outside. A tiny smile played at the corners of Portia's mouth. In the meantime, she would allow herself to enjoy the view.

She started as he cursed suddenly and whirled to face

the silently scribbling clerk. 'By all that's holy, can you not check to see what is delaying the man?'

The scratching of the man's pen stopped. The small sound was replaced by his long-suffering sigh. Casting Mateo a look of extreme annoyance, he slid from his high chair and creaked his way down the hall.

Once he'd gone, Mateo smiled and dropped himself on to the bench next to her. Portia returned his smile. She enjoyed the warm feel of him next to her nearly as much as she'd appreciated his backside view.

She cocked her head at him. 'Rankin is a horrid little man,' she said. 'He's likely trying to goad us.'

'Aye, I began to suspect as much,' said Mateo. 'But I thought we should discuss the question—why? He cannot know exactly what we wish to discuss, and even if he did, why should he seek to unsettle us? Or perhaps he only hopes we will leave? But again, why?'

Portia shrugged. 'I put it down to his ill nature.'

'Surely there is more to it than that? And I give him what he wants, eh? The old one will report that my temper is heated to boiling.' He scrubbed his hands vigorously through his dark curls. 'So—do I look the part?'

She laughed. Impulsively, she reached out and loosened his respectable stock. Tilting her head, she ran a considering gaze down the front of him and then reached out and undid the top button of his waistcoat. 'Now you do.'

She glanced up and her smile faded. Mateo stared and it was not laughter she saw now in his eyes. His smile had faded, taking those tiny, irresistible lines with it, and leaving something intense and speculative that heated her from the inside.

She dropped her hands away from him. 'Thank you for bringing me along.'

'It is nothing.'

'No,' she said firmly. 'It's not.' But it would be better if he did not know just how grateful she felt. 'I know that you wish to do the talking, but I do have some questions I'd like Mr Rankin to answer. I was curious about a few things before, but his treatment of us only sharpens my curiosity.'

'Yes?' He looked suddenly alert. 'What questions do you have?'

Portia breathed deep. 'I'd like to know exactly when J.T. lost ownership of the house. Why did the new owner not take possession immediately? Or why not after J.T.'s death, when every other gamester he'd borrowed from or lost to made claims against the estate? He's been dead for nearly fifteen months. Why wait until now?'

Mateo shrugged. 'Perhaps the new owner did not hear of your husband's death right away.'

She looked wry. 'If he was in England, then he would have heard of J.T.'s death,' she said scornfully.

He sat straighter. Portia could see the questions in his eyes, but she was in no way prepared to answer them. Not here. Not now. She shook her head. 'And it does not explain why he did not make his claim immediately upon winning.'

Mateo sat back and allowed his gaze to return to the dingy window and the unceasing activity on North-brook Street. 'You are right, I believe. There are too many questions here.' He stared intently down the hall-way where the clerk had gone. 'Our decrepit friend has been gone a long time.'

Portia stared as he abruptly rose from his seat.

'Something is not right here,' he said.

She jumped to her feet and followed as he strode suddenly down the hall.

Mateo tried to ignore his sense of foreboding. Likely this Rankin was only passed out from drink, or just the small sort of man who built himself up by irritating and belittling others. He prayed it was some such simple explanation and not a complication that would cause a delay and destroy his company's best chance for the future.

An ornate door on the left looked out of place in this dusty corridor. From behind it came the sound of small, frantic movements and the faint sound of cursing. Portia came up behind him as he reached it. He placed his hand on the knob and cast her a faint look of enquiry. At her nod he pushed it open.

Chaos reigned inside. They stood on the threshold of a small, comfortably appointed office, but comfort was clearly not on the itinerary today. Papers and files were strewn everywhere. The elderly clerk knelt on his knees at the bottom of a filing cabinet, searching frantically through its contents. From behind a richly carved desk piled high with scattered documents rang another loud curse.

'Damn it all, but it *must* be here! Where the hell else would it be?'

Mateo cleared his throat.

The clerk jerked about. Up over the desk rose a set of sandy eyebrows and a pair of small, narrowed blue eyes.

'Well, well, Mrs Tofton,' Mateo mused. 'It does appear that we have come at an inopportune time.'

The piggish eyes were joined by the rest of the man. Mateo caught the scent of alcohol, noted the red, bloated face and ample belly and was reminded strongly of his sea-cook's stories about Davy's drunken sow.

'Yes, yes—a most inconvenient time.' He waved a dismissive hand and attempted an apologetic expression. 'So sorry, but you'll have to come back another day.'

Mateo narrowed his gaze. 'Oh, I do not think it will be so easy, Mr Rankin.'

Just like that the solicitor's barely conciliatory air disappeared. He whirled on his clerk. 'Useless old fool!' he hissed. 'I told you to get rid of them!'

'Ah, but you cannot blame your assistant.' Mateo glanced askance at Portia. 'Anyone will tell you that I'm a most inconvenient fellow.'

She nodded in pleasant agreement. Rankin merely sputtered.

'We are here about Stenbrooke.' He let his gaze roam over the mess. 'We'd meant to discuss a sale of the estate, but I have a feeling there might be some difficulty with that.'

Mr Rankin not only looked like old Davy's sow, he apparently shared her stubborn characteristics. 'I'm not prepared to discuss the business today, sir, with you or anyone else. You'll have to leave.'

Mateo merely leaned against the door frame and crossed his arms. 'Mrs Tofton, something tells me that there is no need for you to start packing.'

Rankin actually grunted. 'She's to be out by Michaelmas.' He turned his narrow little gaze on Portia. 'That's four short weeks,' he said nastily. 'If you haven't started packing, you'd best hop to it.'

'I'm not so sure about that, Mrs Tofton. It would appear that Mr Rankin has misplaced something.' Mateo arched a brow in Portia's direction. 'Would you care to make a wager on it? I'm betting he's lost the deed of conveyance to Stenbrooke.'

'I don't think I'd care to take that bet,' said Portia casually.

A snarl of frustration ripped across Rankin's face. 'Perhaps I have mislaid the document. But that doesn't change the fact that the place no longer belongs to her.'

Mateo stood straight. 'Do you know, I think your brothers would have some colourful cant phrase to describe what Mr Rankin is trying to sell us—a bag of moonlight, would they label it?'

He hid a smile as she considered. 'A bag of moonshine, I believe. Or they might say that Mr Rankin is trying to bamboozle us.' She cocked her head at the solicitor. 'And I do believe that they would be right.'

Musing, Mateo glanced at Portia again. 'Two women alone might have appeared to be an easy target. Perhaps the document never existed.'

Portia pursed her lips. 'He did have the deed last month.'

'It could have been a fake.'

He saw hope flare in her eyes, but then her brow furrowed. 'Much as I'd like to believe that, it did look official enough to me.' She frowned. 'I believed it to be J.T.'s signature. Both Dorinda and I examined the deed, and I asked Mr Newman to look it over, as well. We were all convinced.'

The clerk rose, groaning to his feet. 'Did Mr Rankin not leave you a copy, when he came out to see you, ma'am?'

'Keep quiet, Dobbins,' the solicitor ordered.

Everyone ignored him.

Portia shook her head. 'No, should he have?'

'Well, it's usual in these cases, but not required,' the old man mused. 'Certainly at one point there were three copies of the thing, right here in this office.'

Mateo waved a hand. 'But if none of them can be produced, there is no proof. Stenbrooke will remain yours.'

The solicitor abruptly slumped into his desk chair. 'Mr Riggs will see me drummed out of the county for this,' he moaned.

Mateo could not help but notice that the clerk did not greet this pronouncement with any sort of distress.

'But wait…' Rankin straightened in his chair. 'Perhaps his courier mistakenly took it back with him. Yes, of course!' He slapped a hand on his desk and cast a look of triumph at Mateo and Portia. 'It must be so! So sorry,' he smirked, 'but I'll be in contact with Riggs and soon enough I'll have your copy and one for the courts. I'll file it at the quarter session and that will be an end to it.'

Portia took a step into the room. 'Who is Riggs?' she asked. 'The name on the deed was Averardo.'

Mateo stilled. Rankin's expression fell again.

'Enough!' Mateo barked, suddenly impatient. 'I have had my fill of these games. Mrs Tofton, who is the local magistrate? He can sort through this mess better than you or I.'

'No!' Rankin reached out a pleading hand.

The clerk's mouth twitched. 'The magistrate threatened to ride him out of town on a rail himself, should he catch him in another questionable bit of business.'

'Shut *up*, Dobbins,' Rankin growled.

'Let's go,' Mateo said to Portia.

'Please!' Rankin called. He stepped around the desk. 'You'll put my livelihood at risk, all for a misplaced piece of paper?'

'Yes,' Mateo said over his shoulder. 'And with the same amount of pleasure that you have shown in displacing Mrs Tofton.' He placed his hand on Portia's elbow and stepped towards the door.

It was the clerk who spoke out. 'Ma'am, I'm thinking you'll want to hear his end of it.'

Mateo glanced over his shoulder.

Rankin's shoulders slumped. 'Come back,' he said with a wave. 'I'll tell you.' He looked up sharply. 'But you'll have to agree not to run telling tales to the magistrate.'

Mateo raised a quizzical brow at Portia. She nodded. Together they turned back, and he swept a pile of files from a chair for her. She arranged the heavy skirts of her habit, and once she was seated, he perched on the edge, firmly telling himself to ignore her sweetly spiralling scent. 'Let's hear the whole of it,' he said.

Rankin took his seat again. He shrugged and darted a look of ill-concealed dislike at Portia. 'There's not so much to tell. Everyone knows her husband was a gambler and a wastrel.'

Portia flinched. Mateo leaned forwards, scowling. 'The whole of it, where you are concerned,' he growled.

Rankin returned his glare. 'It's simple enough. Her husband used the estate as a stake in a card game. And lost. My client is someone who I have collaborated with before, handling his business matters in this part of the country. He sent the deed over by courier, along with signed statements of witnesses who were present when Mr Tofton lost his estate.'

Next to him, Portia tensed further. Her fists clenched in her lap and the elegant column of her neck tightened. Mateo had to blink and stop himself from running a soothing finger down the slender length of it.

'I looked everything over carefully. It was all in order. So I travelled over to Stenbrooke to deliver the news,' concluded Rankin.

Mateo listened with only half an ear. His brain was sifting through the man's words, hearing everything that he did *not* say, but his gaze was still caught by the contrast of Portia's creamy skin and thick, honeyed hair. He could see her pulse, beating steadily right at the tip of a richly curling lock of hair. The curl fluttered, shifting just the tiniest bit with each beat of her heart.

The clerk, still hovering at the filing cabinet where his employer had flung him, cleared his throat. Loudly. Then he did it again.

Mateo jerked his gaze away. 'Is there something you'd like to add, sir?'

'No,' Rankin answered for him—and viciously. 'Absolutely, there is not.'

'He come back from the lady's estate chortling over their reactions,' the clerk said defiantly. 'Those ladies were shocked and devastated, and he enjoyed every moment of it.'

'Hold your tongue, old man.' The threat in Rankin's tone was clear.

'I've held it long enough,' the clerk replied. He focused his attention on Portia. 'I am old,' he said simply. 'I worked thirty years for my last employer, but they sent me out to pasture, wanted new blood. I took this job because I thought no one else'd have me. But I can't abide the sick feeling it gives me.'

He raised his chin. 'Don't want to retire; I'd likely go mad with boredom. I'd like a nice, quiet position, though.'

Mateo's mouth quirked. 'It just so happens that Mrs Tofton is the controlling owner of a fleet of merchant ships. I'm sure she could find you something to your liking, should you have something she'd like to hear in exchange.'

Rankin stood. 'That's enough! I've told you what I know—you can't go stealing my employees right out from under my nose.' He cast a malevolent look at his clerk. 'Even if they are traitorous dogs.'

Portia stood suddenly. 'I've had as much of your company as a lady can tolerate, Mr Rankin.' She turned to the clerk. 'Mr...?'

He bobbed his head. 'Dobbins, ma'am.'

'Mr Dobbins. I am certain we could find a quiet task verifying manifests or something similar. I'm sure we could round up a raised desk, a cushioned chair and an increase in pay. Does that sound to your liking?'

The clerk's eyes lit up. 'It does indeed, ma'am.'

She shot a dark look at Rankin, and then held her

arm up invitingly to Dobbins. 'Then let us go, sir. I'm quite anxious to hear what you have to say.'

'Now, just a minute!' Rankin objected, starting around his desk once more. 'I won't have—'

Mateo stepped in front of the man. 'You won't have an office, a business or all of your teeth, should I hear another word from you. Or another word about you, either. As of this minute, this affair is none of yours.' He grasped the man by his oversized waistcoat and pulled him in close. 'Do I make myself clear?'

Mateo pushed him away. Without another word he hastened after Portia and the clerk. They'd reached the outer office and were just stepping into the bustle of the street when he caught up with them.

'Well, Mr Dobbins, I'd like to hear just what you can tell us. Now, before we go any further.'

'Perhaps we could find a spot to sit down?' Portia interrupted. 'Poor Mr Dobbins has had quite a morning. I can feel your arm trembling,' she said kindly to the man. 'There's a bench in front of that bookshop, down the street. Can you make it there?'

'Surely I can, Mrs Tofton, thank you.'

They set off. At the clerk's shuffling gait it took several long minutes to reach the spot. Mateo was bursting with impatience again by the time they arrived. All thoughts of Portia's elegant nape and appealing new confidence aside, his mind was already drifting towards the sea, to the difficulties he was going to have to face back in Philadelphia. He needed to wrap this transaction up, and quickly, before he actually gave into temptation and touched that dancing curl of honeyed hair.

'Smartly, Dobbins,' he ordered once the old clerk

had settled on to the bench and leaned back gratefully into the warmth of the sun. 'Let's hear what you have to offer.'

'Aye, aye, sir,' Dobbins said with a flash of humour in his eyes. He sighed. 'Rankin told you the truth, ma'am.' He smiled at Portia. 'Just not all of it.'

'What is it that you thought I needed to know?' she asked softly.

'Just what you started to find out for yourself. The client Rankin mentioned was Mr Riggs. He's a scientific type, an agriculturist—always trying to find a way to get a bigger, faster crop, or the harvest in quicker. He has a great tract of land outside Marlborough. Longvale, it's called. But he also searches out small parcels of land in different areas and uses them in his experiments.'

'Mr Rankin told my companion that his employer would likely plough Stenbrooke under, but Riggs was not the name on the deed.'

'Exactly, ma'am! Riggs leased a bit of land from Rankin, then asked him to keep an eye out for more in this area. Oh, he found him a few lots, but he skimmed a little cream off the top of the deals, if you know what I mean.'

'And Riggs found him out?' Mateo asked.

'He did. But he told him he would not turn him in—not if he handled this Stenbrooke case, fast and quiet-like.' He looked to Portia. 'Averardo is the one who won your estate at cards. I don't know why he didn't handle the conveyance himself, but he sent the documents out to Riggs, who sent them on to Rankin. Sent them by courier, in fact, and that fellow stayed here while Rankin set the conveyance in motion. Mighty curious man, that courier. High-handed, I'd call him. He asked a lot of questions of Rankin, once he come back from Stenbrooke.'

'What sort of questions?' Mateo demanded.

'Oh, he wanted to know who was with Mrs Tofton, and how did she take the news, that sort of thing.' Dobbins patted Portia's hand.

'And do you believe the courier took the deed with him when he left?'

'Must have done. It's not in that office and there's been no chance to file it with the courts. Won't reconvene until quarter day.'

Mateo felt a surge of hope. All he needed was to find this Averardo before the next quarter day, before there was any chance of that conveyance being recorded. It would be simple enough then to make the man a generous offer. The deed and any copies would be destroyed and Stenbrooke would remain Portia's as if the conveyance had never happened. Most importantly, he could be out of England and on his way to Philadelphia, with no need to wait for another deed to be drawn up, no need to involve clerks, solicitors or courts at all.

Mr Dobbins had reached a similar conclusion. 'You'll want to find Averardo, should you wish to buy Stenbrooke back,' he told Portia.

'Do you know where we might find him?' she asked.

'I don't know the first thing about him. Mr Riggs is the man to ask,' Dobbins spoke kindly.

'Yes, thank you, Mr Dobbins. I've heard of Mr Riggs and his work.' She smiled at the old man. 'Now, what are we to do with you?'

Mateo fished out his purse. 'Are you familiar with Portsmouth, Mr Dobbins?'

'I know where it is,' the clerk replied cautiously.

'Then take this.' Mateo gestured and counted out a fistful of coins to the man. 'Make your way there and in Union Street you'll find offices for Cardea Shipping. Talk to Mr Salvestro—he's the agent there. Tell him that I—' He stopped and cursed inwardly. 'Tell him that *we* sent you. We'll write ahead so you'll be expected. By the time you arrive, they'll have a satisfying position set up for you.' He raised a questioning brow. 'Will you have any difficulty with that?'

'None at all, sir!' Dobbins replied happily.

Portia stood, smiling brilliantly. 'That's settled, then.' She held out her hand to Dobbins. 'Welcome aboard, Mr Dobbins.'

Chapter Five

Perhaps Portia should have felt disheartened. Her simple plan to regain Stenbrooke had suddenly become more complicated. The Michaelmas deadline had acquired a new significance and now she had Mr Rankin working actively against her, instead of just callously executing his duty.

She wasn't in the least disheartened, however. Oddly, and against all reason, she felt elated. Rankin had been vile and rude, it was true, but he had a long way to go before he could match the habitual coarseness of her late husband. Rankin's discourtesy had barely moved her—and it was not only because of her more than passing familiarity with a bully's behaviour.

No—it was because she'd faced it with Mateo at her side. He'd always done that for her, boosted her confidence with his own. Her father, perpetually surprised that he'd fathered a girl after so many strapping sons, had always treated her as if he'd expected her to break, or perhaps just to break into tears. She'd always thought he'd be equally horrified at either occurrence. To her brothers she'd been a nuisance, or an occasionally amusing target, and as for J.T....well, she was not going to ruin her good mood by recalling anything about him. But Mateo had always treated her with a simple acceptance, and she had come to crave that heady feeling of equality.

Today she'd had a taste of it again—and she wanted more. She bit her lip to keep from grinning. Watching him stride up Northbrook Street ahead of her, she knew that that wasn't all she wanted.

Mateo was different in nearly every way from the other men in her life. He just seemed so much *more*. Darker and more handsome, without doubt—also strong enough in character to stand up against the unscrupulous and confident enough to extend a little kindness to the unfortunate. Mateo had never, she felt sure, dragged someone down to lift himself up.

Instead, the opposite held true—he exuded an incredible masculinity that was impossible to ignore. Perhaps it came from being a ship's captain and the air of command that went with it. Perhaps it was the intriguing dichotomy of knowing that his large, calloused hands were equally comfortable gripping the top rigging of a merchant sloop or a lady's hand amidst London's grandest society. Whatever its origin, his appeal was a smoky, nearly tangible thing, reaching out to her and setting her blood to surging until she feared she couldn't contain her response. Despite the difficulties ahead, she felt hopeful and light.

Unfortunately, Mateo's temper was not pulling in tandem with hers. Since they'd parted from Mr Dob-

bins he'd been silent and withdrawn. Lost in contemplation, he'd walked beside her, but without touching her,
until his absorption and his longer pace allowed him
to gradually draw ahead. He had not even noted her
absence, and though she knew he did not deliberately
ignore her, and while she could certainly appreciate
once more the pleasing prospect of broad shoulders,
tight trousers and tall boots, she was not inclined to
allow it to continue.

Already he'd reached the side street that led to the
livery. 'Mateo,' she called as he made the turn. She was
still a good distance behind him.

He did not pause.

She quickened her step. 'Mateo!' She reached the
corner. The crowd was thinner here, but still the street
was busy. 'Mateo! If you pull much further ahead, I'll
lose sight of you completely.'

She saw his head turn and his step falter. He cast
about for her and spun on his heel. She waved at him
and he strode rapidly back to her.

'My apologies, Portia.' He offered her his arm.

'Since I'm to benefit from your contemplation, I suppose I will forgive you,' she said lightly.

'Hmm.'

'Are you thinking of the trip to Marlborough? It's a
good nineteen miles, nearly twenty by the time we reach
Longvale, but we'll be on the Bath road for most of the
trip. We should make it there in a morning's drive.'

'Hunh.'

She tried again. 'J.T.'s curricle is still in the carriage
house at home. If the day is fine, and you don't mind
riding in the open, we could make use of it.'

No response. Perhaps she should try another tactic. 'My ears are purple, your nose is green and since I'm a widow now, I'm contemplating having a torrid affair with a rakehell of the first consequence. I know you've connections to the nobility through your cousin Sophie and that you've made a few forays into London society over the years. Can you recommend anyone who might do?'

'Mmmph,' was the entirety of his reply.

Portia nudged him with an unladylike jab of her elbow. 'Mateo!'

He glanced down at her. 'Yes?'

She rolled her eyes and gave up. 'Are you fretting about how to deal with Mr Riggs? There isn't the slightest need.'

'Is there not? I hesitate to disagree, *cara*, but I have a bad feeling we are about to become mixed up in what your brothers would call a cavey business.'

They'd reached the livery. Portia nodded her thanks as he held the door wide for her to enter the dingy office. 'A havey-cavey business, they might label this,' she corrected. 'While my father would storm about, calling the whole thing a damned hum.'

His eyes widened. 'But he would not approve of you repeating it,' he chided.

'Well, I don't approve of how he handled my inheritance, so we'd be even. In any case, I suppose that the question of whether they would be right or not depends on what Mr Riggs has to say.'

The livery attendant was a boy of about fourteen, sleeping soundly on the one rickety wooden chair. Mateo shook him awake and sent him off to ready their mounts. 'I don't know what caves have to do with any of it,' he grumbled as he offered her the questionable chair.

'I'm sure I don't, either,' she said with a smile. The office was wooden, nothing more than a lean-to attached to the side of an ancient barn. Sun shone through cracks in the boarded walls and ceiling, highlighting the straw dust in the air and touching the shabby room with a hint of magic. Mateo perched himself on an empty barrel and gave every indication of going off into deep thought again.

'But are you not interested in what I have to say about Mr Riggs?' she asked. 'I assure you I know exactly how to handle him.'

'Indeed?'

'Indeed. I am in possession of the perfect weapon, one that will guarantee he will tell us everything we ask.'

'Are you?' he asked with mild interest, running a discerning eye over her sitting form.

'Yes. You see,' she said, lowering her tone and leaning forwards, 'I am intimately acquainted with his mama.'

He choked back a surprised laugh. 'Do you know, that is exactly the sort of thing that might weight the ballast in our favour?' He smiled at her with tepid approval. 'I swear, I've never met a lady so naturally up to every rig.'

Mild interest. Tepid approval. Up to every rig? What utter rubbish. Portia watched his attention wander again and clenched her fists in frustration. There was nothing *mild* about her response to Mateo. Quite suddenly, being treated as an equal became woefully inadequate. She wanted to be seen, to be treated, to be *wanted* as a woman.

Her eyes narrowed. But how to go about it? The old Portia wouldn't have had a clue; would never have attempted it, in any case. She'd do what she'd always done as a young girl, duck her head and accept her own inadequacy.

But that girl didn't exist any more. Like a sharp blade she'd been forged by fire and honed by hardship. Portia was no longer content to wait for what she might be given; she was ready to go after what she wanted.

She stood. Gathering her skirts, she straightened and threw her shoulders out. She took a step forwards, positioning herself so a shaft of sunshine caught the golden frogging on her habit, setting her chest ablaze.

He looked up. 'Well, there's no hope for it,' he said cheerfully. 'I suppose you'll have to come along to Marlborough.'

She froze. Her heart fell and she let her skirts follow it to the packed dirt floor.

'You'd meant to leave me behind?' she whispered.

He nodded.

The gathering cloud of ire inside of her must have shown on her face, because he hastened to add, 'But only because I can travel more quickly alone.'

Speechless, she picked up her skirts again and headed for the door.

He stopped her just as she reached the threshold. 'Portia?' He took her arm. 'Where are you going?'

'We passed a gunsmith, just down the street,' she

snapped. 'I feel the sudden need to purchase myself a firearm.'

His mouth quirked. 'Does someone need shooting?'

She jerked her arm from his grasp. 'Yes. You—for being a great, irritating lout. And me—for being a great, naïve fool.'

'*Cara*, come back.' His tone rang smooth and caressing. And also insincere and patronising. She knew he didn't mean anything at all, calling her *beloved*. She'd heard him use the term with his cousins, with her cousins. She was sure he'd used it once with a scullery maid from her father's kitchens. But she *wanted* it to mean something when he said it to her. 'Surely it cannot be as bad as all that.'

He really did need shooting.

'Tell me,' he said, stepping closer. 'What is the trouble?'

The trouble was that he stood too close yet again. Sensation rippled from the top of her head and took a swirling detour round the front of her, raising her nipples to stiff peaks. She shivered and all the fine hairs on her nape and along her arms stood on end, straining towards *him*, no doubt.

'The trouble is that I have been silently singing your praises,' she grumped.

He grinned. 'It does not sound so bad.'

She crossed her arms in front of her. 'It is. All morning I've been thrilled because we were acting as equals in this endeavour. Now I see I was mistaken.' She turned away again. 'You are no different from any of the men in my family—dismissive and in no way inclined to believe that I have a brain and an idea how to use it.'

'No—not so!' he exclaimed. He grabbed her hand as she tried to walk away again. 'I was rude, it is true. I am most sorry, Portia. Of course we are equals, just as you asked. Partners in this damned rum.'

'Hum,' she said. Which was exactly what her body was about, humming, even while her brain was slowing, ceasing to function altogether. Warmth, thick and rich, spiralled from their clasped hands, crawled up her arm and slid downwards, settling low.

But Mateo had grown serious. 'Truly—I thought only of speed,' he said earnestly. 'You must understand, it is very important that we finish this as quickly as possible.'

Disappointment nearly choked her. Aghast, she could only marvel at her own stupidity. Of course he wanted to be done and gone quickly. Of course his interest in her was only mild at best. She'd come a distant second to adventure nine years ago. She placed further behind his business interests now.

Mateo reached up and squeezed both her shoulders in what was meant to be a comforting grip. Letting his hands slide, he grasped both her elbows and pulled her close. 'Now,' he said with a warm smile, 'was that all that was bothering you?'

It was the smile that did it. She wished he'd snapped at her. She wished he'd agreed that she was a woman, and of no use. But he stood there, smiling that easy, encouraging smile and she couldn't help herself. It blended into all the countless other times he'd teased her, heartened her, made her feel special and *alive*.

Fondness swamped her, along with exasperation and a great flood of hot and molten desire.

'No,' she said. She gripped his arms tight, stood on her toes and leaned in until her breasts pressed against the hardness of his chest.

His eyes widened, and then darkened. His heart beat against hers, quickening to match the racing tempo of her pulse.

'There's more,' she whispered, right before she leaned in further and kissed him.

She'd caught him by surprise. But experience and a seaman's instinct to seize life's bounty as it came had him quickly entering into the spirit of the thing. And perhaps there was another reason, as well. The thrum of a familiar chord sounded in the back of his mind, a twang of awareness and want that he'd been ignoring. He listened to it now, and let his tension melt away, returning her eager kiss, deepening it, in fact, and sliding his hands along the length of her trembling arms. Tenderly, he pulled her in and wrapped her in his embrace.

For several long, delicious moments he indulged them both. Her mouth was sweet, their kiss languid and deep. But then, at last, he settled his mouth against the white, endlessly tempting turn of her neck. And the chord thrummed deeper, more primitive and carnal. Inside him it echoed like a growl of satisfaction. *Mine*.

He had to acknowledge it then, the sense of recognition that had struck him when first she barged into the tavern the other night. It overwhelmed him, sweeping over him like a great wave over his bowsprit, leaving him muddled with longing.

He couldn't think, couldn't formulate a thought past his need to see her as overcome as he. Slowly his lips and tongue travelled, dancing over the pulse point at the base of her elegant throat and on to the one just below her ear. She let out a whisper of a moan, a sound of pure pleasure. The resonance of it, low and throaty, vibrated against his searching mouth and sent a surge of lust straight through him.

She turned her head, capturing his mouth with her own, moving her hands along a sensual path around his ribcage and across the breadth of his back. She trailed naughty fingers down to his buttock, making him writhe against the slow, soft circles she drew there.

Not a nymph, then, his Portia, but a siren, full of mischief and devilry of the most appealing kind. He measured the weight of her breasts in his hands, stroking his thumbs over nipples already peaked in desire. His erection strained further and he pressed it against her. Let her feel what she did to him with her bold mix of confidence and need.

He stilled, his caressing hands slowed. The sudden realisation of where she had come by such confidence struck him like a blow. J.T. *Dio*, she'd been married to that snivelling boy. He'd had the teaching of her, had the right to put his hands all over her, in just the way Mateo did now. And more.

No. It was an image that he could not endure. He kissed her again, purposeful, urgent and hot. He was desperate to drive the image of J. T. Tofton from his mind, the memory of him from hers.

But the heavy fabric and high neckline of her habit frustrated him. He ran his hands along the length of her, delighting in the sweet turn of her waist, rejoicing in the abundant curves of her breasts. He pulled her close, wrapping himself around her, as if in that way he could claim her, make her his own.

She pulled her mouth from his, breathed his name in his ear. Her voice rasped, husky with need.

Portia. He stiffened, torn reluctantly away from desire once more. This was Portia in his arms, tempting him, driving him wild and making him forget.

But he ought to remember. No matter how much he burned for her, he needed to remember who she was and why he was here. Remember that only yesterday he'd accused her of the vilest betrayal. Remember that people were depending on her. That others looked to him for their livelihoods and on top of that responsibility he also carried the weight of a centuries-old family tradition.

How weary he was of carrying so many burdens. He yearned to dump them overboard, leave them behind as so much flotsam and return to the discovery of this new and intriguing facet of his relationship with Portia. But could he do it? No doubt it was exactly what his father would have expected him to do.

He pulled away. Stepped back.

'We cannot,' he said, holding on to her hands, meeting the question in her eyes with regret. 'This has to stop.'

Her eyes filled. She ducked her head. 'Does it?' she asked the floor.

'It does,' he affirmed. He let her go and retreated across the tiny office. 'I'm sorry.'

She raised her head then and took a step towards him. 'I'm not.'

'No,' he said again. 'Portia...' he turned her name into a caress '...my impetuous Peeve, you do not understand all the issues I am faced with.'

'Then tell me,' she said simply.

He ran a hand along his jaw. How to make her understand? Turning away, he braced a hand on the door frame and looked out over the small courtyard and the street beyond. But it was the thought of Philadelphia that occupied him, and a clipper he saw in his mind's eye, heavy in the water as she fought an icy sea.

'First I have to make you understand how things are at home.' He sighed. 'Twenty years ago, Philadelphia was the greatest seaport in America. Our ships, builders and seamen were famous, our reputations earned us the greatest respect. But war and blockades, the rise of other ports, shifting markets, they have nearly broken us.' His head dropped. 'You have been to my home. You know how all of my family is involved in Cardea Shipping, in one way or another. If the ships do not sail, if the warehouses sit empty, then my uncles and cousins and their wives and children do not eat.' He shrugged. 'Yet our port has fallen into an unprofitable pattern of revival and depression that must be broken.'

'And you have an idea how to do that?' She sounded interested, despite herself.

'Everybody does,' he snorted. 'Many of my competitors have turned their backs on the sea altogether and now they ship coal from the interior on crude, box-like boats.' He shuddered. 'I have done what I can, what my stubborn father would allow me to do. I have searched out new markets. I fought to establish a presence in Baltimore's rising hold on foreign goods.' He paused to look over his shoulder and catch her eye. 'Now Cardea Shipping is on the eve of its most important venture.'

He breathed deep. 'Ships from Philadelphia were the first to break the monopoly of the East India Trading Company. Twenty years ago there were forty of our vessels engaged exclusively in regular trade with the East. It is a difficult market, yet the rewards are great. And I mean to revive it.'

He gripped the frame hard in his passion. 'Any day now the *Sophia Marie* will be beating her way home. Near a year and a half she's been gone. My cousin Giorgio captains her—he and her crew will be weary from the long trip from the northwest and the difficult journey around Cape Horn, but her holds will be stacked high with the deep-piled furs that the Chinese adore. I have a warehouse stocked high with the ginseng they crave.'

He turned back to face her. 'The risks are high in a voyage like this, but the odds become more favourable for a caravan of ships. For several years I have toiled, putting together this enterprise. I have spoken endlessly, cajoled shamelessly and forced compromise on a handful of uneasy, rival merchants. I've battled my father and risked my reputation putting this arrangement together. It was to be the biggest opportunity of my lifetime.'

He could see the comprehension in her eyes. 'Until the reading of your father's will.'

He nodded. 'Until I was no longer the head of Cardea

Shipping, nor even the eventual heir to the business. I was only a man whose own father had passed him over, whose father had given control of his business into the hands of a woman a continent away rather than see his son take over.'

'Oh, dear. Oh, Mateo,' she breathed. 'I am sorry.'

'You can imagine the value my judgement holds now. The caravan, the entire Eastern enterprise, began to unravel. My investors have fallen away. The insurers will no longer do business with Cardea Shipping until they hear from *you*.'

She bit her lip, but he pressed on. 'Do you understand now why I must finish our transactions as quickly as possible? Cardea Shipping began generations ago in Sicily. My grandfather brought it to the New World. All my life I've planned to carry on the tradition left by countless Cardea men. This was meant to be the making of the business, setting us up for success for years to come.'

She exhaled slowly. 'I begin to see just why you were so angry with me.'

'I was laughed out of port, Portia, for losing my business to a woman,' he said bitterly. 'I am anxious to restore my reputation, yes.' He met her gaze with a hard, direct stare. 'And what do you think would be said of me, should it became known that we…' he gestured '…were involved.'

'That you were a man of great good taste and refinement?'

He did not smile. 'No, and you are naïve to think so. I have no wish to for ever be the man who prostituted himself to regain his legacy.'

She shrugged. 'It happens every day in the aristocracy.'

He began to grow impatient. 'It does not in my world. And even were we to remove that consideration, still it would not be a good idea.'

Mute, she looked away from him.

'Your father and mine might be gone,' he said, folding his arms in front of him. 'And I have more than a passing suspicion that my father's mind was running along exactly these lines, but do you think I would betray their memories so?'

She waved a dismissive hand. 'There is no betrayal between consenting adults. You don't need an excuse, Mateo, a simple "No" will suffice.'

He should let it go. Clearly she was ready to do so. But for some reason his mind kept scrabbling around and around the idea. 'I only consider the gossip that would arise about you. We were raised as a family in spirit, if not in blood. Your opinion of me must be abysmal indeed if you think I would dishonour that tradition and treat you so shabbily.' Oh, *Dio*. He greatly feared that he was trying to convince himself, not her.

She looked at him squarely. 'You are being dramatic again, Mateo. And you forget that I have been out in society a little. I did pay attention, you see. Married and widowed women have gentlemen admirers all the time.'

'Is that what you want? A gentleman admirer?' he asked bluntly. 'Because your kiss told me that you are more interested in a lover.'

She stiffened. Perhaps he should not have been so crude. But she straightened her shoulders and met his gaze. 'And if I was? You are free and so am I. There would be nothing shameful in such a...relationship.'

She put on a brave front, but he could see the start of tears swimming in the depth of her dark eyes. The sight caused his stomach to clench. 'I do not mean to hurt you,' he said gently. 'It is more than evident that I desire you, *cara*. Perhaps it is because of our history, but I cannot regard you so casually.' He took the risk and approached her again. He caught her hand. 'It is not in me to love you and leave you,' he said softly.

She said nothing, only gazed up at him, hunger in her gaze.

And a warning clanged sharply in his head. 'No— it could be nothing else. We've explored this avenue before, Portia.'

'I know.' He could barely hear the words.

A sudden fear set him to say, 'I am too restless for married life. You, of all people, should know that, Portia. I cannot even stand still for long! Nothing in my life has prepared me for such a thing. I would be abysmal at it.'

'I don't recall asking you,' she snapped.

He raised a brow.

'A kiss!' she nearly shouted. 'I wanted a kiss. I've had it. I thoroughly enjoyed it. But that is all.' She wrenched away from him. 'Men! A lady asks for an inch and they fear you mean to steal a mile!'

Had he been wrong? 'I am sorry,' he said. Again.

'Yes, I know,' she said bitterly. 'And you are not ready to be anything else. I understand. But all of this talk, if you ask me, is the true damned hum. We could have "dallied" seven times by now and no one would have been the wiser.'

He let loose a short bark of laughter. 'Of course they would. People know. They always do.'

As if to prove his point, the attendant and a groom at that moment appeared in the courtyard outside, leading their mounts. Trying to silently convey the full weight of his regret, Mateo extended his hand and led her out to meet them.

But when the groom had gone and they stood alone next to her restless mare, he gave in to temptation once more and touched that wayward lock curling so prettily against her nape. 'Can you see how a dalliance,' he said quietly, 'no matter how tempting, would not be wise?'

She looked up at him, her brown eyes shining, but did not answer.

'You have Stenbrooke to get back to and I must make haste back home. A quick finish to our business and then we must say goodbye once more.' He wrapped his hands about her small waist and lifted her easily into the saddle. She hooked her leg over the pommel and settled in.

It was then that the idea hit him.

'Unless,' he said suddenly, 'unless you would consent to sign Cardea Shipping back over to me, right away? Before we track down this man who's won your estate?' He gripped her leg in his excitement. His mind raced with the possibility. 'It would not be as effective as leaving for Philadelphia right away, but if I were returned to the helm I could get word back, perhaps send the factor from Portsmouth back to start with the insurers...'

Mateo looked up. 'I would not leave you, of course,

until our business was complete.' He let all of the naked need he felt show in his expression. 'I know I have disappointed you, *cara*, and more than once, but you must know that you can trust me to keep my word. Please, would you consider it?'

Her expression had gone carefully blank as she looked down at him. 'No,' she said. 'I would not.' She spurred her mare forwards, and left him behind.

Chapter Six

The ride home passed silent and uncomfortable, but mercifully brief. It wasn't until they'd reached the boundaries of Stenbrooke that Mateo spoke to her. He spurred his mount up next to her mare. 'I'd like to speak to Miss Tofton when we arrive, if I may.'

'Of course.' Portia nodded. She purposefully curbed her bay's passion for being the lead in every group, keeping her reined in close, but Mateo had nothing further to say. When they reached the house he helped her dismount, but also curtly informed the groom to keep his gelding ready, as he would not be staying long.

Portia was spared the need to send a servant for Dorinda; she came running lightly down the staircase as they entered the hall. 'Well,' she asked, breathless with excitement, 'did it go as planned?'

Mateo snorted. 'It did not, Miss Tofton. And I begin to detect an unpleasant pattern. It would appear that nothing in this business is fated to go as planned.' He shot an enigmatic look in Portia's direction. 'I will let

Portia fill you in on the details, but we've had several obstacles placed in our path.'

Undaunted, Portia returned the look, but he had turned back to Dorinda. 'If you please,' he said, 'we'll need your help in overcoming them.'

'We will?' asked Portia.

He ignored her. 'We will be travelling to Marlborough tomorrow morning. As it is a good deal further than this morning's jaunt, I would ask you to come along as Portia's chaperon.'

'I don't need a chaperon,' she protested. 'I'm a widow, not a green girl!'

The expression he turned on her shone distinctly ironic. 'I think it would be wise.'

She folded her arms. 'And in any case, Dorrie is not a good traveller.'

'I believe Mr Cardea is right,' Dorrie interjected. 'I will manage. It wouldn't look well for the two of you to be roaming the countryside unescorted.' Though she looked flustered at the idea, she summoned a smile of approval. 'Not everyone will be aware of your long-standing friendship. And people do talk.'

He sketched a formal little bow of agreement. Portia didn't like it a bit. Was this to be her punishment then? she wondered. Was she to be treated with cold formality because she had refused his self-serving request?

'But the curricle—' she began.

'Is not large enough for three,' he interrupted. 'I shall arrange the transportation.' He bent over Dorrie's hand. 'If you could be ready to depart early in the morning? At eight, perhaps?'

'Of course,' she answered.

He bowed once more and turned on his heel. On the threshold he hesitated. 'It's possible we might be forced to spend the night on the road,' he said over his shoulder. 'You should both pack a portmanteau.' Without a further word or a glance in Portia's direction, he strode out of the door.

She met Dorrie's wide-eyed gaze with brows raised in answering surprise. In silent consensus they both rushed to watch his departure from the drawing-room window.

'What on earth did you do to him?' Dorrie asked in wonder.

Portia hesitated, but gave in to the awe in her companion's eye. 'I kissed him.'

Dorrie gasped. 'You didn't!'

Oh, but she had. She'd waited a lifetime for that kiss and it had been every bit as sweet and darkly seductive as she'd dreamed.

'But, Portia!' Dorrie still gaped at her. 'How could you?'

She raised a brow and swept a hand towards Mateo's retreating form. Her appreciative eye ran again over his broad shoulders, narrow hips and long legs. 'How could I not?'

She'd quite amazed herself, finally reaching out for what she wanted, and the pride she'd felt had only enhanced the pleasure of at long last being in Mateo's arms. A thrill went through her at the mere remembrance. It was heady stuff, being kissed by Mateo Cardea.

He'd kissed her mindless, breathless, until the shabby office, the livery, indeed all the world had dropped away. There had existed nothing in her universe save the two of them and the spiralling heat of their desire. She'd forgotten Stenbrooke, her people, herself. She'd been ready and willing to follow wherever he and their mutual passion led.

For make no mistake, it had been mutual. J.T. might have had occasion to mock her womanly skills, but she knew enough to recognise when a man was in the throes of sexual desire.

Dorrie still stared. Poor thing, she looked utterly perplexed. 'But what did he do?'

'He enjoyed it,' Portia replied firmly. *Thoroughly.* 'Until he recalled that he enjoys running Cardea Shipping even more, and that the running of it will not be nearly as profitable if he allows a "dalliance" to slow his return.'

'I'm sorry,' Dorrie said. She sounded puzzled, but sincere. 'Aren't I?'

'I'm not,' Portia answered with resolve. 'I didn't plan it, but it happened. I took a chance, something I've never done, except here, at Stenbrooke. And it's something we both must become comfortable with, my dear. It's a chance we are taking, setting ourselves up to live alone here. And though it didn't work out with Mateo, I am determined that it will for us, for our home.'

'Of course it will,' Dorinda said stoutly. 'But I still don't know what happened with the solicitor!'

Briefly, Portia sketched an outline of the morning's events.

'Well! Eventful indeed, and still you found time to press yourself on Mr Cardea?' Dorinda's disapproval rang clear. 'You have had a busy morning.'

'Oh, don't scold me, Dorrie,' Portia pleaded. 'Mateo did the job for you.'

'Well, I am glad that he did.' Her gaze was troubled as she pulled Portia away from the window. 'Do not mistake me,' she said. 'Of all people, I know that you deserve some happiness at last.'

She led Portia to the couch and kept a hold of her hand, stroking it gently. 'But I worry for you, dear. It has been long enough—were you discreet, no one could fault you for seeking a little pleasure. But you must be careful.' She hesitated. 'There is something in your eyes when you look at Mr Cardea—and it is in no way discreet. I think your heart is more involved in this that you might realise.' She sighed. 'I don't wish to see you hurt again.'

Portia bit her lip to keep it from trembling. Now she *was* beginning to be sorry she'd ever looked at Mateo Cardea with desire. And the worse part of having to listen to everyone counsel against a liaison was the knowledge that they were right. And not because she would be difficult to leave, although it had been sweet of Mateo to insinuate such a thing. She knew better than to believe it, though. Clearly she was not the sort of woman who could tempt a man away from his other interests. Her husband had proved that point, repeatedly.

She swallowed against the sour taste in her mouth. No, Dorrie had the right of it. Her feelings for Mateo ran too deep. She was supposed to be seeking her independence, not handing her heart over to someone with the power to destroy it.

'You know I appreciate your concern, Dorrie dear, but you may relax. Mateo possesses a plethora of reasons why we should not become more intimately involved. Not the least of which is that he has no wish to prostitute himself while getting his company back.'

'He said that to you?' Dorrie asked, shocked.

'Right before he asked me to turn Cardea Shipping over to him. Now. Before we have Stenbrooke back in our possession.'

Her companion glanced back in the direction of the window. 'I am beginning to rethink my favourable impression of the man.' She turned back, looking troubled. 'What did you answer?'

'I said no,' she said flatly. Was she supposed to just trust him to keep his end of their bargain? Lord, but she'd wanted to. She'd looked down into those pleading, dark eyes and she'd wanted to please him, to ease his worry. Even after he'd rebuffed her advances, even after the repeated offences he'd dealt her, she'd wanted to say yes.

But she'd stopped herself in time. She could not risk it. Every man she'd trusted had put his own concerns before hers. Nothing Mateo had said or done so far had convinced her that he would act differently. His priorities were firmly fixed on himself and his business.

A loudly clearing throat distracted her. Vickers hovered on the threshold, a tray in his hands. 'The post has arrived, Mrs Tofton.'

She knew before he'd crossed the room what was on the tray. She could see the worry and distaste he tried to hide. She glanced at the single letter once, and then tossed it back on to the tray.

'Burn it,' she said.

Dorrie had gone tense. 'Is it from…Reading, then?'

Portia nodded.

Dorrie jumped to her feet. 'Oh, that horrid woman! I felt sorry for her once, you know.'

Portia did not answer.

'Is there nothing to be done about her? It is harassment she's subjecting you to! Perhaps a magistrate—'

'Just burn it,' Portia instructed Vickers. 'Right away.' She turned back to Dorrie, fierce with determination. 'We have to look after our own interests. For if we don't, no one will.'

A sea captain intimately understood the value of patience. Frustrating as it might be to wait out bad weather, he knows to keep his vessel close-hauled upon the wind and wait for fair wind and sea before he unfurls his top-gallants. Many times as a privateer, Mateo had held his breath and his crew at a stop, waiting for his enemy to be caught in exactly the right position for a broadside volley. Hell, at the tender age of fourteen, the men in his mess had lectured him on how to stall his own pleasure, to be sure of his lady's. But not once, in a long and varied career, had Mateo ever had a greater need for patience than he did right now, dealing with Portia Tofton.

She would not trust him to keep his word, but she was willing to take him to her bed? What sort of logic was that? He snorted in disgust. Women's logic—the sort tailor-made to drive him mad.

And therein, perhaps, lay part of the problem. For until she had pressed that deliciously curved body up against him, he hadn't allowed himself to think of Portia as a woman. First he'd painted her as a scheming opportunist; once he'd realised that he was mistaken, still he had not truly looked at her. Instead he'd overlaid her with a picture of the unassuming, unfailingly supportive young girl he'd once known.

In reality, she was neither. Portia Tofton was proving to be far more complex than Portia Varnsworth had ever been. She still was as he'd remembered and expected, but she'd grown, too. No, he had not expected to encounter strength, steel and determination. She'd become a woman of fascinating layers. Were this any other time and circumstance, he'd enjoy nothing more than slowly peeling them away. One by one, he'd work his way from the lovely, rounded outside to the sweet and juicy kernel within.

Dio knew he was tempted. She'd kissed him—so hot and sweet—and he'd longed to loose her hair until those sun-kissed streaks curled about him. Her arms had held him tight, and he'd ached to go further until they were snarled together in a passionate knot. But he suspected that neither of them could tangle limbs without also involving hearts and lives. In the end, she would be hurt, and he was just beginning to wonder if he might not be, too. It would not be wise for either of them to indulge themselves.

Unfortunately, Mateo was a master at indulging himself. Keeping away from her was not going to be easy—especially not now that he'd had such a tantalising taste. He'd never been good at denying himself the things he was not supposed to have. As a child he'd always filched the *buccellati* his *nona* set out to cool. As a young man eager to learn of life at sea, he'd stowed away on one of his father's ships and earned the right to be called a son of Neptune.

And now Portia had lit a great, blazing light in his mind and body. It shone unrelenting on the attraction, the desire and the possibilities between them—and he was going to have to keep himself in the dark.

He sighed. Devil-may-care, his mother had called him with affection. And now, in more ways than one, his past was coming back to haunt him. If he wanted a future, he was going to have to overcome it.

His course was clear: he would keep his distance, exercise a little restraint and do his best to keep them both off the rocks.

He was off to a good start this morning. He'd hired a well-sprung carriage for the trip to Marlborough, and though it was roomy enough, he'd also hired a hack for himself. He was glad enough for it when Portia had emerged from Stenbrooke's front door.

In a spring-green dress with a tightly fitted bodice, she made him wish he could once again don those blinders he'd been wearing. There was no doubting her womanliness today, or her pique with him. Oh, she greeted him with all politeness, but she barely met his gaze, even when he took her hand to help her into the carriage.

And though he'd just set his course for distance and restraint, he couldn't help but admire the view. The square neckline and cunning wrap-around collar of her gown exquisitely framed the creamy expanse of her chest and throat. *Dio*, but he'd been a fool not to see what was right in front of his eyes. He made up for lost time now, staring until she moved past him and all he could see was the few inches of her nape between her collar and bonnet.

And right then, for a shocking instant, he could not catch his breath. Right there. His hand convulsed around hers. He'd kissed her right there and laid claim to that sweet, tender spot. And he wanted quite fiercely to pull her back and do it again.

But then she was in the coach, and her hand left his and the moment passed, thanks be to the heavens. Mateo stood a moment, flexing his hand where it had touched hers. Hell and damnation.

'Mr Cardea,' Miss Tofton said patiently. Mateo started. Was it the first time she'd addressed him? She twinkled up at him, and he thought it likely was not. 'Do you know just how old Mr Riggs might be?'

'Dorrie.' Portia called the warning from the coach, but did not look out of the window.

'What?' her companion asked, all innocence. 'A woman should prepare herself for all eventualities, dear. And just because you have no interest in marriage does not mean that I do not.'

Mateo blanched. Miss Tofton noticed and laughed outright. She held out her hand for his assistance.

With all alacrity he handed her in. Just as he closed the carriage door behind her she held his gaze and met it with a slow wink.

For the first time Mateo began to fear he was out-matched. As quickly as possible, he made sure the luggage was loaded and saw them all off.

Fortune smiled upon them. The weather held fair, the roads were wide and well kept, and the horses were fresh. They covered the first half of their journey in good time. They made Hungerford, the halfway point, by mid-morning. His mood much improved, Mateo called a halt at the Bear Inn.

All lay quiet at this time of day, which meant there was no shortage of ostlers and grooms to come to their assistance. 'Ladies, I confess,' Mateo said as they emerged from the coach, 'despite the beauty of the day, the dust of the road has me longing for the clear wind and clean deck of my brig.' He raised an enquiring brow. 'Since that's not to be had, I'll presume to propose a substitute. I dare say you won't mind a short break?'

If anything, Portia's mood appeared to have worsened. She did not answer, but climbed wearily down, her face set and wan.

'That would be lovely, Mr Cardea,' Miss Tofton answered apologetically. 'I fear neither of us is as seasoned a traveller as you. I, for one, would appreciate a chance to stretch my legs. Thank you.'

'Come, Peeve, look lively!' Mateo had never known her to object to travelling. 'We've made dashed good time. Stenbrooke will be back in your hands all the sooner because of it.'

'Let's hope Mr Riggs will be as co-operative as the weather,' she agreed. Mateo stared at her. Her eyes were closed, her shoulders drooped. It came as something of a shock. Listlessness was not something he'd ever heard or seen out of her.

'Having doubts?' he teased. 'We'll just have to hope he has a high regard for his mama.'

She didn't respond to his sally, and he could see the strain in her expression as she looked about. 'There's the innkeeper.' She pointed. 'Shall I go and bespeak us a private parlour?' she asked.

At his nod she hurried off. Mateo watched her go, then turned his questioning gaze on her companion.

Miss Tofton didn't pretend to misunderstand his look. 'It's my fault, I fear,' she fretted. 'I should have considered that an enclosed carriage...I just didn't think...' She let her words die away.

'It's not motion sickness?' Mateo could not suppress a sailor's disgust for such a notion.

'No.' Her mouth twitched at his dismay. She glanced about at the flurry of men seeing to the horses and carriage. Stepping away, she raised her brows. 'Hungerford is such a pretty little town, is it not?'

Curious, Mateo followed her. 'Yes,' he said for the benefit of their audience. 'The thatching on all the cottages is particularly charming.'

'It is,' she agreed. 'Do you know, I've stayed at the Bear once before. If I recall correctly, there is a lovely little stream just behind the inn.' She cocked her head. 'Would you mind escorting me?'

'Not at all,' he said promptly. He offered her his arm and they strolled around the building.

There was indeed a stream in the back, and it was a pretty spot. The water was shallow, but moved steadily, echoing musically over a tumble of rocks. Sunlight fought through the canopy of overhanging trees and sparkled off the surface.

Miss Tofton was apparently enamoured of the sight. He quelled the urge to prompt her. Better to keep quiet and wait.

The question, when it came, surprised him.

'Mr Cardea, will you tell me how Portia came by that nickname you call her?'

'What? Peeve?' he asked, startled.

Lips pressed together, she nodded.

He thought back. 'It started with J.T., I suppose. My family was at Hempshaw the summer that he and his family moved nearby. All of Portia's brothers were enamoured of the initials he used then instead of his full name, and they began to do the same.'

She smiled. 'And I suppose Portia wanted to follow their example? It sounds like her.'

'She did. She told us all to call her P.V. for Portia Varnsworth. Her brothers immediately warped it to Peeve, and Peeve she's been ever since.'

Miss Tofton regarded him thoughtfully. 'Until you arrived, I've never heard anyone call her by that name, except for her husband, my cousin.' She hesitated. 'It never sounded like an endearment, Mr Cardea, but rather, more of an…insult.'

'Ah. I see.' He did, too. It sounded exactly like something J.T. would do.

'Did you know James Talbot well?' she asked eventually.

Surprised, Mateo nodded. 'I did. We saw a lot of him, both at that first visit when he'd moved to the area, and later too.'

She was quiet a moment. 'I gather, then, that you will understand when I say he was a difficult person.'

Her caution irritated him and unnerved him a little too. She acted as if she were afraid J. T. Tofton was going to jump out and berate her for daring to mention him. Mateo folded his arms. 'He was a whiny snot of a boy,' he said bluntly. 'Never content with his own lot and perpetually jealous of someone else's. I'm sorry, I know you don't like to speak ill of the dead, Miss Tofton, but there's no covering the stink of rotten fish.'

'Of course, you are right.' She sighed. 'Suffice it to say, he did not improve with age.'

Mateo curbed his impatience. 'Well, I admit I was damned shocked to hear that Portia had married him. Forgive my continued bluntness, but I believe that was the first time my regard for her significantly fell.' In fact, he'd congratulated himself on making a lucky escape, for he'd told himself that any woman who had willingly chosen J. T. Tofton would never have suited him.

'Her reasons are her own, and I'm sure I can't speak to that.'

'Then I wish you would just say what you brought me back here to say.'

She gnawed at her lip and regarded him anxiously. 'Will you promise not to reveal what I tell you?'

He hesitated. 'If you wish.'

'Portia has never mentioned it to me. Vickers, her butler, did.'

'Told you what, Miss Tofton?' he asked with exaggerated patience.

'James Talbot hated Stenbrooke,' she blurted out. 'He hated the hard work it required, and resented the money spent on it. After it became profitable, he thought that the income should go into his pocket and not back into the estate. But Portia did what she could, and her father had seen to it that she had her own money to spend.'

She paused, but it was clear that she was just beginning. He waited.

'James Talbot was not…a kind husband.'

Mateo's fists clenched.

'In fact…' her voice lowered yet again '…some would say he was quite the opposite.' She looked away, over the stream. 'He locked her up once, in the tack room of an ancient barn that used to stand at the far boundary of Stenbrooke. Portia thought it wasn't safe, she wanted it torn down. She'd stopped in there to be sure that all of the equipment had been removed. James Talbot did not want to waste money tearing down a building that was falling in on its own. He found her there that day. They argued.'

'How long?' Mateo asked past a tightened jaw.

'He came back to the house, packed a bag and left,' she whispered.

'How long?' he repeated.

'Three days.' Her eyes brimmed with unshed tears. 'The servants looked, but when she was not to be found, they concluded that she must have gone away with him.' She swallowed. 'He laughed when he came home and found her still there. He said it had only been a prank.'

Mateo wished then that J.T. would jump out at them, returned from the dead—so he would have the pleasure of sending him back to hell.

'The next week Portia had the barn torn down. She also wrote and invited me to live at Stenbrooke.'

'I see,' he said. And he did.

'It was a long time before I noticed that she avoids tight spaces, and I never considered that a carriage…'

'I'll take care of it, Miss Tofton,' Mateo interrupted

her. 'Thank you for telling me.' He retrieved her hand and they started back.

'There's another reason I've told you this, Mr Cardea.'

He'd already seen that, too.

'I care for Portia deeply. She means as much to me as a sister.' She gave a bitter little laugh. 'Lord knows, she's been kinder to me than my real sister.' Her voice firmed. 'She's been hurt enough. I would not see her hurt again. By anyone.'

'Nor would I, Miss Tofton.' And he meant it. 'Nor would I.'

Chapter Seven

Portia shifted the cold ham on her plate to a new position. Her adverse reaction to being in the carriage had caught her by surprise. Had she been in a coach since... Well, just since? No, she normally rode everywhere, and hadn't had occasion for a longer trip. And truthfully, she hadn't stopped to consider that she might be affected. Foolishly, most of her resources had been focused on Mateo, while the rest were absorbed with her plans to get Stenbrooke back.

And just perhaps, without those two evils, she might never have been affected at all. But the gloom and sense of confinement in the carriage had merely echoed her larger situation. She was effectively trapped by her dependence on Mateo Cardea. His word and his willingness to help her were all that stood between her and homelessness.

Well, not homelessness. She could have a home with Anthony, or perhaps eventually with one of her other brothers. But when she thought of returning to that life, to feeling extraneous and beholden, to existing at the mercy and whim of her family and expected to feel grateful for it, that's when she truly started to feel sick. The air in the coach had grown thick and her throat had begun to close. She'd struggled to hide her distress from Dorinda, but truthfully, if he had not stopped here at Hungerford, she might just have hung out of the carriage door and broadcast her anxiety all along the Bath road.

She cast another look towards the parlour door. 'Where do you suppose Mateo has taken himself off to?' she asked. She was torn between dreading a return to the coach and wishing to get the day's travel over with.

No, she reconsidered wearily, she wanted it *all* over with. She wanted to be back home, with Stenbrooke safely hers, and Mateo Cardea gone from her life again. Then, and only then, would she be not only independent, but she'd also be safe. And if that was a contradiction or didn't make sense, then she didn't much care.

'He said something about needing to speak to the stable master,' Dorrie answered. 'Would you pass me the plate of scones? They are quite good.'

Portia did, keeping her eyes averted. Dorrie's appetite was in no way diminished by the trip. In fact, her companion appeared unusually cheerful since she'd come in from her short walk around the inn.

They both jumped as the door banged open.

'Are you finished, ladies?' Mateo asked with flair. 'Are we ready to get back to the road?'

'We've finished, Mr Cardea,' Dorrie assured him. 'But come, we'll keep you company while you eat.'

'No need! The landlady has packed me something for the road. If you please...' He beckoned. 'We have to make some changes and I wish to be sure they are acceptable.'

Portia shrugged in reply to Dorrie's mystified glance. Together they rose and followed him outside.

'What is it, Mateo?' she asked, sweeping the yard for a clue. There were no vehicles in sight save for some other traveller's open landau.

'As we drove in, I spied a wobble in the back end of the coach,' he explained. 'The wheelwright's been to look at it and he says there's a problem with the axle.' He frowned. 'We can't take a chance on it; he says it could go at any time.' He waved towards the landau. 'This is the only replacement available.'

He looked with concern at Dorinda. 'Miss Tofton, I worried that you would prefer an enclosed carriage, but will you mind the change terribly?'

Dorrie practically beamed up at him. 'Not at all! We'll be all right, won't we, Portia?'

Portia regarded them both with suspicion. The thought crossed her mind that perhaps she had not concealed her distress so successfully.

'We could perhaps find a local carriage we could hire, but I'm not sure how long it would take, or if we would be successful at all.'

'I think it will be all right, don't you, Portia?' Dorrie repeated. 'I did bring along my parasol, just in case something untoward should happen.'

Portia opened her mouth. Whether she meant to probe or to protest, she wasn't sure. She sensed a conspiracy. But abruptly, she shut it again, determined to let it go. The prospect of travelling in the open, with the wind in her face, was too delicious to pass up.

'Good,' Mateo said with satisfaction. 'Let's be on our way, then, ladies.'

The remainder of the trip passed quickly. Mateo still rode, but several times he brought his mount close by the open landau, so that conversation was possible. Other times Portia felt the weight of his gaze upon her, but she was too happy with the sun and the breeze to let it bother her. And when her own gaze wandered over to linger on him, well, she decided not to let that bother her, either. He looked magnificent with the sun lining the sharp angles of his face and the wind playing with his dark curls.

She loved to watch him ride; he had such a comfortable and natural seat—and as often happened, her mind spun away, creating the image of him striding easily across a heaving deck, masterful and in command of all he surveyed.

It was an exceedingly pleasant way to pass the time—but apparently not an acceptable one. Dorrie reached over and wrapped her on the wrist with her parasol.

'Dorrie!' Portia objected.

Dorrie merely raised her eyebrows. Then she relented. 'What was he like as a boy?' she asked with an understanding smile.

Portia tilted her head, considering. 'A great deal of fun,' she answered quietly after a second's thought. 'Busy, I would say. Never still, always on the go. Up to every rig and row my brothers could get into, but he always had time—and a kind word—for the girls too.'

Dorrie's brows went back up. 'Generous indeed.'

'He was, truly,' she mused. 'It was rare for a boy to be so accepting of others, at least in my experience.' She smiled in remembrance. 'When he was happy, you could feel it inside of you—and you could scarcely feel any other way.'

'It's a shame we haven't seen him really happy.'

'Yes, it is. Perhaps it is because of his heritage, but he feels things deeply.'

'Sounds familiar,' Dorrie said with a grin. She leaned forwards. 'And what sort of girl were you, Portia?'

The infatuated sort. But she didn't say it. She gave a little smile instead. 'Perhaps you will not credit it, but I was a fun sort, as well, if not in the same rowdy way as my brothers.'

Dorrie did not get a chance to reply, as Mateo drew his mount close in. 'Marlborough is just ahead,' he called.

They swept into the great wide main street of the town and Dorrie exclaimed at the crowds of people. A vendor gave them directions and within minutes they were on their way north.

It was not too long before it became clear that they had reached Longvale land. First the road narrowed to a track and Mateo was forced to ride ahead of the landau. Then the land opened up and they found themselves surrounded alternately by well-tended fields of grains and odd little plots, different from anything Portia had seen before. One was filled with large mounds of soil, out of which stretched a massive tangle of ground-creeping plants. Another had been ringed with young trees, to which a criss-cross system of rope had been strung. Immature vines climbed the rope and spread out, creating an oddly beautiful, floating green surface. Portia's curiosity was piqued long before they reached the house, and then it flared to even higher heights.

None of the attention so carefully shown on the land had been extended here. Weeds choked the gravel drive, shutters hung askew, and slate tiles sagged from the roof. Portia shared a bemused glance with her two companions as the landau rolled to a stop.

No groom came running. No one emerged from the house. An ancient post listed at one side of the drive. Mateo tied his hired hack to it and directed the driver of the landau to circle around and search out the stables.

Dorinda bit her lip as the carriage rattled away. Portia smiled encouragingly and took her hand as they followed Mateo across cracked stones to the door.

No knocker had been hung. Mateo pounded a fist upon the door and when there was no answer, he pounded again, long and hard. He'd just raised his fist a third time when the door opened a crack.

A young woman's face peered out at them, timid and puzzled, as if she'd never seen a visitor at the front door. 'Yes?' she asked.

'I am Mr Cardea,' Mateo said gently. 'My companions and I are here to see Mr Riggs.' He ended by flashing the maidservant his most charming smile. Portia had to bite back a grin when the girl blinked, flushed and then adjusted her cap.

'You're wanting to see Mr Riggs?' she repeated.

Again her brow creased as if this was a completely new idea.

'Indeed we are.' Mateo tried the smile again. 'May we come in?'

She thought about it. Portia could not determine if she was generally a slowtop or if she had been dazzled by Mateo's charm. The latter, likely, for she straightened suddenly and opened the door. 'Yes, do come in,' she invited, dipping a quick curtsy.

The three of them advanced into a dark, panelled hall in sore want of a cleaning. Dorinda huddled close.

'Wait right there,' the maid said, pointing to a gloomy corner. 'I'll see what's to be done with you.'

'What's to be done with us?' Dorrie repeated in a whisper. She leaned against a wall as if to steady herself. 'The offer of a seat, perhaps? Or a drink to clear the dust of the roads? I'm exhausted. All I wish to do is lay my head back for a moment's rest.' A look of horror crossed her face. 'But I wouldn't dare! What sort of man is this Mr Riggs, to keep such a house?'

'I'm beginning to have an idea,' Portia answered. Suddenly some of the observations she'd heard from the man's mother began to make sense.

'I don't care how old he is,' Dorrie said suddenly. 'I don't care if he is as handsome as sin and rich as Croesus—you are not to even *consider* marrying him! The thought of you living in all this disorder would drive me mad.'

Mateo smiled, while Portia regarded her with a grin. 'This disorder only drives you mad because you've no prospects of setting it to rights. Give you a free hand to wage war against it and you'd be as happy as a pig in swill.'

Her companion looked momentarily diverted by the thought, but she had no chance to respond before heavy footsteps echoed from the back of the house.

'Visitors,' declared the stout woman who emerged from the shadowed hall. She looked them over with disapproval. 'Ain't dressed for it, neither.'

Even Mateo's legendary charm had become strained. 'Indeed,' he answered non-committally. 'And you are?'

'Mrs Pickens. Housekeeper.'

'Very good,' he said with a nod. 'Would you be so kind as to inform Mr Riggs we are here? And perhaps find a comfortable spot for the ladies to wait?'

'No use waiting. There's a problem in one of the fields. He won't be back 'til nightfall.' She shrugged. 'That's if he don't decide to sleep in the barn.' She half-turned away. 'Best bet's to come back near daybreak. You might catch him in for breakfast then.'

Portia stepped forwards. 'We really must speak to him today. We have an urgent matter of business to discuss. Can he be summoned from the fields?'

'Aye, but he won't come,' the housekeeper said dourly. 'Most folks know not to come to the house. If you want to speak to the master, you'll have to go out to the fields.' She wrinkled her nose and ran an assessing eye over the three of them. 'I got boots of all sizes. Some of them will likely fit the ladies, but there ain't nothing I can do 'bout your hems.'

Beside her, Dorinda uttered a long, stuttering sigh.

'Boots for me, please,' Portia agreed. 'But please,

cannot you find my companion a quiet spot to rest and wait?'

'No decent place to be had, 'cept for the master's study.' She studied Dorinda. 'Come back to the kitchens with us,' she invited. 'More comfortable, and I just put on a pot o' meadowsweet tea. Good for the joints,' she explained.

'It sounds lovely, thank you,' Dorrie accepted with relief. But she cast an anxious glance at Portia. 'Will you be all right without me?'

'Perfectly,' Portia assured her. 'Now, I'll take those boots.' She shot a look at Mateo. 'And a pair for Mr Cardea, should he feel the need to change.'

'No need at all,' he replied. 'I've quite resigned myself that my boots will not survive my acquaintance with you, Portia.' He grimaced. 'Let's just hope they are the only casualty.'

Only Portia could contrive to look completely fetching while striding across farmland, wearing bulky work boots and an old linen wrapper dragged from the bottom of a storage bin. Mateo spent a few minutes watching her carefully, but she appeared to be fully recovered from her earlier lethargy.

He felt relieved, and restless because of the intensity of that relief. Though she'd always been quiet—at least when he was around—she'd always been full of interest and enthusiasm once you looked past the surface. But her companion had conjured an unpleasant image of what Portia's married life must have been like, and he couldn't shake the ugly picture from his mind. It disturbed him to think of all that quiet, industrious energy subverted by cruelty or negligence.

He hardly had time to dwell on it, thank goodness. The boy dispatched to guide them had been promised a slice of berry pie on his return, and he set a brutal pace. Portia literally took it in her stride, and indeed appeared remarkably at home crossing fields and jumping ditches. She never stalled until they skirted a damp meadow planted thick with tall, rough stalks, hairy leaves and drooping pink flowers.

She stopped and broke a stalk off. 'Comfrey,' she said musingly.

Mateo was far beyond the area of his expertise. 'Is that significant?'

'Only unusual, to see an entire plot of it planted,' she returned. She waved to their impatient escort. 'I'm sorry. Lead on.'

Clearly Portia had landed smack in the middle of her area of expertise. Watching her, with Miss Tofton's story fresh in his mind, the significance of Stenbrooke and all that it must have meant to her became suddenly clear. More than a childhood passion for gardening and landscape had gone into that magnificent estate. Stenbrooke must have provided both purpose and escape. To keep her home and live her life according to her own choosing—it would be the ultimate victory, the symbol of triumph over all that she had endured.

The idea added another level of commonality to their already dangerous understanding of each other. It also added another dimension to his determination to see both their goals met.

His master was just ahead, the boy told them, pointing to a field of spindly grain stalks. Mateo shared a smile with Portia as the boy left them at a run, and together they crossed to the far edge of the field, where a group of labourers had gathered in a loose circle.

The men parted as they approached, and he saw that they watched a man wielding a shovel. He was of middling years, and dressed as a gentleman, but his breeches were shabby, his waistcoat stained and the string of curses coming out of his mouth would have earned any sailor's respect.

'Mr Riggs.' Mateo stepped closer. 'I apologise for the interruption, but we'd like a moment to speak to you.'

'Not now.' The portly man spoke without looking around. He knelt down in the dirt and pulled a clump of scrawny plants up by the roots. He shook the dirt free, spraying it everywhere, and began to examine the root ball closely, grumbling under his breath all the time.

Mateo's patience had met its end. 'Sir, we've come—'

His gruff speech was interrupted when Portia laid a hand on his arm and squeezed. The wry twist of her mouth surprised him, but not nearly so much as the slow wink of her eye.

She stepped forwards and knelt down next to the obnoxious man.

'Drainage is fine, roots are healthy,' he said without looking at her. 'But just look at this barley; it's got barely a whisker, let alone a beard.'

'Too many heavy feeders?' she asked.

Riggs started at the sound of her voice, and at last his head whipped around.

Portia maintained her serious expression and gestured across the field. 'Have you tried beans?'

The man's eyes grew rounder. 'And clover,' he said grudgingly.

'Had the sheep in?'

He nodded.

Slowly she peeled her gloves off. Riggs and his labourers stared as if she'd sprouted two heads. Mateo wondered what under the deep blue sky she was up to when she looked over her shoulder and handed him her gloves.

Every man in the field held his breath as she knelt down, close to the earth. She peered at the hole Riggs had made, then scooped up a handful of soil. Cradling it, she picked through it. She closed her eyes, brought it close to her face and sniffed deeply. She squeezed her fist tight around it, and then examined the soil again. 'I can see you've added malt waste,' she said thoughtfully. She met Riggs's gaze. 'Have you tried marl?'

Mateo saw respect bloom on the man's face and surprise show on the labourers'.

'Aye,' Riggs answered her. 'It was the last thing I tried. It's been three seasons I let this field rest. I thought 'twould be ready again.' He kicked at the row of spindly stalks. 'But you see the results.' A crafty look grew in his eye. 'So then, will you make a suggestion of what I should try next?' He allowed open amusement to colour his voice and Mateo saw several of the surrounding men smirk.

Portia stood, clapping her hands together, then wiped them on the rough linen of her wrap. She took her gloves back from Mateo, but did not don them. Instead she waved them negligently to indicate the sparse field of grain. 'Plough it all in,' she said curtly. 'Now, have you a river or tributary on your land?'

'I do.' Riggs popped to his feet, as well, and Mateo was surprised at how sprightly he moved.

'Then I would dredge up a goodly amount of river mud,' Portia instructed. 'Lay in a store of fish, grind them and mix it in with the mud. Spread the whole mess over your field and plough it under, good and deep.' She grinned. 'It stinks to high heaven, but it works wonders.'

Riggs's jaw dropped. 'By God, I've never thought of such a thing—but it sounds as if it just might work.' He stuck out a grubby hand and Mateo bit back a smile as Portia took it with her own. 'Who the h—?' He checked himself. 'Who the blazes *are* you?'

'Lady Portia Tofton,' she said briskly.

Mateo stared. He had not heard her use her heredi-tary title since he'd arrived. Not that he'd given it much thought, but he'd supposed that she'd given it up on her marriage.

'We've come to discuss some important business with you,' she continued. 'But I'm pleased if I've been of some help.'

'Business?' Riggs eyed her up and down in a fashion that set Mateo's teeth on edge. 'It's enough of a shock to find a woman who understands agriculture. Will you tell me now that you've a head for business, too?'

Mateo edged closer. 'We want to discuss an acquain-tancc of yours, sir. Mr Averardo.'

'Never heard of him,' Riggs said. He also never took his eye off of Portia.

She took a deep breath. Mateo wished she hadn't. Riggs appeared to enjoy it far too much.

'Mr Riggs, I am the owner—was the owner—of property south of Newbury. Stenbrooke,' she said gently. 'Perhaps you recall it?'

'Newbury?' he beamed. 'Ah, then you're a Berkshire girl! Wonderful country, is it not? No place better than Wiltshire and Berkshire for research into important agricultural developments.' He took her arm and, turning her away from Mateo, led her a step or two to one side. 'You'll never see so many different terrains situated so close. Why, do you know that on this acreage alone I have high chalk plains, a lowland landscape and deeper-lying vales? Three separate soil systems in one estate! Not to mention the nearby river valleys, the—'

'Stenbrooke, Mr Riggs?' Mateo interrupted, following the two of them. 'You might recall sending your solicitor, Mr Rankin, to serve a deed of conveyance on the property—even though your name was not to be found on the deed.' He raised a brow. 'We were wondering how that came about?'

The man reddened. He clapped his hand to the milling, chatting men still standing about. 'You heard the lady, lads! Fetch the plough and get this blasted barley tilled under—and then we're for the river.'

The men scattered and Portia laid a hand on the man's arm. 'Please, Mr Riggs. That deed of conveyance has gone missing. I need to find it, so I can get Stenbrooke back.'

'I can't discuss it!' He seemed genuinely upset. 'It's not my business to share with you or anyone.'

'It's my business, sir,' Portia asserted. 'And you made it yours when you sent Mr Rankin to my home.'

'Would never have done it, had I known...' he waved his hand ineffectually '...had I known you.'

'I love Stenbrooke, just as you obviously love Longvale. Berkshire is indeed a remarkable country. I would be heartbroken to leave it.'

'I am all sympathy, my lady, but there is nothing I can do.'

'Of course you can. You can tell us about Mr Averardo.'

Riggs rubbed his fingers vigorously over his ears, as if he could block out the sound of her request. 'Don't know the man, I tell you!'

Mateo's frustration was building. 'Then how did the deed to Stenbrooke come into your possession? Why were you involved at all?'

Mute, Riggs shook his head.

Hell and damnation. Mateo's fists clenched. Was he to be thwarted at every step of this miserable business? He took a menacing step towards the man, determined to wring the information out of him, if need be.

But once again, Portia stalled him. She stepped in close to Riggs and wrapped her hand around his arm. She breathed deeply and smiled at the man. 'Perhaps you have not realised, Mr Riggs, that my father was the Earl of Winbury? I grew up at Hempshaw, also in Berkshire.'

Riggs stared at her, clearly not understanding what that information had to do with anything, but also clearly grateful for the reprieve. Mateo hadn't a clue what she was up to, either, but after her earlier success, he was willing to play this out her way.

'You've been to Hempshaw before, I believe, sir? At

least, I thought I recalled that you had escorted your mother there on at least one occasion.'

Horrified comprehension dawned on the man's face. Mateo could only hope it boded well for them.

'That's right—' Portia smiled '—I can see that you do recall it. My mother was the Countess of Winbury. Our mothers were the best of friends. I am still in contact with your mama, in fact.' Her smile grew slightly knowing. 'She's such a dedicated correspondent.'

Riggs gave a massive shudder. 'Well, I know it. You have my sympathies, if you are on the receiving end of her acid pen.'

Portia managed to look shocked. Mateo hid a smile.

'That's not a very chivalrous thing to say about your own mother, sir,' she chided. 'She's a lovely woman.' She paused and regarded him in a considering manner. 'But I admit she does seem to be a bit obsessed with your unmarried state.'

'Twenty years and I've heard of nothing else,' he moaned.

'Well, now that I've been to Longvale I have a greater insight into her objections. Your house is in a deplorable condition and your person is not much better. I don't mean to be rude, sir, but you could do with a bath, a hair cut and a trip to the tailor.' The mischievous smile returned. 'Clearly you are in want of a woman's guidance.' She darted a quick glance in Mateo's direction. 'In my next letter I shall tell your mama that I am in complete agreement with her. I dare say she will be very grateful to have her maternal urgings validated. *Very* grateful, indeed.'

Mateo gaped at her. The minx! He'd accused her of

blackmailing him into marriage and now she used the threat of marriage to blackmail Riggs. *Dio*, but it was a brilliant strategy. *She* was brilliant. He had to fight the mad impulse to laugh out loud, and the more insane urge to grab her up by her arms and kiss her, hard and long.

Except that her strategy appeared to have backfired. Instead of blurting out the information they were after, the repulsive man was running an evaluating eye over her. As if she was a prized filly at a horse fair. Mateo's heart began to pound.

'Well, I might actually consider my dear mother's feelings in this matter, were the chit in question one with a brain in her head and an understanding of what I'm doing here.' The lecherous devil leered at Portia. 'Damned if I wouldn't like to shock the old woman by presenting her with my wife!' Mateo watched him gnaw the inside of his cheek, considering. 'It would seem to solve your problems, as well, Lady Portia. What do you say?'

It was Portia's turn to gape. Her mouth actually dropped. Ah, but she was hoist by her own petard! Mateo had to recognise the humour in the situation, then, even though he could swear the man's words had started a red haze around the edge of his vision.

Portia recovered quickly. She threw another glance his way and then let loose with a gay laugh. 'Oh, Mr Riggs, you flatter me! Your mother will in no way consider me eligible to be your bride.'

'Certainly not,' Mateo agreed. 'Lady Portia is a widow, childless and likely too old, besides.'

This time she did not feign to look at him, although

her lips tightened. She looked absolutely lovely, even covered with mud and awash with annoyance.

'But how happy she will be to hear you are finally ready to take her well-meant advice!' she exclaimed. 'Of course you will be expected to find a fresh young bride. Your mother will likely insist that you spend the Season in London next spring, looking over the new crop of available young ladies.'

'She knows I can't do the Season,' Riggs said, aghast. 'The spring planting!'

'You'll have to count on missing part of the summer, for likely your young bride will wish to marry from her own home,' mused Mateo. 'Oh, and the autumn will be taken up with a bridal trip.'

'At harvest time?' Riggs shook his head. 'No. I've said it all along—marriage is a bad idea.'

'But imagine the rewards,' Portia cajoled. 'A lovely young woman, and likely children to follow. She'll keep your house, see to hiring more servants and make your life so much more pleasant!'

'Yes,' Mateo said sourly. 'She'll run through your money, expect you to keep regular hours, eat regular meals and keep her informed of your whereabouts at all times.' Mateo shuddered right along with their victim. 'And the people that will be about! Young hostesses must prove their mettle, mustn't they? There will be dinners and house parties and you'll have to do the pretty with all your neighbours—'

'Enough!' Riggs nearly shouted. 'I know what you're trying to do, but the devil of it is, it's likely to work! Lady Portia, I beg you, do not start my mother off on a tear. My nerves won't take it!' He sighed. 'But, truly, I cannot help you.'

'Tell us what you know,' Mateo said simply.

He drooped in defeat. 'All right, but come, you've quite worn me out. I need a drink.' He led them to the corner of the field, where an earthenware jug rested in the shade. He tipped it up and took a long draught, then offered it around. Both Mateo and Portia declined.

'It's just tea, not rotgut,' he clarified. 'It's gone cold, but it's good none the less.'

'No, thank you. The deed? Do you have it in your possession?' asked Mateo.

'What? No. I sent it on weeks ago.' He heaved a great sigh and settled to the ground, leaning back against a tree. 'There are a couple of stumps there.' He indicated with a wave of his hand. 'You're a strapping fellow,' he said to Mateo. 'Roll them over here and you two can sit.'

Mateo wrestled one of the wide remnants over and Portia perched herself upon it. He leaned against a tree and invited Riggs to continue.

'I handled the business for a friend,' he said with a shrug. 'I owed him, you see. Could hardly refuse.'

'Why not?' Portia asked.

He took another drink and wiped his mouth on his sleeve. 'It all started with Bright Early Morning.'

Mateo and Portia exchanged a look.

'Finest specimen of a racehorse I believe I've ever seen.'

'A racehorse?' Portia looked as startled as Mateo felt.

'Yes. It was a project of mine.' Riggs's expression lost focus and he gazed up into the canopy overhead. 'I thought to develop a special feed. Something to increase endurance, strengthen the bones, give a horse an advantage in a race. I proposed the plan to a friend, a man mad for racing and involved in breeding horses. I talked him into it, you might say.'

'Ah,' Portia said suddenly. 'The comfrey!'

'Yes, that was a component. We kept her on a special diet of my design. And she looked so damned healthy! Sound and strong—and fast, too. I thought we'd struck upon something big. We entered her in the Oxford races. My friend and I both bet heavy on her.'

'What happened?' asked Mateo, although the answer seemed obvious.

'She nearly did it, nearly won. They were turning into the last stretch and she started to pull away from the pack. Another jockey saw her making to leave them, and he jostled her—set his mount against her hard and deliberate.'

'Oh, no.' Portia's face fell.

'Aye. She went down in a tumble. Shattered a front leg and a back. Had to be put down right there on the track. Another colt was caught up in it, too. They tried to save him, but after a day or two, had to give it up.' He shook his head, closed his eyes and drank again. 'Worst day of my life.'

'But what does Bright Early Morning have to do with Stenbrooke?' asked Portia.

'My friend, the breeder, he lost his most promising filly. He lost a fortune. And he lost a good bit of his reputation, as well.' He turned pleading eyes to Mateo. 'You see, don't you? I owed him. Money, but more, too.

It was a debt of honour.' He looked again to Mateo for understanding.

And Mateo knew what he meant. 'So he asked this of you? That you deliver the deed to Stenbrooke?'

'Among other things, but, yes. He sent the paperwork by courier. But at the time we were having major drainage problems in an important field. So I sent the fellow on to Rankin so he could handle it for me.'

'And it was not Averardo who asked this of you?'

'No, it was Dowland—Lord Dowland, I should say.'

Mateo knew him. Had met the baron, in fact, when he had attended the festivities of his cousin Sophie's wedding to Lord Dayle. Near to Mateo's age, Dowland was full of enthusiasm for racing, and for Parliamentary reform. And he was something of a kindred spirit. Together they had cut a swathe through Dorset, mourning Charles's loss of freedom and celebrating their own.

'Who is Averardo to him, though?' Portia asked.

'I don't know. I barely looked the papers over, just sent the courier on to Rankin.' He paused. 'It was the courier's idea, now that I think back on it. He said he could see how busy I was, and suggested that the matter was straightforward, and something that could be handled by a subordinate.'

Mateo snorted. 'I've never heard of a less straightforward matter of business in my life.' He stilled. 'Nor a more inventive courier.' He fixed Riggs with a hard stare. 'All copies of that conveyance have gone missing, sir. Rankin thought it likely that this courier had brought them back to you.'

'The hell you say!' He bit his lip and shot an apologetic glance at Portia. 'Sorry, my lady, but, no, I got a note from Rankin stating the matter was done, and I've neither seen nor heard another word on the matter since.' He added with irony, 'Until today.'

'And would you perhaps recall the name of the courier?' Portia asked.

Mateo nodded. In a situation abounding with odd circumstances and unusual practices, this courier appeared to be the only common thread.

'No, that's not something I would...' He paused. 'Wait.'

He ran a hand over his brow, leaving a streak of dirt behind. Mateo declined to inform him of it and enjoyed a petty surge of satisfaction.

'I do recall something. It was an Italian name, Lawrence—no. Lorenzo or something like. I only thought twice of it because the man was so damned pretty. He looked like he'd stepped straight out of a painting from one of the Renaissance masters.'

'Is there anything else you might remember? Anything that might help us?' Portia asked.

Riggs just shook his head.

'We put a scare into your man Rankin. He's likely trying to track those deeds, as well. I doubt he'll bestir himself too far...' Mateo noted that Riggs had the grace to flush '...but if he finds a copy and files it with the courts before we can track this Averardo down, then our situation becomes more complicated.'

'I was little more than a go-between in this damnable situation,' Riggs said bitterly. 'And now I regret even that much.'

He could not regret it as much as Mateo mourned the thought of another delay. 'We'll need to speak to

Lord Dowland next, it would seem. Parliament's out, so he could be anywhere—at his seat or anywhere on the racing circuit. You wouldn't happen to have an idea just where we could find him, would you?' Try as he might to stop it, still bitterness leaked into the words as they left his mouth.

'He has a fine stud in Lambourn. He spends most of his time there, these days. You'll find him there,' Riggs said with assurance. 'We're trying the special diet again, and this time we are starting while the animal is young. He's looking over the likely candidates.'

Portia rose from her rustic seat. 'Thank you for telling us what you know.'

'You won't write to my mother?' He shuddered and climbed to his feet, as well.

She smiled. 'No.' Her head nodded towards the men behind him, hitching up the plough. 'Good luck with your field.'

'I'll call Rankin off if I can,' he promised.

'Thank you.'

Mateo flinched when she bent and kissed the man's grimy cheek. He took her arm and they started back on the long walk to the house. Portia strode along in earnest silence, for which he was grateful. In his mind he began to calculate distance, money and, above all, time. Precious days ran like water through his fingers. The harder he gripped, the more slipped away and each drip of a lost second echoed a mournful death knell for his future.

Chapter Eight

Portia watched Mateo's frown grow as they made their way back to Mr Riggs's run-down house. By unspoken consent the three of them politely declined Mrs. Pickens's gruff offer of a room for the night. Thankfully, Dorrie had only a short time to fuss over Portia's muddied hem before the landau was brought around. Her companion gazed back on the place thoughtfully as they pulled away.

'Do you know, I think we've discounted Mr Riggs's possibilities too quickly,' she mused.

Portia rolled her eyes. 'Oh, hush, Dorrie.'

The shadows lengthened as they headed towards Marlborough and the glower on Mateo's face kept apace. Guilt churned in Portia's stomach. She knew he was concerned over lost time and his need to be gone. She sighed in relief as they drove into town just as the last light slipped from the sky.

Stacks of carriages, post-chaises and coaches lined up outside the Castle Inn, but there were still rooms to be had. No private parlours were available, however, so the three of them ate a simple meal in the public dining room. Still and silent, Mateo picked at his food. Portia watched, the knot of anxiety in her stomach growing with each monosyllabic sentence he uttered. Guilt stabbed her. It was just so *wrong* to see his restless energy frozen, his ever-changing expression immobilised into one haunted expression. She could take no more.

'Excuse me, please.' She stood. 'I need to speak to the landlady.'

She pushed her way through the busy room, wishing fervently that she had never kissed Mateo Cardea. The signs were plain upon his face. She'd been in his shoes, could nearly feel his misery and increasing panic as if it were her own. He was trapped, just as firmly as she. Every time they caught a glimpse of light, the tunnel stretched out longer.

She made her way towards the back of the inn. It was quieter here, with the bustle and hum of the common rooms replaced by only the occasional tread on the stair. Portia found her way to a dark corner and covered her face with her hands. Somehow the fact that she'd kissed Mateo—propositioned him, practically—made it all that much worse. It added an element of awkwardness for him and a sense of anguished hopelessness for her.

For as stupid and futile as it might be, she still wanted him.

He'd refused her advances, made it clear that he valued his agenda over hers; he'd even ticked off to Mr Riggs all the reasons why she was unmarriageable, as if it were nothing more than a market list.

But he'd also let her shine today, in a way that her husband, her brothers, even her father would not have allowed. It had been she who had won Riggs over, because Mateo had not pushed her aside or felt threatened by her expertise. Even when her plan hadn't gone as she'd expected, together they had made it work. And she'd used her title again, she marvelled. She hadn't planned on it, it had just slipped out—and she hadn't even flinched. It had felt good. Almost, for a moment, as if she was whole again.

She'd been riding high as they left that field. He hadn't once made her feel awkward, or out of place. Instead she'd been buoyed by a feeling of success and self-worth—until she'd seen Mateo's face and realised what it had cost him.

She rubbed her brow repeatedly with her fingertips. Now all she could feel was exhausted by the emotional extremes of the day. For so long she'd kept herself insulated from exactly this sort of emotional tumult. It was safer to wrap her passion up into her gardens.

But it was also lonely. She'd managed to hide from that consequence for a long time. She'd brushed it aside and told herself that it was more than a fair trade. Until she'd burst into that inn in the middle of the night and found Mateo Cardea again.

Now all she wanted was to burrow into his arms and allow his kiss and the touch of his hands to chase the sadness, the awful, intense *aloneness*, away. Only he could do it, bring her back from that lonely edge, connect her solidly to the world once more.

But she couldn't ask it of him. So she determined to do what she could for him instead.

She brought her hands away from her face and pushed away from the wall. And froze. A gentleman stood just a few feet away, staring at her with a furrowed brow. Her heart started to pound. It was dark this far back inside the inn, and quiet.

'Are you all right, ma'am?' The stranger stepped closer. He wore a look of concern.

'Yes, of course. Thank you.' Portia stepped away, nervous. Long, dark locks framed his face, caught back in a queue. She'd seen plenty of men around the docks with hair like that, but never a man in the garb of a gentleman. The combination was incongruous.

She jumped as a bang, then a curse, sounded down the hall. The harried landlady emerged from a room, burdened with a load of dirty linen.

'Let me help you with that, Mrs White.' Portia hurried to the woman's side. She didn't look back at the stranger. 'I was wondering if you could answer a few questions for me.'

Mateo left the stables, his feet dragging as he headed back inside the inn. Tonight he missed the sea, with an intensity that only another sailor could understand. *Dio*, but he longed for the vast, empty ocean about him and a clean wind at his back. The sea challenged a man, it was true. Constantly she tested his skills and endurance, but she also gave him the sense that he was master of his own destiny. Prove yourself worthy, and she gifted you with the certain knowledge that the world was yours for the taking.

But here? Here nothing was certain, and his destination was complicated by the needs of others, and clouded by deceit. The opportunity for a simple trade with Portia had long since disappeared. Worse, his suspicion that someone was working to manipulate this unlikely chain of events only solidified as time passed and complications arose. But who would enact such an elaborate play? For truly, he began to feel as if he'd been playing a part prescribed to him by some unknown author—and he didn't even know the full cast of characters, let alone understand the plot.

Mateo had neither the time nor patience to play a pivotal role in someone else's drama. He was captain of a merchant ship, not a damned green-room dandy, and he knew what to do when a headwind tried to force him in a direction he did not want to go. He was prepared to beat an upwind course. Now he just had to inform his crew.

He wound his way through the sprawling inn, making for the back stairs. He'd just started up when he heard a door slam, somewhere deeper in the bowls of the place. A moment later he heard his name called.

'Mateo, wait!' Portia rushed from the shadows to join him on the stairs. 'I wish to speak to you!'

And was this not just what every seaman sent ashore dreams of—a beautiful girl waiting for him, eager for his company? Her skin glowed in the faint light, flushed with eagerness or exertion, and her eyes sparkled. She'd changed her gown, and although this one carried no field dirt about the hems, its deep v-shaped neckline tempted Mateo's thoughts in a very earthy direction.

'Will you come up to our room?' she asked.

'I will, if you agree to play chaperon. Miss Tofton

appears to be growing dangerously marriage-minded. I don't want to be caught in a compromising position.'

'Oh, stop.' She sounded perversely irritated. And that led him to feel perversely amused.

'I was just on my way there,' he said. 'I have something to discuss with you and Miss Tofton, as well.'

He gestured for her to proceed ahead of him, and then spent the rest of the two flights of steep stairs regretting that bit of chivalry. Her rump swayed above him, at nearly eye level and just out of his reach. His pulse quickened, his body stirred and he congratulated himself on the plan he meant to propose—one that would grant him a timely reprieve from Portia's tempting presence.

They'd nearly reached the second-floor landing when they met a couple of men coming down, carrying between them a wide, unwieldy trunk. The sweat and strain of their faces was testimony to the weight of the thing, their speed as they rounded the landing indicated their eagerness to be relieved of it. Portia pressed up against the stairwell wall to let them pass, but the damned thing shifted and swayed in her direction as the first man started backwards down the stairs.

Instinctively, Mateo reached out for her. He pulled her close, pressed her tight against the wall and shielded her body with his. The trunk thumped into him, scraping heavily across his back as the men cursed and struggled to regain their grips.

'Sorry, guv!' one of them called as they continued their descent.

He didn't respond. He was pressed full length into Portia Tofton—and he had no inclination to pull away.

Ever so slowly, she lifted her head. Their gazes met. And the world shrank, contracting mightily until nothing existed save for the two of them, and the retreating clatter of the men and their burden. Her eyes darkened, even as all the tension ebbed from her body. Desperately, Mateo wished he could close his eyes and savour this delicious sensation; her gradual moulding to the front of him.

Was this—this heart-pounding, breath-stealing moment—the reason his father had left the family legacy to Portia? Had he been so convinced that throwing them together would lead inevitably to this tortuous, physical longing? For the first time in his life, Mateo was tempted to do exactly as his father wished.

He stepped back instead, but her gaze remained locked with his, and he was damned if he could look away. The air between them had come alive. It pulsed with awareness, and pure, undeniable need.

There was no denying it. He had to kiss her. He might expire on the spot if he didn't. He reached for her, already anticipating the yield of her mouth against his, the feel of her exquisite curves filling his hands. His hands closed around her waist, cradled the generous swell of her hips. She reached up…and the slam of a door sounded above, followed by the fast approach of a set of footsteps.

Her arms dropped. He released her. They turned away from each other just as a gentleman reached the landing above.

'Good evening,' the man said with a tip of his hat. Judging by the hint of a smile on his damned pretty face, he had an idea of what he'd interrupted.

Mateo murmured an indistinct reply. He'd just indicated for Portia to precede him when a niggling memory
caused him to turn and glance at the man again. But
the fellow was gone already; he could hear his footsteps
continuing on down the stairs. Mateo shrugged. Silent
and tense, he followed Portia to the room she shared
with Miss Tofton.

Her companion was comfortably ensconced there,
Mateo noticed irritably. He'd asked her to come along
expressly to prevent such tantalising interludes. What
good did she do him, curled up by the fire like a cat?

'I was wondering where you'd got to, Portia, and
was just trying to summon the energy to come and find
you!' Miss Tofton said. 'Good evening, Mr Cardea. I
hope you find your room as comfortable as we do ours?'

'I do.' It was the damned stairwell that had proved
uncomfortable. 'I'd like to speak to you ladies about
where we go from here, if you don't mind.'

'Of course.' Portia perched herself on the edge of the
bed. 'I was going to ask the same of you.'

Mateo swallowed and went to lean against the
mantel. 'I'm afraid you'll object to what I have to say,'
he began.

At the same time, Portia had looked to Miss Tofton
and warned, 'You won't like what I mean to propose.'

He met Portia's startled gaze while Miss Tofton
looked from one to the other. 'Well,' she said briskly,
'let's get this unpleasantness over with, shall we?'

'I would normally encourage the lady to go first,
but I have a matter of importance to discuss,' he said
regretfully. 'I can scarcely believe there's been another
leg added to this wild-goose chase, but it's clear we need

to get to Lambourn next—and we need to get there as quickly as possible.' He paused. 'I've been enquiring into the state of the roads between here and there.'

'There are no direct routes, just a maze of narrow country lanes,' Portia interrupted. She shrugged. 'I've been asking about, as well.'

'It's not terribly far as the crow flies, perhaps twelve miles or so north-east, according to the ostlers. But a larger coach cannot travel that way. We'd have to travel back to Hungerford, take the road north and east to West Shefford, and then turn west towards Lambourn. It will double the distance and just take too long.'

'I agree,' said Portia. 'The best route is the most direct, but it must be taken on horseback, as there are places we would need to leave the roads altogether to cross over the chalk plains.'

'Yes, exactly.' He could only be grateful for her understanding. 'That's why I'd like you and Miss Tofton to return to Stenbrooke while I go alone.'

'What? No! I agree that Dorrie should return home, but the *two* of us will continue on to Lambourn.'

They glared at each other.

'Wait just a moment, both of you.' Miss Tofton sounded distinctly grumpy. 'Portia, you mentioned that Mr Riggs promised to stop that solicitor—Rankin—from pursuing this matter. If that's so, then why are we still in a tearing hurry?'

Mateo struggled for patience. 'Rankin is an unknown. Riggs may be able to stand him down. He might never even have lifted a finger against us after we left. Or he might be the mean and stubborn sort to do all he can to hurt us, despite anything Riggs says, just because we crossed him. We cannot know.'

He hardened his voice, just a bit. He wanted them both very clear on the urgency with which he needed to be done with this. 'But even if you remove him from consideration, I am still facing an important time issue. I must get back to Philadelphia soon, if at all possible. I am, of course, thrilled to even have the opportunity to get Cardea Shipping back, but if I delay much longer, this escapade will have cost me more than a few months' time and the loss of my pride. It will cost the company the rewards and opportunities resulting from several years of struggle and hard work.' Earnestly, he faced the two women. 'My family's fate is inextricably bound up with the success of the business. In a hundred different capacities, they make their livings and stake their futures on it. If I fail at this, I fail them, too.'

Portia's chin went up. 'Don't distress yourself, Mateo. I've no mind to let this linger on any further than need be, cither. I'm tired of feeling as if an axe is about to fall on me. Where is that damned deed of conveyance? Who is this Averardo? Will I be able to keep Stenbrooke or be turned out on my ear? I need to know.' She gestured to her companion. '*We* need to know.'

She stood suddenly, and crossed to the other side of the bed. 'That courier... I haven't been able to get him from my mind.' She looked over her shoulder at him. 'Doesn't it begin to feel like we are being manipulated? As if this Averardo, whoever he is, doesn't wish to be known?'

'I'd reached the same conclusion,' Mateo confessed. 'I think he's purposefully putting obstacles between us.

It only adds another element of urgency to this mess we are in.'

'All right,' Miss Tofton said. Her voice rang with disapproval. 'I accept that all speed is necessary, but all the original objections to the two of you travelling alone still exist.' She sighed. 'I know I'm not a bruising rider like you, Portia, but I will do my best.'

Portia crossed the room again to kneel at her companion's feet. 'I'm afraid it will be too rough for you, dear,' she said gently.

'She's right, though,' Mateo said quietly. 'It would be easier were I to go alone.' After the stairwell, she had to have an inkling how true a statement that was. He stared down at her. The light of the fire caught in her hair and flowed, molten, through her heavy locks. Her eyes, though, were hidden in shadows. 'You can trust me, Portia.' It came out in nearly a whisper.

He wanted her to trust him, so intensely he ached with it.

She put her head down on Miss Tofton's knee, and his heart fell.

'In my head, I know that is true, Mateo.' Her voice was muffled in her companion's skirts. Suddenly her head snapped back up. 'But I've played the docile daughter, sister and wife for too long, and I'm less than satisfied with where it's got me.' She shook her head and stood. 'It's less about trusting you than it is about learning to trust in and rely on myself.' Her jaw set and determined, she met his gaze. 'I'm going with you.'

Mateo breathed deeply, waiting for his pride to pound annoyance and disappointment into submission. 'All right.'

Miss Tofton still wore a disapproving frown. 'How long will it take you to get to Lambourn and see the baron?'

'A few hours' ride to arrive. Not long to discuss it, provided we find him home. A full day, then, to see the business done,' Mateo calculated.

Miss Tofton's chin lifted. 'Well, then. I will take the carriage back to Hungerford and await you at the Bear. Meet me there once you've talked to your baron.' She let loose a weary sigh. 'Then perhaps we can go home.'

Portia said nothing, just looked to him. Mateo scowled. Should he expect the pair of them to place their trust in him at this late date? Apparently not. He gave a curt nod.

Portia reached down and gave her hand a squeeze. 'If it's any consolation, Dorrie, I promise not to ravish him on the ride over.'

Mateo snorted and pushed away from the mantel. 'You'd best get some sleep. We'll need to depart early in the morning.'

'I'll just ask Mrs White to have a maid awaken us at dawn.' She took a step towards the door and then stopped. 'I'll also be sure that *two* mounts will be readied in the morning.'

He nodded and she swept from the room. With a sigh of resignation, Mateo bent low over Miss Tofton's hand. 'I'll be sure that the driver has the landau's top up for you.'

She rose from her chair and stopped him as he turned for the door. 'I can't help but notice that you did not make me a promise similar to Portia's.'

No, he hadn't, and what he likely needed was a

damned vow of chastity. He glanced towards the doorway where Portia had disappeared, and was distracted by a sudden thought. 'Miss Tofton—does Portia normally use her title?'

The lady frowned. 'No. As the daughter of an earl, she could, of course, choose to use the honorary title, but I've not heard her addressed as Lady Portia in years.' Her scowl deepened and she regarded him thoughtfully. 'Do you mean to say you've heard her refer to it?'

He nodded. 'She used her title today, when she introduced herself to Mr Riggs.' He paused. 'Do you think it is significant?'

'Yes,' Miss Tofton said quietly. 'Yes, I do.'

'What does it mean, then?'

She frowned at him once more. 'It means that you had better make me that promise, Mr Cardea.'

He laughed and this time he kissed her hand as he bent over it. But he didn't promise.

Chapter Nine

The lane they followed narrowed further as Portia and Mateo grew close to the town of Albourne. For some time now there had been nothing to see save for the massive hedgerows on either side. But while the view was restricted, the noise was immense. The thick walls of crossing hawthorn branches provided a home for hundreds of warbling, chirping, twittering and peeping songbirds. They'd set a good pace, but the combination of hot sun, monotonous surroundings and cacophony of sound had lured Portia to a pleasant daze. When the concert suddenly ceased, it was a shock. She jerked to attention.

Her bad-tempered, piebald mount swivelled her ears, puzzled by the sudden absence of sound. They fixed forwards when a jingling of traces sounded ahead, around a curve in the lane. A squeal followed, and then a string of curses. Portia met Mateo's questioning look with a shrug, and they approached the turning with caution.

'What the devil?' Mateo exclaimed.

They were met with the curious sight of a high-balanced rig *backing* towards them.

'There must be someone coming this way,' Portia explained. 'There's no room to pass.' She studied the vehicle advancing towards them, end first. It barely fitted the lane, brushing the hedges on either side with its wheels. 'We'll have to go back.'

They retreated nearly half a mile, until they reached a wide turn that left room to manoeuvre. Patiently they waited while the gig made its slow way back and squeezed into the narrow space left. The driver, a red-faced young man, continued to swear and bemoan the scratched paint on his rig.

At last, then, they got a clear look at the cause of the ruckus—a placid-faced farmer driving a cart loaded high with stacks of hay. He ignored the cursing young blade, but tipped his hat at Mateo and winked at Portia. This last bit of insolence pushed the young man past his limit. He cracked his whip over his poor team's heads and went thundering back down the way they'd all come.

Laughing, Portia and Mateo followed at a more reasonable pace.

'I have some sympathy for the fellow,' Mateo confessed. 'That's exactly how this enterprise has felt: one step forwards and two steps back.' He shot Portia a crooked smile, the first that she'd seen since before they'd met Mr Riggs. 'I'm sorry if I've been as crotchety.'

'I think we might be excused, even if we were to curse a blue streak to rival that young man's,' Portia said, returning his smile. 'Heaven knows we've reason enough.' Her smile twisted a little. 'And heaven knows I heard worse when I tagged after you and my brothers.'

'And J.T.' He'd gone still, tense.

'And J.T.,' she agreed. She chose not to meet his gaze.

Mateo was suddenly blinded by a flash of insight. J. T. Tofton was not the sort of man who would appreciate his wife having a rank higher than his own. Had he insisted that Portia abandon her rightful title and take up his name instead?

He turned his gaze ahead. 'We should reach Albourne shortly. If you don't mind, I'd like to ride through. Mrs White packed us a huge luncheon; I thought perhaps we'd find a likely spot off the road to eat, after a while.'

She agreed. Soon the hedgerows ended, and the lane widened as they drew near the little town. They were quickly through, and the road out opened up again, and Portia gradually became aware that the quality of the silence had changed. Tension radiated from Mateo. He held his face carefully expressionless.

She waited.

Eventually he broke. 'I don't know that I've adequately thanked you, Portia, for giving me a chance to get Cardea Shipping back.'

'Of course you have. But it's I who owe you thanks, and perhaps an apology. My simple plan did not turn out as we expected, did it?'

He grunted. 'Well, neither of us could have predicted all of this.' He tilted his head, indicating the countryside about them. 'But I was wondering if getting Stenbrooke back would be enough.' He paused delicately. 'Miss Tofton mentioned debts, a pile of them that emerged after J.T.'s death.'

She felt herself colouring. 'Thank you for your concern, but we've managed. I've met all the honest debtors who have come knocking.'

'She also mentioned...indignities.'

Portia kept her tone carefully even. 'I believe Dorrie has been talking a bit too much.'

His brow lowered and a grim light shone from his dark eyes. 'If someone has bothered you, if a man, perhaps, has been importuning you...' His voice fell away.

'No man has importuned me,' she said, telling the truth, just not all of it. 'I'll be all right, Mateo. Dorrie and I will both be all right. We'll live a happy life at Stenbrooke, I promise you. You may rest easy.' She gentled her tone. 'But thank you for asking.'

He nodded. They grew silent again. Portia tried not to dwell on how his concern warmed her. The undulating downs did not provide much of a distraction, though one loomed soon enough when they reached a ridge and the track they followed veered sharply south.

Mateo pulled to a stop. 'Now we leave the lane and head out across the plain.'

'It's forbidding, isn't it?' Portia asked. The open, rolling landscape, empty of anything save dry, waving grass and the occasional planted field, made her feel small.

'We shouldn't be out there long. Believe it or not, there's a stretch of wood ahead, the ostlers said, a thin remnant of an ancient forest. When we reach it, we turn north and should intersect another useful lane.'

They rode on. The sense of isolation was nearly complete. Occasionally her horse would shy from a breaking ground bird, but the absence of any tree cover or variation quickly grew to be as monotonous as the hedgerows. She caught sight of a dark smudge on the horizon and wondered if it might be the beginning of the wood Mateo had mentioned.

Closer proximity revealed it to be a burial mound, instead. It was quite the longest one she'd ever encountered. The most prominent feature in the landscape—indeed, the only one—she found her eye inescapably drawn to it. There were several ploughed and planted plots in proximity, but a wide swathe of undisturbed plain had been left to surround it.

Mateo dismounted as they drew close, running a curious eye over the length of the thing. 'Shall we stop? It may be the only shade we see for a while.'

'Let's,' Portia agreed. She let him see to the staking of the horses while she unpacked the saddlebags. Mrs White had thoughtfully folded a large linen square in with her hearty luncheon. They had the makings of quite a nice little picnic.

'Come, sit down,' she beckoned. Mateo was pacing around the curved end of the mound, eyeing it with interest. He obeyed her summons, and took a seat a little apart from her. Leaning against the thing, he downed a long swill of Mrs White's apple cider, then patted the turf-covered mound behind him. 'This I have not seen in Pennsylvania, though it reminds me of the ceremonial lodges the savages build. I'm sure you can tell me why the English would fashion a hill in such a desolate spot. Does it serve a ritualistic purpose?'

She smiled around her sandwich. 'It's a burial mound.'

'As in, filled with the dead?' He wore a slightly horrified look.

She nodded. 'There's no need to be frightened, though. I've heard of the occasional ghostly figure at these sights, even unearthly spirit hounds, but I believe they mostly show up during the solstices.'

His hand hovered over the food, deciding. 'I'm not frightened. I just hate the thought of them, trapped in the dark, mouldering in the earth, drying, decaying.' He shuddered.

She put aside her sandwich. 'Thank you so much for that vivid description.' She looked at him closely. 'So no burial for you, then?'

Juice dripped down his chin as he bit into a peach. Portia found herself licking her own lips. *Stop.*

'Aye, but it'll be a burial at sea, like any good sailor.'

She shivered. 'So you'd prefer being devoured by sharks and crabs? I don't see as that has any more appeal.'

'Ah, but it does. For I'll become part of the great, living sea.' He sighed. 'Free in the vastness of the ocean.'

His eyes unfocused and she took the opportunity to drink in the sight of him. Someone should paint him, she decided. His constant energy had been harnessed for the moment as he leaned back, one arm propped on a raised knee, wearing a contemplative expression on a face turned up towards the sun… She sighed.

'I'll be the wave that slaps against the shore, the breeze that lifts the sail of some lucky brig.' His tone vibrated with intensity.

'The hurricane gale that sinks ships,' she said wryly.

'Only my competitors, perhaps.' He laughed.

She turned away from the beautiful picture of him smiling at her. He was stealing all the pieces of her heart, one smile, and one touch at a time. It frightened her, but it also stirred her temper—towards him, for staying resolute in pursuit of his goals, and towards herself, because she did not.

'I was wrong, then. You make a good case.' She sighed. 'Crossing the ocean was one of my favourite parts of visiting your family in Philadelphia. I loved the ship at night, when all grew quiet. I would stand at the rail and feel as if I were alone with the wind and the stars and the sea.'

Reaching out, she ran a hand over the rough turf. 'Perhaps these men have become part of this land,' she suggested. 'It seems likely that they might have loved this place as much as you love the sea.'

'If they wished it, then I hope it is so,' he said quietly.

She looked out over the plain. Suddenly the place did not seem so sad and desolate, not when the sun shone brightly as she sat in the blowing grass, amidst the buzz of insects and with the sky so brilliantly blue overhead.

'It really is lovely here, isn't it?' she asked with wonder. 'It's hard to believe, while sitting here in such tranquility, that someone might be scheming against us.' She turned back to him. 'It does seem so to you, too, though?'

'We've had only a hint here and there. I suppose we cannot prove it, but I feel the truth of it.'

She understood just what he meant. It almost felt like a tickle, at the very edge of her consciousness, a hint of a forming pattern taking shape in her mind.

Their dark thoughts had broken the spell of the place. Mateo shifted restlessly and climbed to his feet.

'I'll pack the rest of this away,' she told him. 'Let's go on.'

They rode companionably close, without speaking. It was to be found in silence, too—that connection she'd been craving. It rippled through her, setting her alight, making her very aware of how close his leg was to hers. He rode just a stride ahead of her. If she nudged her horse just a little, then their legs might brush. She didn't do it, though. Instead she looked her fill, following the solid curve of his booted calf up to his muscular thigh, and climbing higher to where he sat firmly in his saddle.

Firm. A very good word.

'What did you mean to do, Mateo,' she asked, mainly to distract herself, 'if I had refused to sell my interest in Cardea Shipping?'

'Hmm? Oh, I had a few ideas.'

'Such as? Or are you not comfortable sharing them with me?'

'Packet boats,' he said. 'The *Lady Azalea* is my own ship, not the company's. I thought to use her to start up a business with a regular schedule of packets from Philadelphia to English and European ports. There are a few very successful enterprises out of New York; I thought to give them a run for their money.'

'You've family here in England. I know Papa told me your cousin Sophie had married into the aristocracy. Did you never consider a life here, perhaps?' She tried with all her might not to betray the blind, breathless hope that suddenly sprouted inside her.

He laughed. 'No doubt Sophie would see me set up somehow, but can you see me giving up the sea?'

Hope withered away. She sighed. 'No, I suppose not.'

'What a challenge that would have been, though,' he mused. 'To have the run of a business from the start.'

'I'm sure you would have made a success of it,' she said stoutly. 'But there'll be no need, if we can just track down the elusive Averardo.'

He looked back. 'I'd forgotten what a good listener you are, Portia. It pains me to remember all the adolescent twaddle I poured into your ears when we were young. But I always felt better after talking to you.' He turned his gaze towards the plain. 'Perhaps that is why my father tried so hard to see us married, back then.'

'Do you think this is what your father hoped for? Why he wrote his will the way he did? Was he hoping that we would be thrown together like this?'

He glanced back at her over his shoulder. 'In all likelihood. I'm sorry that he did not appear to have considered your feelings when he came up with the idea.' He sighed. 'It is just like him, though. Everything must always be his way. He knew but one way to run a shipping company, had one clear-cut vision of how a merchant gentleman should conduct himself and considered marriage the only route to happiness.'

He rode on quietly for a moment. 'Do you know, if your father were still alive, I'd suspect *him* of conspiring to carry out my father's wishes and drawing out this process. The whole mess just reeks of the two of them.'

'I'd be inclined to agree with you. Your father was at Hempshaw not long before my father died, did you know?' She sighed. 'I was married by then, of course, but I came back for a short visit. Even though Papa was mostly bedridden at that point, they were having a grand time of it. I know his visit was a great comfort.'

'I knew of it, although I believe I was pursuing contacts along the Rio de la Plata at the time.'

Her mouth twisted. 'The irony is that if my father were still alive, J.T. would likely never have gambled Stenbrooke away. He was more than a little intimidated by Papa. It wasn't until after he had gone that J.T. began to really run amok. If Papa had been alive, he would never had got himself killed so—' She caught herself.

He'd twisted around in his saddle to watch her. After a moment's pause she continued. 'If I had not needed your help with Stenbrooke, Mateo, I would have just handed Cardea Shipping right back to you.' She stared ahead at him. 'It's what I'd do now, if so much weren't at stake.'

He checked his mount, holding him in until they were riding abreast. He met her earnest gaze with a direct one of his own. 'I know,' he said simply.

He fell silent then, and so did she. Portia felt oddly as if he'd relieved her of a burden, one which she hadn't even known she'd carried. She enjoyed the feeling, relished the peace of just being in his company, as she'd done so often in the past. She'd just noticed the dark line ahead that surely must be the wood they were watching for, when he spoke suddenly, startling her.

'Why, Portia? Will you tell me why you married a buffoon like J.T.?' He grimaced. 'Even his name was an affectation. I never understood it. What was wrong with just plain James?'

She gave a little smile, although there was no

humour behind it, and tried to avoid the first question by answering the second. 'Well, there you've hit upon your answer. You knew him. Nothing plain was ever good enough for J.T.' She did laugh then. 'Dorrie always called him James Talbot, though he hated it. He had an uncle in Virginia who'd first called him J. T. He loved it, and thought it sounded exotic, like something from the American frontier.'

'Perhaps it would have made sense, had his interests lay in that direction. But they didn't, did they? As far as I know, his inclinations centred on drinking, gambling and wenching. He never showed the least interest in anything involving hard work.'

'No, he did not.' She said it flatly. Forbiddingly.

He chose not to notice. 'And yet you married him. Knowing that about him, knowing that he'd always been envious of your brothers, of their position and rank and their life of relative ease. Still you married him.'

She maintained her stubborn silence.

He stared at her for several long moments. She nudged her mount until the piebald picked up a bit of speed and pulled ahead.

'Portia, please,' he called. 'I want to understand.'

'There's no need to go into all of that,' she bit out.

He drew abreast of her again. 'Perhaps I only feel a need to pay you back for all those times I talked and you listened. Perhaps I've just had too much damned time to think over the last few months—about my life, about my family and my father.' He paused. 'About you.'

His tone grew harder, almost angry. 'Or perhaps I just wish to make myself feel better, but I cannot fathom how you could have ended up with that bastard. Portia, please. I want to know.'

His insistence opened up something ugly inside of her. The anger that had stirred in her earlier grew, clawing its way out and up, emerging from her suddenly tight throat in a torrent of bitter words.

'Well, that does change things, does it not? You want to know. And I, of course, will cast all my own inclinations aside to oblige you.' She sniffed. 'Every day you make it clear how much more important your wants are than my own. But I warn you—you may not enjoy getting your way in this case. For you see, I married J.T. solely to get what *I* wanted.'

She'd shocked him. Good. She *liked* shocking him. Forget Stenbrooke—as of this moment her only goal was to continually and increasingly shock the hell out of Mateo Cardea.

Unfortunately, she's also spooked her mount. She shied, sidling sideways. Portia settled herself deeper into her seat and brought her under control.

Mateo's face hardened. 'Calm yourself,' he ordered.

But she was in the grip of madness and pique and the sudden urge to push him away, just as he'd done repeatedly to her. And what better way than to reveal all the dirty truth behind her marriage?

'No. You asked—repeatedly—and now I shall answer. No doubt you wonder what I could have wanted enough to make me marry a man like J.T.? I'll tell you, Mateo. I wanted a *life*.'

The incomprehension on his face only fuelled her anger.

'I was one and twenty years old. My mother was

gone, my father was failing. His health had been growing worse for a long time, but he was full of male pride and mortally determined not to let the world know it. I was the only one left at home—and so it fell to me to help him. Land steward, secretary, nursemaid, I did a little of it all while my brothers pulled mad pranks at school and revelled in low living in London.'

She paused for a breath and reached down to soothe her skittish horse. The forest loomed closer now. She could clearly see the mixed line of oak and chestnut at the edge of the plain.

'When it became impossible to hide Papa's illness, Anthony moved home. My brothers gathered and one of their main topics of conversation was what they were to do with me.'

Mateo made a sound of protest and she gave a bitter laugh.

'Anthony was betrothed, and did not believe that his new bride would wish for me to be hanging about, interfering with her control of the house and her new role. But none of the others wanted me—having an unmarried sister about would interfere with their pleasures. They'd nearly convinced Anthony he had no other choice when J.T. offered up a new solution. "I'll take her off your hands", was his exact wording, if I recall correctly.'

Mateo's grim expression lightened just a bit at that. 'Eavesdropping again, were you?' he asked.

She lifted her hand in a gesture of futility. 'What else was I to do? They were deciding my future over drinks, as if I were the leftover runt of the litter.' Resentment spilled out of her. 'I suppose I should have been grateful that none of them thought to put me in a bag and drown me.' She took a moment to gather herself. 'They took J.T.'s offer to Papa. At first he flatly refused, but I badgered and bullied him until he agreed.'

'You *wanted*—ah, you knew Stenbrooke would come to you on your marriage,' he said quietly.

'Yes. It was a plan that worked for everyone. My brothers were rid of me. J.T. elevated himself from a country squire's son to the son and brother-in-law of an earl; he took my dowry and used it to run with my brother's set, to live the fast town life his father refused to finance. And I didn't care, because I got Stenbrooke—my own home, my own life and the chance to live there alone for much of the year.'

They'd nearly reached the edge of the forest. Without comment, Mateo urged his horse north. She followed and for a few moments they travelled parallel to the wood line in silence. But this time it was an uneasy stillness, and it did not last.

'One thing I don't understand,' Mateo said eventually. 'Surely you had other choices. You did have a Season, did you not?'

Her anger had ebbed a little as she finished her story, but now it surged anew and quickly rose to new heights. 'Choices,' she said flatly. 'Do you really not understand how few of those a woman in my position possesses? Yes, I did have a Season. It's hard to believe I didn't take, isn't it? Me, with dirt under my fingernails, more interest in landscape and horticulture than fashion and flirting, and brothers to torment anyone who might look past all that?'

She glared at him and furiously fought back the

sudden tears that threatened to flow. 'Do you profess to be surprised that no man wanted me, Mateo? I don't know why you should, when you've shown repeatedly that you do not!'

Her fury set her mount off again. The piebald reared, dancing on her hind feet. She clamped down and held on until the horse settled and then she launched herself out of the saddle. Furious, she tossed the reins at Mateo, not even waiting to see that he caught them. Then she stomped the few paces remaining and entered the sheltering embrace of the forest.

Only instinct allowed Mateo to snatch her reins out of the air. Shock actually held him rooted to his seat for a moment afterwards. He stared after her, his mind frozen under the onslaught of a veritable gale of emotion.

Guilt blew at him the hardest. The men in Portia's life had indeed failed her, and, judging by her last remark, he ranked high in their number. It was a truth he'd been avoiding, but the sudden certainty of it sent him reeling off balance.

He slid down to the ground, craning to catch a glimpse of her while he tethered the horses, but she'd disappeared into the murky distance. Impatient, he called her name as he followed her into the dense covering of oak and chestnut. 'Portia!'

No response. He shook his head. Distance—it was exactly what was missing between them. It seemed it should be there, a natural blockade resulting from years apart, their awkward past and the innate differences in their personalities. Instead they'd stepped without a hitch into the old closeness they'd shared—and the distance between them felt as if it was shrinking by the minute.

He went further into the wood, noting the change in atmosphere. The light broke through only intermittently here, and the air felt several degrees cooler. The constant breeze that swept across the plains did not reach this far in, it only set up a constant rustle in the tops of the trees. He could hear nothing else, in fact, save for the crunch of his footsteps on the bracken-covered forest floor.

'Portia?'

Indeed, this must be the remnant of an ancient forest, for some of the trees were massive. Mateo began to feel ridiculous, as if they played at children's games once more.

'Portia! *Cara*—come back!'

'No.'

Well, it was a reply at least, and it came from ahead and to the right.

'Go back, Mateo. Better yet, go on. Wait for me at the road.' Her voice sounded thick, with an embarrassed, nearly pleading note colouring her words. 'I need a few moments alone.'

Ah, he was close. He thought she might be behind the oak ahead.

'Now, Portia,' he said. 'I may have proved myself a prying lout and likely an overbearing pain, as well, but I am a gentleman. I cannot leave you here alone. You might be eaten by wolves.'

'There are no wolves in Wiltshire.'

He *was* close. He could practically hear her blink. He

crept up to the massive tree on silent feet. 'Wild boars, then?' he said, peeking around the massive trunk at her. 'Ferocious badgers?'

She cut him a scathing glance. 'No, and no.' She pushed herself away from the tree, away from him. 'And I'm not one of your dockside doxies in any case. I'm a country woman—I can take care of myself.' She raised a haughty brow at him. 'And clearly that is a skill I must fully develop.' Her gaze fell away. 'You're more of a danger to me than any wild creature.'

He sucked in a breath. 'Portia. *Cara*, I …'

Her hand hovered over her chest, as if she were in pain. 'No. You cannot cover this with laughter or fix it with glibness. I am not a child to be jollied out of my ill humour.' Her eyes narrowed. 'You were the first one, Mateo—the first man to break my heart.'

His heart sank. 'But I thought… All those years ago… When I wrote you, you were as incredulous as I at the idea of a marriage.'

Disappointment weighed down her expression. 'You knew. I will not believe you didn't know how I felt about you.'

He had, of course. 'I'd hoped it was a childish infatuation, one you'd got over.' He'd wanted desperately to believe it, so that he could carry on with his chosen course without an added burden of guilt.

'I had to be grateful—you rejected me in the nicest possible way, giving me a chance to salvage my pride and hold my head high.' She sighed. 'I was young, a naïve girl who'd spent most of her life tearing up her father's gardens. I knew I didn't have anything to offer you, to hold your interest or compete with the excitement of a privateer's life.' She turned away. 'But it still hurt. My feelings for you were real and it took me a long time to get over them.'

She humbled him with her honesty. 'I'm truly sorry, *cara*, for the hurt I caused you.'

'And then you came back, and I discovered that I had not fully banished those feelings—they were still there, buried deep inside. But I couldn't trust either of us enough to let them out.' She shook her head. 'I thought losing Stenbrooke, getting involved in all of this—' she gestured '—was the worst thing that could have happened to me. To either of us. But now I'm beginning to think it's been a gift.'

He snorted. 'You'll have to explain that convoluted theory.'

'Truly—the situation has forced us to step back and evaluate, to reaffirm what is important to us. And it's given us a chance to get to know each other again. For a long time you were an ideal to me, but now I feel as if I am growing to know the man underneath.' Her chin rose. 'And I'm happy to have shown you the woman I am now. I have flaws and foibles.' She grimaced. 'But I have strengths, too—far more than the girl you used to know.'

Tenderness welled within him. 'Portia, you are a lovely, incredible woman. I hope you will never let anyone tell you otherwise.'

She took a step closer to him. Her eyes went dark as they locked with his. 'Say it again, Mateo,' she asked. 'When you say such things I begin to believe them.'

Almost involuntarily, he stepped back. 'Portia…'

'What? When we are done with this business, whether

I have Stenbrooke back or not, I'll be starting a new life. I'm no longer a girl, a daughter, a wife. I'll be my own woman and I'm not going to hide away any longer.'

Mateo swallowed.

'I find a certain justice in the thought that the man who broke the girl's heart should help shore up the woman's,' she said, her voice gone husky. She took another step closer.

'That's enough,' he said. He had a sudden empathy for her skittish mount. He was feeling unaccountably unsettled himself. 'Aside from all the pain that I've already dealt you, there are too many other reasons for us not to contemplate…' His sentence trailed away.

'Contemplate what?'

'Whatever you're contemplating,' he said firmly.

Her dark eyes glittered in the dim light. 'What are the other reasons, again?'

Did she think to mock him? 'You know what I mean.'

She stilled. 'Ah, yes,' she said. 'Your profits.'

'Yes,' he ground out. 'Such matters are important to me, I cannot deny it. Largely because they are important to my family and their legacy. But there is more to consider. I also think of the future.' He reached out and took both her hands, and was surprised at how cold they felt. 'Not just the future of Cardea Shipping, but of my own future. And yours, too.'

Her chin went up again. 'I'll take care of my own future, thank you.'

'Yes, you will. And you'll do it at Stenbrooke, should we ever see this business through.' He sighed and enclosed both of her chilled hands inside his. 'We are very different people, *cara*. The story you just told and nearly every word you've said to me since I arrived have proved that.'

'I don't know what you mean,' she said unsteadily.

'You longed for nothing more than your own home. You fought for it and you won. It was a victory and you celebrated by putting down roots, and making Stenbrooke part of you.' He shook his head. 'This is something I could never do.' He met her gaze and let the regret he felt show. 'Our futures lie down very different paths.'

'I thought I had made it clear.' She pulled her hands from his. He found out how successfully he'd warmed them when she placed them squarely on his chest. 'I'm not asking for your future.'

He pulled away and let loose a bitter laugh. 'So you think now, at this moment. And I think I've already done enough damage.'

She closed her eyes. 'Perhaps you are right. We are different. I need Stenbrooke and you need to be free. But it feels as if we've stumbled into this place out of time, a spot between our pasts and our futures, where we can just be. And we can *be* together, if we wish it.' Her eyes opened again and her gaze connected hotly with his. 'I spent my past alone, Mateo. I'll likely spend the future the same way. I don't want to be alone here, too.'

He stared at her, standing in a dappled pool of sunlight and shadow, naked hope and desire on her lovely face, and he was frozen in an agony of indecision.

What should his next move be? He knew what he wanted it to be. He wanted to make her happy for once, here in this moment. He wanted to bury his hands in her hair, lay her down on the forest floor and prove to her once and for all how lovely she was, inside and out.

He moaned in frustration. There was no good choice. He would hurt her now or hurt her later.

She reached for him, burying her fingers in his cravat and pulling him close. 'You cannot deny that there is passion between us,' she whispered. 'I can feel it in the beating of your heart.' She brushed soft lips across his. 'And it matches the rhythm of my own.'

Her boldness captivated him. *Layers.* There they were again. And this was the sweetest, most tempting layer of Portia Tofton he'd seen yet.

'Damnation,' he said. All objection, all thought of right and wrong and consequence, was lost in a haze of desire. He gave up, gave in and pressed his mouth to hers.

Willingly, happily, her heart filled with joy, Portia lost herself in Mateo's kiss. *Yes.* This. This is what she'd ached for, for nearly half of her life, it seemed. His arms came around her, wrapping her tight and she was gone.

No, not gone. *More.* With Mateo she was a brighter, better version of herself. He looked past the tight, con-tained picture she showed to the rest of the world and gave her the beautiful gift of acceptance.

His kiss grew more demanding and she abandoned thought and answered with her own fierce need. Her hands moved, measuring the breadth of his chest and shoulders, dragging into the dark abundance of his curls, and at last, digging beneath layers of linen and camlet to touch silky hot skin underneath. At last.

He shuddered beneath her hands. 'Dear God in

heaven,' he moaned, and then he returned the favour, burying his face in the sensitive curve of her neck while he busied himself with the fastenings of her habit.

She gasped when he spread the fabric wide. Impatient, he tweaked her straining nipples through the fabric of her chemise. He urged her several steps back and she went willingly, until she came up against the thick tree trunk that she'd hidden behind a few minutes ago. That delicious feeling of connection swept over her again. She was part of him and he of her and somehow they both belonged in this strange place at this exact time. His fingers flew through the ties and tiny buttons of her shift and stays and at last all barriers were gone and suddenly she was bare to his touch.

Except that he didn't touch. He put his hands to her shoulders and pressed her back against the rough bark of the tree. An inarticulate growl of pleasure rumbled through him as he looked his fill. The cool forest air caressed her and her breasts swelled. Her nipples rose stiff with longing for him to do the same.

'So beautiful,' he whispered. And then he was bending down, hovering over her while his breath, hot and sweet, teased one tight peak. His finger drew tempting circles about the other.

She arched her back, silently begging for more.

'Tell me, *cara*,' he said, his voice gone rough with desire. 'You started this, damn you. Now tell me what you want.'

And she did, because with Mateo she knew that she was safe, and that he would hear her.

'Touch me,' she asked in a voice that she barely recognised. 'Do it now, Mateo.'

His tongue darted out, flicked over her and she nearly wept with pleasure. For long moments he kissed and laved and sucked while she moaned and sighed in incoherent, ever-increasing need.

Suddenly he stood and pushed himself between her thighs. Instinctively her legs widened to admit him. The hard, iron-hot length of him pressed against the intimate spot between her legs, and she moved against him in anticipation. Reaching down, he began to lift her heavy skirts up and out of the way.

'Wrap your leg around me,' he ordered.

She did. A pang of unease rippled through her. It had been a long time since she'd been so open and vulnerable to another, on many levels. But then he smiled down at her and she knew. She could risk anything with him.

His fingers traced a soft path up her leg, and the last of her anxiety vanished. At the top of her garter he lingered, teasing her soft skin and making her breath come quickly. Slowly his fingers climbed, ever higher, until they found the hot, wet core of her.

Their simultaneous groans echoed through the trees.

He slicked a finger deep inside of her, and then up to the swollen centre of her desire. Back and forth in her silken folds he stroked.

Her breath began to come in gasps. Lightly he rubbed and deeply he plunged, winding the spring of her need until she was ready to explode.

His fingers eased higher, danced faster over her. Her hands came away from him, her arms flattened behind her, against the rough tree trunk. She sobbed his name as her body strained towards him.

He answered with a firmer stroke. With his other hand he reached up and grasped her nipple. And that was the end of her. Light flashed behind her eyes as her universe broke apart. Wave after wave of pleasure and relief racked through her. Again she cried his name, and she reached for him, clutching tight lest she be spun away by the violence of her release.

He held her tight until she ceased trembling. Over and over he peppered her brow and temple with soft kisses. 'Beautiful,' he murmured. 'You are beautiful, Portia.'

It was a gradual process, but slowly up became up again, and down, down and she returned to herself. She felt light, happy and utterly content with the world around her. Straightening, she met Mateo's mouth with hers. He kissed her deeply, greedily. She welcomed him and reached for the fall of his trousers.

Frustration mingled with regret in his expression as he set her hand from him.

'But, Mateo—'

He shushed her. 'I am content. I am happy to have given you pleasure,' he said softly against her hair.

She pushed back and stared up at him. 'I know enough of men to recognise that for the lie it is. Why won't you let me—?'

'*Dio*, you are making this more difficult. God knows I want to, it's practically killing me not to!' He gathered her in again. 'But the risks are too great.'

'If you worry you might get me with child, you needn't. I never conceived during my marriage. Yet another failure,' she said bitterly. 'The doctors said it might never happen.' A stab of longing shot through her womb at the idea of a baby, but she sobered when she considered what a pregnancy would mean to him—a snare at worst, an obligation at best.

'That is not what I meant, although it is a valid concern. You are like the plants that you love so much, *cara*—at last you've found the perfect spot and you've sunk your roots deep. You will thrive at Stenbrooke.' He gave a self-deprecating laugh. 'But I am the albatross; I need a strong wind and miles of space around me.'

He took her hand. 'So if I'm given the choice to hurt you now or hurt you more later…then I have to choose now.' Frustration throbbed in his voice as he cursed again. 'You've given me so many things, Portia. Your friendship, my company, and now a moment I will treasure for the rest of my life. All I can do in return is to make the choice that will cost you the least amount of pain.'

She supposed it made sense, if you looked at the world through the warped lens of a man's eyes. He was doing as he'd done before—appeasing her pride, taking the blame on his own shoulders. Was she supposed to feel grateful? She did not. Perhaps he was right and gratitude would come later, but right now she was fully occupied fighting off the cold, familiar shock of rejection. Again.

Chapter Ten

The door to the stable office stood propped open. Inside, a group of men hovered around a table. From the grubbiest stable boy to the richly dressed baron in their midst, as one they ignored the dim light and pored over scattered, dog-eared copies of the *Racing Calendar* and the *Stud Book*.

'Topgallant is out of Three Sheets by Easy Breeze,' one of the men said soberly. 'That's top blood—and the rumour amongst the legs is that he's fast. We might find him hard to beat.'

Another man stabbed his finger at the open *Stud Book*. 'Too bad she wasn't covered by Into the Wind, or it'd be no problem,' he cackled.

To a man, they all groaned.

'Catch that?' he grinned. 'Three Sheets Into the Wind? A horse like that'd be lucky to find the finish!'

Reluctant laughter swept through the room even as a sense of nostalgia rippled through Mateo. There was something to be said for this—the camaraderie and bonding of men from different walks of life by a common purpose. He'd spent many a similar happy moment in the company of his crew.

He stepped out of the doorway and forwards into the room. 'I'm of the mind, my lord, that a horse with a grand name like Topgallant is bound to come out the victor in any race.' He smiled at the man seated at the centre of the group.

They all looked around in surprise. Lord Dowland stood, then grinned in pleased recognition. 'Cardea! You sea dog! I haven't clapped eyes on you since Dayle's wedding! What in hell's blazes brings you to Whit-court?'

'Well, there is a matter of an outstanding bet between us. If I recall correctly, you still owe me money.'

'I most certainly do not!' The baron smiled through his mock outrage. 'That poor devil only fitted twenty-four sausages in his mouth, not twenty-five! I believe it is you, sir, who owes me!'

'You were too lost in your cups to count correctly, my lord,' Mateo said with a quirk of his lips. 'And for that matter, so was I.' He sobered a little and stepped forwards to clasp Dowland's hand. 'But I haven't come to call in a wager; instead I'm here on a bit of business.'

'Come in, then, man! Come in! Let me introduce you to my men—the best bunch of trainers, jockeys and grooms in the south of England!'

'Thank you, I'd like that, but perhaps I should first introduce you to my…associate.' Mateo reached behind him into the shadows at the doorway and pulled Portia forwards. 'My lord, may I present Lady Portia Tofton?'

He met the slight lift of Portia's raised brow with a wink and gave her a little push.

There was a scramble as men and boys straightened or hastened to stand. Portia dipped a curtsy and graced them all with a lovely smile.

'Tofton?' a dirty young man said, mouth agape. 'But ain't that the gent who done got himself killed racin' carriages? The one who—'

His words were abruptly cut off as someone clapped a hand over his mouth and pulled him roughly to the back of the group. Mateo stared at Portia's whitening face.

Lord Dowland stepped smoothly into the breach. 'Lady Portia.' He bowed low. 'How pleased I am to meet you. You are welcome at Whitcourt, as well.' He gazed at her, his face carefully composed, considering.

'Yes,' she answered his unasked question wryly, and ran her gaze over the room full of curious faces. 'That was indeed the gent I was married to.'

An excited murmur broke out. The baron waved it down. 'Forgive us our ill manners, my lady.' He slapped a hand to Mateo's shoulder. 'Well, then, if the two of you will spare me just a moment, I'll give these louts their instructions and they can get back to training my horses. Then we can retire to the house and discuss your business.'

'Thank you,' Mateo said quietly. He pulled Portia closer. 'We'll just await you outside.'

They retreated to the expansive courtyard. Curiosity ate at him. Something had definitely passed between Portia and Dowland, something they all knew about J.T.'s death. Something that he did not.

Yet he did not think he could ask. He had no right to expect one level of intimacy when he'd so thoroughly rejected another. She strayed from his side, left the cobbled court and walked over to watch the yearlings in a nearby paddock. She was quiet now, as she'd been all afternoon, since they'd left the wooded site of their tryst behind.

And he? He'd been quietly frantic, more impatient to find this elusive stranger and finish this business than even before. The image of her in that enchanted glade, gorgeous in her half-dressed state, glorious as she came undone, had been branded for ever into his mind. Portia might be content with their slow progress and time for reflection, but he feared he might not ever be content again. Nor was he so eager to shine a light on his past mistakes. He'd rather make up for them and move on.

He stared at her, slim and straight at the fence, a candle lit by her amber-in-the-sun hair. The distances between them were insignificant on one level, and insurmountable the next. It would be unconscionable of him to take advantage of her without committing fully on all of them. But, damn, it would be the best ride of his life.

Sighing, he moved over to stand beside her at the rail.

'Look at them.' She gestured towards the frolicking colts. 'Constant, joyous motion. It reminds me of you.'

He laughed. 'Standing still was never my forte.' Not in a physical, mental or emotional sense. He liked motion. He craved progress in pursuit of his goals. And perhaps even more valuable, he'd found a moving target was much harder to hit with veiled criticisms and barbed judgements.

They stood in silence for a few moments more. 'While we are here, it would be best, I think, were you to stick close to me. It's been a long time since I've been in Dowland's company, but even years ago he had a certain...reputation.' He grimaced. 'Not that I mean to disparage our host, but he is one who is also constantly in motion—from one woman and on to the next as quickly as possible.'

Her face stayed carefully bland. 'I don't believe there is cause to worry. I can't even tempt the men I throw myself after.'

Incredulous, his gaze snapped to hers. 'Is that what you think? That I am not tempted?' He snorted and a bay colt nearby answered him. He and Portia both grinned, lightening the tension of the moment.

Ridiculous, truly, that she could entertain such an idea. Where was that steely core of confidence that had got her so far on this bizarre venture? He leaned in close. 'You may put that idea straight from your mind, Portia Tofton. Have you not looked in a mirror and seen yourself in that habit? Do you tell me that you did not choose that golden frogging because it brings out the gold flecks in your dark eyes and the sunny streaks in your hair?'

She flushed and he continued. 'You've tempted me nearly every moment since I've set foot back in England. You'd tempt the dourest vicar, let alone an acknowledged rake like Dowland. Now *stick close*.' He tucked her hand under his arm and cursed himself for a damned fool for letting her know the truth of how she affected him. But at this moment, her shaken assurance seemed more important than his pride.

He lowered his voice. 'If our circumstances were the least bit different, I would have had you up against that tree quicker than a flash. I would have buried myself in you and likely have knocked the damned tree down with the force of my desire.'

He took satisfaction from the deep flush across her fair skin and the surprise in her eyes. Then he turned them both to meet the baron as he emerged from the stable office. He ignored the curious look the man tossed between the two of them.

'Now then,' Dowland said with a smile, 'shall we go on to the house?'

This was a working stud farm, not Dowland's no-doubt-impressive seat, but it was attractive and welcoming none the less. When he and Portia had left the high plain behind, they'd reached the downland of rich, green turf—and here it flowed right up to the stone manor house. A few outbuildings flanked the manor in a pleasing arrangement and Mateo could see that someone had begun a garden in the back. But the stable buildings were the centrepiece here. Built of the same stone as the house, they were immaculate and fully occupied. Box stalls looked out to a clean, cobbled yard. Fenced paddocks and freshly raked training rings completed the picture.

Dowland took them on a brief tour, pride and pleasure ringing clear in his tone, but at last he directed them towards the house. As they approached, he veered off on a path leading towards the side of the house.

'You won't mind if we skip the front entrance and

enter directly into my study, will you, ma'am?' he asked Portia with a sheepish expression. 'My son is teething and was up half the night. He's likely asleep and my wife, as well. There will be less fuss and bother—and less chance of waking either of them—if we just sneak in the side.'

Stunned, Mateo stopped dead in his tracks. 'Incredible! Dowland, you've married?' He ignored Portia's pointed grin.

The baron laughed. 'Yes, old man, it happens to the best of us.'

'My congratulations, of course. I hadn't heard a word of it.' He had to hurry to keep up as Dowland opened a wide a set of double doors.

'Sorry, Cardea, but you'll have to carry the bachelor's torch on your own now.' He waved them into his light and comfortably furnished study. He held out a padded leather chair for Portia. 'Cardea and I cut a wide swathe through the ladies of Dorset when first we met, Lady Portia, but I confess I'm quite content to tend the home fire now.'

He waved Mateo towards a matching chair and seated himself behind a handsome cherry desk. 'I also confess I'm quite curious to discover what has brought the two of you here.'

Portia spoke up. 'Your friend Mr Riggs advised us to speak to you, my lord.'

'Ah, Riggs.' Dowland leaned back in his chair. 'Brilliant man, if a bit barmy, eh?'

'We found him very helpful…' she paused '…if a little eccentric.'

Mateo would have used a stronger word himself, but Dowland seemed content.

'Well, I shall endeavour to be as helpful and less eccentric, shall I?' The baron looked to Mateo. 'What is it, Cardea? Are you ready at last to trade your clipper in for a thoroughbred?'

'Not in this lifetime, lubber.' Mateo laughed, but then settled into a more serious tone. 'Actually, we're here to discover what you can tell us of a man named Averardo.'

The baron frowned and Mateo sat forwards. Something moved behind the man's eyes. 'Averardo? It's not a name I recognise right way. Is there a particular reason that I should do so?'

Portia's heart fell. Not again.

She'd come to the realisation this afternoon—after the worst few minutes of her life fell so closely on the heels of the best—that Mateo was entirely correct. It would be best if they found this stranger quickly, made their bargains and completed their transactions in as little time as possible—before she made an even bigger fool of herself.

That meant that now was not the time for another stumbling block, and yet another person who'd never heard of the man who threatened Stenbrooke.

Mateo's expression mirrored the exasperation she felt in her gut. 'Incredible,' he muttered again.

She sighed deeply.

'Lord Dowland,' Mateo said with exaggerated patience, 'you appeared to be somewhat familiar with Lady Portia's husband. Perhaps you will not be surprised to hear that he apparently gambled her estate away—to a man named Averardo. A man whose existence we begin to doubt.'

'I knew nothing of it,' Portia said. 'That is, until a solicitor showed up with a deed of conveyance with Averardo's name on it. A solicitor sent by Mr Riggs, who in turn says he did so at your request.'

Understanding blossomed on the baron's face. And something else—remorse, perhaps? Just a twinge of anxiety. He kept his silence, but stood and quietly crossed the room to close the door.

'I gather you've recalled the matter?' asked Mateo.

'I have, now that you explain.' When he was seated again, he crossed his fingers in front of his mouth. 'I do not know how much help I'll be, but I'll tell you what I know—' He held up a hand. 'Provided you promise not to mention the matter to my wife.'

'Agreed,' Mateo answered without hesitation. He and the baron both looked to Portia now. Disappointment and reluctance warred with her need to know.

'Portia?' Mateo's brows flagged his disbelief.

She nodded and shifted uncomfortably, wondering just what she might be asked to hide.

The baron mimicked her uneasy movements. 'Yes, well, it is somewhat of a delicate matter.'

Mateo's mouth twisted. 'Let me take a stab in the dark. You agreed to handle the matter for someone else, a friend, perhaps.'

Dowland shot him a look of surprise. 'Almost. I did—but not a friend, exactly. For the Countess of Lundwick.'

The name meant nothing to Portia. She looked to

Mateo and saw incredulousness creep in. 'You didn't!' he exclaimed. 'I've heard of the woman—even seen her in action. She's a better strategist than most military officers I've met. You don't mean to say…' His words trailed away and he stared at his friend.

The baron nodded.

'But she's married!'

Dowland glared at him.

'And near old enough to be your mother, besides!' Mateo remonstrated. But Portia saw the grin dancing at the side of his mouth.

'Yes, but she's a beauty none the less, and quite the most determined woman I've ever met. Her husband is a member of the Jockey Club and heavily involved in racing. She is left alone and to her own devices—'

'Far too often for society's comfort!' Mateo laughed.

'And once too often for mine. I was drunk—a good three days beneath the mahogany.' He ducked his head. 'My dear Lady Portia, I do apologise for the coarseness of this conversation.'

'As you've shown you knew my husband, I'm sure you realise that none of which you speak is new to me.'

The pain she felt at uttering this must have shown. He hurried to add an assurance.

'Oh, no. Please do not think this a recent development. My…liaison with the Countess was long before I met my wife.'

'A fact for which she is eternally grateful, I am sure.' Her tone was as dry as her mouth.

'That is the point; I don't wish her to become aware of it at all. Unfortunately, I left the Countess in possession of some rather…damning information. I never gave it a second's thought, though, until just months ago, when she thoroughly enjoyed rubbing my nose in my carelessness.'

'So she blackmailed you,' Mateo said flatly.

'I suppose you could call it that. Though it was done very prettily and in the sweetest tone imaginable. She assured me that she would *not* whisper such choice titbits in my wife's ear if I handled a delicate matter for her.' He glanced apologetically at Portia yet again. 'I'm sorry, but after the scandal of your husband's death, I was not in the least surprised to learn that he had also gambled away your home. The Countess told me the man who had won the estate was unable to claim it himself. She claimed that the timing was important and asked me to see it done.' He looked away. 'I was not inclined to refuse. I am quite fond of my wife, you see, and hated to think that something so unimportant to me might be dreadfully painful to her.' He sighed. 'In truth, I was relieved that what the Countess asked was not more...unsavoury.'

Portia kept her gazed fixed firmly on her hands in her lap. Nothing about this episode in her life had been savoury.

'Dowland,' Mateo said in a strange, strangled voice, 'did the Countess give you the papers right then?'

'What? Oh, no. She sent them later.'

Portia did look up then, and straight into Mateo's eyes. 'By courier!' they said together.

Mateo leaned in towards the desk. 'Tell us about the courier.'

The baron frowned. 'He did ride an exceptionally fine mare,' he mused. 'Fifteen hands, I'd say, well developed and the softest grey colour, like the breast of a dove.'

Portia could not help but laugh. Mateo cast his eyes heavenwards.

'Anything you can recall about the man himself, Dowland?'

'He had an unusual name. Foreign. Wait, I'll have to think a moment.'

Portia met Mateo's gaze again. Breathless, they stared. And waited.

She couldn't stand another second, of anticipation or of Mateo's warm regard. 'Might it have been Lorenzo?' she suggested.

'No.' The baron leaned back in his chair, his face a study of concentration. 'Stranger than that. Cormi… Corsica…' He sat straight up. 'Cosimo—that is it!'

'Cosimo?' Portia repeated, disappointed. Was it not the same man, then?

'What did he look like?' asked Mateo.

'Hmm. Tall, if I recall correctly. Well done up, for a servant, I thought. His clothes were plain, but of good quality. Well-favoured, I would have to say. I remember thinking that the Countess might have turned in a different direction for her pleasures.'

He sat straighter. 'I also remember thinking that I wanted the job done as quick as possible. My wife is in a delicate state again, you see, and at that point she was feeling particularly unwell. I didn't wish to be gone from her for long, nor did I wish to answer many questions as to what I had to do. We were fresh out of all the trouble that occurred with Bright Early Morning—I assume Riggs told you about that?'

Portia nodded.

'Suffice it to say that I was steeped in enough misery and not looking forward to bringing it on to someone else—on to you, in short. That's when I hit upon the idea of having Riggs handle it for me.'

'It was your idea?' Mateo asked. 'This Cosimo did not suggest it?'

'No, it was my notion. Riggs was feeling particularly guilty and I thought he might be better for something to do. The man needed something else to think of besides the accident. So I wrote him a long letter and asked the courier to continue on to Longvale and make his delivery there.'

He scrubbed a hand across his jaw, clearly thinking. 'The man appeared struck by the notion. I thought it was because he knew his mistress intended me to carry out the deed. I assured him it would be taken care of.'

Mateo stood. Portia watched him as he walked over to the double doors and stared out. She knew he wasn't seeing the afternoon sun falling softly over the lush green landscape.

'Do you think that *he* might be Averardo? This courier?' she asked suddenly.

Mateo turned. 'It's possible, I suppose. But why? Why place so many barriers between you? Why would he not just tell you himself that he was taking over Stenbrooke? It's almost as if he's toying with you.'

Her mouth twisted bitterly. 'Perhaps he is a former friend of J.T.'s. It does seem like something his crowd would do, out of sheer malice.'

He stared at her for a moment. 'Perhaps it is as I said before and the conveyance is a fake.'

'That would be the best possible outcome,' the baron said. 'Although the documents appeared to be correct. It would be a lot of trouble to have witnessed accounts and everything else made up or forged.'

'And what am I to do? Sit at home and wait for someone to show up and throw me out? Or not, because it is all a hoax?' Anguish stabbed through her. 'I cannot do it. How could we live with such uncertainty?'

Mateo slammed a hand against the door frame. 'Then why all the subterfuge? None of this makes a damned bit of sense!'

'Lord Dowland, would your Countess be likely to know what all of this is about?'

Wry, he said, 'If there's the smallest bit of skullduggery afoot, then the Countess is *highly* likely to know about it. That is, if she's not thoroughly entangled in it.'

Before Portia could reply, the study door swung open.

'Reginald!' sounded a bright, happy voice. 'Your son has something to show you!'

A pretty woman with tired eyes stood on the threshold, a toddling child clutching tightly to her hand. They advanced into the room and Portia saw the moment when she realised her husband was not alone.

'Oh! I do apologise. I had no notion you had company.'

Lord Dowland's face had changed, softened. It cost Portia a pang to see it.

'Come in, dear,' the baron said, standing swiftly. 'An old friend has come to visit. This is Mr Cardea, and this is *his* friend, Lady Portia Tofton.'

'How do you do?' The baroness dipped a curtsy. She

was hampered when the child at her side objected to the presence of strangers and hid behind her skirts.

The baron coaxed him out and took him up in his arms. 'Cardea, Lady Portia, this strapping fellow is the next Lord Dowland. Now come, my boy,' he wheedled, 'take your finger from your mouth long enough to say hello!'

The boy opened his mouth, but kept his finger firmly in place towards the back. 'Ungh!' he said.

His father was able to correctly interpret this. Obligingly he peered into the boy's mouth. 'By George, look at the size of that one! Well done, my boy! It's no wonder you've been wearing your mother's nerves to a frazzle!'

The boy, reminded of her existence, reached for his mother. Smiling, she took him and he snuggled close, emitting a sigh of utter bliss before laying his head on her shoulder. From his perch he granted his father a sloppy baby grin and turned a magnanimous eye to the rest of them. A chubby king, surveying his domain with satisfaction.

They made a beautiful picture. The three of them, complete and happy. It seemed almost a sacrilege to witness their moment of contentment. Portia glanced away, looked to Mateo to gauge his reaction to the family's tranquillity—and caught him in an unguarded moment. He stared, white-faced at the scene, an odd intense emotion washing pale his tanned complexion. If Portia had been forced to label it, she would say it looked like… pain.

But the baroness had spotted an incongruity in her perfect world. 'Reginald!' she scolded. 'You haven't even sent for a tray? Your friends must think us incredibly inhospitable!'

'It's quite all right, Lady Dowland,' Portia assured her. 'We've come on business, truly, not a social call and we won't intrude much longer.'

'Nonsense, you must stay for tea at least.'

'I wish we could, ma'am,' Mateo replied. His expression had cleared. 'But our business is pressing and it sounds as if we'll have to be setting out for London.' He looked to the baron. 'Am I right, Dowland? London is where we'll find the answers to our remaining questions?'

A worried frown wrinkled the baron's brow. 'I should think so, but you'll have to be fast. The…men you seek should be there now, but they are racing enthusiasts. They'll be leaving for Doncaster soon for the running of the St Leger, and then back to Newmarket.'

Portia stood. 'Then we must be off.' She smiled. 'It was lovely to meet you all.' To the baron she said, 'Thank you for your help.'

He shifted his stance. 'It was nothing, really, the least I could do.'

The baroness glanced outside. 'But there are only a few hours of daylight left. Perhaps you should stay the night and set out in the morning.'

'They are pressed for time, dear.' Her husband went still, pondering, and then his head came up suddenly. 'Of course! I can loan you my post-chaise. It's very well sprung and my teams are the fastest you'll find on the roads. I'll be happy to send one of my men along as postillion.' He clapped Mateo on the back. 'You'll be halfway to London before the night is out.'

'That is very kind of you, but we've left my companion in Hungerford and must meet up with her when we leave here. A post-chaise will likely not seat three comfortably.'

'No.' The baron's face fell. 'It has just the one front-facing bench on the inside.' He glanced at Mateo. 'But there is the outside seat in the back, over the rear wheel.' He shrugged. 'It's by far the fastest option.'

Questioning, Portia met Mateo's gaze. He turned away and looked out of the doors again. She could almost see him weighing their options, calculating time and distance and measuring days in his head. He turned back.

'It's enclosed. Will you manage?'

She thought about it. 'A post-chaise?' She turned to Lord Dowland. 'Is it the travelling chariot sort? With the glass panel in front?'

He looked startled at the question. 'Yes, it is.'

'Then I should be all right.'

'I would feel better if you would allow me to help you in this way.' The baron meant it, she could tell.

Mateo's gaze held hers first, then moved to Dowland's. Grimly, he nodded.

Chapter Eleven

Damned if Dowland hadn't been right. Mateo marvelled as the post-chaise moved smartly along, especially once they reached the well-travelled roadway in West Shefford. The beautiful Berkshire countryside passed by in a blur. They'd likely reach Hungerford in less than an hour's time.

It had been a long day. Portia sat next to him on the bench seat, far enough away so that the bounce and sway of the carriage did not jostle her against him. Out of the corner of his eye he watched her, and tried hard not to be caught at it.

The line of her limbs, the way she sank into the padded bench—they spoke of her weariness. Even as he watched, she tilted her head back to rest and closed her eyes. She wouldn't sleep, though. Her trust only extended so far, and she was too noticeably *not* touching him to be truly relaxed. A sigh escaped him.

Her hair was falling again. Did it ever stay put? The strands lay, a delicate adornment to the slender column of her neck, pointing the way to *his* spot. The spot he loved to kiss, longed to taste again. When he touched his tongue to her there, she made the most delicious sounds in the back of her throat.

He closed his eyes and sought to distract himself before he began to think too hard about touching his tongue to all the other delectable parts of her.

That stable boy's outburst rang through his head again. And the carefully blank faces of all those other men. What did they all know about J.T.'s death? It seemed wrong, a disgrace that the world should know something so basic about her life while he did not.

He opened his mouth to ask her.

'You had a very strange look on your face today,' she said into the silence.

He resigned himself to waiting a little longer. 'Did I?'

'You did—when Lord Dowland and his wife and son were grouped together, looking like an artist's rendering of the perfect young family.' She rolled her head on the cushion to look over at him. 'You looked as if it hurt, seeing them like that.' After a moment she continued. 'I wondered…were you perhaps thinking of your father? Of the problems you had with him?'

'No,' he was surprised into answering. It was a difficult subject, his family, one he never spoke of, nor often allowed himself to dwell on.

But Portia was the one person, perhaps, who would understand. It felt important, suddenly, that she did understand.

'It's just that—it struck me—the way that boy lay his head down on his mother's shoulder. That little sigh.

Such peace. I felt it, right here.' He pressed a fist to his gut. 'And I knew, suddenly, that I hadn't felt such a thing since my own mother died.'

She nodded. Quiet fell over the carriage again. Except, of course, for the rumble of wheels and the pounding of hooves and the jingle of harness and trace.

'Have you been seeking it, do you think? For peace?' She wasn't looking at him any longer.

He pondered his answer. 'No. My father used to ask me much the same thing. He'd get so upset with my wandering, pursuing new imports and markets and contacts. What was I doing? Why could I not stick to the tried and true? What was I searching for? He'd ask it with such exasperation. I used to answer him quite truthfully: nothing.'

He set his own head back against the cushion. 'I don't think I've been searching. Instead I've just been keeping busy…distracting myself. Perhaps so I wouldn't have to think about what I was missing.'

Her gaze had fastened on him again. He could feel the weight of it, a substantial thing that made his skin flush with warmth. He kept his own gaze directed towards the glass panel in the front, where the road unravelled over the steady rise and fall of the horses. 'It shames me when I think of what we spoke of yesterday—about becoming part of the vast ocean. Suddenly I'm thinking about what I've done with *this* life—and I realise I've wasted so much time. I think I've only been skimming the surface of life, afraid to look too deep.'

Her head shook in disagreement and she followed his gaze forwards. 'I don't believe that at all. You delved deep enough all those years ago, enough to see a young girl's loneliness and offer her your friendship. You looked hard enough to notice her feelings and treat them gently. You weren't skimming when you worked so hard and long for your family and their legacy or when you acted as a good friend and example to my brothers.' She reached out then, and touched his face with gentle fingers, forcing his head to turn, his eyes to meet hers. 'Perhaps it is only your own needs that you are afraid to look too closely at.'

He stared, unable to even begin to summon a response to that.

Her hand fell away. She stretched and yawned. 'Now, I am extremely weary. We have a short while before Hungerford, yes?'

Still silent, he nodded.

'Then I think I'll take a quick nap.'

And to his amazement, and utter gratitude, she did.

Portia did sleep a little, lulled by the rhythmic sway of the carriage and the warm feeling of having returned a little of Mateo's kindness. Her last thought, before she drifted off, was that perhaps he should be happy that she did not repay some of his more painful lessons.

The postillion's calls as he pulled his team to a stop awakened her. The Bear Inn loomed, large and hulking in the last of the day's light. They left the horses in their harness and went in together to fetch Dorinda.

They found her, looking very smug and awaiting them in a private parlour.

'I hope you've no room reserved for the night,' Mateo warned before Portia had even fully withdrawn from her companion's embrace. 'We must go on tonight.'

Dorrie's face fell. 'Must we?'

'I'm sorry, but we do. I've nearly given up on making it home in time to see my ships fitted for the Orient.' His face hardened. 'Months of work, this has cost me, and perhaps the best chance for my family's future. But by God, I am going to see this through, and quickly, before he has a chance to throw even more obstacles in our path.' He waved a beckoning hand at Dorrie. 'The horses are standing. We're to London as quick as we can manage.'

Dorrie sighed, but looked resigned. 'I'll assume, then, that your mission did not go well?'

'It went exactly as well as last time,' Mateo said sourly. 'Which is not saying a great deal.'

'Then you'll be happy to hear that I accomplished something here,' she announced, 'although not as much as I'd hoped.'

'What is it, dearest?' Portia asked. 'You look like the kitchen cat that's just lapped a whole bowl of cream.'

Her companion squared her shoulders and drew herself up to her full height. 'I believe I've met your mysterious courier.'

Portia gasped.

'What?' Mateo nearly shouted. 'What did he say? Where is he now?'

Dorinda winced.

'Dorrie, please, tell us what happened. How did it come about?'

'Of course, but should we not speak in the carriage? I thought we were in a hurry.'

'We were, we are, but you'll have to tell us now.' Portia could hear that Matco was losing patience.

'We have new travelling arrangements, dear. Mateo will be forced to ride outside. Come, let's have your bags loaded while we hear your story. Then we'll go on.'

'He arrived before me,' Dorrie said after the luggage had been dispatched and they had all settled uneasily about the room. 'He'd just bespoke the last private parlour. I was understandably dismayed when the landlord told me there were none left; I'd said I'd meet you here and I was not going to wait in the public room.' She shivered. 'I'd just decided to take a bedroom when he spoke up. He was still lingering and must have overheard me talking to the innkeeper, because he offered to share his parlour. He said he would not need it for long in any case.'

'What did he look like?' Portia asked, more than a little curious.

'He was very handsome,' she answered on a little sigh. 'Tall, with hair even darker than yours, Mr Cardea. Cut too long for my taste,' she told Portia, 'but a very dashing fellow, none the less.'

'Did he give you a name?' Mateo asked.

'Yes, that was my first clue as to who he might be. He used another exotic-sounding name: Giovanni.'

'He used yet another with Lord Dowland,' Portia told her.

'What makes you sure it was him, Miss Tofton?'

'I was not sure at first. He made pleasant, unexceptional conversation. He asked where I was from and I told him I lived now in the vicinity of Newbury. He said he'd been there, but knew it very little. We talked of London and the foreign places he had travelled. We had a light meal brought in, it was all extremely pleasant.' She made a face at Mateo. 'I'm getting there, Mr Cardea, don't look so impatient.'

'I do apologise.'

Portia was glad to hear a twinge of humour in his reply.

'I had told him earlier that I was awaiting friends. We'd just finished our tea when he asked if we would be returning to Stenbrooke once my friends arrived.' She paused and shot them a significant look. 'I had never mentioned Stenbrooke by name, you see.'

Admiration flooded Portia and she allowed it to show. 'That was so quick of you, Dorrie! What did you do?'

'I pretended that I did not notice. I answered his question and told him I wasn't sure of our plans. Then I asked him if he wouldn't mind a small fire to chase the evening chill. When he went to see to it, I slipped some laudanum into his drink.'

Portia gasped again. 'Dorrie! You didn't!'

Mateo only laughed, but Dorrie was preening at the approval in his face.

'You know I always carry a small vial, dear,' she said. 'A lady never knows when she's going to need it.'

'And did he drink?' Mateo asked.

'No,' she said with chagrin. 'I'm afraid I must have given it away. Perhaps I watched him take up his cup a bit too avidly.'

'There's a lesson for you,' Mateo said. 'The next time you think to poison someone, you'll know better.'

'Mr Cardea! Laudanum is not poison. I merely

thought to put him to sleep, so he would still be here when you arrived.'

Portia could barely contain her impatience. 'But what happened?'

'He raised the cup to his lips, but then he hesitated. He met my eyes over the rim and then he set it down. He smiled brilliantly at me. Then he arose and took my hand, kissing it in the most improper fashion.' Her tone had grown a little wistful. 'He told me I was a woman to be reckoned with.' A flush spread across her face. 'Can you imagine? Me?'

'Certainly I can,' Portia said stoutly. 'It was a wonderfully brave thing to do.'

'He left then, most cordially, but not before he asked that I be sure to give you both his regards.' She heaved a heavy sigh. 'I'm sorry, Mr Cardea.'

'There is not the slightest need for you to feel sorry, Miss Tofton. I applaud your ingenuity. It would seem none of us is as crafty as our nemesis.'

'It must be Averardo—they must be one and the same. There's no other explanation for the way he's playing with us.' Irritation grew hot in Portia's chest. 'And if he is, there is still no explanation for it!' Her fists clenched. 'I suppose I should just be grateful that he did you no harm, Dorrie, but I am growing wretchedly tired of being manipulated!'

'I know, dear.' Dorrie's tone was comforting. 'Have you any idea what he's about, Mr Cardea?'

Mateo did not respond. His gaze had lost focus. Portia exchanged a glance with Dorrie. He stared into the fire, his mouth moving silently.

'Mr Cardea?'

'I'm sorry,' he said distantly. 'All of those exotic names—surely they mean something. I'm trying to recall…Lorenzo, Cosimo.' He looked up suddenly. 'And, yes, Giovanni! Medici!'

Portia stared. 'Excuse me?'

'Yes, I'm sure I'm right. Prominent Medici names, all!'

'Medici?' Dorrie's face twisted in confusion.

'Yes, yes. It's been nagging at me and I finally remembered. It's something my father spoke of. It was when he was trying so hard to convince me to—' He stopped, flushing. 'When he tried to convince me to abandon the idea of a privateer's cruise.'

And suddenly Portia flushed too, because she knew just what else his father had been trying to convince him of, at the same time. Marriage. To her.

'They planned for us to move to Portsmouth, do you recall?' His voice sounded only slightly strangled.

She nodded. She couldn't have forced an answer past her tightened throat if her life had depended on it.

'I was to open the office there. When I…when it did not work out, he hired someone else to do it, a man named Salvestro. He praised the man's performance repeatedly throughout the years and always made specific mention of his name because it also belonged to the first prominent Medici.'

'They were merchants, as well, yes?' Dorrie asked, frowning in concentration.

'They were a family who started out in trade and grew into one of the greatest dynasties in Italian history. It was my father's dream to see his family prosper in that way. I drove him mad because I would not co-operate.'

'But you worked long and hard for Cardea Shipping!' Portia protested.

'Eventually I did, but never in quite the direction he wished to go. And always without the proper degree of seriousness,' he said with a wave of his hand.

And that was likely another reason why he needed so strongly to prove himself now, she realised.

He stood abruptly and his chair nearly tipped over behind him. 'I knew that this had the taste of my father's handiwork smeared all over it! But how? Why? I'm tired of the manipulation, as well, and I'm damned tired of being one step behind.'

He started towards the door. 'We should go, ladies.' He halted. 'Or should we, at that? Perhaps we are just playing into his hands?'

Portia stepped up beside him and laid a hand upon his arm. 'What choice do we have, truly?' She squeezed. 'Let's see this thing through. All of us, together.'

'You're right, of course. But damn it! You know I've always been one to lay my own course.' He shook her off, then held the door and gestured for them to proceed. 'Let's go then. The postillion says his teams can make it to Reading tonight. We can get a short night's rest and we'll be in London early tomorrow afternoon.' His tone grew grim. 'Just in time for a social call.'

They'd reached the narrow hallway. At his words, Dorrie came to an abrupt halt. Impatient, Mateo pushed past her. 'I'll just be sure everything's ready.'

'Reading?' Portia winced as Dorrie grabbed her arm and stalled her. Her companion's whisper sounded harsh in her ear. 'We're stopping in Reading? Do you think that's wise?'

'This is the first I've heard of it,' Portia said, trying to calm the sudden racing of her heart.

'But *she* lives in Reading. Every time those horrible, impudent letters arrived, they were posted from Reading. And all the papers, when they wrote of her origins, they called her an *innkeeper's daughter.*'

'I know that, Dorrie.' The thought of running into… *her* was bad enough, but to do it with Mateo at her side… She shuddered.

She struggled for composure. 'But we'll be getting there late and only stopping for a few hours' rest.' She grimaced. 'There are at least three inns in Reading that I can recall. We're not likely to run into her.' She frowned. 'And even if we do, what can she do? I've done nothing wrong.'

Dorrie sighed. 'As if we weren't facing trouble enough.' She folded her arms stubbornly. 'It's asking too much of you, I'll just explain to Mr Cardea—'

'And tell him what?' Portia's chin lifted. 'Lord, Dorrie, I would like to keep just one of the many humiliating episodes of my life to myself! Does the world need to throw evidence of every one of my shortcomings in his face? Please, I cannot stand the thought of him looking at me with…with pity and with…*knowing.*'

'But, there's a chance—'

'It's a chance I'll take,' she said firmly. 'Because the odds have got to be higher that nothing will happen at all.'

Chapter Twelve

It was late when they arrived in Reading and the streets lay dark and quiet. Dorrie clung to her side as Portia climbed wearily down from the post-chaise. Mateo had already completed his transactions with the postillion and the stables, now he went ahead of them into the inn to make arrangements for their short night's stay. Portia watched him go, in the torchlight only an indistinct form topped with broad shoulders and a tangle of dark curls, and considered how different her mood might be right now, had Dorrie done as she'd suggested and gone home.

Ouch. Dorrie was still very much present, as evidenced by the vice-like grip she was maintaining on Portia's arm. Her head bobbed and swivelled like a weather vane, searching corners and shadows with nervous, darting looks.

'Relax, please, Dorrie. It's late. No one is about at this hour.'

'No one we'd wish to meet,' she returned.

'Come, let's go in then.' They followed in Mateo's footsteps and found him finishing with the innkeeper.

'Is she all right?' Mateo leaned in close as the landlord called for their baggage to be carried up to their rooms. He nodded towards Dorrie, who had steered Portia as far from the public taproom as possible and was now scanning the darkened hallways. 'What is she looking for?'

Portia shivered. Fatigue seeped into her very bones and undermined her defences. The warmth of his breath on her cheek only served as a reminder of everything she longed for and could not have. 'I think we're all just tired,' she said, crossing her arms in front of her.

'Indeed we are.' Dorrie had come back. She claimed Portia's arm once more. 'Thank you, Mr Cardea, but I'm taking Portia straight up to our room.'

'Goodnight, then.'

His gaze followed them, a palpable sensation down the length of her spine as they climbed the stairs. Portia wanted to turn back, to meet his eyes and allow him to see all the turmoil and fervent desire seething inside of her. She did not. And not just because she feared the lack of a similar conflict in his eyes. Though it took all of her will, she kept her face turned forwards, towards the future. Because soon enough this would be over and that's what she'd be left with. Her future, alone and independent, just as she'd wished.

She did as Dorrie bade, kept her gaze down and followed her companion's swinging skirts into their small room. Just the one bed, big enough to share, an empty wash stand, a small table and one chair before the unlit fireplace. Dorrie shut the door with a sigh of relief. Portia stared at the bed with a mix of longing and regret.

Had she ever been this tired? Had any woman ever been subjected to a day so filled with soaring highs and despairing lows? And would she ever stop wondering what might have been with Mateo, had circumstances been different?

With a sigh she sank down on to the foot of the bed. She smelled of horse, of wind and sun. And passion. She wondered if Dorrie could detect it, if she already knew what she had begun with Mateo today, in that dark, secluded wood. She thought of tomorrow, when she would see London again, wear a pretty day dress instead of this increasingly heavy habit, when she would meet a wicked Countess and perhaps discover the reason they'd been sent on this frustratingly wild ride.

She leaned her head against the bedpost. What she truly longed for—quite inexpressibly—was a bath. A long, steaming bath in which she could close her eyes and examine the triumphs and soak away the humiliations of the day—and prepare herself for the gains and losses of tomorrow.

Not a practical wish in the middle of the night. Abruptly, she stood. 'I'm going back downstairs, Dorrie, to request some hot water—enough to wash in, at least. I can't even begin to imagine climbing into bed in this condition.'

'Poor dear,' Dorrie crooned, 'you've been through half of Berkshire today.' Her companion sat beside her on the bed. Sympathy and a perhaps more disturbing understanding showed in her face as she reached over to tuck a stray curl behind Portia's ear. 'I'll go; you stay safely here and rest. I'll ask for coal for the fire, too, so you won't catch a chill.'

It wasn't worth an argument. The door snapped shut behind Dorrie and Portia closed her eyes and leaned again against the bedpost. Mateo's room was right across the hall. Was he falling straight into bed? She hoped he dreamed of her tonight. She hoped all the wicked, erotic sensations of the day—the sight of her bare breasts, the damp feel of her, and the sensuous sound of her release—had been burned into his brain. It was no less than he deserved. No less than she had already suffered, locked for hours on the inside of that post-chaise, reliving the taste and feel of his hands and lips and tongue all over her.

She jumped as the door opened again. 'Hot water and coal are on the way,' Dorrie said from the doorway. 'The landlord's sending a girl right up. Since we are not retiring right away, I'm going back to the kitchens to see if I can find us a bite to eat.'

'Thank you, Dorrie.'

'Sit down, dear.' Dorrie nodded towards the comfortably plush chair in front of the fire. 'You look exhausted. I'll be right back.'

Portia pushed away from the post. She had to stop this. She could not continue daydreaming over Mateo. Their paths were clear and separate. He'd made his stance plain. She would only make herself miserable and him ill at ease. They had enough trouble to contend with, without her rampant desire adding to everyone's discomfort.

She curled into the chair, staring into the empty hearth. But that was the trouble, wasn't it? She didn't feel uncomfortable with him. She only felt right, happy, at home in his regard for her.

They'd crossed a boundary today, and not just in a physical sense. She'd been deliberately prickly since he'd arrived, had worked hard to show him only the strong, determined, independent side of her. Until today. Today she had cracked. She'd let him see her soft, flawed interior—and he'd met it with the same simple acceptance and admiration that he'd shown before.

Heady stuff, that. She felt a sudden pang of sympathy for some of J.T.'s opium-eating friends. She could easily come to crave something that felt so good.

More significant, perhaps, Mateo had gifted her with a glimpse inside of him, as well. For all of his insouciance and charm, she knew him for a deeply private person. Laughter and smiles were his shields and he'd allowed her to slip past them today. It had felt like a beginning, a tantalising glimpse of the deeper, more meaningful rapport that could exist between them. Except that it never would exist. Instead, tomorrow they faced the end. One way or the other, they'd go their separate ways.

The thought nearly stole her breath.

But life was short and full of hardships. And truly, Portia knew herself for one of the fortunate few. Whether her plans for Stenbrooke were granted or not, she'd been given the gift of a new beginning—and this time around she was determined to do things differently. She'd reached for a way out last time. She'd accepted the least evil of all her options and tried to make the best of it—or so she'd told herself.

But was it the whole truth?

Now was the time for truth-seeking, was it not? Now, at this time, when her future poised, teetering, on the brink of what might be, perhaps she should look deep and accept her own truth.

She did not want to—but she feared she was to be given no choice. All the platitudes and excuses she'd used to reassure herself were flaking away. She dropped her head in her hands, tried to block out the comprehension that rose like the sun within her. But there was no escaping it. She'd accepted James Talbot because she'd been afraid. Afraid to stand up to her brothers. Afraid they were right and she wouldn't ever be anything but a burden to the people she loved.

And that wasn't all. She delved even deeper into the ache that lay buried at the heart of her and winced at what she found. Mateo had hurt her, and her unsuccessful Season had frightened her. Before she'd fully recovered, her brothers' disregard had wounded her further. And she'd given in to that hurt and fear. She'd been afraid that no other man would ever want her. She'd been afraid to even try—she'd never fought for her chance at happiness.

It was an ugly, painful realisation—but worse was the sudden thought that she might be doing it again. Was she fixating on Mateo because it was easy? Because he was here? Was she dredging up old feelings because despite all of her talk, she was afraid to be alone?

The door opened with a bang behind her, startling her out of her bleak thoughts. Peering around the high back of her chair, she saw a servant girl backing into the room, burdened with an armful of towels, and a pitcher of hot water, with a heavy coal bucket hanging off one arm.

'...inconsiderate...out of bed...heating kettles in the dead of night...' The girl kept up a continuous, discontented rumble as she made her way into the room.

Portia started out her chair. 'Let me help with that.'

'Oh, no!' came the sharp, indignant reply. 'You want hot water in the middle of the blasted night, you'll get it. My papa runs the best inn in Reading, with the best service! Anyone will tell you. A thousand times a day I have to listen to it, on and on...'

Portia shrank back in her chair. Her nerves were too frazzled to deal competently with such blatant disrespect, her emotions too raw. The woman's grumbling continued as she deposited her burdens at the wash stand. Carrying the coal, she crossed the room to the hearth. Portia curled tight into the chair, out of the way, and watched the back of her head as she quickly built up the fire.

'Thank you,' she said quietly as the coals flared to life.

'Not at all,' the girl returned, her voice heavy with sarcasm. She shot Portia a quick glance of dislike over her shoulder. 'If you suffer a longing for fine French cuisine, just say the word, my papa will have me on the first packet to Calais.'

But Portia sat frozen, arrested by what she'd just seen.

The woman finished, rose, and managed to dip a curtsy that oozed mockery. By the growing light of the fire, with the woman in full view now, Portia could see it all: the ruin of a once-pretty face, marred by a network of reddened scars that ran across one side of her face and disappeared under the wilted linen of her cap. The girl noticed her changed manner and shot her a look of scorn. Head high, she flounced across the room to the door.

She paused on the threshold. Portia's nails dug into the padded arm of the chair.

It couldn't be. But it was.

After all of Dorrie's precautions—Portia bit back the sudden, mad urge to laugh.

It was her. Moira Hanson. Her husband's mistress.

Behind her, one hesitant footstep sounded, back into the room.

'It's you, isn't it?' The girl's voice rang low now, incredulous. Slowly she retraced her steps, stopping at the side of Portia's chair to stare down at her. 'It is! I've seen you, once before,' she said wonderingly. Then she laughed, an ugly, brittle sound. 'It was at the theatre. You were with your fine, fancy friends. Me and J.T. had a box, not far away. You never even saw us...' her mouth twisted '...or what we got up to, right there under your nose.'

Portia kept her gaze locked on the fire. 'Thank you for the water.' She gestured. 'And for the fire.' She had to work to keep her voice neutral, flat. 'That is all I require.'

'Oh, no!' Moira said, low and vicious. 'You'll not get off that easy. Did you think to come here and lord it over me? Is that why you're here—making demands in the dead of night?'

Portia looked up then, focusing on her narrowed,

mean eyes, and pointedly not on her disfigurement. 'I had no idea you were employed here.'

'I'm not *employed* here, Miss High and Mighty. My father is the landlord.'

It was the scorn in her voice that did it. Dread and chagrin began to turn to anger and indignation. *She* had been the victim in this mess, not this greedy little harpy. It had been a horrible, humiliating, tragic episode—but none of it had come through Portia's actions.

She stood. 'That would be *Mrs* High and Mighty, as you would have good cause to know.'

The other woman's eyes narrowed. 'You've come to gawk at me, haven't you? Have a laugh at my expense?'

'Don't be ridiculous.'

'Me? You're the ridiculous one, so fine—you think you are.' Moira stepped forwards. Her voice rose. 'I don't care who your father was, you weren't woman enough to keep your husband happy.'

'That is enough. Just please go.'

'You think you're better than me?' the woman shrieked.

Portia shook her head.

'Why haven't you answered my letters, then? Tell me that.'

Portia raised her chin. Her heart ached at the thought of the wicked taunts and hurtful accusations that had been in those letters. How she'd love to give as good as she got, just this once. Make this vulgar strumpet eat every one of the hateful words she'd spewed at her, in writing and in person. But they had each paid a steep price already, and Mateo slept just across the hall. She shrunk at the idea of him being witness to this woman's vitriolic hatred. It would be her last, greatest humiliation.

The door opened again. Portia flinched, but it was only Dorrie, carrying a covered tray. She stared. It took a moment for her to recognise the confrontation taking place in the room, and then all her colour drained away. 'Oh, no,' she moaned.

Moira laughed. 'Oh, yes, I'm afraid so. You thought to humiliate me? You've done enough already!' She gestured towards her marred face. 'You ruined my life! And it's time you paid.'

'Please,' Portia asked. 'This is neither the time nor the place. Just go.'

'You don't know how right you are, *my lady.*' The girl nearly choked on a sob. 'This is not the place, not *my* place. Do you know how long it took me to get out of here? To make my way to London and break into the right circles? But I had done it! I was on my way to becoming one of the most glittering courtesans in history! I had my own rig, my own servants. And now here I am, back again, fetching and carrying for every loose screw on their way in and out of Town.'

She slammed the coal bucket down with a horrendous crash. 'It's all gone now!' A harsh, broken sound erupted from her chest. 'You *owe* me!'

'I'm sorry for what happened to you.' Portia firmed her voice. This woman had to be made to understand, finally, here and now. 'Truly I am. But your misfortunes came about due to your own actions. They've nothing, *nothing* to do with me.' She glared at her. 'Do you see me endlessly blaming you for the loss of my husband?

Let us not speak of who owes whom! We've both paid enough. It's over.'

'It's not over for you, is it, you spiteful, prideful bitch?' Moira's voice rose to a screech. 'You've got a future, haven't you? You can find another poor, unsuspecting sod to marry you. Look at me! No man will touch me! What am I supposed to do?'

Suddenly Mateo's form filled the doorway. Hair tousled, his eyes heavy with sleep, he scowled at Portia. 'Damnation,' he grumbled. 'What's going on here?'

Cold despair washed over her. Mute, Portia watched Moira take in his loose linen shirt, tight breeches and bare feet.

'Is this him? The next one?' the other woman spat. 'Don't be taken in by her.' She pointed a spiteful finger. 'Her heart is cold, but the rest of her is worse. If you've a wish for a warm bedmate, then keep looking.'

Portia clenched her shaking hands and raised her chin.

'Portia? Who is this little shrew?'

Mateo came further awake and quickly recognised the danger of his position. The only tom in a cat fight? Not a good place to be. He rubbed the last bit of sleep from his eyes and began to tally the butcher's bill.

One down, it would seem. Miss Tofton slumped against the wall next to a tray-covered table, her hand in front of her eyes. The remaining two combatants still faced off. Portia—looking rumpled but lovely with colour flaring high in her cheeks—shot daggers at someone who appeared to be a serving girl—one whose pretty face had been marred some time in the recent past.

'I'm sorry,' he said to Portia's opponent, 'but you appear to be upsetting Lady Portia. This, you understand, is a sacred duty that has apparently fallen to me. I can't have you interfering.' He raised a hand and beckoned. 'Come, then. I'm sure you understand. I'm afraid you'll have to go.'

'I'm not going anywhere until I've had my due,' came the snarled reply.

Clearly the serving girl was unhinged. Or didn't know when she was bested. Or both. 'Portia?' He turned to the only reasonable-looking person in the room. 'Who is this…person?'

Her chin high and her eyes blazing, she answered. 'She's the woman who killed my husband.'

The servant girl gasped and reared back. Her face went bright red, and then deathly pale. Mateo knew just how she felt.

'No!' she gasped. 'That's not true. It was your fault, you cold bitch! If you'd been any kind of wife, he'd never have chased after me! And if you'd given him the money he needed, we never would have made that bet, never been in that street…' She broke down, sobbing, and threw herself against Mateo's chest.

Other guests were beginning to gather in the hallway behind him. Mateo tried to put the girl away, but she pounded at him with her fists. 'Just look at what she did to me!' she cried.

'Please, miss. I mean, ah, madam? Pull yourself together.'

Instead she collapsed in a heap at his feet. Mateo

reached down to lift her up. She fought him. He dropped her and she attacked his legs, clawing and scratching in time with her sharp, sawing breaths. 'Not my fault,' she moaned repeatedly.

Portia turned away. Mateo was desperate for help. He turned to her companion. 'Miss Tofton,' he pleaded.

The girl clutched his ankles and sobbed harder. 'Miss Tofton, please!'

Portia's companion took pity on him. Her face shifted, a mask that wavered between anger and pity as she knelt down, captured the girl's hands and pulled her in close.

Mateo heaved a grateful sigh. Carefully he eased away and went to shoo the audience away from the door and back to their rooms. When he returned, Miss Tofton was assisting the girl to her feet. The fight had gone out of her. She leaned into the older woman, her face turned away.

'I'll just take her downstairs,' Miss Tofton said quietly.

Portia still faced the fire, her back to them all. She did not respond.

'Will you need help?' Mateo asked quietly.

The older woman shook her head. The girl's sobs had quieted now. The rasping catch of her breath faded as Miss Tofton steered her into the hall and towards the stairs.

Quiet settled over the room. Mateo waited.

And waited. Portia neither moved nor spoke.

'Portia,' he began.

'Just go, Mateo.'

'But I—'

'Please, go. I cannot take any more tonight.'

At a loss, Mateo fell back on the tried and true. He summoned a smile. 'Come now, Portia! Don't fret. You're the clear winner in this skirmish.'

That got her moving. She rounded on him, eyes wide and clearly aghast. He winced. It was not the effect he'd been hoping for.

'Winner?' She'd gone from aghast to incredulous. Not a far trip, and not one that favoured him in any way. 'Is that what you see here? A battle won?' She whirled again and began to pace, as if she could not contain her outrage. 'I cannot decide if it is because you are a man, or if you merely possess your own particular brand of obtuseness.' She threw him a scorching look. 'Would that I were a man, then, to see things in black and white.' She snorted. 'Most of us, and women most of all, know that life is lived in all the grey areas in between.'

She folded her arms and glared at him. 'And in a horrible, dirty grey area such as this, there are no winners.' She turned away again. 'We are all losers.'

'Perhaps I might see better if I knew what I was looking at,' he said quietly. 'I think it's time you told me just what this was all about.'

Silence again.

He was not going to be put off. 'Clearly it involves J.T. I may be a clown, Portia, but I'm not stupid. I know there's something I haven't been told, something about his death that everyone else seems to know.'

'It's no secret,' she said bitterly. 'It's a sordid tale that made every paper and a hundred broadsheets across the kingdom. I'm surprised you didn't hear of it in Philadelphia.'

'Tell me.'

'I'd rather not.' Her shoulders slumped. 'I don't think I can.'

He let out an explosive breath. 'Of course you can.' He crossed the room, stood between her and the obviously fascinating fire in the grate. Tenderly he cupped her face in his hands. 'I'm beginning to believe you can do anything, Portia Tofton.' He let his hands drift down, over her shoulders, down her arms. He grabbed up her hands. 'Come. We're going to talk, but not here.'

She was distracted enough not to object. 'Where, then?'

He stood in the hall, her hand warm in his. His palms itched, tingling from that brief touch, eager for more. Looking about, he considered his options. His gaze slid past his own door, and kept on sliding. The lower part of his anatomy stirred, pointing in that direction. No.

'Aha!' He pulled her down the darkened hallway, to the stairs. Faint light drifted up from below, along with the sound of masculine merriment from the public rooms. He swept an extravagant hand, indicating the top step. 'Your seat, my lady.' He raised a brow. 'As long as you promise to behave. I recall what happened the last time we were in a stairwell alone together.'

'Nothing happened!' She was blushing, he knew it. He wished he could see it clearly.

'Only because we were interrupted. You were going to kiss me, though.'

'Is that how you recall it?' She settled down on

the top step and glanced archly up at him. 'Strangely enough, I remember that *you* were on the verge of kissing *me*.'

He dropped down next to her, leaned in close. 'Oh, that's right, *cara*—I was going to kiss you. Damned thoroughly, too.' He retreated, rested back on his elbows in a completely non-threatening pose. 'But I promise—no kissing tonight.'

Dio, was that a look of disappointment on her face? Suddenly he was grateful for the dim light. It was better if he didn't know.

Footsteps sounded below. Slow and methodical, they climbed steadily upwards. 'At least we'll know if we're to be interrupted,' he whispered. They slid over towards the wall, leaving a path open.

Miss Tofton wearily rounded the turning below. She stopped, surprised to see them there.

'How is she?' Mateo asked softly.

'Sleeping.' Portia's companion gave a wan smile. 'I told you, you never know when you might need a little laudanum.'

Portia let loose a great sigh.

'The landlord sends his apologies. I explained, and he understands the situation, but still asks if we could leave early, before she awakes.'

Mateo nodded.

'Shall we head back to our room?' Miss Tofton asked Portia pointedly.

'I'll have Portia back to you in a little while,' Mateo answered for her.

A silent communication passed between the two

women. Miss Tofton sighed. 'Come soon. You need your rest.' She climbed past them. 'Goodnight, Mr Cardea.'

'Goodnight.'

After a moment the door closed behind her and they were left in the comforting darkness. Portia had tensed up again beside him; he could feel her unease radiating through the small space that separated them.

He kept silent.

And at last she relented, slumping against the wall beside her. 'I don't know where to begin,' she said.

He shrugged. 'At the beginning?'

'No,' she said definitely. 'There's too much hurt between now and the beginning. I'll just stick with the end.'

He nodded. Her head turned, tilted questioningly.

'I'm nodding,' he said.

She laughed, but it turned into a sigh.

'She was his bit of muslin?' he prompted.

'Yes, she was his mistress, obviously. Not his first—he made sure I was fully aware of that—but without a doubt she was his most notorious. They were together quite a while—I wondered if they didn't have real feelings for each other.'

His fists clenched. A sound of protest slipped out. 'Sorry,' he said. 'Go on.'

'It was quiet enough at first, and I was preoccupied with Stenbrooke, and with my father's health. But then the rumours and scandals began. I found out later it was because she wasn't content just to be his mistress, she wished to be famous, acclaimed, sought after.'

'Ah, but don't we all?' he murmured.

'No, we don't,' she said firmly. 'Some of us just wish to be left alone.'

And if that wasn't a telling statement, then Mateo had never heard one.

'At first he appeased her by getting up to mischief *with* her,' she continued. 'He dressed her up like a man and tried to sneak her into his club, but they were both tossed out before they'd barely made it past the door. He bought her a gleaming white high-perched phaeton with blue trim and a matched white team to pull it—and she had their manes and tails dyed blue, as well. He gave her lessons and she drove it all over town, always with a little blue-grey greyhound beside her on the bench.'

'Ah, yes, she sounds an exact match for J.T.'

'I think she was. They might have been happy together indefinitely.'

'Were it not for money?' he guessed wryly.

'J.T.'s lack of it, more specifically. She became more demanding. She wanted a certain, expensive, diamond necklace and he didn't have the blunt for it. Perhaps it was just an excuse—for she announced that she was moving on to a new protector with deeper pockets.'

'Poor J.T.,' Mateo said mockingly.

'He was desperate to keep her. He came to me, demanding money, but I hadn't any to give him—and I wouldn't have given it, in any case. He went back to town and made a bet with her. He would race her through the streets of London, each in a high-perch phaeton. If he won, she would stay with him. Should she win, he'd buy her a necklace *and* let her go with his blessing.'

'Oh, Lord,' he whispered.

'They set the reservoir at Green Park as their destination. All their low friends and members of the *demimonde* gathered to cheer them on.'

Mateo's teeth ground together. 'Were your brothers there?'

'No, thank goodness. I like to think that they would have tried to talk some sense into him.'

Mateo was not so generous, but he let it rest.

'They barrelled down Curzon, then he took Half-Moon Street and she took Clarges. They met at Piccadilly and were racing towards the end when they came upon a carter carrying a load of wooden faggots. His nag had broken down. They never had a chance. The carter was killed outright.'

'And J.T.?'

'He was crushed under someone's wheels. He lived in agony for a couple of days. Long enough for me to arrive—at which point he soundly berated me for ruining his life.'

'Consistent to the end,' Mateo said bitterly.

'The papers reported every dirty detail. And while all of England rebuked him for his careless disregard of safety and consequence, he blamed me for all the shortcomings of his life. Had I been a better wife, he would have been happy in Berkshire. Had I not been the dull, sturdy type more interested in playing in the mud, he wouldn't have had to stray. Had I not poured all of his money into the wreck of the estate, he could have lived happily in London.'

Hate this hot and potent must be a sin. Mateo couldn't help it; he dearly hoped that J. T. Tofton currently occupied a particularly nasty corner of hell. He clenched his fists and struggled to breathe evenly.

'A futile, meaningless death,' she finished bitterly, 'that in true Tofton fashion, managed to hurt a great many people.'

She sighed. 'You can see what happened to her. I suppose she's been here since the accident. About six months afterward, she began to write to me, demanding money.'

Mateo sat up straight. 'You didn't give it to her?'

'No, though she threatened to take her case to the courts, since she had lost her livelihood.'

'Ridiculous.'

'I still had my hands full paying off all of J.T.'s legitimate creditors. But I did take in the carter's family, brought them to Stenbrooke. Somehow she heard of it and her letters increased in number and malevolence.'

'My poor girl.' He gave in to overwhelming temptation at last and touched her. Softly, he stroked her hair, ran a slow, comforting hand over the gloriously thick mass of it, then on into a deliberate caress down the delicate length of her neck.

She tucked her legs up and ducked her head away, pressing her forehead to her knees. 'So there you have it,' she said, her voice a bit muffled. 'Now you are privy to every last humiliating moment of my life. Every hurt, every tragically wrong decision, every mistake I've ever made. I've done it all in one day—laid myself bare before you, both physically and emotionally.' She turned her face away, towards the wall. 'God knows what you must think of me.'

He froze. Reached out a hand, then let it drop. 'I

think you are the strongest woman I've ever met.' He said it quietly, fervently, with all the conviction he could summon.

Her head shot up. 'Well, you couldn't be more wrong!' Her tone rang cold and sharp. 'I'm selfish, not strong. If I were strong, I would never have married J.T. in the first place.' Tears ran down her face. They glistened, catching the soft light and stabbing him straight through the heart.

Perhaps she was right. Perhaps she was not strong yet, but she damned well was on her way to getting there, after oppression and hardship had done its best to beat her down.

'You are not selfish.' His voice registered barely above a whisper. 'You are incredibly brave, and I am awash in admiration of you. Life is hard. But you don't run. You don't hide. You meet it head-on, you take your blows and, by God, you keep on fighting.'

There were those layers again. He'd been judging her on the tough, outer layer she'd developed in the years since he knew her. The one she'd needed in order to survive all the blows life had thrown her way. And he had delivered some of the worst, he realised with horror. But at her core still lived an uncertain girl. A little bruised. Most definitely alone. Such strength and hope it must have taken for her to risk herself again— with him, who hurt her first and perhaps most of all.

He'd done everything wrong. Hurt her again and again with practically every word, every encounter. Now was his chance to make it up to her.

Yet he hesitated. It was terrifying having such insight into another person—because it was never one-sided. He could see through the window they'd opened between them, straight into her soul—and she could see him just as clearly.

A delicate, dangerous situation. One he'd spent his life carefully avoiding. To allow someone full view and sincere knowledge of your true self? He shuddered. It granted them such power, such ability to do real harm. His mother's death had proven how horrendous the pain could be when you were left alone at the window. His father had shown that it was just as bad when the window was deliberately closed.

And in his and Portia's case, the pain was a certainty. Their lives were too different, too separate for the window to last. The wrenching hurt of separation was inevitable. He would have to leave soon. And this would make it so much harder. There would be no deflecting this hurt, no outrunning it with a quick wit or a busy schedule or even a fast ship. It would live with him, inside of him. Already he missed her impudent mouth and her stubborn independence. The sweeping curve of her nape and the feel of her breasts spilling out of his hands and into his mouth. If he took this step, he'd have so much more to haunt him, so much that he knew would be impossible to forget.

But for her he would face it. She'd shown such bravery, risked so much, and she needed to know how beautiful she was—how good and strong and lovely—on the inside and out.

He'd been silent too long. She'd turned her head on her knees and was watching him.

Abruptly, he stood. He reached a hand down towards her. 'Come with me.'

She stared up at him. 'Where?'

Impatient, he beckoned again. 'There's a gorgeous view waiting for us—and we need to see it together.'

Chapter Thirteen

Just what she'd expected to happen after wrenching her emotions out and displaying them for Mateo, she wasn't sure, but Portia knew it hadn't been this.

Her hand gripped tightly in his, he pulled her away from the stairs and down the hall. He paused in front of his room. Shook his head. Then he dropped her hand and pushed her to the wall. 'Wait here. Just for a moment.'

Bemused, she watched as he left her. She was grateful for his kind words. Intensely so. He'd listened to her without judgement, responded with sensitivity and generosity. Just as he always did. Her shoulders slumped. When would she learn? Why could she never stop wishing for more from him?

And just what was he up to now? Gingerly, he tested the knob on the door next to his. 'Locked,' he whispered. Taking a step back, he cast a measuring look up and down the hallway.

'Mateo,' she said low. 'I should go back...Dorrie will—'

'No! Stay here,' he hissed.

He headed down the hall, passing one door by, stopping and listening at another. Finally he hovered in front of the last door on the opposite side. He pressed his ear against it. Ever so slowly he turned the knob. The door swung open. Holding a commanding finger towards her—a silent order to stay put—he disappeared inside.

She waited. Several quiet moments passed, then a soft glow of light emerged from the room he'd entered. He leaned out of the doorway and beckoned her.

She shook her head and raised questioning hands at him.

With a huff of exasperation that she could hear from this distance, he stalked down the hall towards her. 'You never backed down from a single challenge your brothers threw at you,' he whispered. 'Are you going to turn craven now?'

She reared back and stared into the challenge in his face. 'No!'

'Then come on, Peeve.'

She balked at the nickname, digging in her heels.

Very seriously, he turned and gripped her by her shoulders. 'I can only begin to imagine what you might feel at the sound of that nickname, but do you want to know what it does to me?'

Did she? She wasn't sure. She only looked at him beseechingly.

'It takes me back, to a blissful, happy time in my life. It brings to mind a stubborn little girl in plaits and a pinafore, a girl who never once backed down from any challenge her brothers could dream up. It conjures up a shy, pretty adolescent, who could none the less pull off elaborate pranks that boggled the mind, a young woman who listened, without judgement or recrimination, in a way that I've never encountered since. It reminds me of you, Portia, and all the laughter and anger and joy and tears that we've shared.'

Each word was a gift, a surprise that burst inside of her, utterly defeating the cold insecurities dragged up by the night's events. Portia blinked back tears.

'So I will stop using it out loud, if you insist, but you should know that you'll *always* be Peeve to me.'

He wrapped a warm arm about her and guided her to the open room, while she struggled to regain her equilibrium.

It was another guest room, but clearly for a different level of guest. This one loomed spacious, with a high, wide bed, a screen and a standing mirror in the corner and an elaborately carved wardrobe along one wall. He'd lit several candles and placed them on the mantel. She folded her arms. This room did lack one important thing.

'Mateo?' She turned to find him closing the door after them. The click of the lock sounded loud in the quiet. 'There are no windows in here.'

'I know.' He went past her to the corner of the room.

'Then how exactly are we to share the view?' She suppressed a wry grin. 'You aren't going to ask me to view your sketches, are you? My mother did warn me about such things, you know.' She ran a finger along the thick down coverlet on the bed. 'If you are not careful, I'm going to think you bent on seduction.'

'I don't have any sketches,' he said. His voice strained as he lifted the large mirror. She stared. The thing was as tall as he. He placed it carefully in front of her. 'I had something altogether more lovely in mind.'

He came to stand behind her, placed his hands on her shoulders and turned her so that she squarely faced her reflection. 'And I am absolutely bent on seduction.'

'You are?' It came out as a squeak. She swallowed past the sudden lump in her throat and met his gaze in the mirror.

'Of course.' He waved a negligent hand and sat on the foot of the bed. 'But first, I want you to look—' he gestured towards the mirror '—and tell me what you see.'

Her heart tripped, then took off at a run. 'Mateo, I—'

'Ah, ah…' He wagged an admonitory finger, then pointed at the mirror. 'Tell me.'

His nonchalant declaration had left her whole body a-tremble, but in no way was she going to give him a chance to change his mind. She bit her lip and did as he bade.

'What do you see?' he asked again, softly.

Her fingers went to her collar. 'Buttons undone and red, puffy eyes?'

'Look again,' he ordered. 'Look deeper.'

She rather liked this autocratic side of him. She definitely liked what it was doing to her insides. She tore her gaze from his and looked again. 'A dishevelled widow lady who has just had a shouting match with her dead husband's mistress,' she said ruefully.

He sighed. 'I'm disappointed in you, *cara*. Clearly you need a lesson.' He stood, stepped behind her and pressed his body close to hers. 'Shall I tell you what I see?'

His breath stirred her hair, seared her scalp and the top of her ear. She shivered, delighted with the delicious feel of it. Gooseflesh travelled down the length of her arm and her nipples tightened. 'Yes.'

He reached up, plucked a pin from her hair, and cast it on to the bed. 'I see courage,' he breathed. 'The sort that never backs down from hardship, but isn't afraid to ask for help when it's needed, either.'

Another pin followed, then another. Her hair sagged, heavy and loose. 'I see a good mind and a saucy spirit— a combination that makes every moment in your company a joy.'

Her spirits soared, even as her hair tumbled down. He watched it fall in the mirror, and she caught the blaze of excitement in his eyes. He moved closer still and buried his face in the length of it.

Intent and aroused, she stared at their reflections. Almost, she could see herself through his eyes. Certainly she did look different, with her hair tumbling down over both of them and her body pressed back into his.

He inhaled, a great, gulping breath as if he were a drowning man and she a sky full of clean, fresh air. 'I see a great heart.' He breathed into the heavy mass, his eyes meeting hers in the mirror's reflection. 'One that is able to forgive the callousness of an old friend and even the misplaced wrath of a shallow, deluded woman.'

Oh, Lord. The warmth of him sent the blood rushing to her skin. His scent engulfed her, so rich and exotically different from her own. *Man.* It spoke to her and awakened long-neglected yearnings. *Mateo*, it said. Longing and heat spiralled inside of her, pooled in her belly and sent her answer back to him.

So long it had been—but, no, that was not a thought she could finish. She'd never felt like this. Mateo's body awakened hers, his sheer physical presence sent ripples of excited sensation all through her.

But his words—his words flowed over her, inside of her. They were a balm to her cracked soul, soothing hurts she'd scarcely been aware of.

His hands clutched her hips, steadied her against him as he nuzzled her neck. 'I could sing your praises all night long, if you'd like,' he whispered.

'Touch me instead,' she answered. 'Show me, Mateo.'

Against the small of her back she felt him stirring, growing in response. 'See?' he said. 'Clever enough to know what she wants—and courageous enough to ask for it.'

'Stop talking now,' she said, turning in his arms. Rising up, she traced her finger softly over those lovely, tiny lines at the corners of his eyes. 'I love these,' she whispered. He smiled and they deepened under her touch.

She claimed his mouth with her own. He tasted of wine, vibrant and rich, of hot lust and wild desire. Or perhaps that was her. Her mouth slanted over his, their tongues danced and their souls tangled.

His fingers drifted up, over her curves and into her hair. They dug into her scalp and she arched in pleasure. He accepted the silent invitation and buried his face in the nape of her neck. Then suddenly he was working at the intricate fastenings of her habit. He'd got most of them undone and reached inside before she'd caught her breath.

'Wait,' she gasped. She smiled up at him. 'It's my turn.'

She stepped back, and trailed a teasing finger across his chest. She moved slowly, inching her way until she stood behind and to one side of him. She met his gaze in the mirror and cast him a slow, sultry smile.

'Minx.'

She stood on her tiptoes and pressed her mouth close to his ear. 'Only with you,' she breathed.

He moaned.

She didn't waste her breath on words. Instead she let the press of her body and the soft whisper of her caress tell him of her gratitude and of her desire. Lightly, she ran the tips of her fingers up his sides, across the expanse of his chest. His nipples pebbled, tiny echoes of her own arousal, and she brushed a light caress there too.

In the mirror she watched him. His avid gaze followed the sensuous path of her fingers. Suddenly his eyes lifted and locked with hers. 'Are you going to tell me what you see?' he asked hoarsely.

Her hand stopped at the edge of his trousers. Beneath it, his belly heaved and the heat of his flesh seared her.

'You, Mateo. Only you. That's all I need to see.'

He stilled. Time slowed and an incredibly long moment passed. 'Portia,' he said quietly and in a voice full of regret, 'I want you, more than you could possibly imagine. But we cannot go further until we both acknowledge that this can only be temporary.'

She pressed a kiss against the hard muscle of his

arm, then stepped in front of him and snuggled into his arms. 'Do you remember what I said—?' She closed her eyes and shook her head. 'Was it only earlier today?' She chuckled and smiled up at him. 'We're in a unique position, caught between our pasts and our future. We'll likely never see another time like this in our lives.' With a raised brow and a challenging grin, she reached down and cupped the fullness of his erection. 'We might as well make it memorable.'

Mateo groaned and thrust himself further into her hand. Memorable? Every second he'd spent with her in his arms had already etched itself into his soul.

He reached out and quickly finished the job he'd started earlier, plucking and pulling until her habit was undone and falling to her waist. She wriggled her hips and it dropped, leaving her feet buried in a puddle of fabric and the rest of her clad only in her undergarments.

He made short work of them, too. In mere seconds, it seemed, she stood naked, unveiled before him. Candlelight flickered over her curves, shadows danced over her high, pink-tipped breasts. He let his gaze wander lower, over the thatch of her curls, darker than the honey-and-amber locks on her head.

She bit her lip and smiled at him, grabbing the waistband of his trousers. 'Play fair, now,' she admonished. Swiftly, her fingers moved over the buttoned placket and at last his erection spilled free, leaden with arousal.

She sighed in appreciation and touched him with delicately dancing fingertips. An erotic path she traced, over the top and down the length of him. He swelled impossibly high.

This, then, was why he'd spent so long denying them this. Her strokes grew firm; he grew—incredibly— harder and he knew that her touch had become a necessity, like air for his starving lungs.

Dio, yes. He wanted to breathe her in.

He kissed her again, open and intense. Excitement surged through him. He was going to learn her every curve, every contour, both inside and out, and he was going to start right here, exploring her mouth with abandon.

But soon enough, he needed more. Bending his knees, he lifted her and placed her on the bed.

She laughed. He caught his breath again at the sight of her hair in the dim light. A glorious welter, it slid over her shoulders and around her breasts. They called to him, teased him with the smallest glimpses of tightened nipples and darkened areolas as she moved.

He answered. He pursued her on the high bed, approaching with all seriousness until he loomed over her. And then he dipped his head and ran his tongue over a shyly peeking bud. The room shrank as he suckled, first one gorgeous breast, then the other, until nothing existed save for the caress of her hair, soft against his face, the little gasping sounds of her pleasure and the feel of his hot breath against her wet flesh.

At last she dug her fingers into his hair, lifting his face up to hers.

'Come to me, Mateo. I've waited so long.'

No man could resist such a sweet summons. But incredibly, he hesitated. He had to be sure.

He pressed a kiss on her mouth, then turned over on to his back. A hairpin jabbed him and he fished it out, then threw it aside. He laid his head back against the pillows and his mouth quirked. Her fascinated gaze was locked on to his straining erection. Impressive already, even to his own eyes, it jumped a little, stretching impossibly under her regard. 'Come and take what you want, Portia,' he rasped.

She glanced at his face, puzzled, then her brow cleared. Her eyes widened. And she smiled.

She crawled up and over him, her eyes alight with excitement. Leaning down, she tantalised him with a long, hot kiss, and then she positioned herself, open and inviting, over him.

Already she dripped, hot and silky with need. She teased, touching down on just the very tip of him, and a groan travelled up and out of him.

Without any further warning, she sank down. And down and down.

God help him.

There were no words to describe the sensation. He was harder than iron and she was giving way before him, her inner passage clenching, then relaxing as she took him in.

Easy.

But she was hot and tight and he was greedy and nearly beside himself with pleasure. He couldn't do it, couldn't wait. In a flash he had her lifted off the bed, and then underneath him. And he did it without breaking their incredible, intimate contact. 'All right?' he asked, while he still had enough sense to comprehend her answer.

She moved, wiggled, adjusting. Her sex pulsed, coaxing him further, higher, longer. And then she nodded.

Thank God. Gripping her hips, he began to move.

She met his thrusts with eagerness, hunger. He adjusted slightly, lifted his hips and settled into slow, rhythmic strokes.

'Mmm,' she said, and arched her back. Her fingernails carved little wounds into his shoulders. He had it right, then.

In the shifting light he saw her face sharpen with need. 'More,' she whispered.

Yes. His body echoed her. Almost against his own will he began to thrust faster. She tightened, pulling him even deeper.

'Portia.' It was a question. An order. A prayer.

'Yes,' she answered. Then she let out an exultant, strangled cry.

He was gone. Over. Lost in a tumult of surging, throbbing joy. Almost, it was too much. He hung, balanced on the knife's edge between madness and bliss—and then came down hard on the side of bliss.

He could heartily recommend bliss.

Slowly, he returned to himself, happy to find Portia just as thoroughly boneless and content as he. Her head lolled. She gave him a sleepy, satisfied smile and a huge sigh. It was the most beautiful sound he'd ever heard in his life.

He disengaged, rolled them into a comfortable position, and buried his face into the sweet curve of her neck.

'There,' he said into her damp flesh. 'Try to forget that.'

Chapter Fourteen

Portia had worn her finest day gown, a lovely striped linen in varying shades of green and ivory, but she realised with sudden certainty that it was not near fine enough for an audience with the Countess of Lundwick.

She stood, staring like a country yokel at her surroundings, at the immense marble hall, at the collection of priceless curios and the grand, sweeping staircase. And this was just the entrance hall.

She was an Earl's daughter herself, for goodness' sake. She'd grown up on a large estate with a big, rambling, ancient house. She'd danced at balls, drank tea, listened to music and dreadful poetry at some of the most prominent houses in Town, but never had she witnessed such an ostentatious—but somehow also flawless—display of wealth.

A stiffly reserved butler handed them off to an only-slightly-less-rigid footman, who escorted them to a drawing room where they could await the Countess's pleasure.

Dorrie entered first. She came to a dead halt just a step into the room. Portia crowded in behind her, and was forced to go around to make room for Mateo. She followed Dorrie's gaze around the opulent room and her mouth dropped open.

'It's as if we're inside a pastry,' marvelled Dorrie.

'Or a boudoir,' Portia answered, taking in all of the laces and flounces and rich pastel fabrics.

She flushed. Perhaps, after last night, she just had boudoirs on her mind. And who could blame her? She glanced at Mateo, to gauge his reaction.

He said nothing. Loath, no doubt, to add to the meagre number of words he'd allotted to them this morning.

He met her gaze suddenly, and she was taken aback by the bleak shadow that crossed over his features. 'Portia, I'd like a word with you, if you please.'

'Of course.'

He held out his arm, an oddly formal gesture, and she took it, wondering where he meant for them to go. But he only crossed to the window at the far end of the room. They stood there a moment, while he gazed back at the decadent décor and out to the street below, anywhere but at her.

Her heart began to thrum in sudden panic. All of last night's laughing charm had converted to pensive silence. Why?

Perhaps it was her—though she was a widow, her experience was not extensive… No. She cut loose that thought almost as soon as it blossomed. Last night had been wonderful—in his eyes, as well as hers. His tenderness had told her so, as had the joyous urgency of his touch.

Did he know something, then? Or suspect something about what they might learn today? Brow furrowed, she waited.

'There's something I should tell you, *cara*, though it's not easy for me to say.'

She nodded.

'God only knows how this will turn out today.' Each word emerged reluctantly, like a tooth that must be tugged out by the root. 'But if something happens, and we are not able to save Stenbrooke, I won't expect you to give up Cardea Shipping.'

She jerked back a pace. 'Mateo, I—'

'No. I didn't bring this up for discussion. I'd rather not talk about it at all.' He paused. She could practically see him gathering fortitude. 'But I want you to know that I believe that all you'd need is a little coaching, and you'd do a good job with it. You've proved yourself several times over. You've a good head on your shoulders. More important than any of that, though, I want you to understand how much I value your kind and generous heart.' He lifted an ironic brow. 'You'll acquire more Cardeas than you'll know what to do with—all those uncles and cousins are still employed as agents and clerks and captains and mates.' He faltered a little. 'I know you would do your best for them and take care of them as if they were your own.'

He'd shocked her. Never had she been so taken aback, or so deeply, deeply touched. Tears welled in her eyes. She bit her lip. 'No one has ever paid me a bigger compliment, Mateo.' Her voice fell to a whisper. 'Thank you.'

He reached for her hand and gave it a squeeze. Across the room, the door swung open again. Together they turned to face the future.

The Countess of Lundwick stood poised on the threshold, prettily framed.

In direct contrast to the room they occupied, she was clad in the sort of simple elegance that only an abundance of money could buy. It was a brilliant manoeuvre, and one that only enhanced the stunning perfection of her beauty. For a beauty she still definitely was, for all that she was old enough to be Portia's mother.

She swept a beaming glance across the room, shining joy indiscriminately upon them all. Then her gaze settled on Mateo and she stilled.

'Mr Cardea.' She nearly floated across the room, her arms outstretched.

Portia bristled. The expression in the Countess's eyes as she ran her gaze over Mateo could only be deemed *hunger.* The older woman clasped his face in her hands and kissed both of his cheeks.

Her irritation fled, turned to bemusement, really, when the Countess then turned immediately to her— and with the same avid interest. It was not a sensation Portia was used to—to be gazed upon with something that looked almost like…covetousness.

'Lady Portia.' Portia's cheeks flamed as she found herself greeted in the same continental manner, and also subject to a soft caress over her brow and along the line of her jaw.

'My darlings,' the Countess breathed enthusiastically. She reached out a hand to them both. 'I am so glad you've come to me at last.'

Portia shot a quick, baffled glance at Mateo. He looked just as dumbfounded as she felt.

'Lady Lundwick.' Mateo sketched a bow. 'Clearly you know who we are. Might we also assume you know why we've come?'

'But of course!' The Countess turned a beguiling smile on him. 'At least, I presume you are here to discuss Averardo, no?'

Portia stared. Her heart sounded suddenly loud in her ears. It gave her such a jolt of pleasure and relief—to have someone actually verify the man's existence. She'd almost come to believe he was a myth.

The door swung open once more. She turned, almost expecting, in this day of surprises, to see the elusive Averardo himself. But it was a different entity altogether who rather absently entered the room.

'Lundy!' the Countess exclaimed brightly. 'Just see who has come!'

'Can't! I'm off, my love!' The Earl, for Portia assumed 'Lundy' to be the Earl of Lundwick, was the very image of a life lived hard and well. Wide, where he had once been broad and soft where he had once been firm, he still possessed a degree of handsome appeal. 'I've just come for a proper goodbye, then I'm to Tatts for…' He faltered as he took in the trio of visitors. 'Well, now! Look at this. They've come at last, have they?'

'Yes, they've only just arrived.' The Countess crossed the room to greet her spouse with a fond kiss. Together they turned and smiled upon their bewildered guests. 'Aren't they lovely?'

Portia felt befuddled, as if she'd stepped into a waking dream. After all the trials, hardships, horses, carriages and questions, this elegant, affable couple was not what she'd been expecting to find here. She reached over to reclaim Mateo's hand.

'Very happy to have you all,' boomed the Earl. 'Sorry I can't stay.' He leaned down and kissed his wife once more. 'Enjoy them, my dear, and I will see you tonight at the Ashfords' ball?'

The Countess waved him off and opened the door wider as a maid came in, wheeling a cart spread with a lavish tea. 'Now, my dears, we will have tea. You can introduce me to your friend...' she indicated a wide-eyed Dorrie '...and then, we shall talk.'

Torn between amusement, frustration and impatience, Mateo waited. He waited through tea and sandwiches and cakes, through awkward silence punctuated by stilted small talk, presided over by an inexplicably delighted Countess. And when their hostess at last set down her dish of tea, he leaned forwards.

'Averardo, my lady?'

She laughed, an appealing little trill of good humour. Nearly everything about her was appealing, in fact. He could well understand the Earl of Lundwick's choice, although if he recalled, there had been a buzz of scandal at the time, due to her age and her obscure background.

'Yes, Mr Cardea. All in good time. First I would like to offer my condolences on the loss of your father.'

He blanched. 'Thank you.' He sharpened his gaze. 'Did you know him?'

'I did.' Her bright countenance faded a little. 'A very

long time ago.' She turned troubled eyes towards Portia. 'And your father, as well, dear. His death was such a shock, being the first. It quite frightened me, I confess, for I am not in the habit of contemplating my own mortality.'

No one seemed able to conjure an appropriate response to that. After a moment she straightened. 'Well, then. I know you must be anxious indeed to hear what I can tell you. But first, I would ask a favour. I want to hear something from you.'

'What is there about us that could possibly interest you?' Portia asked her. 'Forgive me, my lady, but I find myself quite at a loss here.'

The older woman gazed at her fondly. 'I long to hear about your journey, dear.' She sketched in the air with her hands. 'How you got *here* from *there*.' She smiled. 'Though it is a loathsome prospect, I have been forced to acknowledge that I have reached a certain…maturity in my life. Though it's a slight compensation, with age does come a little wisdom.' She smiled. 'I will share with you some of the most important lessons I have learned.'

Intent, she leaned forwards. 'It is true that destinations are important. People need goals to achieve satisfaction. But more important than even achieving your goals is the *journey*—the path you take in pursuit of your ambitions.' She glanced slyly at Mateo. 'And most crucial of all? The people you travel with. Those are the things that make life worthwhile and reaching your objective palatable.'

Mateo stared at the woman. She sat, her head tilted in earnestness, her toe pointed, hair still dark and face still largely unlined. A fey, gorgeous creature. She radiated contentment, like a cat curled before a fire. He greatly resented being her plaything.

She glanced askance at him, with her wise, knowing eyes and sudden suspicion bloomed. A *snap* echoed in his head. His brain had just sorted the pieces of separate puzzles and realised they fitted together into a breathtaking whole. It seemed an impossible notion.

He returned her look, and then, quite deliberately, he decided to give her what she wanted.

'I, for one, have experienced an incredible journey on my way to your drawing room, my lady. It started in anger—but ended in something else altogether. Along the way I've experienced frustration, exasperation—' his eye fell on Portia '—but also laughter and admiration.'

'Tell me,' the Countess urged with a smile.

So he did. He told her of Rankin and his disgruntled clerk, of Riggs and his wasted field, of Lord Dowland and his horses and his young family. But mostly, he spoke of Portia. He waxed enthusiastic over her passion and skill for landscaping, over her incredible knowledge, over her sensitivity and quiet strength. And when he was finished Portia sat with a reddened look of bashful joy, Dorrie gazed at him with a thoughtful, worried expression and the Countess—she watched him closer still, with undeniable cunning, but also extreme satisfaction.

'Is that what you wished to hear?' he asked her gently.

'It is indeed.' She drew a deep breath. 'And so I shall tell you what you wish to hear.'

'Averardo?' asked Portia.

The Countess nodded. 'That is one name by which he is known. There are others.'

'Like Lorenzo and Cosimo? The names of the Medici?'

She laughed delightedly, but it was respect that shone in her eyes. 'Very good, Mr Cardea. And why not? The Medici were self-made men—they worked and schemed their way into prominence. They made themselves great, but they also lifted others—men of art and science and architecture—into greatness.'

'My home...' Portia swallowed and Mateo winced at how difficult this was for her. 'This man won my home, in a card game with my late husband.' She glanced over at Mateo. 'We wish to buy it back.'

'I do not think he will take your money, Lady Portia,' the Countess said gently. 'But I also do not believe that he will take your home.'

Portia looked stunned. 'But...but why?' She swept an encompassing arm. 'Why put me—all of us—through all this?'

The Countess regarded her kindly. 'I cannot say. You will have to ask him that yourself.'

'I'd be happy to do just that.' Portia's eyes flashed with anger and Mateo wondered if perhaps he should warn the Countess about the danger of underestimating her. 'Do you know where we can find him?'

The older woman shrugged. 'I do not know, precisely. He is a mysterious figure.' She flicked her fingers. 'He comes in, he goes out. One never knows when one will see him next.'

Portia stared at her. She threw down her napkin and started to stand.

'To your knowledge, my lady,' Mateo interjected, 'has Mr Averardo ever gone by the name of Salvestro?' He asked the question smoothly, as if the answer were of no consequence whatever.

She met his gaze directly. 'Yes, Mr Cardea, I believe he has.'

Click. Another piece of the puzzle snapped home. The revelations were coming fast, but he could see that Portia followed his line of thinking, at least to a degree. 'But, Mateo, you said that Salvestro was your agent in Portsmouth…that means…your father knew him, hired him… He's been *working* for you, for all these years…' Her face hardened and she turned to the Countess with determination. 'I'm sorry, my lady, but surely you know more. We must see this man, and straight away.'

Calmly, the Countess poured herself another dish of tea. 'Do not fret so, my dear. He will come to you when the time is right.'

'The time *is* right—right now. Mateo stands to lose too much if we delay any further.'

'Then perhaps you must give Averardo reason to come to you.'

Portia was on her feet. 'This is preposterous. Do you think this is some sort of game? The course of all our lives is at stake here.'

Mateo's mind was racing. He stood. 'Come, ladies. I think perhaps our journey is over.' He levelled a hard look at their hostess. 'Sometimes life's journey takes you to places you've no wish to see.'

Portia tried a last time. 'Please.' She turned a pleading gaze upon the other woman. 'Won't you tell us what we need to know?'

The Countess patted her hand. 'All will be well, dear. You must trust me.'

Portia drew back. Her face set, she walked away.

Mateo bowed low over the lady's hand. 'Thank you. I understand that you have said what you can.' He paused. 'And, perhaps, done what you can.'

'You are very welcome, Mateo,' she said softly. She gazed after Portia's retreating form. 'I hope she will forgive me. Will you bring her to visit again?'

He stared down at her, made note of the wistful tone she allowed to creep into her voice. 'Eventually, perhaps.'

Outside they waited for the post-chaise to be brought from the livery. Several times Miss Tofton opened her mouth to speak, but each time she closed it again and shook her head. Portia stared blankly out at the traffic for several long minutes before she turned to him.

'Mateo—the same man, all along? All through this… wasted excursion, but further back, as well? We suspected Averardo and the courier might be one and the same. But I'm afraid I don't understand. Was he also the same man your father mentioned, the one he hired—to take your place here in England?'

She reached out. Proprietarily, she grasped his hand. 'Perhaps he's been after your dream all along,' she said as if she were thinking out loud. 'Perhaps he's after your legacy.' She stared up at him. 'Perhaps he thinks I will make the trade with *him*, Stenbrooke for Cardea Shipping.'

He blinked. 'I confess, I hadn't even thought of that.'

'You hadn't? But something occurred to you in there, I saw it in your face. What does it all mean?'

He tugged his hand free and captured both of hers. He kissed them tenderly, even as she stared in amazement.

'Peeve, I'm going to ask you do something. I ask it, knowing full well that it may be the most difficult thing you've ever attempted.'

She breathed deep. 'Of course. What is it?'

'For both of our sakes, I need you to trust me. Completely. Implicitly.' He feared that she would realise how everything inside of him hovered, awaiting her answer. 'Can you do that? Will you?'

Her hands spasmed, clutching his. Silence grew thick between them. 'Yes. Of course I will.'

His heart lurched, his chest expanded. Beside them, the post-chaise rolled to a stop.

'Where are we going?' she asked, not taking her eyes off his.

'To see someone I've journeyed with in the past.'

Chapter Fifteen

'The knocker's up,' Mateo said in relief. The post-chaise drew to a halt in front of the Bruton Street town-house. 'We're in luck.'

He instructed the postillion to wait. When the door swung open, he flashed his most charming smile. 'Batten down the hatches, Fisher. I'm afraid it is an American invasion.'

'Yes, Mr Cardea,' the butler answered formally. 'I am duly frightened.' He opened the door wide and bowed Mateo and the ladies in.

'Before you start counting the silver, will you inform Sophie of our arrival? It might be something of a shock,' he added ruefully.

'It would only be a shock if I were able to inform her, sir. Lady Dayle and the children are currently in Kensington.'

That did deflate Mateo a little. Sophie's help he knew he could count on. Of her husband's he was not so sure. 'And Lord Dayle?' he asked.

'I believe he is in his bookroom. I'll just go and see if he's at home, shall I?'

Mateo grinned. It took true skill to convey sarcasm through a stiffly proper demeanour. 'Thank you, but step sharply now,' he called. 'There aren't enough valuables in the entrance hall to keep me interested for long.'

Fisher's stately pace never faltered.

'There are likely a hundred inns within a mile of here, Mateo,' Portia said. Worry created shadows beneath her eyes. 'Perhaps we should just find one for the night?'

'That wasn't exactly a warm welcome, Mr Cardea,' Miss Tofton chided.

'Nonsense. Fisher expects me to light a fire under his bowsprit. It's no more than the man deserves—a name like that and do you know he's never set foot in the smallest dinghy?'

'Fisher!'

Mateo turned in anticipation. The call came from above, not from the bookroom down the hall.

'Fisher—I'll need an umbrella. The sky looks as if it's going to open up.'

Mateo stepped forwards as Charles Alden, Lord Dayle, husband to his cousin Sophie, appeared at the top of the stairwell, fastening his cufflinks as he came. 'Fisher?'

'Sorry, Dayle. I sent him off to find you.'

The Viscount's head popped up. 'Cardea?' His face lit up in shock. 'By God, Cardea, it is you, you soup-swilling son of a sea-cook!'

Mateo laughed. 'You're improving, Dayle. I could almost use that one without shame.'

'Yes, well, a man should never stop striving for excellence. In all things.'

His cousin-in-law had reached the hall. He reached out and pulled Mateo in for a bracing hug and forceful thump on the back. 'What are you doing here, Mateo? Does Sophie know you're in England?' His eye fell on the two ladies, silently watching. 'And who is this you've brought with you?' He let his arm fall from Mateo's shoulder and shot them both a blinding smile.

Mateo stepped protectively towards Portia and her companion. 'You're an old married man now, Dayle,' he objected. 'Turn it down a bit and allow me to introduce an old family friend, Lady Portia Tofton, and her companion, Miss Tofton. Ladies, this is the Viscount Dayle.'

'Tofton?' Dayle frowned.

'Yes, *that* Tofton,' Mateo said in exasperation.

Portia curtsied, and came up with a grin. 'One might just as easily say, *that* Lord Dayle. I believe I've heard just as much about you, my lord, as you might have about my late husband.'

Dayle laughed. 'I dare say that could be true. But people change, do they not, Lady Portia?'

'Some do, my lord,' she answered non-committally.

'And some are just destroyed by their own stupidity. Come, Dayle, I've been dragging these two ladies all over the south of England for days now. I was hoping you'd redeem me and put us all up for the night?'

'I hope you're planning on staying longer than a night? Sophie will skin us both if she misses you. She and all the rest of the family are up to their elbows in

Mother's latest project: an orphanage in Kensington. They'll be wanting to give you the grand tour.'

Mateo purposefully did not commit to anything. 'Thank you, Charles. I knew I could count on you.'

'Not at all. Look, here's Fisher. Where have you been, man?' Dayle called to his butler.

Fisher's eyes flicked in Mateo's direction. 'Counting the silver, my lord.'

'Not a bad idea, with a pirate in the house. But now I need you to see to these ladies.' He cast a sympathetic look at Portia. 'I'd wager they'd like a hot bath, and perhaps a tray in their rooms?'

'Oh, yes, thank you, my lord,' Miss Tofton piped up.

Mateo noted that the offer of such homely comforts had dazzled the companion where Dayle's blinding charm had not. Perhaps days spent under the influence of his own considerable charm had granted her an immunity.

'There's a post-chaise out in front that will need taking care of,' he informed Dayle.

'Fisher will see to it, won't you, man?' Dayle leaned in confidingly. 'He's the most sought-after butler in town, Cardea—he can do any number of things at once, and all brilliantly well.'

Portia looked back once as the ladies were led away. Mateo nodded encouragingly. Dayle observed this silent communication, but did not comment. Neither did Mateo.

'Come on. Let's find some brandy. You look like you could use one.' He laughed. 'You're the perfect excuse to keep me from Lady Ashford's ball tonight, and for that I owe you.'

Dayle waited until they were settled in the bookroom with cigars and brandies before he eyed Mateo's relaxed slouch with scepticism and asked, 'What sort of trouble are you into now?'

'I wish I could say it was the usual sort, but I'm afraid it's gone a bit worse than that.'

'You know I'll help, in any way I can.'

Mateo blew a smoky cloud of relief. 'Thank you, Charles.' He sat up straight. 'Here's what I'll need.'

Chapter Sixteen

Early morning light painted Mayfair with a dazzling brush, reflecting off immaculately swept steps and bright, shining windows. On Bruton Street, the sun sparkled off Lord Dowland's newly washed post-chaise and flashed amidst the jingling traces of the freshly harnessed team.

Lord Dayle worked fast. Portia ruefully eyed the carriage and then her agitated companion.

'Are you certain about this?' Dorrie asked, her tone low with concern.

'It's as good a plan as any,' Portia sighed. 'Averardo has watched us so closely all along, he must be doing so now.' She tried not to peer about the seemingly empty street, but it was a difficult urge to conquer. 'Even if he's not watching himself, he's likely hired someone to keep an eye on us. We have to make this look authentic.'

'You know I don't like leaving you.'

'It's just for a short time. I'll follow you home soon enough, perhaps as early as tomorrow if Mateo's plan works.' She gripped her companion's hands. 'We have to finish this. And when we do, Stenbrooke will be ours and we'll never have to worry about losing it again.' She smiled. 'And I will be travelling alone this time, not in Mateo's company. So you may relax.'

Dorrie lifted an ironic brow.

'I'll be all right, Dorrie. I promise.'

Her companion's mouth twisted wryly. 'Yes, I know. You trust him.' She sighed. 'And that's as good a recommendation as I'll ever hear.' She hugged Portia close, and then stared intently into her face. 'Now I wish you would begin to trust yourself.'

Portia swallowed.

Dorrie relented, and hugged her once more. 'Now, I hope to see you tomorrow.'

Portia nodded, her throat too thick to speak. Part of her returned the sentiment. She firmly squashed the other part.

Behind them the door opened and Mateo and Lord Dayle emerged, blinking into the bright sunlight. Mateo carried a travelling case in his hand.

'Well, I hope all of this sun presages an easy journey for you, Miss Tofton.' Lord Dayle bent low over Dorrie's hand. 'It was a pleasure to make your acquaintance.'

'And yours, as well. Thank you for your generous hospitality.' Dorrie curtsied and then extended a hand in Mateo's direction. 'Mr Cardea…' She stopped and gave a little shake of her head.

Portia's eyes filled as Mateo ignored the outstretched hand and pulled Dorrie in for an embrace. She forgot her tears, though, when she saw him whisper something in her companion's ear.

'I think that is precisely what I'm afraid of,' Dorrie told him tartly, but her eyes looked suspiciously bright, as well.

'Portia will be home with you soon,' Mateo told her as he handed her into the chaise.

'Goodbye, Dorrie!' Portia called as the vehicle moved away. She watched and waved until it turned a corner, and her companion was gone.

But there was no time to brood. One of Lord Dayle's grooms was already leading a saddled horse up. Mateo lost no time before strapping his case behind the saddle. Once he had it secure, Lord Dayle grasped his hand and gripped him tightly on the shoulder.

'It was damned good to see you, Cardea. I hope next time you'll be able to stay a while.'

'I will. Give Sophie my regrets.' He winced. 'And my apologies.'

Lord Dayle laughed. 'Yes, you'll have hell to pay when next she sees you. Sure you won't reconsider?'

'I wish I could.'

Portia felt the impact when his eyes slid to her.

Lord Dayle cleared his throat. 'Well, then. I'll let you two say your goodbyes.' The Viscount gave her hand a squeeze and retreated inside the house.

Silently, Portia turned her gaze to Mateo. Mere inches of pavement separated them, but in her heart she felt the gap between them widening. She jumped a little when he reached out suddenly to grasp both her hands.

'I've an idea how we can ensure this appears convincing.'

Her mouth quirked. 'Do you?'

He leaned in and pressed the softest kiss upon her. It was a feat of strength not to lean in and silently ask for more.

'I'm not sure I'm convinced,' she said when he pulled away.

A laugh bubbled up. 'Perhaps you can drum up a tear or two?' He kissed her hand and then climbed into the saddle.

Their eyes met once more. 'What did you whisper to Dorrie?' she asked suddenly.

Her favourite laugh lines appeared at the corner of his eyes. 'I promised her I would do the right thing.' And with that he nudged his horse and was on his way.

Portia stood rooted in her spot for a long time, long after he had turned the corner and disappeared into the London traffic. Her reaction came startlingly close to her companion's; she very much feared Mateo did intend to keep that promise. Tears did come then, easily. She let them fall. One last look over her shoulder at Lord Dayle's welcoming home, and then she did as she'd been bid, and walked away.

Berkeley Square was a green blur that she passed right by. She followed Berkeley Street all the way down to Piccadilly, then crossed into Green Park. She kept her directions firmly fixed in her mind and tried her best to walk casually. She was supposed to appear self-absorbed and not horribly on edge at the idea of being observed and followed.

The park was nearly empty at this time of the morning: a wide, green expanse occupied by only a rider or two, and a few children with their nurses. Portia ambled along her prescribed route, until she found a bench near the reservoir. She sat, staring over the peaceful scene.

She waited. And she tried desperately not to *think*.

A bank of clouds passed over, blocking the sun. The water before her grew nearly black beneath it, a painful reminder of storm-swept eyes that darkened in anger, and lit up in laughter, and softened in love. The tears started to fall again.

She ducked her head as a finely dressed gentleman passed on the nearby footpath. He tipped his hat to her, but came to a halt when he glimpsed her face. 'Miss? Are you in need of assistance?' He whipped out a handkerchief and presented it with flair.

'No, thank you. I'm all right.' She wiped at her tears, but did not take the handkerchief.

Sheepishly, he stuffed it back into a pocket. 'Don't know why women don't carry the cursed things, when they are so often in need of them.' He smiled and plopped down on the bench beside her. 'Now what's amiss? You're too pretty to be so sad.'

Portia's tears dried as she stared at him. Her eyes narrowed. 'But I know you. Don't I?' She considered his impeccable clothes, his handsome features…and his long, dark hair, which, tied tightly back, was not noticeable immediately. 'Yes. I saw you at the inn in Marlborough.'

She saw the truth of it in his face, but before he could answer a horse thundered up behind them, pulling to a stop right behind their bench. Portia turned as Mateo swung down from the saddle.

'My, that was fast, Peeve.' He cast a hard look at the

man on the bench beside her. 'I see you've met your brother.'

Her heart stilled. The gentleman jumped to his feet. But Mateo was watching him with a mock frown. 'Or perhaps he's mine?'

Mateo had never quite realised how many reactions—and at such a clip, too—could show in a man's eyes. Like the swiftly turning pages of a book he saw the rounding of surprise, the swift narrowing of anger, the hardening of calculation and, finally, a rueful easing of respect.

Fluid and graceful, the gentleman—his brother?—slid back into his seat. 'Now there's a question for the ages,' he said wryly. 'And one I wish I knew the answer to.'

Portia glanced wildly from him, to Averardo—for lack of a verified name—and back again. 'What are you talking about?'

But their adversary's gaze never left his own. 'How did you know I'd follow *her*?'

Mateo smiled and lifted a shoulder. 'One thing I do know about you—you're not stupid. Given the choice between the three of us, *I'd* certainly choose her.'

Portia still looked bewildered, and increasingly not happy about it. He noticed the tracks of tears on her face and his stomach clenched.

'Mateo, it's extremely bad manners to throw a statement like that out and not explain it. I thought we suspected this man of trying to steal your company?'

'Steal your company?' Averardo straightened in surprise. 'Oh…' he grinned '…the Portsmouth office. You worked that out, did you?'

'Somebody had better begin talking to me,' Portia said through gritted teeth.

'It's the story, *cara*,' Mateo said gently. 'The story that so occupied your father and mine through all those years. If I've put all the pieces together correctly, then the Countess of Lundwick had at one time, a very different name.' He smiled at the dawning realisation in her eyes. 'La Incandescent Clarisse.'

'But she—' She went still, then turned to the man at her side. 'Then you are—'

'Indeed. I am her son. But your father's, as well? Or his?' He gestured in Mateo's direction and breathed deep. 'We shall never know.'

'For years they searched,' Mateo said. 'But when did they find you? Where?'

'When I was fourteen years old, they found me. In Nice.' He drew a deep breath. 'When your fathers were thrown into that Naples prison all those years ago, my mother was left alone. Her home had been destroyed; she was reputed to be harmed or dead. It was then, when she begged sanctuary at the home of a friend, that she met Teodoro Donati. He was a wealthy merchant, and he was, naturally, enchanted. He offered her his protection and took her home to Nice.' He grinned. 'Quite frankly, I think my mother had had enough of notoriety. Donati sympathised with her, petted her, and treated her like a lady. She was in her element.'

'Did they marry?' Portia was clearly caught up in the story.

'Eventually. Donati was also no fool. He wed her

after she gave birth to me. She lived happily with him until his death, a spoiled, happy wife.'

Mateo had caught the undertone of tension in Averardo's voice. 'And you? Were you happy, as well?'

He hesitated. 'Yes, for the most part. Always it was clear I was part of the Donati family, but not truly of it. When your fathers approached me with their story, I was…relieved. He eyed them both solemnly. 'They were great men. I would have been proud to have been sired by either of them.'

'But why did they never tell us?' Portia said almost angrily.

'I believe your mother fell ill, soon after they found me,' Averardo said to Mateo. He shrugged. 'I suppose they did not want to upset her. After that…well, we had already established a clandestine relationship. But they were attentive and very kind. They had me tutored in English, and made sure I had a gentleman's education.'

Another surreptitious glance. 'They had expectations, as any father would. Leandro took me into the shipping business in small ways and there were other opportunities, as well. Between their patronage and my contacts with the Donati family, I have had a varied career and done very well.'

'But the will and the conveyance and all of this…' Portia waved wildly. 'How did it all come about? Why?' she asked, clearly growing upset.

Averardo put his hand over hers. Mateo told himself firmly not to mind.

'Your fathers loved you both very much. They worried for you both. Some years ago they concocted this scheme…' he laughed '…and several variations, as your circumstances changed.' He rolled his eyes at her. 'For one, I am very thankful they did not press me into challenging your husband to a duel, but it was a near thing.'

Portia's face flamed. Mateo hitched his mount to a nearby sapling before crossing to the bench and perching on the arm next to her.

'I felt bad enough cheating him out of your estate,' Averardo continued. His face lit up in remembrance. 'Oh, was he in a frenzy! I began to quite enjoy it. But when I did not immediately press my claim, he relaxed. I swear, I think he forgot all about it as the months passed.'

'Yes, he might have,' Portia said bitterly. 'Stenbrooke meant nothing to him. But it was more likely he just wanted to avoid my wrath while he could.'

'Your fathers finalised their plans just before your papa died,' Averardo told her gently. 'They told me what they had done, and asked for my help.' He took a deep breath. 'They had done so much for me, and, truly, they believed that this was their best gift to you.'

'Gift?' Portia cried. 'But Mateo has likely lost a great opportunity! When I think of the anxiety and the anger and all of the...' Her voice trailed away and she looked to Mateo for support.

'The journey,' Mateo told her. 'The chance for our lives to converge again—that was what they considered a gift.'

'You do see,' Averardo said, nodding in approval. 'I have not given you enough credit.'

Mateo glanced down at Portia. 'They are still match-making, the pair of devils,' he said simply.

'They sought to give you an opportunity,' Averardo

corrected. 'Your father, in particular, Mateo, felt very strongly about it. He gambled his life's work because he believed that you would make the most of it.' He stood. 'Whether you do or not is entirely up to you. I will send the deed to Lord Dayle's house.' He tipped his hat and stepped away.

'Wait!' cried Portia. 'I finally have a brother worth knowing! You can't go now!'

Averardo hesitated. He looked over his shoulder, his face softening. Then he cast a questioning look in Mateo's direction.

'I just have one question.' Mateo said.

Averardo turned. 'Yes?'

'What is your *name*?'

'Not Cosimo, I hope,' said Portia with a shudder.

His expression remained serious. 'Not many people know my true name.' He took a deep breath. 'Marcus. My name is Marcus Donati.'

Mateo extended a hand. 'Welcome to the family, Marcus.'

Chapter Seventeen

A cheery fire burned in the grate of Lord Dayle's bookroom and Portia sat before it, warmed through. Mateo's acceptance of Marcus had enabled them all to return to the Viscount's town house where Marcus had presented her with a thick roll of papers. With a flourish, he had said, 'The conveyance on Stenbrooke. I doubt it would have held up, in any case, as is it not even in my legal name.'

Portia had none the less greatly enjoyed feeding the thing to the fire and watching it go up in smoke.

Now she drowsed in a comfortable chair and let the men's animated talk flow over her. Sleepily, she let her gaze roam over the pair of them. Last week Dorrie had been the only thing preventing her from feeling completely alone in the world. Today she had a new brother. And a lover. She sighed. Yesterday she had been worried that her longing for Mateo sprang from a fear of being alone. Tonight she knew that some deeply buried part of her had thought him safe precisely *because* he was certain to leave her alone.

For so long she'd dreamed of independence, of finally having control of her own life. Thanks to these two men, she finally had it. Even more importantly, she knew she deserved it. But for the first time she feared it wouldn't be enough.

She closed her eyes against the pain of that realisation.

When she opened them again, the room had gone quiet. A glance told her that the fire had burned low. Mateo sat in a chair nearby, watching her.

'Did you know that you snore?' he asked conversationally.

She sat up. 'I do not.'

'You do. Just the tiniest rasp.' He got up, crossed over to her and cupped her jaw with his large, calloused hand. 'It's adorable.'

'I'd wager you snore, as well,' she said irritably, 'but I doubt it's adorable.' She was perversely annoyed because she didn't know for certain.

His other hand rose to frame her face. 'It's our last night together,' he said quietly. 'Everyone else has gone up to bed.'

She leaned into his caress. He kissed her then and she knew that she'd been right, this was not enough. She would miss the incredible connection they shared, miss the comfort of his company, the sure knowledge that he knew her thoughts almost before she did, and found them amusing and worthwhile. Years loomed ahead, years that suddenly seemed empty because they wouldn't be filled with him.

But he'd said it himself—they were so different. He

needed the sea, needed a sense of freedom just as he needed air to breathe. And he needed the chance to show the world what he could do. He could never be happy if he was forced to give those things up.

And was she any different? She spared a moment's thought to the idea of giving up Stenbrooke. A wrenching pain squeezed her heart, and a healthy dose of fear, but she thought she could do it. A lifetime with Mateo would be more than a fair trade.

But the same, she feared, could not be said of him. And what would happen to her heart if he refused the idea? Or worse, if he agreed and came to resent being tied to her?

'You're thinking too loud,' he said softly in her ear. 'And tonight is for feeling. You can think tomorrow.'

She sighed. But he was right. So she would savour the moments that they'd already shared and she would fill this night with more. Her arms crept up around the expanse of him and buried themselves in the tangle of his curls. She kissed him with all the longing in her past and future.

He pulled her tightly against him, as if he could not get close enough. There was a desperate urgency in them both that fuelled their feverish touches, but which somehow added another layer of tenderness to every caress.

Time slowed to a crawl. Perhaps it stopped altogether as they played, touching, tasting, laughing softly with each button that came undone and each tape that came untied. At last he was standing naked and she was left only in her stockings. She bent to undo the rosebud fastening of her garter.

He put out a delaying hand. 'Don't. I like them.' He fingered one frilly garter admiringly. 'Especially the roses.'

'Well, what did you expect?' she said tartly. 'No doubt if I were a dockside doxy I'd have fish, or anchors or something nautical on my garters.' She laughed. 'What do you suppose the Countess has on hers?'

He didn't answer. Not with words. Instead he dropped to his knees and pressed a hot kiss to the tender skin her stockings left bare.

She gasped.

Torture. That's what it was. He nipped and teased the soft flesh of her thighs, even moving behind her and paying lavish homage to the back of her legs. His hands roamed down over her calves and up over her buttocks, setting her to squirming.

'You said you trusted me.' His warm breath tickled her right through her stocking.

'I do.' It was a vow.

'Then put your hands on the arm of the chair.' His voice was soft, but there was a ring of command in it, as well. Her heart pounded, but she did as he asked.

'Lower,' he said. 'Brace yourself on your elbows. And spread your legs.'

She did, swallowing back a surge of anxiety. She was open before him, on display, exposed and vulnerable. But it was Mateo who asked, Mateo who had taken such tender care of her spirit, she could not but trust him with her body. Tense, she waited.

'You are beautiful,' he whispered. 'Gorgeous.' He slipped a finger along her woman's crease as he said it and she started, then groaned in pleasure.

She was wet and ready for him. His fingers lingered, teasing back and forth, threatening her sanity. He reached further and teased the swollen centre of her passion. Her sex pulsed with arousal.

'*Dio*, but I cannot wait. I wanted to make this last all night long, but I have to be inside of you.'

'Don't wait,' she said. And discovered that there was a power in her ability to overthrow his control.

He raised her from the chair and positioned himself behind her, between her legs, the length of him a burning brand against her. She gasped as he pushed gently across her achingly wet folds.

And then he slid home, entering her fully on one hard thrust. She cried out at that pleasure, at the wonderful stretching of her body and the incredible pressure of his.

He clutched her hips and began to move. She ached with the joy of it, with the intensity of her need, and she pushed back against him, demanding more. He gasped for breath, his grip on her tight, his thighs tense against her own.

His pace began to grow more frantic. He reached around and cupped her, his finger finding her swollen bud. It was all she needed. With a cry she went over, shaking, shuddering, her body gripping his in waves of undulating pleasure. And he followed, crying out with a hoarse voice as deep inside her he throbbed to a violent release.

Eventually they stilled. Mateo withdrew gently from Portia's body and, still holding her tight, he twisted so that they landed in the chair, with her on top of his lap. Softly he kissed the honeyed glow of her hair.

'It's not enough,' he whispered. 'I want more, all of you, in every way. I want you all night long, to make up for the nights ahead.'

'Mmm.' She gave a tiny wiggle against him, not lifting her head from his shoulder.

He laid his head against hers. 'I've come to care for you, Portia.'

Her finger drifted across his chest. 'I know.'

He pulled back, a little annoyed. 'You know?'

She smiled lazily up at him. 'You might not have said the words, but you've shown me in a hundred ways.'

'I didn't mean for it to happen,' he said testily. 'In fact, I tried damned hard to prevent it.'

'I know,' she said again, but her smile took some of the sting from her words. 'I care for you, too, you know.'

'It's incredibly foolish of us.' He sighed.

And it was. The Countess of Lundwick might spout on about journeys, but it was Portia who had come the farthest. *Dio*, but he was proud of her—of the tough determination she'd shown in the face of adversity and the extraordinary courage it had taken to allow him past it.

He'd seen the fierce joy in her eyes when that deed of conveyance had gone up in flames. She'd battled hard for her independence and now she had won it. He'd done his best to help her reach it—how could he even think about asking her to give it up now?

It would be the height of selfishness to consider it. And the height of foolishness, as well. He clenched his teeth. More than just geography and temperament kept them apart. This was Portia's chance to live her dream, bask in her triumph. She deserved the opportunity to stand on her own two feet, to discover her own strength firsthand.

'I'll have to leave tomorrow,' he said.

She nodded. 'You'll take a piece of me with you.' Her voice shook with feeling.

He reached out to caress her, stroked her hair. And ignored the fact that his hand was shaking, too. 'It's the most precious gift anyone has ever given me.' He lifted her chin and stared into her gold-flecked eyes. 'I will treasure it always.'

'Tonight is a gift, too,' she said, reaching for him. 'For both of us.'

He pressed his lips to hers. 'Then let's make the most of it.'

Chapter Eighteen

The *Lady Azalea* rocked, resisting the tug of the tidal surge. Mateo stood alone on the quarter deck, enjoying the feel of the wind washing over him, waiting for the tang of sea air to fill him with anticipation and joy. Deliberately, he faced south. The sea was there, just beyond the mouth of the harbour. A siren, she tempted him with her call. For the first time in his life, he hesitated to answer.

Over the last week he'd found one reason and then another to delay their departure. His chief mate was growing restless, his crew had begun to look at him in wonder. Still, he could not bring himself to give the order to heave anchor and cast off.

Other voices filled his head, drowning the siren's song. His father's rang loud and often. *What are you looking for, son?* Portia's often followed. *Have you been looking for it, do you think? For peace?*

He had not been looking for it. But it had found him anyway. Because that's exactly what Portia gave him:

peace and companionship, calm acceptance and uncon-
ditional trust. All the things he'd refused to acknowledge he'd been seeking as he wandered.

But the real beauty, the great, grand wonder of Portia
was that she also gave him adventure and desire, opposition and laughter. Everything that he'd embraced as a
substitute, and come to crave.

In Portia he'd found everything, all rolled up in a
saucy, delectable package.

Dio, but he was a fool to even think of leaving her
behind.

His mind churned as he stared unseeing at the busy
harbour. Perhaps, just perhaps, there was a way. Deliberately he turned from the rail and went to his cabin.
Now anticipation set his heart racing, but he held himself in check, adopting calm as he sharpened a quill and
pulled a fresh stack of paper from his drawer.

He had a lot to put down, and it took quite a while.
He had just finished, and was sealing a thick packet
of documents when his mate knocked and entered the
cabin.

'Oh, there you are, John,' Mateo said pleasantly.
'Order me up a boat's crew, please. I'm going ashore.'

The man looked at him in surprise. 'Actually, the
boat's manned and ready, Captain. We've just had a
signal. There's a passenger wanting to sign on.' He
paused, considering. 'We can fit him in if we bunk
Hatch in with the men.'

'Good, but tell him and the crew, too, that it will be
several days, likely a week before we set sail.'

'Another delay, Captain? The crew will—'

'The crew will do as I say, as always. Anyone who

wants to question that can head ashore and find berth on someone else's ship. Now go and make sure that boat is manned, John.' He handed over the sealed packet. 'And see that this is delivered. I've written down the address. I'm going to Berkshire. You'll have the ship while I'm gone.'

'Aye, sir.'

The boat weaved through the harbour traffic and Mateo fought the urge to hurry the men as they pulled. The Portsmouth docks loomed ahead, indistinct in the evening light. Mateo's mind ranged ahead, trying to calculate how long it would be until he could reach Stenbrooke, trying to anticipate Portia's reaction to his plans.

The pier was closer now, but quiet at this time of the evening. A lone figure stood there, watching them come in.

Mateo started, then rose half out of his seat. Surely not?

'Strongly now, men! Pull! Put your backs into it!' He narrowed his gaze and peered across the water. His heart nearly burst with joy as he cupped his hands and shouted across the water. 'Peeve! What in blazes are you doing here?'

She waved, but didn't answer. The boat pulled along-side and Mateo was scrambling out and on to the pier before the men had even pulled in their oars. With a laugh, he swept Portia up into his arms and twirled her wildly about. 'How did this come about?' he asked joyfully. 'And where is Dorrie?'

'Dorrie is in Wiltshire,' she said with a smile. 'I wrote to Mrs Rankin and told her we had been to call on her son. I sang Dorrie's praises and made sure to mention how struck she had been with the potential of Longvale. She received an invitation to visit, and, if I'm not mistaken, Mr Rankin and his mama are even now evaluating *her* potential.' She cast a dark look over his shoulder towards a bustling dockside tavern. 'And just where were you going?' she asked suspiciously.

'To Berkshire.'

A tiny grin fought its way through her severe expression. 'Why?'

He lifted a shoulder. 'I'm two and thirty years old. I thought perhaps it was time I started listening to my father.' He looked steadily at her. 'Would you care to travel along with me?'

'It sounds lovely, but I couldn't. I've just booked passage to Philadelphia.'

His mouth dropped. 'You're the passenger?'

'If you'll have me.'

He gathered her into his arms. 'Oh, I'll have you.' He bent to kiss her, but pulled away at the last second.

She pouted.

'I feel it's only honourable to inform you of the change in my circumstances, Peeve.' He frowned down at her. 'You may wish to reconsider your passage.'

She raised a questioning brow.

'I'm afraid I'm no longer the sole owner of a shipping company. I just turned fifty percent of it over to Marcus Donati.'

She gasped. 'Oh, Mateo! I cannot believe it!'

He smiled. 'I'm done with skimming the surface. I'm diving in and soaking up everything life has to offer.'

He ran a finger along the tempting sweep of her nape. 'And the best it has to offer is you.'

Her eyes filled. 'Still, it is a generous gesture—and I know how difficult it must have been for you.'

He shook his head. 'Not at all. I'm going to let him hold the reins for a while. He deserves a chance at the family legacy. If he hurries, he might still join the fleet to Canton, but even if he does not, with his contacts in Italy he'll make a good go of it.' Sobering, he asked, 'Well, what of it, Peeve? Will you turn tail and run back to Stenbrooke now?'

Clearly holding back laughter, she bit her lip. 'I cannot.'

'Why not?'

'Wait.' She reached down and dug into her portmanteau and held out a thick packet of her own. 'I signed a deed of conveyance, granting it to Marcus Donati.'

He sucked in a shocked breath. 'You didn't!'

'I'm nearly seven and twenty years old. I thought it was time I stopped letting fear make my decisions for me.' She bit her lip. 'I had to take the chance. I had to ask. You mean more to me than Stenbrooke ever could.'

Very gently, he reached out and took the parcel from her hand. Then he turned and with a mighty heave, threw it out into the harbour.

'Mateo!' she gasped. 'Why did you do that?'

'Because I can't let you give Stenbrooke up, after you battled so hard to keep it. And in any case, we're going to need it.'

Her shock was quickly done in by curiosity. 'We are?'

'We are,' he said firmly, then leaned down and kissed

her soundly. 'Packets, Peeve! A business of my own that I can have the running of from the ground up! We'll have the best of both worlds: earth and sea. I'll have a fleet of ships to manage, but we'll need a retreat, a place where we can get away from the bustle of the docks, the pressures of business, a place to make babies and watch them run free.'

Tears shone in her eyes again and she nodded vigorously.

'Perhaps we can live part of the year in England, and part in Philadelphia. Perhaps we'll build a new home in Le Havre or on the Rio de la Plata.' He grinned. 'You can have a garden for every climate.'

'I don't need a home in every port. All I need is you.' Her arms clutched him tightly. 'We only have one life, Mateo.' She smiled. 'One journey. I want to travel it with you.'

'One life,' he whispered. 'Let's make it memorable.'

* * * * *

Special Offers
Regency Ballroom Collection

Classic tales of scandal and seduction in the Regency Ballroom

Scandal in the Regency Ballroom
On sale 4th April

Innocent in the Regency Ballroom
On sale 3rd May

Wicked in the Regency Ballroom
On sale 7th June

Cinderella in the Regency Ballroom
On sale 5th July

Rogue in the Regency Ballroom
On sale 2nd August

Debutante in the Regency Ballroom
On sale 6th September

Rumours in the Regency Ballroom
On sale 4th October

Scoundrel in the Regency Ballroom
On sale 1st November

Mistress in the Regency Ballroom
On sale 6th December

Courtship in the Regency Ballroom
On sale 3rd January

Rake in the Regency Ballroom
On sale 7th February

Secrets in the Regency Ballroom
On sale 7th March

A FABULOUS TWELVE-BOOK COLLECTION

 Save 20% on Special Releases Collections

Find the collection at
www.millsandboon.co.uk/specialreleases

Visit us Online

0513/MB416

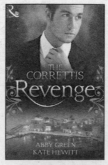

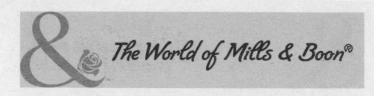

The World of Mills & Boon®

There's a Mills & Boon® series that's perfect for you. We publish ten series and, with new titles every month, you never have to wait long for your favourite to come along.

Blaze.
Scorching hot, sexy reads
4 new stories every month

By Request
Relive the romance with the best of the best
9 new stories every month

Cherish™
Romance to melt the heart every time
12 new stories every month

Desire™
Passionate and dramatic love stories
8 new stories every month